BROKEN beautiful HEARTS

BROKEN

beautiful

HEARTS

KAMI GARCIA

{Imprint}
MAKE YOUR MARK

NEW YORK

*For every girl who is struggling
and doubting herself—
Speak your truth.
You're stronger than you think.*

[Imprint]
MAKE YOUR MARK

A part of Macmillan Publishing Group, LLC
175 Fifth Avenue, New York, NY 10010

Library of Congress Control Number: 2017931494

ISBN 978-1-250-07920-6 (hardcover) / ISBN 978-1-250-07923-7 (ebook)

Our books may be purchased in bulk for promotional, educational, or business use. Please contact your
local bookseller or the Macmillan Corporate and Premium Sales Department at (800) 221-7945
ext. 5442 or by e-mail at MacmillanSpecialMarkets@macmillan.com.

Book design by Natalie C. Sousa

Imprint logo designed by Amanda Spielman

First edition, 2018

1 3 5 7 9 10 8 6 4 2

fiercereads.com

If you dare to steal this book, borrow it without permission, or maliciously destroy it,
you will be doomed to "just friends" status with your crush—and it won't be
Peyton and Owen's brand of *just friends*.

The shell must break before the bird can fly.

—ALFRED, LORD TENNYSON

CHAPTER 1
When the Stars Align

I BELIEVE EVERYTHING happens for a reason and usually the reason sucks. I also believe the laces from my eighth-grade soccer cleats are good luck, Adele is the most talented singer to ever walk the earth, and popcorn without butter is just corn.

But more than any of those things, I believe that if you're lucky—at least once in your life—you *might* have a perfect day. A day when all the stars in your personal universe align and your dreams seem possible.

The crazy part?

I think today might be mine.

Except Dad isn't here.

The thought bears down on me, but I push back against it.

Today might be the only perfect day I'll ever get. Dad wouldn't want me to waste it.

I pick up the letter on my desk and reread it for the tenth time since it arrived yesterday.

> Dear Miss Rios,
>
> After careful consideration, the women's soccer staff at the University of North Carolina at Chapel Hill believes that you have the qualities we are looking for in a student-athlete. As the head women's soccer coach at this university, I want to formally offer you early acceptance and an opportunity to play soccer for the team that has won 21 out of 35 NCAA national championships.
>
> Please understand that this acceptance is contingent upon you:
> - maintaining the recommendation of your high school coach
> - remaining in good academic standing
> - continuing to demonstrate strong leadership and soccer skills
> - playing in your current position, center forward, next fall.

I've wanted this for as long as I can remember, but now that it's actually happening, it doesn't feel real.

"Peyton?" Mom calls from downstairs.

"Coming." I fold the letter and tuck it in my bag.

I gather my dark, wavy hair into a ponytail, pull it through an elastic, and take a quick look in the mirror. My wardrobe consists of a steady rotation of skinny jeans and cargos that show off my long legs, layered tanks and fitted henleys, and ankle boots. Today is no exception.

I do my standard two-minute make-up application—concealer under my eyes and berry-tinted lip balm that doubles as blush.

Now I just have to find my black boots.

"You're going to be late," Mom yells.

"Coming!" I bend down and check under the bed—a pair of balled-up soccer socks; my elementary school yearbooks; a bottle of nail polish; old issues of *Soccer 360*; a Luna Bar that's hard enough to use as a hammer; and . . . my boots. I drag them out by the laces and put them on.

Dad's dog tags slide back and forth on the silver chain hanging around my neck. I never take them off. When I insisted on wearing them to the Spring Fling with my strapless dress, Mom figured out how to pin the tags inside the dress so they wouldn't be as noticeable. I would've worn them either way.

On the way out, I grab the black leather jacket draped over the chair next to my door, under a poster of my soccer idol, Alex Morgan. The jacket belonged to my dad. I slip it on. The sleeves hang past my fingertips and the leather is cracked, but I love it anyway.

I jog down the steps and walk into the kitchen.

Mom holds up a brown muffin. "Do you want one to take with you?"

"Not if it has oats, nuts, dried fruit, or seeds in it."

She breaks the muffin in half, which takes some effort because it's as dense as a hunk of fruitcake. Dad used to do all the cooking. He was Cuban and every morning started with café con leché—strong Cuban coffee with steamed milk—and thick toast with butter. After he died I took over the cooking, but I couldn't bring myself to keep eating the same breakfast Dad used to make me. Now Mom is determined to learn to cook, too. Muffins are her latest experiment.

I rummage through the pantry. "Do we have any doughnuts?"

"Doughnuts are pure sugar. They don't qualify as breakfast." She pours a cup of coffee and hands it to me.

I add milk and sugar. "Then why do doughnut shops open at five o'clock in the morning?"

"It's one of life's great mysteries." Mom takes a bite of the muffin and scrunches up her nose when she thinks I'm not looking. "Have you told Tess yet?"

"Nope."

"I'm surprised you held out this long."

"I want to see the look on her face when I tell her."

"What about Reed?" she asks.

I haven't heard from my boyfriend yet this morning. "He worked late. He's probably still asleep. And it will be more fun to tell people in person."

I down the rest of my coffee and put the cup in the sink. "I'm taking off."

"Drive carefully," Mom says as I walk out the door.

I toss my bag in the back seat of my red Honda HR-V and slide behind the wheel. The road is carpeted with colorful fall leaves from the oaks and maples on my street. My neighborhood is only twenty minutes from downtown Washington, DC, and ten minutes from the outdated mid-rise apartment buildings in Tess' complex. But you'd never know it.

My street looks like it belongs in a small town—the huge trees arching over the road, the Cape Cod–style homes, and the "tiny library" on the corner that reminds me of a pink dollhouse.

On the drive to Tess', I try to come up with a cool way to tell her about UNC. But I've got nothing. We both know that colleges mailed out early admission and athletic scholarship letters this week. If I show

4

up at her door holding a folded piece of paper, it's too obvious. Not that it matters. Even if I don't manage to surprise Tess, she'll still make a big deal about my news. That's what best friends do when something amazing happens to you.

I park next to Tess' building and I start to get out with the letter in my hand. But at the last minute, I drop it onto the passenger seat for her to find when she gets in. I jog up the concrete steps, avoiding the crumbling stair the city was supposed to repair two years ago. I punch in the security code for the front door.

I'm dying to tell Reed my news. A benefit of dating my best friend's brother is that when I come over to hang out with one of them, I get to see them both.

Seven months ago, Reed was just Tess' hot older brother—until a party, four games of beer pong, and a car ride changed everything. Tess and I weren't the only juniors who showed up at the epic spring break party at Chicken Johnson's house. But we *were* the only juniors stupid enough to play beer pong with Chicken and the wrestling team. The guys were all seniors like Reed, and they outweighed and outdrank us.

After I spent an hour in the bathroom holding Tess' hair while she puked, Reed carried her out to his car. He looked hotter than usual, in a pair of jeans that hung low on his hips and a gray 18TH STREET MIXED MARTIAL ARTS T-shirt that outlined his muscular chest. He wasn't over-the-top gorgeous. The combination of Reed's blue eyes, crooked nose, buzzed black hair, and brooding expression was more gladiator than pretty-boy.

But he had sexy nailed.

Tess passed out in the back seat, and I ended up riding shotgun. It was a first. Tess always sat in the front, and I preferred it that way. I'd harbored a monster crush on Reed for years, but I didn't really know him—or do things like sit next to him in the car . . . or *talk* to him.

I didn't say a word until we got back to the apartment, except for the occasional "uh-huh" to make it seem as if I was participating in the conversation. Reed carried Tess to her room and deposited her on the bed as I stood in the doorway.

"Make sure she takes Advil when she wakes up," he said as he walked toward the door—and me.

I froze and Reed had to squeeze by me to get through the door. He moved to his left and I moved to my right, and I ended up with my back against the doorjamb and my face inches from his collarbone.

He wrapped his arm around my waist and looked down at me. "You have really pretty eyes. They're sort of gold."

People had complimented the color of my eyes before. From certain angles, the contrast between my light brown skin and dark hair made the hazel flecks in my brown eyes look gold. But this was the first time a hot guy was saying it.

"They're just brown."

"Golden brown." Reed brushed my hair over my shoulder and his fingers grazed the back of my neck. I bit my bottom lip and held my breath.

His eyes lingered on my mouth. "Do you know how sexy that is?"

At that moment, with my heart racing and Reed touching me and staring at my mouth, the only thing I knew was that I wanted him to kiss me. He ran his thumb across my bottom lip, and I gasped.

Reed tightened his hold on my waist and backed me out of Tess' room, pulling the door closed behind him. His hand slid down to my ass and he leaned into me. "I should've done this a long time ago."

I had to remind myself to breathe.

When Reed finally kissed me his lips were rough from years of fighting. But I didn't care. His mouth kept finding mine—over and over.

"I want to kiss you again," Reed whispered. "Tomorrow. And the next day. And the day after that. How does that sound?" He kissed me again.

Then he pulled back and flashed a cocky smile. "You want to get something to eat tomorrow night? I have a fight, but that won't take long."

It took a moment for me to realize he was asking me out. With his battered good looks and scraped knuckles, Reed wasn't homecoming-king material, but that didn't have a negative effect on his social life. He had a reputation for being protective, wild, cocky, and *fun*—something that had been seriously lacking in my life.

Girls stopped Tess in the halls at school to dig for information. Did her brother have a girlfriend? Where did he hang out? Would Tess put in a good word for them?

Reed Michaels—the object of their affection—had spent the last ten minutes kissing me, and now he was asking me out on a real date? How could I say no?

Why would I?

"Yes."

It's hard to believe that night was seven months ago.

I was stumbling through my life back then, trying to figure out how to keep going without my dad, and Reed helped me through some of the low points.

On the other side of the apartment door, something heavy hits the floor with a thud.

I knock and Tess yells, "Just a sec."

She opens the door, holding her braids together behind her head with one hand. "I'm almost ready."

"That's what you say every day." I follow her inside, dodging the binders and textbooks spilling out of her backpack onto the floor.

"I dropped it." She kicks the bag and another book slides out. Tess huffs and finishes braiding her pale blond hair. It reaches past her shoulder blades, but she never wears it down. Right now she's in a braiding phase. She secures the braids behind her head and rolls the rest of her hair around them to form what looks like a crown. I have no idea how she does it. I can barely make a neat ponytail.

I gesture at her hair. "This is new."

"What do you think?" She tucks a few uncooperative strands behind her ears. "It's kind of warrior-princess. Right?"

"I have no idea what that means, but it looks cool." I glance down the hallway behind her. "Is Reed sleeping?"

"Yep."

Reed knows how much I wanted to get into UNC. Maybe I should wake him up and tell him? Then he could go right back to sleep.

Or he could end up in an awful mood for the rest of the day.

I'll let him sleep.

A few months ago I wouldn't have thought twice about waking him, and I probably would've jumped on his bed to do it.

"Did he get home late last night?" I ask.

"Super late. And he looked like crap." Tess looks away with a hint of guilt in her eyes. She bends down and collects the mountain of crumpled paper, pens, and textbooks. She tries to shove it all back into her bag, but it won't fit the way she's jamming it in there.

"Was he at an underground fight?" I ask.

"He didn't say. But his hands were banged up when he came home, and he was walking around holding a bag of frozen peas against his jaw."

Reed got involved in the underground fight scene two months ago.

He figured out that he could make more money in one night's worth of street fights than he could earn in two weeks training other fighters at the gym.

He dragged me along one night to watch him battle it out in a parking structure while people placed bets. Bloody and brutal, with no rules or referees, the fights barely resembled MMA—or any sport. And Reed loved every minute of it.

"I'm worried about him, Tess. He could get hurt." She's never seen an underground fight firsthand. "Whenever I try to talk to him about it, we end up arguing."

She tugs on the zipper of her backpack, but it still won't close. "Please don't be mad at him. I don't want him in those fights any more than you do. But my mom can't cover the bills on her own."

I take the bag from her and reorganize it so everything fits. "I'm not mad. Just worried. If he gets caught, he'll get kicked out of the league." And that will be the end of his dream of competing in the UFC.

When we first started dating, Reed and I used to talk on the phone at night, dreaming out loud. He would climb the MMA ranks until a sponsor, or a high profile trainer, recognized his potential. I'd play soccer for a Division I college and get recruited to play professionally after I graduated.

"He's doing it for me," Tess says softly.

"You can't blame yourself." I work the zipper of her backpack until it closes. "Reed makes his own choices. No one tells him what to do."

She smiles a little. "Like someone else I know."

"I'll take that as a compliment."

Tess laughs and her blue eyes light up. She and Reed look nothing alike, but they have the same amazing blue eyes. Ocean blue—like the water in the photos of my grandparents on the beach in Cuba, before they immigrated to the US. I've never seen water that blue in real life.

On our way out, I notice a hole in the drywall behind the front door. "What happened? It looks like someone punched a hole in it."

Her eyes dart to the damage. "Close. Reed and TJ were messing around in the hallway when Reed was opening the door. TJ slammed into him, and they hit the door so hard that it swung around and the knob went through the wall. My mom wasn't happy. She's making Reed fix it."

There's something weird about the hole, but I can't figure it out.

Tess opens the door, and her mom is standing in the hallway, fumbling with her house keys.

Mrs. Michaels gasps. "I didn't hear you coming out."

The shadows around her eyes are darker than usual. She's probably coming off a double shift at the café. Tess holds the door open for her mother.

"Thanks, sweetheart." Her mom wanders inside like she's sleepwalking. She tries to hang her keys on the wall hook, but she misses and they drop on the floor.

I rush to pick them up.

"I'm sorry. I don't know what's wrong with me." Mrs. Michaels yawns.

"You worked eighteen hours straight and you're exhausted," Tess says, rushing to the kitchen.

Her mom smiles at me. "How's everything going with you, Peyton?"

"Good." *Better than good.* And suddenly, I feel guilty about it.

Tess returns with a coffee mug and hands it her mom.

"Thank you." Mrs. Michaels eases herself onto the sofa, takes a few sips of her coffee, and sets the mug on the end table.

"Do you need anything before I leave?" Tess asks.

"No, I'm fine." Tess' mom unties her apron and tosses it on the chair. "Go ahead to school." She rests her head on the arm of the sofa and closes her eyes.

We tiptoe out of the apartment and Tess locks the door behind us. On the way to my car, she walks along the edge of the curb putting one scuffed brown boot directly in front of the other as if she's on a tightrope. It's obvious she hasn't heard from any colleges yet.

Now I wish I hadn't left the letter on the passenger seat.

When we get to my car, I try to hop in first and grab it, but Tess is faster. She picks up the letter and flips it open.

"Wait—" I reach for it, but she's already reading.

"Holy shit." She looks over at me. "You got in! Why didn't you say anything?"

"I wanted to tell you in person, but it didn't seem like the right time."

She closes the letter and places it on the dashboard. "Why? Because I'm feeling sorry for myself?"

"Tess . . ."

"Stop. This is the biggest thing *ever*." She grabs me by the shoulders and shakes me. "You got into UNC! You're going to be the next Alex Morgan!"

I break into a huge smile. "Doubtful, but don't jinx it."

"You can't jinx the inevitable." She looks away. "Before you ask, nothing came for me and I'm *fine*."

"It's okay to be worried."

Tess leans her head against her window. "What if I don't get a scholarship anywhere?"

"Letters only went out two days ago. Lots of people are still waiting," I remind her. "And this is only the first round of academic scholarships.

With your GPA and test scores, you'll get one." We both know a soccer scholarship is a long shot for her. Tess is a great player, but she doesn't stand out on the field the way she does in the classroom.

She starts to say something, but I add, "And I'm *not* saying that just because you're my best friend."

"Grades and test scores might not be enough."

"You're also a member of chorus and the yearbook committee, which is impressive considering you're a total lyrics slayer and the only decent photos you take are selfies." The corner of her mouth turns up, so I keep talking. "Plus, you have twice as many community service hours as the rest of us."

"Appearing well-rounded is more work than an actual job." Tess hugs her legs and rests her chin on her knee. She's not snapping out of it.

Time to shift into best-friend overdrive. "Didn't you tell me that five percent of students who are offered scholarships turn them down?" I intentionally quote the wrong percentage.

"Nine percent. The article said most people pass because they get accepted to a school they like better or another college offers them a bigger scholarship."

"And then . . . ?"

She realizes what I'm doing and rolls her eyes. "And *then* the scholarship committee moves to the next person on the list. You made your point."

"My work here is done." I cut through the gas station that shares a parking lot with 7-Eleven, throw my Honda into reverse, and execute the smoothest parallel parking job of my life.

"That was impressive for a girl who failed her driver's test twice." Tess tries to keep a straight face.

"I only jumped the curb once." When I hit the curb, the test administrator's clipboard slipped out of his hands. He tried to grab it and whacked his forehead on the dashboard. Then he failed me on the spot. I picture his puffy cheeks and pinched red face and I burst out laughing—which makes Tess crack up, too.

We dissolve into hysterics until she gets the hiccups and I yell, "Side cramp."

"Thanks for cheering me up," Tess says between hiccups. "What would I do without you?"

I tilt my head toward a woman walking out of 7-Eleven holding a glazed doughnut. "You'd probably starve."

On the way to school, we binge on sticky doughnuts and extra-rich hot chocolate. We manage to arrive on time, along with the second wave of students that skate in just before the bell everyday.

"Does Reed know about UNC?" Tess asks as we walk through the huge double doors. "I mean, did you text him or anything last night?"

I give her some serious side-eye. "And violate the code? I'm offended."

We both smile and say it at the same time: "Best friends before boyfriends."

CHAPTER 2

Perfect Day

THE FIRST THREE periods of the day go by without a hitch. In chemistry class, the teacher was out sick. She left our assignments on the board for the substitute, but one of the slackers erased them. The sub didn't have a hard copy, so the period turned into study hall. At Adams that means pop in your earbuds and listen to music or play games on your phone.

When I arrived at English, my teacher handed out pop quizzes as we walked into the classroom. I'm not great at recalling details about topics that don't interest me—like *The Metamorphosis*, the gross novella we're reading about a man who turns into a cockroach. But on today's quiz, I actually knew most of the answers.

Third period is always the easiest part of my day, aside from lunch. My art teacher, Mrs. Degan, encourages us to experiment and set our own artistic parameters. She says we could be one brushstroke away

14

from genius, the way her last name is only one letter away from *Degas*. I spent the class period working on my current work of genius, an attempt at a cubist self-portrait that makes me look like a LEGO minifigure.

The letter from UNC feels like a good luck charm in my pocket.

For once, I'm not cursing the fact that I have first lunch—or *break-fast*, as most people would call a meal you eat at ten fifty-five in the morning.

On my way to meet Tess on the quad, I call Reed, but his phone goes straight to voice mail. I don't bother leaving a message. He's probably still asleep or I would've heard from him by now. He can't go more than a few hours without calling or texting me, and he knows I was waiting for a letter.

Maybe I'll ask him if he wants to skip the party tonight. Things have been off between us. Some alone time together is just what we need to get back on track.

The diner is already packed when Tess and I get there. Seniors are allowed to eat lunch off campus, and this place quickly became our go-to spot. It's a huge step up from the vending machine selections we were stuck with last year, unless we wanted to risk eating the mystery meals in the cafeteria.

We squeeze past the people waiting for seats at the counter.

Tess points at a booth in the back corner. "Lucia and Gwen found a table."

Our friends are leaning across the table talking, their faces obscured by almost identical curtains of long, brown, spiral curls. They're the same height and body type, and from this angle they could pass for twins. But the similarities end with their hair.

Lucia is Afro-Latina, with Puerto Rican roots, and her skin is a rich coppery brown that makes Gwen's pale, rosy Irish complexion look pasty. Lucia's curls are natural and Gwen uses a weird-looking curling iron to create hers.

Lucia is determined and outspoken, and her goals are more important to her than any guy. Gwen is always on the hunt for her next boyfriend and when she finds Mr. Right Now, she'll spend all her time with him.

It gets me thinking and I turn to Tess. "You know how some people say it doesn't matter if you date jerks because every relationship is a learning experience?" I ask.

"By 'some people' I'm assuming you mean Gwen?"

"Do you think it's true?"

"No," Tess says immediately. "That's what people say when they know they're dating assholes, but they don't want to walk away. Look at my mom. It only took one jerk to ruin her life."

Tess means her dad.

I'm not sure if I agree with her take, but I understand where she's coming from.

The moment we get to the table, Gwen pounces. "So . . . ?"

Tess sits next to Lucia, and I slide in beside Gwen.

"I didn't get anything," Tess says.

"*Yet*," Lucia says, swinging her dark hair over her shoulder.

Gwen tugs on the sleeves of her oversize hoodie. "I've got nothing to report, either."

"I got an offer from Stanford," Lucia says, as if it's no big deal. "They only gave me a partial ride, but they're covering most of the tuition and my athletic expenses, so my parents can swing it." She's downplaying the acceptance because she doesn't want to make anyone else feel bad.

Tess smiles. "I'm really happy for you."

"Don't forget about us when you make new Ivy League friends," I say.

Lucia laughs. "No chance. I've been trying to forget about you guys for years, and it hasn't worked."

"You deserve it." I ball up a napkin and throw it at Lucia. "Even if you are a pain."

"Just don't bring it up around Lorenzo," she says. "He's acting like a huge baby because he wanted me to go somewhere close to Virginia Tech. Like that's gonna happen."

"You should be nicer to him," Gwen says.

Lucia pops a fry in her mouth. "If it's so important to him, he can find a college near Stanford." She points a fry at me. "You're up, Peyton."

I slide Dad's dog tags back and forth on the chain. "I didn't get a scholarship. . . ." I try to play it cool, but a smile tugs at the corners of my mouth. "But one school offered me admission and a spot on the women's soccer team."

Gwen drums her palms against the tabletop. "Which school? Spill!"

"University of North Carolina."

"No freaking way!" Lucia shouts.

The guys in a booth across from ours look over at us and smirk.

Lucia stares them down. "There's nothing here for you," she says, motioning between us girls. "So turn around and mind your own business."

One guy's face reddens and the other two laugh, but they still turn around.

"What did Reed say when you told him about UNC?" Gwen asks. "He must be happy that it's not too far away."

"I haven't had a chance to tell him yet. He worked late," I say casually. Tess is the only one who knows about the underground fights. "He's probably still sleeping."

Gwen and Lucia exchange looks.

"It's eleven thirty," Gwen points out. "Must be nice to sleep all day."

"Like you've never slept later than that," Tess snaps. "He literally got home in the middle of the night."

Tess is always the first person to defend her brother. With a deadbeat for a father who took off before Reed and Tess started elementary school, Reed was the one who worked at the gym, at fourteen, to help out with the bills. He was the one who showed up at our soccer games to watch Tess play.

Gwen backpedals. "I didn't mean anything by it."

Tess stands up and grabs her bag.

"Where are you going?" I ask.

"I need some space."

"Don't leave, Tess," Gwen pleads. "I'm sorry. I didn't know your brother worked so late."

"Now you do," Tess says as she walks away.

Gwen puts her head down on the table. "Why did I say anything?"

"She'll get over it," Lucia says. "Just leave her alone until practice."

I feel bad for Gwen, but she should know better. Nobody gets away with criticizing Reed in front of Tess. Not even me.

CHAPTER 3
Striker

AFTER SCHOOL, I'M the first person on the field for soccer practice. The letter makes me want to get out here and earn it. I stand in the center of the field, passing the ball from knee to knee. This is the place where I feel most at home—the most like me.

It doesn't hurt that soccer reminds me of Dad. He taught me how to play and I loved the game from the first kick. Mom says I would've slept with my kid-size soccer ball if she had let me. Dad had dreamed of going pro, too. It turned out he was a better Marine than a soccer player.

Losing him made me realize that we can't control everything that happens in life. The universe has its own plans and we don't get a vote.

But soccer has always been the one thing I could control—not whether my team wins or loses a game. That's out of my hands. But the way I play and the effort I put in—that part is my choice.

"I heard somebody on my team was accepted to the University of

19

North Carolina." Coach Kim strolls toward me with a bag of balls slung over her shoulder. "You've worked so hard for this, Peyton. I'm proud of you."

"Thanks. I wasn't sure if it was going to happen."

She pulls the drawstring on the bag and dumps out the balls. "I was sure enough for both of us."

"It's not a done deal. I still have to maintain my grades, and I'll need a recommendation letter from my coach at the end of the season."

"That might be a problem," she said, teasing me.

"And I have to train harder than ever so I'll be ready to start 'in my current position' for UNC in the fall, or something like that. The letter looks like a contract."

"That's standard language. Coaches have a limited number of open spots on their teams. They have to make sure they're offering those spots to athletes who will be ready to fill them nine months from now." She tosses me a ball, and I head it back to her. "So go warm up."

Lucia is the next person out of the locker room. "You always beat me out here."

"What can I say? You're slow."

She blows out a puff of air. "Whatever. You wouldn't win as many games without me."

"I can't argue with that."

Lucia and I have been playing together on school and select teams since fourth grade. She's the best goalkeeper in our high school division.

I lob the ball at the bottom right corner of the goal. Lucia isn't ready and she almost misses it. But she dives for the ball and makes the save.

"I almost got that one by you."

"Because I wasn't ready," she says, calling me on it.

The rest of our teammates trickle out of the locker room, and Coach Kim takes a few minutes to get updates from everyone. Then she splits us into two teams for a scrimmage. When she blows the whistle, everything except the game fades away.

I dribble the ball down the field and look for an opportunity to pass. I'm a center forward—a striker, like Alex Morgan. It's my job to score goals and create opportunities for my teammates to score. It's an offensive position that requires more than just soccer skills.

I hear Dad's voice in the back of my mind. *A striker has to have guts and take risks. You have to know when to pass or when to take the shot. There will be shots that look impossible, but they aren't. Sometimes the difference between winning and losing is taking that shot when you get the chance.*

"Peyton! On your left," Imani, another forward on my team, shouts.

Gwen is coming up next to me on the outside. Lucia is playing goalkeeper for the other team, and she'll stop any ball within her reach before it hits the net. The bottom corner of the net is my only chance. Gwen is right on top of me, her feet slipping into the spaces between mine as she attempts to steal the ball.

"Peyton, over here!" Imani raises her hand to let me know she's still open. She doesn't see Tess behind her.

Today still feels like my perfect day, and on your perfect day you have to take the shot. I kick the neon-green Umbro ball, and it rockets toward the bottom left-hand corner of the net.

Lucia realizes where the ball is going and dives for it. The green ball skims the fingertips on her glove and sails into the net. The other girls on my scrimmage team shout and clap. Scoring on Lucia doesn't happen often.

You have to know when to pass or when to take the shot.

After practice I check my phone. Reed still hasn't called or texted me. He never goes all day without sending me at least one text. I grab my bag and call him as I head out to my car. His phone rings six times.

Where the hell is he?

I'm about to hang up when he answers. "Hey. I was just about to call you."

"At five o'clock? Why not just wait until tomorrow? You're obviously busy since I haven't heard from you all day."

"My phone died. Why are you so mad?"

"Colleges sent out letters two days ago." Tess and I have only mentioned it twenty times in the last week.

"Yeah?" Reed asks as if he's hearing the information for the first time.

"*Yeah?* That's all you have to say?"

In the background, voices mix with the familiar sound of weights hitting the gym's rubber floor mats. Someone asks Reed a question that I can't make out.

"Reed?"

"Hold on, Peyton." Reed says something to the person in the background. I only catch bits and pieces of his end of the conversation. "He's early. . . . Did he bring everything? I'm coming. . . . Give me five."

I'll count to ten and then I'm hanging up.

I'm on six when Reed gets back on the line. "Sorry. I'm training a new guy. He doesn't have the drills down. So the letters went out? Are you worried you won't get one?"

"I already did. Something my boyfriend should know." The excitement of telling him is completely gone.

"I *told* you my phone died." An edge creeps into his voice.

"We should talk later."

"Don't hang up. I'm being an asshole." Reed's tone changes completely, and now he sounds sweet. "I'm sorry. You said you got a letter. From where?"

"University of North Carolina. The coach wants me to play on the women's soccer team." Part of me still can't believe it.

"I knew you'd get in." He sounds excited. "You can fill me in tonight and we'll celebrate at the party. Meet me at my place at nine. The guy I'm training is waiting. I've gotta go."

"Reed—"

"I'll see you at nine. Love you." He hangs up without waiting for me to say it back.

I'm still annoyed when I get to Reed's a few hours later, and I'm definitely not in the mood for a party. As I walk up to the building, my phone pings with a text from Tess. She already left for the party with Lucia.

sperm donor called. go easy on Reed.

Any chance of Reed having an epiphany about the state of our relationship is gone now. *The Sperm Donor* is how Tess refers to their father. He gets drunk and calls once or twice a year to lay into one of them— usually Reed.

The fighter, Reed "The Machine" Michaels, owes at least part of his success in the cage and the underground fights to his father. Reed has eighteen years' worth of rage churning inside him, and his father's calls fuel that fire. It's hard for me to imagine how he feels. All the memories

I have of my dad are good, and the few memories Reed has of his father are terrible.

I take my time climbing the stairs to the apartment. Should I bring up the call if Reed doesn't? When I reach the third floor, I hear voices coming from inside an apartment.

"I gave you all the extra money I had, like I do every month," Reed says.

"I know," his mom says. "And I wish you didn't have to."

"You sure about that?" he demands.

"Do you think I like asking you for help? It's the last thing I want. But I'm short on the rent."

"I just told you that I don't have any more money. What the hell do you want from me?" He shouts so loud that it makes me jump.

I've never heard Reed yell at his mom or Tess. Even when I argue with him he always stays calm. Pissed off, but calm.

"Now you're gonna cry and make me feel like shit?" Reed asks. He's not yelling, but his tone is intense. "I'm out of here."

I back away from the door just as it opens, and Reed charges out of the apartment. He almost walks into me but catches himself. He glances from the apartment to me and seems to calm down. "How long have you been out here?"

"A few minutes." My throat is so dry I barely get the words out.

He closes his eyes for a second and takes a deep breath. "I shouldn't have done that. Shit."

I touch his arm. "What happened? I've never heard you yell at your mom before."

"Because I don't." He turns away and paces the hall. "My piece-of-shit father called. He was drunk, as usual. Talking shit about how we ruined his life. I said I don't know how we could've ruined his life when he never sees us."

"What did he say?"

"Not much. It pissed him off and he hung up." Reed takes a deep breath. "Tess left for the party, and as soon as she was gone, my mom started complaining about how she can't make rent. Asking if I could work extra hours when I'm already working as hard as I can. I just lost it." He glances at the door as if he's considering going back inside. "Let's get out of here."

"Are you sure you don't want to apologize to your mom? I can wait out here."

"Not now. She needs some space." He takes my hand and leads me toward the stairs. "I'll drive."

I look back at the apartment door, imagining Mrs. Michaels crying on the other side. Why isn't he going back inside to apologize?

We get in Reed's car and for a few minutes neither of us says a word. The houses get larger and more opulent the closer we get to the party.

Reed steals a glance at me. "I'm sorry I didn't call you earlier today."

"It's fine."

"No, it isn't." He reaches over and rubs the back of my neck and smiles. "You got into UNC. That's a big deal. I'm really proud of you." His mood does a complete one-eighty, as if the scene back at the apartment never happened.

"Thanks." I'm not sure how to react. Reed's moods have been all over the place lately, but I've never seen him shake a bad one this fast.

"Like I said earlier, we're gonna celebrate tonight." He squeezes my shoulder, and I give him a weak smile.

"If you really want to celebrate, let's go somewhere by ourselves. I'm not in the mood for a party."

Reed frowns. "I need to get out of my head, you know?"

"And you can't do that alone with me?"

"Sure. But sometimes it's easier when there's a lot going on. We can go out tomorrow night, though. Is that cool?"

It's not cool. Not even a little.

But I'm not in the mood to argue. "Sure, whatever."

"Don't be mad." He turns into Quail Landing, the wealthy neighborhood where high school students throw parties and let strangers trash their homes whenever their parents leave town.

"I'm not mad," I lie. We talked about the offer from UNC for all of two minutes.

My perfect day doesn't feel so perfect anymore.

CHAPTER 4
Little Black Box

THE FACT THAT I asked Reed if we could spend time alone tonight and we ended up at a kegger sums up the current state of our relationship.

"You sure you don't want a drink?" Reed holds out a plastic cup. "It's your night. We should toast your acceptance."

"But you're not drinking," I say. He never drinks the night before a fight.

"I'll toast with this." He holds up the can of Coke he's drinking.

"That's okay. We can celebrate next week at Bourbon Steak." It's our favorite restaurant downtown. We made a reservation weeks ago just in case I had college news to celebrate.

"Is that next week?" he asks.

I know what's coming. "Yes. On Thursday night. It will be nice to spend some time alone."

He puts down the plastic cup. "About Thursday. I'm working late. But you can pick another night."

"It took weeks to get a reservation. You can skip one night at the gym."

"I wish I could."

He's bailing on me. Again.

"Forget it. I don't want to go anymore." I'm not trying to guilt Reed into changing his schedule. I mean it.

"I thought you'd be in a better mood tonight."

"I was until you bailed on me for the tenth time."

"Hi, you two." Tess enters the kitchen, her cheeks flushed and her hairline sweaty from dancing. She twists her hair into a knot, studying us. "What's wrong?"

"Nothing." I cross my arms and watch a guy beer-bong a six-pack.

"Peyton is pissed off because I wanted to come to the party," Reed says.

Was he paying any attention to our conversation?

"I'm *not* pissed." *But I'm getting there.*

"You look pissed," Tess says.

"I'm *annoyed*, and it has nothing to do with the party."

"Right." Reed exhales loudly. "She's mad because I can't go to dinner on Thursday. I've gotta work."

"You didn't even remember we had plans." When did I become the girl who begs her boyfriend for attention? And how fast can I get rid of her?

"That's not—" he says, but I cut him off.

"I don't want to argue. It's one stupid dinner. It doesn't matter."

Reed's phone pings and he reads the incoming text. "Hold on."

Sure. Why not? It's not like we were having a conversation or anything.

Reed wanders away from us, focused on whatever he's typing. Without looking up, he holds up two fingers and says, "Give me two minutes."

"More like twenty," I say loud enough for him to hear.

If he was actually listening.

Tess nudges my shoulder with hers. "I know Reed is a pain in the ass sometimes, but tonight it's not his fault. He's always a little off after the Sperm Donor calls."

She's probably right, but over the last two months, making excuses for her brother has become Tess' full-time job.

"It's not about whether or not he loves me. Something is going on with him, and it's not just the phone call. Something changed. He's different." I didn't realize how much until I heard him yelling at his mom.

Tess stares at the floor.

"Whatever it is, go ahead and say it," I tell her.

"Maybe it's not Reed."

How can she play dumb with me? I've seen the way Tess tiptoes around him like she's navigating a minefield when he's in one of his moods.

"So you think I'm the problem?"

Tess shakes her head. "No. That came out wrong. I meant maybe it's things between you two that changed. You're upset because Reed is at the gym all the time, but he has to train more if he's going to fight in the middleweight division."

"It was his idea to move up a weight class," I remind her.

"I know. I tried to talk him out of it. But he thinks he has a better chance of making it into the UFC as a middleweight."

"It's more than that." We're missing something. I lean against the wall and watch a new beer bong competitor get into position.

This is not how I envisioned celebrating my big news. I reach for my phone to check the time, wondering if it's too early to head home. But it isn't in my pocket. Nothing but lip balm, house keys, and Reed's car keys. God forbid he carry anything except his phone. I pat down my coat. "I lost my phone."

"It's probably in the car, like the last three times you lost it. I need to run to the bathroom and then I'll help you find it," Tess says.

The line for the bathroom is six people deep. I can't wait that long. "All my voice mails are on it."

Tess knows that by *all* I really mean *one*—the last message from my dad. It's the reason I've had the same phone for a year and a half, even though it barely holds a charge.

"I bet it's in the car," she says. "Don't worry."

"I'm just going to run out and check." I leave through the back door.

Outside, a stone retaining wall snakes down the hill beside the house. The wall separates a paved footpath from the long driveway. My arm scrapes against the rock as I rush toward the steps at the end of the walkway that lead down to the street.

Reed parked his car across from the steps, and I can't get it unlocked fast enough. I search for my phone in the front seat and between the crevices of the center console.

Nothing.

Think. Retrace your steps.

When we got in Reed's car I tossed my jacket in the back seat. My phone could've fallen out of the pocket. I lean between the front seats and grope around.

Come on. Please be here.

What if it's not?

My chest tightens. I can't lose Dad's message.

Reed's car is full of junk—hand wraps, sparring pads, sweaty T-shirts, and empty energy drinks. His smelly gym bag is open on the floor. I dig through it until my fingers hit something rectangular and smooth.

A box.

I take it out of the bag, expecting a cheap plastic box like one Reed uses as a first aid kit. But this box is glossy black cardboard, like a gift box.

Reed doesn't do surprises, and he thinks presents are a waste of money. The only gift he has given me in the seven months we've been together was for my birthday. And Tess and Mrs. Michaels don't have birthdays anytime soon.

My stomach bottoms out.

All the time he's been spending at the gym . . .

What if Reed hasn't been there every night?

Things have been off between us for a while and I'm not a fan of his recent mood swings, but I'd *never* cheat on him. That doesn't mean he wouldn't.

The box doesn't have a store name or logo printed on it, and it's a weird size—too big for a bracelet and too deep for a necklace. A watch, maybe?

I open the lid.

At first, I'm not sure what I'm looking at—small glass bottles and a folded sheet of paper? Then I lift the paper and see the slender objects tucked beside the bottles.

Syringes.

My hands shake and the bottles clink against one another. Most athletes who play at my level know about PEDs, performance-enhancing drugs. Using PEDs—or doping—gives athletes an edge. Strength, speed, or stamina—the results depend on the cocktail. I turn on the dome light and examine the labels.

Reed's cocktail of choice? Steroids.

Even as I stare at the evidence, I can't wrap my mind around this. Reed has a fight record that most amateur fighters would kill for. Why would he risk his future in the sport he loves? And his life?

Why didn't I see the signs?

His short temper and unpredictable mood swings.

The underground street fights.

The way he yelled at his mom.

Even the fist-sized hole in the wall in Reed's apartment. Picturing it now, I realize why it looked strange. The hole was too high to have been made by the doorknob.

So many things haven't added up over the last two months. I should've realized what was going on. Why didn't I connect the dots?

I'm done wondering.

Reed is going to connect them for me.

I close the box and shove it into the huge pocket of Dad's leather jacket as I get out of the car. Something is glowing on the ground, next to the curb.

My phone.

A text from Reed illuminates the screen.

where are u?

I pocket my phone and head back to the house, feeling raw.

When I look up, Reed is standing at the top of the stone steps, craning his neck as he scans the yard. He sees me and waits for me to catch up with him.

"Hey. I came out to find you," he says as I walk up the steps. "Tess said you went out to the car."

He's smiling.

I'm not.

I look around. This isn't a conversation I want to have in front of an audience, but I don't see anyone nearby. The retaining wall separates the stairs from the driveway and tall hedges block the view to the house.

Reed tries to put his arm around me, but I walk past him.

"Are you still pissed off about dinner on Thursday?" he asks.

"We need to talk." I'm not ready for this conversation. It's like standing on the edge of a swimming pool when you know the water is freezing. You just have to jump. "I found something in your car when I was looking for my phone."

I reach into my jacket pocket. Reed's skin pales when he sees the box. I hold it out between us, resisting the urge to chuck it at him.

"That's not mine."

I wave the box in front of him. "It was in *your* bag."

"TJ needed somewhere to put it." Reed looks everywhere but at me. "It's his."

"If you're going to lie, you should look the person in the eye when you're doing it."

"I'm not—"

"Don't treat me like I'm stupid. Tell me the truth or I'm going to walk away and I will *never* speak to you again." He opens his mouth to say something and I point at him. "*Never.*"

I pace in front of the retaining wall, toying with my dog tags.

Reed glances over his shoulder, checking to make sure no one is around. "I can explain."

This is really happening.

"I needed to put on some muscle fast. The guy I'm fighting in a few weeks outweighs me by fourteen pounds. I was going to stop after the fight. But I need this win to make it into the tournaments coming up if I want to book bigger fights." He's talking fast and pleading with me with his big blue eyes. "And what if Tess doesn't get a scholarship? She'll need money for tuition. If I don't attract some attention and get a sponsor, I won't be able to help her."

"Don't use Tess as an excuse. If you get caught, you'll be banned from competing altogether."

"Nobody will find out." He sounds so casual about it, like I caught him with a beer.

"Really? What if they test you?"

"They never test at this level unless someone gets reported or caught on-site. And I'm careful."

I exhale dramatically. "Well, that changes everything. I didn't realize how much thought you had put into cheating and pumping your body full of poison. I feel soooo much better now."

Reed's jaw muscles twitch. "It's not really cheating. I still have to win in the cage."

"Keep telling yourself that." I shove the box against his chest. "Take this. I don't want to touch it for another second."

Reed crams the box in the pocket of his cargo jacket, as if I'll forget it exists if it's out of sight.

"You've been lying to me for . . . how long, Reed? Two months? Or longer?"

"I told you I'm gonna stop."

"When?"

He rubs his hands over his face. "Soon."

34

I expected him to say *now* and beg me to forgive him—or help him. "Not good enough."

"What the fuck is that supposed to mean?"

"It means you have to choose right now. Me or the drugs." I watch him and wait for him to make the right choice and pick me. But the longer he doesn't say anything, the more my heart breaks. What happened to the boy who brought me mashed potatoes every day for a week after I had my wisdom teeth removed? The boy I gave every part of myself to?

It doesn't matter.

He's gone.

"I just need a little more time," he says finally.

"You made your choice. We're over." Saying the words hurts even though I'm the person saying them.

He presses his palms against his temples. "Okay. This is a lot for you to take in. But don't throw away the last seven months."

"*You* threw them away."

"A couple of months. That's all I need. After the tournaments I've got coming up I'll stop. I swear."

A minute ago he said he'd stop in a few weeks. Now it's a couple of months?

"You don't have to make me any promises, Reed. This relationship is over. I don't want a boyfriend who chooses drugs over me."

The color drains from his face. "You're pissed and you need some time to think," he says, in the soothing tone he uses when I lose a soccer game. "We should talk after you calm down. I'll take you home."

"There's nothing left to talk about. I'll get a ride from Lucia."

I try to walk around him, but Reed steps in front of me. "Are you running away from me?"

The accusation pisses me off. "Running? I'm not even walking fast. You're paranoid. That garbage is screwing with your head. And I don't run from anyone. I'm *walking* away because there's nothing left to say."

"Why are you being such a bitch?"

He did not just call me a bitch.

"Excuse me? Who do you think you're talking to? I'm not one of your fangirls begging you to hook up with me while you're all sweaty after a fight."

"I'm talking to you like you're my girlfriend, who won't cut me a break." The muscles along the back of his neck bulge. When did they get so big?

"I'm not your girlfriend anymore."

He bristles. "Stop saying that. We're not breaking up."

"Even if you hadn't been lying to me—which you have—do you think I could stand by and watch you poison yourself? I care about you."

"You *care* about me?" He jerks back as if I slapped him. "You're supposed to *love* me, not *care* about me. Or was that bullshit?"

"It's a figure of speech. Get a grip." But he doesn't have one anymore. I see that now. "This conversation isn't going anywhere."

I try to walk away, but Reed catches my arm. "We can leave together."

"There is no *we* anymore."

"You can't break up with me because of this, Peyton." His voice wavers. "I need you."

"I'm sorry." A knot forms in my throat. I turn toward the walkway that leads up to the house. I can see it over his shoulder. But Reed tugs my arm. "Let go."

"Not until you say we'll work this out. That you love me and we're still together," he pleads.

"I can't." I try to pull away, a little harder this time.

Reed's grip tightens and his fingers dig into my skin.

"I'm not messing around anymore, Reed. Let go." I jerk my arm and he pulls me toward him with so much force that I hit his chest. He releases my arm, but I can't get past him. He's too close.

His nostrils flare and he's breathing fast. "Yesterday you were kissing me. And now you don't want me to touch you?"

He jabs at my shoulder with his fingers and pushes me back a few steps.

"You're pushing me? I don't think so." I try to slip past him, but no matter which way I go he's right there blocking my path.

"You're breaking my heart, Peyton. You know that, right? And you don't even give a shit." He pushes me again, harder this time. I glance over my shoulder. The stairs are behind me.

"Stop it! The steps are right there!" I look around for help, but I can't see past the hedges.

"After seven months, that's all you have to say to me?" His mouth forms a hard line.

I catch a glimpse of Reed's arm moving through the air. Rocketing toward me.

His palm slams against my chest and it knocks the wind out of me.

The ground seems to slide out from under my feet, and I fall backward. I swing my arms, trying to regain my balance. But it's too late.

I'm already falling. . . .

My stomach plummets.

There's no up or down.

Colors blur and sounds bleed together.

My shoulder hits the step first, absorbing some of the impact. I grab for the retaining wall, but I can't catch ahold of anything. I'm half rolling, half skidding down the remaining steps. I see the ground, and I put my hands out in front of me to break my fall. But my knee hits the ground first.

My kneecap smashes against the concrete.

A shot of pain hits the back of my knee and splinters up my leg. A scream rips from my throat, and I manage to roll onto my side.

Reed is standing at the top of the steps, with his arms crossed. He shifts in and out of focus. I blink hard, and my vision sharpens.

For the first time, I see something different in Reed's eyes when he looks at me.

Rage.

I try to process what's happening, but my thoughts are jumbled. All I want to do is get away from him. I shift my weight to try to move. Pain shoots down the back of my leg behind my knee. I cry out, but my voice sounds strange, like it belongs to someone else. Like I'm not crumpled in a heap at the bottom of the stairs, looking up at the person who put me here.

"Are you okay?" someone calls out.

I turn my head and see two people running toward me. That's when I realize that I'm lying on the sidewalk where the steps and the retaining wall end, and now people can see me.

"A girl fell down the stairs," someone shouts.

The pain shoots down the back of my knee again. Strangers crowd around me. At least I'm not alone with Reed.

He jogs down the steps, playing the concerned boyfriend.

If that asshole doesn't stay away from me—

"Peyton? Oh my god!" It's Tess.

Everything will be okay now.

Tess rushes over and kneels beside me. She brushes the hair out of my eyes. "What happened?"

"We were arguing," Reed says. The rage is gone. Now he looks panicked. "Peyton shoved past me, and I guess she lost her balance."

The words hit me like bricks.

"I tried to grab her arm, but I wasn't fast enough." Reed hesitates as if he can't bear to say the next part.

"And she fell."

CHAPTER 5
Shattered

AT FIRST, THE words don't make sense.

I look at Tess. "I didn't fall. Reed pushed me."

For a second, Tess stares at me as if she couldn't have heard me correctly.

"That's not what happened, Peyton," Reed says calmly. He kneels beside me, and I recoil.

"Get away from me!"

"Peyton? What's wrong with you?" Tess' voice trembles. "Reed would never hurt you."

"You lost your balance," he says patiently.

"You mean *after* you pushed me?"

Tess' eyes dart between her brother and me. "Maybe it seemed that way, or—" She glances at the people crowding around us and presses her lips together, making it clear she doesn't want them to hear our argument.

Another shot of pain races up behind my knee and I hold my breath until it subsides.

Oh god. It must be serious if it hurts this much. I can't even bend it. How can I play soccer if I can't bend my knee?

Lucia and Gwen push their way to the front. They drop down at my side, between Reed and me—providing a buffer without realizing it.

Tess takes out her phone. "We should call an ambulance."

"No! Just take me to the emergency room." I need a doctor to look at my knee. My whole body aches, but I try to push up with my elbows and get into a seated position. Another flash of pain races up the back of my leg and I suck in a sharp breath.

"I don't think you should move," Reed says. "What if you hurt your back?"

"I don't give a shit what you think!" I shout. My friends and the other people gathered around us seem confused.

Tess and Lucia support my back and help me sit up. My injured leg is stretched out in front of me, but I can't move it more than an inch without sending another shock of pain through my body. I'm not sure if I can stand, but I doubt it.

And there's no way I can walk.

"You'll have to carry her to the car, Reed," Tess says.

He looks at me and I lose it. "Don't even think about touching me."

Reed rubs the back of his head. "Come on, Peyton. Don't do this. Just let me carry you so we can get you to the ER."

I ignore him and turn to Tess. "Find someone else. Anyone else." She looks hurt, as if I'm talking about her.

"I'll get Lorenzo," Lucia offers.

I nod and grit my teeth against the pain. The back of my knee feels like a rubber band that's being pulled too tight, and the smallest movement sends daggers up my leg.

"Are you okay?" Tess squeezes my arm.

"It just hurts," I manage.

And I'm scared to death. What if it's my ACL? Or a fracture? What if there's permanent damage?

Tess turns to Reed. "I don't understand what happened. Were you guys still fighting about how much you've been working?"

His eyes flash to mine.

"Go ahead, Reed. Tell her."

He looks at Tess. "It's a misunderstanding."

"You're a lying asshole." The sight of him makes me sick. I look over at Tess. "He's been doping. When I went out to the car to look for my phone, I found his stash in his gym bag."

"I told you it's not mine," he says.

"You admitted it was yours."

"No." He stays calm. "*You* kept saying it was mine."

Tess holds up a hand, cutting us both off. "Then whose is it?"

"It belongs to a friend." Reed glances at TJ. "Someone on my team."

"Think about it, Tess," I plead. "Reed's mood swings and his temper, the street fights . . . it's because he's doping."

"Please don't do this, Peyton," Reed whispers, loud enough for Tess to hear. "I know you think the drugs are mine, but they're not."

Tess' bottom lip quivers, and her eyes flicker between her brother and me. She pulls her arm out from under my hand, making it clear she believes Reed.

My eyes burn and I blink back tears. One escapes and rolls down my cheek.

Thankfully, Lucia and Lorenzo plow through the crowd. He bends down next to me and Lucia hovers behind him.

"Are you in a lot of pain?" he asks loud enough for everyone to hear.

At least people think I'm on the verge of tears because of my knee and not my best friend's betrayal.

I sniffle. "I don't feel great."

Lucia squeezes his shoulder. "Let's get her to the hospital, babe."

"On it." Lorenzo picks me up gently, but even the smallest movement hurts my knee.

Reed rushes to his car and opens the passenger door, as if he thinks he's driving me.

"I'm not going anywhere with him," I tell Lorenzo.

Reed hears me and stands on the sidewalk with his shoulders sagging. He doesn't look like the kind of guy who would push his girlfriend down the stairs. But that's exactly who he is, even if I'm the only person who can see it.

The crowd around us begins to whisper. Lorenzo stops, unsure what to do or where to go.

Lucia takes over. "Tess, why don't you drive Reed's car? He can ride to the emergency room with Lorenzo and me."

Reed nods at Tess, as if she needs his permission. "Peyton has the keys."

I take them out of my pocket and hand them to Lorenzo.

I don't want Reed to come to the ER. I never want to see him again. How could he do this to me? My mind keeps going back to the same thought.

What if there's permanent damage?

Lorenzo helps me into the back seat, and I clench my teeth against the pain.

"We're parked all the way on the other side of the house, so we'll be a few minutes behind you," Lucia says.

"Can someone call my mom?" I ask.

"I will." Tess whips out her phone and she jogs around to the driver's side. When she gets in the car, I listen to her side of the conversation.

"She's okay," Tess tells Mom.

No, I'm not.

"I mean, she hurt her knee. But other than that she's okay. Umm . . . She fell down the stairs."

"I didn't fall," I say under my breath.

Why doesn't she believe me?

"We're in the car now. She's right here. Hang on." Tess tries to hand me the phone. "Your mom wants to talk to you."

If I talk to Mom I'll fall apart, and I have to hold it together until I get to the ER. "I'm all right, Mom," I yell, loud enough for her to hear me. "I just want to go to the hospital."

Tess gets back on the phone. "Your mom says she's on her way."

The pain has finally caught up with me, and my whole body aches. My eyelids feel heavy, but I fight to keep them open. I'm not letting down my guard with Reed standing outside the car.

When we finally pull away from the curb, I let out a sigh of relief as the crowd grows smaller and smaller through the rear window. Reed stands in front of everyone, watching me.

There's so much I want to say to Tess, but I'm exhausted.

I'll just close my eyes for a minute.

I feel the ghost of Reed's hand on my arm and the pressure from the final push, and my body jerks. My adrenaline spikes and then it bottoms out again, like the crash you experience after pulling too many all-nighters.

"The ER is only five minutes away," Tess says, her fingers wrapped tightly around the steering wheel.

"He pushed me, Tess. I swear."

Her eyes meet mine in the rearview mirror. "Maybe it seemed that way because you bumped into him and he tried to grab you. It could've felt like a push."

"But that's not what happened."

"Reed would never hurt you. He cares about you more than he cares about himself."

How can I get through to her?

Trashing Reed won't work, so I try another approach. "I know the difference between someone pushing me and someone trying to grab my arm. It was a push. Reed lost his temper and flew into a rage."

"The drugs weren't his," she says firmly.

"Tess, all the signs are there—"

She cuts me off. "He's been moody and temperamental because he's *exhausted*. He trains nine hours a day, seven days a week. Then he coaches fighters for another four or five hours before he goes to a sketchy location to fight so we can afford food and electricity."

There's no way to get her to believe me right now.

Tess pulls into the hospital driveway and stops near the glass doors to the ER. She leaves the car running and hops out. "I'll be right back."

Once I'm alone, the panic hits me full-force. Some of the shock of Reed pushing me has worn off, and now all I can think about is my knee.

What if I can't play soccer anymore? Permanent damage could keep me off the field—and end my career before it begins. Every once in a while you hear about a situation like this on the news. A high school athlete blows out a knee or an elbow during senior year, and it's game over. What else will I do if soccer isn't an option?

Nothing. I'll do nothing.

Going pro has been my dream for as long as I remember.

The folded acceptance letter is still tucked in my back pocket.

I don't have a plan B.

Tess returns with two nurses, and the three of them to help me out of the car and into a wheelchair. Inside, a nurse wheels me through a pair of double doors that lead to an examination area, where hospital beds are lined up along the walls and separated by privacy curtains. Once I'm settled in a hospital bed, Tess sits with me as the nurse takes down my personal information.

"Can you tell me where it hurts and describe the pain?" the nurse asks.

"I've had some shooting pains, but there's also a weird pulling feeling. Is that bad?" I ask.

"I'm not a doctor, sweetheart. But don't worry. This is an excellent hospital." The nurse takes notes on a form attached to her clipboard. "How would you rate your pain, on a scale of one to ten? One being no pain and ten being unbearable pain."

"If I don't move my knee, it's around a five. But if I bend it, the pain shoots up to an eight or nine."

More like a ten.

I'm trying to be brave. A ten seems like a pain level of someone who survived a car crash, not a fall down the stairs. But if the nurse asked me to rate how scared I am right now, it's a twelve.

"How did you hurt your knee?" the nurse asks.

If I say Reed pushed me intentionally, he might get arrested. If Tess weren't in the picture, I would've called the police already.

But Mrs. Michaels can't support herself and Tess on her own. She tried before and it didn't go well. It seemed like every year they were moving into another crummy apartment. When Mrs. Michaels ran out of friends' couches to crash on, Reed started working even more extra hours to help out.

"I fell down a flight of stairs," I say.

"Did you hit your knee against anything?" She scribbles more notes on her clipboard.

"My kneecap hit the ground."

"On the sidewalk," Tess adds, wringing her hands.

The nurse finishes writing. "A doctor is going to come and take a look. Can I call someone for you?"

"I already talked to her mom," Tess says. "She's on her way."

"I'll be back to check on you in a few minutes." The nurse pulls the privacy curtain around the bed, and Tess and I are alone again.

"Thanks for not saying anything," she says.

"I know you don't believe me, but I'm telling the truth."

Tess presses the heels of her hands against her temples, like she's fighting the worst headache of her life. "I don't know what you want me to say. You're my best friend. I want to believe you. But we're talking about Reed. He's my brother. He wouldn't lie to me. And he loves you. He'd never hurt you."

Until tonight I thought the same thing. "I know you want to believe him, but he admitted the drugs were his. That's what we were fighting about before he—"

"It's a misunderstanding." Tess' tone turns harsh. "That's the only explanation."

Not the only one.

Before the argument escalates, I hear Mom's voice on the other side of the curtain asking for me. "I'm looking for my daughter, Peyton Rios."

"Mom?" I call out.

A moment later, she pulls back the fabric and rushes toward me, trapping me in a hug. "Thank god you're okay. What happened?" Mom stands and looks from me to Tess.

"I'm going to the waiting room." Tess tries to part the curtain, but she can't find the opening and she has to walk past Mom to go through the other side. Normally, Tess would give her a hug, but not today.

Mom takes my hand. "What's going on?"

I try not to cry. "We were at the party, and I went out to Reed's car to look for my phone. But I found something else."

"What?" Mom leans closer and her dark hair swings forward.

"He's doping. I found steroids in his gym bag."

"I don't understand. What does this have to do with your knee?" The moment Mom asks the question, recognition flashes in her eyes. "What happened to your knee?" She says each word slowly, giving them weight. "Tess said you fell down the stairs."

"I did." I nod as a tear runs down my cheek. "Reed pushed me."

My mother narrows her eyes. "Reed did this?" Her expression is ice cold, and it has *Wife of a Force Recon Marine* written all over it. "I'll be right back."

"Mom, don't!" I try to push myself up in bed. "Mom!"

She storms past the other beds and walks through the automatic doors that lead to the waiting area. For a split second, I panic. What if she does something stupid and Reed gets angry and hurts her, too?

An image of my mom standing at the window, in her nightshirt, flashes through my mind. I was eight or nine. Dad was away and Mom heard someone outside. She told me to hide under the bed, which I did for two minutes before I scurried down the stairs to see what I was missing. She was standing in front of the bay window in our living room with a baseball bat resting on her shoulder and the phone in her hand. She called 911, and the police came. Nothing happened, but after watching her that night, I knew that if someone had been out there, my mom would've protected us.

I watch the doors that lead to the lobby, waiting for Mom to come back. Instead, Lucia and Gwen walk in.

"Over here." I wave.

They both look freaked out.

"What's going on out there?" I ask.

Gwen sits on the edge of my bed and bites her nails. "Your mom just cussed Reed out."

"Then she ran him out of the ER." Lucia looks impressed. "She told him to get his ass out of the hospital or she'd run him over with her car."

I take a deep breath. I love Mom for doing it, but I wish Tess wasn't here to witness my mother's wrath. "What did Reed do?"

"He just kept apologizing and saying it was a big misunderstanding and that he loved you," Gwen says.

Lucia drops down into the chair beside the bed. "And your mom kept telling him to shut up and get out of her sight. She also told him to burn in hell a few times."

I've seen Mom in action. It's easy to picture her unleashing on Reed. "What about Tess?"

"She left with Reed. I mean, she had to. He's her brother." Gwen fiddles with the remote control for the bed. She presses a button and the bed rises like the chairs at the hair salon. "Sorry."

"Stop messing with that thing," Lucia snaps.

Gwen shoots her a dirty look. "Don't boss me around."

"Where's my mom now?" I ask.

"She's talking to security so they won't let Reed back in the ER," Lucia says. She makes eye contact with Gwen, who immediately

49

glances in my direction. She catches herself and looks over her shoulder, in an obvious move.

"Real subtle. Who wants to tell me what else is going on?" My voice cracks.

Lucia curses in Spanish under her breath. "We don't want to make you feel worse, but I have to ask . . . What really happened between you and Reed?"

I lie back against the pillows and stare at the ceiling. "You don't believe me, either."

"I didn't say that." Lucia looks me in the eye. "But you were in a lot of pain after you fell and you were so upset. I—"

Gwen cuts in. "You mean *we*."

Lucia glares at her. "*We* just want to hear it from you."

"Reed pushed me down the stairs. Is there anything else you want to know?"

"Like, *pushed you* pushed you? On purpose?" Gwen asks.

"Yes." I search their faces, trying to figure out if they think I'm telling the truth. I never thought my friends would doubt me about something this serious.

Gwen shakes her head. "It doesn't make sense. Before your mom came out to the waiting area, Reed wouldn't shut up about how worried he was and how much he loves you. It didn't seem like an act."

"Maybe he believes what he's saying, but that doesn't change the fact that he's lying," I say.

Lucia nods.

Does that mean she believes me?

Behind Gwen, I catch a glimpse of Mom through the slit in the curtain. She's coming toward us, and I don't have a chance to ask.

"We should go and let you talk to your mother," Lucia says. "You're going to be okay."

Gwen doesn't say anything. She just waves as they walk away.

Mom pulls the curtain around my bed closed.

"What did you do?" I ask.

"I got rid of that bastard, and I told him to stay away from you."

"But Tess was there."

Mom sits on the edge of the bed and rubs my arm. "I wish that hadn't been the case, but I couldn't let Reed sit in the waiting area after what he did to you."

"Tess doesn't believe he pushed me. I'm not sure if any of my friends do. Everyone thinks I'm *confused*—that it was some kind of misunderstanding. But you believe me? Right?"

She leans over and takes my cheeks in her hands. "You're my daughter. I will always believe you. I also know that if you weren't sure about what happened tonight you would admit it. You're rational and clearheaded like your father. And you have great instincts."

"If my instincts are so great, how did I end up here?"

CHAPTER 6
Robo-Girl

MY LIFE IS divided into two time periods—*before* Reed pushed me down the stairs and *after*. In less than twenty-four hours, I went from being a star player on the girls' varsity soccer team with a boyfriend who loved me and an offer letter from UNC to being an injured athlete with a blown-out knee—courtesy of my steroid-abusing ex-boyfriend.

After my visit to the emergency room, two MRIs, and three appointments with Dr. Kao, a highly respected orthopedic surgeon, the doctor gave me an official diagnosis. I had a ruptured PCL—the ligament that runs behind the knee to stabilize it—and damage to some of the surrounding cartilage.

I needed surgery.

Now it's three weeks later and I'm in Dr. Kao's office again, sitting in the same chair, waiting for the post-surgery verdict. I hook my thumb in the middle of the chain around my neck and slide Dad's dog tags from one side of the chain to the other. Dr. Kao opens the folder on her desk and skims a page, her expression unreadable.

My future is written on that page.

What if she says I can't play soccer anymore? Or if she says I can, but when I get back on the field again I suck? I'm not sure which is worse.

Playing soccer is the only thing I've ever wanted to do. I don't have a backup plan. Obviously, I'll get a degree in something when I graduate from college. But I have no idea *what*.

Dr. Kao flips through her notes. "I have good news. Peyton's post-surgery MRI looks better than I expected. I was able to repair the PCL with the allograft Achilles tendon without causing the knee any additional trauma."

Mom exhales like she had been holding her breath. "Thank god."

Hope swells in my chest. I'm desperate for good news.

Mom turns her wedding ring back and forth on her finger, a giveaway that she's worried. "What happens next?"

Dr. Kao swivels her stool toward me. "You'll meet with a physical therapist three to four times a week to strengthen your quadriceps and regain your range of motion. If everything goes well, you should be out of the leg brace soon."

She's referring to the black brace strapped to my leg that looks like black body armor from a sci-fi movie Dad loved called *RoboCop*. Two bars run up the inside and outside of my leg, secured by three adjustable straps that wrap around my leg—at the top of my thigh, and above and below the knee. Circular hinges allow me to bend my knee, but it feels awkward.

"When can I start playing soccer again?" It's the only information that matters to me.

"The ligament needs time to heal." Dr. Kao points at my MRI glowing in front of the light box. "You're lucky the kneecap didn't shatter."

Nothing about this situation feels *lucky*.

"How much time, exactly?" I rake my hands through my hair.

"Four months. But you should be able to resume normal activities in four or five weeks." Dr. Kao keeps talking, but I'm not listening.

"*Four months?* That's almost half the year." I knew I'd be out for the rest of the fall season, but four months? I do the math. "It's November now. . . . I could miss the spring season."

My high school doesn't offer spring soccer, so Lucia and I play on a select team that travels all over the country—a team that's more competitive than the varsity team at Adams. We start playing in March. Even if my knee heals by then, Dr. Kao isn't going to let me throw on a uniform and run straight onto the field. I'll probably need more physical therapy, and my select coach will ease me back in slowly.

This isn't happening.

I stand up too fast and my chair skids backward. I'm not used to the brace, and it throws me off-balance.

Mom catches my arm and steadies me, her hand shaking. "We'll figure it out. It will be okay, Peyton."

I sit and slouch in the chair. "I'll lose my spot at UNC. How is that *okay?*"

Dr. Kao shifts on her stool.

"You can't be the first athlete to sustain an injury. They must have protocols for situations like this." Mom turns to Dr. Kao, her expression hopeful. "Don't they?"

"I already know how it works. It's all in the letter." Which I practically have memorized. "The offer is contingent on how I perform this year and my ability to start for UNC next year. Division One teams can't afford to take chances on injured players." My voice cracks.

The office walls are covered with autographed posters and framed thank-you letters from college and pro athletes whose careers Dr. Kao saved.

I look at Dr. Kao. "Is there anything we can do to speed up the process? Anything at all?" Tears roll down my cheeks. "Please. I have to play in the spring."

"I know this must be hard to hear, Peyton," Dr. Kao says calmly. "But if you start playing before the PCL heals properly and you sustain another injury on the soccer field, you will end up back on my operating table."

It didn't happen on the field.

Mom panics and hammers Dr. Kao with questions about recovery rates and physical therapy. I wish the questions in my head were as simple to answer.

What if I had stayed home instead of going to the party that night? Or if I hadn't found the box in Reed's gym bag? What if I had figured out he was doping sooner?

Would I be sitting in this chair right now?

The answers don't matter, because I'll never know.

CHAPTER 7
Burning Bridges

MOM KNOCKS ON my bedroom door and pokes her head into my room. "Do you need anything?"

I'm still trying to process the conversation in Dr. Kao's office. "No. I'm okay." The words sound ridiculous coming out of my mouth.

Nothing about this situation or the way I feel is okay.

Mom twists her wedding ring on her finger. "Has anyone called?"

She means Tess.

"Not yet."

The last three weeks have been miserable without my friends, especially Tess. I've talked to her on the phone a handful of times, but the calls didn't involve any real conversation—just meaningless chitchat between awkward silences. I couldn't mention my knee or share my fears about the surgery and my future without it sounding like an attack on Reed.

Gwen completely bailed on me after she left the ER. Conflict of any kind makes her nervous, but I never asked her to take sides. I guess I'm better off knowing that our friendship wasn't worth a single phone call.

At least Lucia didn't ditch me. She still calls and stops by to hang out and drop off my classwork. She's also the only one of my friends that showed up at the hospital the day of my surgery. Gwen texted me—the only time since the night I was in the ER.

But I expected Tess to be there. We've been best friends forever. Some things are bigger than being stuck in the middle between your best friend and your brother.

Friendship is bigger.

She texted me with a lame excuse about having the flu.

Instead of Tess, I got Reed.

According to Lucia, he hung out in the parking lot, hiding from my mom and calling Lucia for updates. He's playing the heartsick ex-boyfriend with everyone, including me. He texts and calls me constantly—begging me to give him another chance or to meet him somewhere to talk. Like that's ever happening.

Soon everyone will know the truth about him.

"Do you think they'll get the test results before the lab closes tonight?" I ask Mom as she rearranges the soccer trophies on my bookshelf.

"They should . . ." Mom says. "Reed went in this morning."

Lucia texted to tell me the test was today, but she didn't know what time. "How do you know the test was in the morning?"

"Reed's mother told me when she called earlier to inform me what a terrible parent I am."

I scoot closer to the headboard and sit up straighter. "She actually said that?"

Mom nods. "Among other things. There was lots of nonsense about how Reed would never use drugs or hurt you. I stopped listening after she told me he used to volunteer at an animal shelter."

"That's actually true."

"Then I feel sorry for those dogs." Mom has been on a rampage since she saw me in the emergency room and I told her who put me there. That was *before* we found out the extent of the damage to my knee. "I still think we should've pressed charges against him."

"It would hurt Tess more than Reed. Mrs. Michaels already works two jobs and she still can't cover their rent and the bills without his help."

"I care about Tess, but she's not my daughter," Mom says.

I'll never forgive Reed. The moment he pushed me, a switch flipped inside me. It severed the bond between us along with the feelings I had for him. But I still can't send Reed to jail—not when Tess loves him so much and he's the only thing standing between Tess and an eviction notice.

"When the drug test comes back positive, he'll get kicked out of the league. For Reed, that's worse than spending a few months in jail," I remind her.

Mom gathers a pile of dirty clothes. "I'm going to toss this load in the wash and do a little stress baking. Any requests?"

"You choose."

She leaves my door open on her way out. "Yell if you need anything."

I check the time. Three o'clock. Classes ended for the day at two thirty.

Tess should know the truth soon, if she doesn't already. But what will that do to our friendship? Will things ever be the same between us if Reed gets banned from the league? I'm the one who reported him. Will Tess think about that every time her mom works an extra shift?

My cell phone rings and Tess' number appears on the screen. This won't be an easy conversation. She's probably hysterical.

I take a deep breath. "Hey."

Tess sniffles on the other end of the line. "How could you do this to me?"

"Do what?"

"Lie to me," Tess says between ragged sobs. "You were supposed to be my best friend. I trusted you."

Were.

The word knocks the air out of my lungs. "I didn't lie."

"The results of Reed's drug test came back, Peyton. They were negative."

For a second, I'm not sure if I heard her correctly. "Then the results are wrong. They need to test him again."

My head spins like I'm stuck on a ride that's moving too fast.

"Did you even think about how this would affect me?" Tess chokes back a sob. "Reed would've been banned from competition and the gym. And I would've ended up sleeping in the car, with my mom, in the Walmart parking lot. Without my brother's help, her paychecks would last us two weeks."

"I'd never do anything to hurt you, or your family, Tess."

"You already did."

"But I—"

The line goes dead.

The test came back clean.

How is that possible? Even if Reed stopped doping—which I don't believe for a second—the drugs would still be in his system three weeks later.

I flip open my laptop and type in a search for *beating drug tests for performance-enhancing drugs*. Dozens of blog posts and articles pop up: BODYBUILDING TIPS: DRUG TESTS YOU CAN (AND CAN'T) BEAT, MASKING PERFORMANCE-ENHANCING DRUGS, and URINALYSIS: AN ATHLETE'S BEST FRIEND.

The articles lead me down a rabbit hole of forum posts outlining different ways to conceal PEDs in a test, including the most effective cleanses, ointments, and herbal concoctions to get the job done. From consuming ridiculous amounts of water and taking diuretics to dilute any traces of PEDs in your urine to using testosterone patches or an ointment called The Cream to mask steroids—the options are endless and readily available online.

Lucia told me that Reed had willingly agreed to the test. Now I understand why.

A blood test was the only real threat—and passing the urinalysis basically guaranteed that Reed wouldn't have to take one. His trainer wouldn't push for a blood test and risk losing his best fighter, not when he has Reed's clean test results to wave around.

My phone pings and I check my texts. Unknown. That means it's Reed. I blocked his phone numbers, so now he calls from his friends' phones.

test came back clean. it's all good.

It's all good?

What is he referring to, exactly? Getting away with pushing me down the stairs and lying about it? Beating a drug test and destroying my credibility? Or ruining my relationship with Tess?

I want to respond with a cruel comment that will hurt him, but I stop myself. Not because I want to be the bigger person in the situation. I just want him to stop texting and calling, and anything I say to him—positive or negative—will just encourage him.

So I do nothing.

A minute later, he texts again.

miss u. can we talk?

The house phone rings in the hallway.

"Reed? Is that you?" I hear Mom say. "Hello? Whoever this is, stop calling my house."

"Was it Reed?" I call out.

"I don't know."

From the moment the gossip junkies at school heard about what happened at the party, I've been inundated with emails, social media messages, and—the latest—prank calls and texts. The fact that I haven't been to school, or anywhere else except the doctor's office, for the last three weeks hasn't deterred the haters.

Team Reed—his friends, girls who want to hook up with him, other athletes who think I'm trying to destroy his future in MMA, and the bandwagon haters—instantly branded me as a bitter ex-girlfriend or "a girl trying to get attention."

Reed's clean drug test will give them another excuse to rally.

A handful of supportive messages also showed up in my inbox. Most of those were from anonymous senders or girls I don't know very well who had been physically attacked by someone they knew—school bullies, a family member, or someone they were dating. People hadn't believed them, either.

My phone pings again. Reed will probably keep texting me all night. I glance at the message and I suck in a sharp breath. I don't think this one is from Reed.

watch your back bitch

Another text appears on the screen.

you can't stay home forever

The house phone rings again.

"Where's the cordless?" Mom calls from the hallway.

"In here."

She pokes her head in my room, and I point at Dad's chair. "Under Dad's jacket."

Mom digs through the clothes and finds the phone.

"Hello?" She tucks it under her chin, picks up one of the T-shirts piled on the chair, and starts folding. "What did you say?"

The color drains from her face and she drops the shirt.

"Who is it?"

Mom hangs up and stares at the phone. "I don't know. But he was threatening you."

"Are you sure it wasn't Reed?"

"Positive. I would recognize his voice."

"What did he say?"

The phone rings again, startling me. Mom's finger hovers over the buttons on the cordless. "Don't answer it, Mom!"

She ignores me and stabs one of the buttons.

A few seconds pass.

"I'm calling the police." She hangs up and hurls the phone into the hallway, watching it roll across the carpet.

"Mom? Was it the same person? Tell me what he said."

"I don't want to repeat it." She twists her wedding ring, her hands shaking. "It will upset you."

"The way it's upsetting you right now?" Seeing her so rattled makes me nervous.

Mom touches a framed photo of Dad on my dresser. He's not wearing his Marine Corps uniform or cammies. He's dressed in his red-and-white league soccer uniform, with a ball tucked in the crook of his arm. "If your father were here, he would know exactly how to handle this."

"We can deal with it. Just tell me what the guy said."

She takes a calming breath. "He said, 'Watch your back, bitch. You can't stay home forever.'"

The same thing someone texted me.

A prickling sensation spreads up the back of my neck, like dozens of tiny spiders crawling over my skin.

"Who calls someone's home and says that kind of thing?" Mom paces in front of the bed. "I hope the people who have been harassing you feel terrible when they finally find out the truth about Reed."

"That's not going to happen." My throat feels like it's closing up. "Tess called. Reed passed the drug test. No one will believe me now."

Mom stares at me in shock. "How could he have passed?"

"I was online trying to figure that out. It's easier than you think."

The phone rings again.

"Don't answer it this time, or he'll keep calling," I tell her.

"Fine." Mom presses her fingers against her temples. Her nerves are frayed. "I'm going to get a glass of water and take something for my headache. Do you want a snack? You haven't eaten much all day."

"No thanks."

She rubs her neck and walks into the hallway.

The phone rings again.

"Unplug it," I yell, but the doorbell rings and drowns out my voice.

"You've got to be kidding me," Mom yells.

I stand up slowly. The *RoboCop* brace throws off my center of gravity and I'm not used to it yet. As I walk into the hall to unplug the landline, the doorbell rings again.

"I'm coming!" Mom shouts.

The phone is still ringing and I yank the cord out of the wall.

"What in the hell are you doing here?" I hear Mom ask.

"I want to see Peyton, if that's okay." The sound of Reed's voice knocks the wind out of me, and I reach for the wall to steady myself.

"Is this a joke?"

I peek around the corner.

"No. I took my drug test this morning, and it came back clean." Reed sounds excited, like a kid. "Didn't Peyton tell you?"

"She stopped caring about your life when you pushed her down the stairs. But I'm *thrilled* to hear that you found a way to cheat on the test."

"I didn't—"

Mom points at him. "Don't you dare show up here and lie to me. Now, get your ass off my property or I'll have you arrested and you can spend some time in jail, where you belong."

Reed backs up and steps off the porch. "Can I just talk to her for one minute? I'm trying to make this right."

"You want to make things right? Tell the truth. Peyton doesn't deserve to be harassed because of your lies."

"Who is harassing her?" Reed's voice sounds deeper—and colder—his anger simmering just beneath the surface. "Tell me who it is and it won't happen again."

"Are you going to push them down the stairs, too?"

Why is she provoking him? If she pushes him too far, he could snap.

Mom starts to close the door. "I'm reporting this little visit to the police. Don't come near my house again."

Reed tries to say something, but Mom slams the door so hard that a framed piece of my little-kid artwork falls off the wall and hits the floor.

"Did he leave?" I ask.

"He's probably still outside somewhere." Mom paces, twisting her wedding ring back and forth on her finger. "I need to call Hawk."

If we've reached a Hawk-level situation, Mom is panicking.

Mom's older brother is an all-around badass. He was in Dad's Force Recon unit, but Hawk was the only Recon operator in their unit who made it home from Iraq. My uncle said goodbye to the military, and now he's a private security consultant.

His specialty?

Risk assessment and crisis management.

"Mom, this isn't a crisis."

"Someone is threatening you. Reed is calling constantly and now he's showing up here. I'm afraid to leave you alone when I go to work." She takes out her cell phone. "And what about school?"

"This will blow over."

"Do you honestly expect me to let you go back to school on Monday so we can test that theory?" she asks. "You're going to have to transfer or we'll get you a tutor."

"I can't just transfer to another school. Reed screwed up my knee and lied to everyone about it. He tested clean, and now people think *I'm* the liar. If I run away, he wins."

"This isn't a game. There's no winner. If your father were here, he'd say the same thing." Her voice cracks.

But he's not.

My chest tightens, with the familiar longing for my dad. "Mom, you're overreacting."

"It's better than losing my daughter." She dials my uncle's number and retreats to the kitchen.

I spend the next twenty minutes eavesdropping on Mom's call with Hawk.

"I don't need the risk percentages," Mom says. "If you think he's dangerous, that's all I need to hear."

Not good.

I pace in the hall outside the kitchen, but Mom's side of the conversation isn't giving away much.

"Are you sure it won't be too much trouble?" she asks. "You're on your own and you have the boys."

My pulse ramps up.

Mom can't be thinking what it sounds like she's thinking.

I storm the kitchen the moment she hangs up. "I'm *not* going to stay with Hawk."

He lives in Mom's hometown, in Tennessee, with his twin sons. The last time we visited was six months before Dad died. I haven't gone back since then. It's too hard. Now Hawk visits Mom whenever work brings him near DC.

"Your uncle agrees with me. Staying here is dangerous. Someone is threatening you, and we have no idea if Reed is involved. And Reed is stalking you."

"Fine. I won't go back to school until this dies down. I'll do the home tutoring thing. But I can't leave. It will look like I'm running away."

"I don't care how it looks."

"But I do." I'm not letting Reed's lies force me out of my school—or DC.

Mom crosses her arms. "It's not your decision."

"A small town like Black Water probably doesn't even have a physical therapist. I can't lose my scholarship. I won't let Reed take that, too."

"There are two state universities less than forty minutes from Black Water, and a major city an hour away. Hawk is going to make some calls, and I'll call Dr. Kao in the morning."

She has it all figured out.

"I *can't* live with Hawk. He'll want to talk about what happened to Dad."

My father died in a cave-in, in a tunnel underneath an abandoned building. Hawk was on the roof of another building nearby, keeping watch and listening on the two-way radio. He heard everything. He was also at the recovery scene and, later, he read the autopsy report.

But I don't want to know the details.

"Hawk is your uncle and he loves you. He's not going to talk about what happened to your dad unless you have questions," Mom promises.

"I won't. Ever."

Mom touches her wedding ring. "One day you might want to hear the whole story."

My chest tightens like a hand is squeezing what's left of my heart. "I already know how it ends."

CHAPTER 8
Black Water

MOM ORGANIZED MY temporary move and transfer to Black Water High School in less than forty-eight hours. The threatening phone calls were a serious motivator. We received three more calls after Mom got off the phone with Hawk. Mom reported the threats to the police, but there wasn't much they could do, so we just unplugged the phone again. The police suggested filing for a restraining order to keep Reed away from me, but Reed was out of control. It would take more than a piece of paper to intimidate him.

I didn't get another text from the prank caller, but Reed texted me eleven times, which was more annoying.

The morning we left, I lugged a huge suitcase out of my closet and filled it with armloads of clothes. Clean or dirty—everything made the cut. How was I supposed to know what I'd need in Tennessee? My family had always visited in the summertime, and it was November.

I packed the important things last—my soccer cleats, even though I wouldn't need them; the framed photo of my parents from my nightstand; a raggedy stuffed bunny I slept with, a birthday gift from Dad when I turned five; and the crooked friendship bracelet Tess made me in elementary school.

When it was finally time to leave, Mom couldn't get me in the car fast enough. I wasn't in the mood to talk, so I let her listen to mind-numbing soft rock stations.

The fall soccer season was supposed to be my victory lap, after three years of leading the girls' varsity team to the state championships. Then in the spring, I'd showcase my skills with my select team. The hard part was supposed to be over, but now it was just beginning. Hawk came through on the physical therapy front—the only detail about this move that mattered to me. A doctor who specialized in sports therapy agreed to work with me.

Six hours into the drive, Mom turns off the radio in the middle of "The Piña Colada Song," which means she wants to talk.

"Does Tess know you left?" she asks tentatively.

"Lucia told her." The only one of my friends who seems to believe me. "I'm sure Tess doesn't care. The last conversation we had lasted less than a minute and she called me a liar. I haven't heard from her since then."

Mom turns off at the next exit. "The truth will come out eventually. It always does."

"That's a cliché."

"It also happens to be true."

After the last three weeks, I'm not holding my breath.

The off-ramp merges onto a narrow two-lane road without a McDonald's or a gas station in sight, just a green sign that reads: BLACK

WATER 20 MILES. Crooked wooden fences wrapped in barbed wire separate the road from miles of pasture. Aside from the occasional weather-beaten barn, there's nothing out here except cows.

Lots of them.

"Is this the road we usually take?" I look out the window in time to see a huge black cow taking a dump near the fence. "I don't remember it being so . . . farm-like."

"I took the back roads. Your dad preferred the highway. But Black Water is 'farm-like' no matter which road you take to get there. Before they built the grain processing plant, the only thing that came out of Black Water was Division One football players."

"Football is archaic."

"Don't let your uncle or anyone else in town hear you say that," she teases.

It doesn't bother me if everyone hangs out at football games. I'm planning to spend all my free time rehabbing my knee.

Up ahead, I see the high school stadium. A white letterbox sign next to the parking lot reads, WARRIORS VS. STALLIONS. FRIDAY NIGHT.

The parking lot is full of pickup trucks and Jeeps.

"It's like we're at a country music concert."

"That means we're in the right place." Mom pulls into the first free parking space and takes out her phone. "Before we go in, I need to check my work email."

My knee is achy and stiff from the drive. "I'm going to stretch my legs."

As soon as I get out of the car, it feels better.

Mom wasn't exaggerating when she said everyone in Black Water loves football. I've never seen so many cars at a high school game. Even stranger, there's nobody else out here except a kid riding a skateboard and three guys, who look like they're in high school, drinking beer on the tailgate of a pickup.

Back home, there were usually more people hanging around outside the stadium than filling the seats inside.

The skater weaves between the trucks, dodging side mirrors like a pro. He coasts into the row next to ours. His hair is buzzed on the sides, with a short strip of hair running down the middle of his dark brown scalp.

Maybe this town isn't as different from DC as it looks. A black kid with a fauxhawk wearing high-top Vans and an old-school Green Day hoodie is a good sign.

The skater does an ollie and the board does a perfect flip, righting itself in midair. He's about to nail the landing when someone darts between two cars and kicks the board out from under him. I recognize the asshole with the mullet. He's one of the guys I saw drinking in the back of the pickup.

The kid lands on his butt and winces.

The guy with the mullet laughs. I'm surprised he has the guts to laugh at anyone else when he's sporting a bad '90s haircut and a T-shirt that says: THE HIGHER THE TIRES, THE CLOSER TO GOD.

The jerk's friends wander over, cracking up like idiots. The taller guy has pockmarked skin and a unibrow. His buddy has two separate eyebrows, but he doesn't seem to know his shirt size. His T-shirt is stretched over his gut like a sausage casing. These two shouldn't be laughing at anyone, either.

The tall guy with the unibrow points at the skater. "Looks like you need some practice, Tucker. Maybe you should go back to California and hang out with the other skate freaks."

Tucker stands, brushes off his jeans, and picks up his board without a word. He either knows the drill or he's smart enough not to antagonize them. He keeps his head down and stays close to the parked cars, giving the three guys a wide berth. He almost makes it past them when the jerk with the mullet lunges to the side and snatches Tucker's skateboard out of his hand.

Tucker tries to grab it, but he's not fast enough. "Give me my board, Garrett. Why are you hassling me? I didn't do anything." He doesn't have a Southern accent like Garrett and his friends. Maybe he really is from California. I feel bad for him. He looks at least two years younger than the guys bullying him.

Garrett leans the skateboard deck against his shoulder. "You made me look stupid in class today because you couldn't keep your mouth shut."

"Because I answered a question right?" Tucker asks innocently.

"I bet he did that shit on purpose." The guy with his gut hanging out eggs Garrett on.

Garrett nods. "Yeah. I was thinking the same thing." With his free hand, he grabs the front of Tucker's hoodie and yanks the kid toward him.

Tucker is so much shorter than Garrett that he has to balance on the balls of his feet. "I swear I wasn't trying to make you look bad."

"But you did." Garrett tosses the skateboard to his friend. The guy with the unibrow catches it and brings the board down hard against his knee. The deck snaps in half.

"No, man! Come on." Tucker scrambles to collect what's left of his skateboard. As he bends down to pick up the pieces, Garrett plants his work boot against Tucker's chest and shoves him backward.

Mom comes up behind me. "What's going on?"

She follows my gaze and sees Tucker hit the ground—and three older guys laughing at him. Mom narrows her eyes.

I know that look.

"I'll be back." Mom marches between a Bronco and the truck parked beside it. For someone who is paranoid about my safety she rarely worries about her own.

I catch her arm before she makes it past the front of the Bronco. "You can't go over there alone, Mom."

"Of course I can."

"I'll go." I try to squeeze by her.

"You just had surgery, Peyton. You're staying here. I can handle those Neanderthals. But call Hawk and tell him to come out here anyway. Those three boys need a good scare." Mom takes off before I can stop her.

I pull out my phone and follow her. I don't think I have Hawk's number. It's not like we call or text.

Shit.

Where's Mom?

"Leave me alone," Tucker pleads.

Garrett grabs Tucker and hauls him to his feet.

I catch a glimpse of a figure darting between two cars near Garrett and his friends. It's another guy.

Mom cuts between two trucks and yells, "Get your hands off him!"

Garrett and his friends look over at Mom. They don't notice the mystery guy charging toward them.

The new guy on the scene grabs Tucker and tears him away from Garrett, simultaneously clamping his other hand around the jerk's neck.

"What the—" Garrett can't get the words out.

The mystery guy tightens his grip on Garrett's throat. "If you want to

74

start shit with someone, let's see how well you do against somebody your own size." He shoves Garrett away from him. "Only a punk would pick on a freshman."

Garrett coughs and rubs his throat. "You'd better watch it, Owen."

"Or what?" Owen laughs and shakes his head like he thinks Garrett is pathetic. "I'm right here. But you'd better bring your friends, because you're going to need help."

The other two guys take a step back to make it clear they aren't accepting Owen's challenge. Garrett puffs out his chest, but he keeps his mouth shut.

"That's what I thought." Owen points at Tucker's broken skateboard. "And you're paying to replace his board."

"The hell I am."

Owen walks up to Garrett and looks him in the eyes. "Those tires on your truck look expensive. How much would it cost if you had to replace one of them? A lot more than a skateboard, I bet."

It takes Garrett a second to catch on. "Stay away from my truck, Owen."

"Like I said, you're paying to replace his board." Owen steers Tucker toward the stadium. "Let's go. We're done here."

Tucker looks back at my mom and nods—a silent thank-you, as if he knew she would've stepped in.

Owen turns in our direction.

He looks right at me. His expression is a complicated tangle of emotions I can't unravel. There was a time when I would've wanted to try to do some untangling, after watching a good-looking guy swoop in and rescue someone. But I'm done with complicated.

CHAPTER 9
Friday Night Lights

MOM BREATHES A sigh of relief when Garrett and his friends take off. "I guess Black Water isn't as boring as I remember."

"I've had enough drama in the last three weeks. Boring might be good. Maybe they have boring hot dogs inside." I walk toward the stadium. That's when I see the entrance.

It's a tunnel.

I *don't* do tunnels.

Mom notices it, too. "I'm sure there's another way in."

We circle around to the side of the building and find another entrance.

Inside the stadium, the field spreads out before us.

A commentator's voice crackles over the loudspeaker. "Another interception by number seven, Cameron Carter!"

The crowd's approval thunders through the stands that rise up above us.

The loudspeaker crackles again. "Touchdown! The Black Water Warriors are giving the Spring Hill Stallions an education tonight, ladies and gentlemen!"

"This is a high school stadium?" I ask Mom over the noise. "This place looks big enough for the NFL."

"Not quite. But people in Tennessee take their football seriously." Mom cranes her neck in search of my uncle. "All the stores in town close on Friday nights."

"Sissy!" Hawk calls out. He's the only person who calls my mom Sissy instead of Sarah—or, if we're in Black Water, Sarah Ann.

My uncle waves from where he's standing several rows up. At over six feet tall and built like a tank, he's hard to miss—gray buzz cut, neat beard, and a kind face. Grandma used to call it a face you could trust. Mom waves back, beaming at her older brother. They don't see each other often, but you would never know it when they get together.

I look around and take stock. The stands are packed with friendly faces—parents and grandparents wearing Black Water Warriors scarves and wool jackets, a German shepherd sitting on the bleachers next to its owner, and lots of people sporting blue-and-white face paint to support their team.

There are more letterman jackets and school colors in the crowd than I'm used to seeing back home. But, otherwise, the people my age aren't dressed much different from the students at my school.

At least I won't be the girl from out of town, who dresses weird.

Unless something has changed since I visited two years ago, I'll probably be the only half-white, half-Cuban girl in Black Water. This place isn't exactly a melting pot. But it's nice to see some brown and Asian faces.

Mom and I weave between people carrying cardboard boxes full of hot dogs, fries, and six-packs. When we reach the narrow steps that slope up to the top of the stands, Mom lets me go first. "Are you sure you don't want any—"

I glare at her and she stops talking.

Holding the handrail, I take the steps one at a time. If my knee gives out, I'm not falling on my ass in front of half the town—maybe the *whole* town, judging by the number of people here.

A pair of hiking boots stops on the step above me, and before I have time to look up, an arm swings around my waist. Adrenaline surges through my bloodstream.

Hawk lifts me up, and my feet dangle in the air. "At the rate you were going, the game would be over by the time you get a seat."

I'm not that lucky.

Instead of using the steps, Hawk walks up the middle of the bleachers, dodging the people seated on them.

"Put me down."

He ignores me. "Almost there."

"Is she all right?" a woman calls after us.

My cheeks burn.

Before I protest again, Hawk lowers me to the ground. "Door-to-door service."

I sit on the cold metal bench without a word, watching Mom walk up the steps like a normal person.

My uncle takes a seat beside me. "Everybody needs a little help once in a while."

Once in a while, I could handle. But people think I need help all the time now. They take one look at the *RoboCop* brace, and they rush to open doors and pull out chairs.

And I hate it.

On the soccer field, my mind was always in control of my body. I decided if I was too tired to keep running. I decided whether or not to quit. Now my body is in control. I have a knee that gives out with no warning, and I couldn't run the length of a soccer field if my life depended on it. Dr. Kao claims it will just take time.

But what if she's wrong?

Hawk leans forward, with his elbows propped on his knees, studying the field.

I spot Mom at the end of our row. The people in the first few seats stand to let her scoot past them. She sits beside me and puts her arm around my shoulders. "What did I miss?"

"Not much." I lower my voice. "It's just football."

"Fourth and ten. Stallions' ball." A flurry of activity takes place on the field. "Interception by the Warriors!" the commentator shouts.

People around us leap to their feet, cheering madly, and the sudden movement makes me jump. Mom notices and squeezes my shoulder. Hawk puts two fingers in his mouth and whistles.

A man who is way too old for blue-and-white face paint turns to my uncle. "Your boys are tearing up the field tonight. Think they can keep it up until the championships?"

Hawk smiles proudly. "That's the plan."

Two huge guys on the field bump chests and yank on each other's helmets. When they turn around, CARTER is printed on the backs of their jerseys.

"Wait. Those giants are the Twins?" I ask. Not possible. The last time I saw them was a year and a half ago, at Dad's funeral, and they were stocky, but they look taller and even bigger now.

Hawk nods. "Yep. Right there. Number seven and number eleven."

The cheerleaders break into a routine. I give them credit. They make backflips and handsprings look easy. The rest of the game passes with more backflips and the Twins mowing down players from the other team.

After the Warriors slaughter the Stallions, Hawk waits until the stands empty out before he gets up and walks in front of me as we make our way down the steps. At the bottom, the Twins stand off to the side, patiently shaking hands with adults waiting in line to congratulate them. They're definitely taller and their features are more defined. A few cheerleaders hang out next to my cousins, smiling as if they personally contributed to the win.

One of the Twins notices Hawk and waves. "Over here, Pop."

I have no idea if he's Christian or Cameron. Most identical twins don't look exactly alike. Subtle differences, like the curve of a jawline or the slant of an eyebrow, help people tell them apart. But Christian and Cameron are mirror reflections of each other—the same broad shoulders and square jaws, blue eyes and dirty-blond hair, and milky white skin and boyish smiles.

"That was one hell of a game, boys." Hawk clamps a hand on each son's shoulder.

"Did you see me take down their receiver?" one of my cousins asks, sweaty blond hair flattened against his skull.

His brother elbows him out of the way. "Yeah, yeah. That was *after* I sacked the quarterback."

"You both did your part." Hawk sounds as if he's used to the Twins competing for his approval. "How about you both try not to embarrass yourselves in front of Aunt Sissy and your cousin?"

"Which one is which?" I whisper to Mom.

"Cameron is number seven and Christian is number eleven," Hawk says. He must have dog hearing.

Cameron sees me and grins. "You look so much older."

"So do you guys."

Christian looks at me and elbows his brother. "This is gonna be a problem."

Cam nods. "I was thinking the same thing."

I cross my arms. "Why would I be a problem?"

"Not you," Christian says. *"This."* He moves his hand up and down in front of me, like he's referring to what I'm wearing—or he thinks I'm such a mess that they need to hide me in the house. "We don't want the guys at school—"

"Talking about me?" I finish for him.

Cam gives me a weird look. "He was going to say *looking* at you."

"I think the Twins are giving you a compliment," Mom says.

"Oh." I feel like a jerk, but I'm relieved my cousins aren't embarrassed to be seen with me. "Don't worry. I'll be able to handle your friends."

Christian looks unsure. "I wouldn't bet on it."

"You can't bet on anything because you don't have enough money to buy a pack of gum, loser," Cameron fires back. Within seconds, the Twins are shoving each other like ten-year-olds.

"That's enough, boys," Hawk says, and the Twins stop.

"There's a party at Titan's," Cameron tells Hawk. "We'll take Peyton with us and introduce her to everyone."

I have zero interest in meeting people tonight. I'd rather sit through another football game. "Thanks, but I'll pass. I'm worn out from the drive." I yawn for effect.

Cameron's eyes dart to my brace. "You're probably not ready to go to a party after what happened at the last one."

"But things wouldn't have gone down like that if we'd been there. Your ex would've been the one who '*fell*'"—Christian makes air quotes—"down the stairs."

My stomach lurches.

The Twins know what really happened to my knee. The one thing I don't want anyone in Black Water to find out.

"I think you embarrassed her," Cam whispers to Christian loudly. "Change the subject."

I glare at the Twins.

A crease forms between Christian's eyebrows as he tries to come up with something. Cam elbows him. Christian shoves him back. "I'm working on it."

What are the odds these two can keep a secret?

Suddenly, Christian blurts out, "Buck Richards kissed a hot girl after the game in Knoxville last week and it turns out she's his cousin—twice removed, whatever that means."

The secret-keeping odds don't look good.

CHAPTER 10
Treading Water

I LOOK OVER at Mom, but she's too busy staring down my uncle to notice. She obviously didn't know Hawk told the Twins the truth about my knee.

Hawk rubs the space between his eyebrows and clears his throat. "I'm sorry, Peyton. I should've checked with you or Sissy before I said anything."

So much for Mom making sure Hawk didn't tell anyone.

"But they won't say a word about it. *Right*, boys?"

"No, sir," Cam says.

Hawk looks at Christian, who says, "I won't even breathe."

My uncle nods. "All right, then. Why don't you do everybody at the party a favor and hit the showers."

The Twins jog off, and I'm stuck with Mom and Hawk and I sense a heart-to-heart conversation coming. I'm tired of answering the same depressing questions. Am I in any pain? Am I having a hard time getting around? Am I worried about losing my scholarship?

All of the above.

"Where's the restroom?" It's the only place they won't follow me.

Hawk points toward the main entrance. "Straight down on the left. You can't miss it."

"Thanks." I take off, determined to get out of earshot before they start talking about me.

In the restroom, a faucet drips below a huge mirror decorated with BLACK WATER WARRIORS bumper stickers. I lean against the wall and let the cold seep through the back of my jacket.

My phone vibrates in my pocket.

Wow. Mom waited a whole five minutes before checking on me.

But it's not Mom.

Tess' name glows in green letters.

Did she figure out I've been telling the truth? Maybe Lucia got through to her. I answer on the second ring. "I'm so glad you called."

"The last time we were alone together you said you had nothing left to say to me." Reed's voice taunts me from the other end of the line. "I'm hoping that's not true."

"Then prepare to be disappointed. If I wanted to talk to you, I wouldn't have blocked your number." My heart pounds. "Why do you have Tess' phone? Let me talk to her."

"She went inside to get something and left her phone in the car. Like you said, my number is blocked."

"It hasn't stopped you from calling."

"I miss you, Peyton." The regret in his voice feels like spiders crawling over my skin.

84

"Put Tess on," I manage.

Reed takes a shallow breath, as if the conversation is hard for *him*. "I doubt she'll talk to you."

"And who do I have to thank for that?"

"I begged you to give me another chance. That's all I wanted." He sounds sincere, like the boy he was when we started dating. "I'd never hurt you."

"Are you delusional?" I fire back. "You *did* hurt me." Why am I still talking to him? I should hang up, but it feels good to unleash some of my anger. He deserves it.

"It was an accident."

Something inside me snaps. "Was lying about pushing me down the stairs an accident, too?"

"I never wanted any of this to happen, Peyton. But you backed me into a corner. If you'd just given me another chance, I could've fixed everything. I wasn't trying to hurt you. I love you."

A bitter laugh escapes my lips. "Keep telling yourself that, but don't try to sell it to me. I was *there*."

"I get it. You're not ready to forgive me. But I know you still love me, and I'm not giving up on us."

The sound of Reed's voice—a voice I used to love hearing—sickens me now. "I don't care what you do as long as it doesn't involve me."

I hang up just as the door to the girls' bathroom squeaks open. I duck into the nearest stall. Blue-and-white cheerleading skirts pass by the space between the stall door and the wall.

"Christian is totally playing games again," a girl says in a slow Southern drawl. "A week ago he said he wanted to 'get serious about our relationship.' Then last night we got in this huge fight and he said we needed a break."

Her friend gasps. "Oh my god, April! He broke up with you?"

"*Taking a break* isn't the same as *breaking up*." April sounds annoyed.

"They both have the word *break* in them."

I try not to laugh.

"Don't be so literal, Madison. It doesn't matter. I was about to tell Christian it was over anyway. I'm sick of waiting for him to grow up. He isn't the only hot guy in Black Water."

"But he *is* the hottest," Madison says. "And y'all will get back together. You always do."

"That's the problem. Christian thinks I'll wait around forever. So I'm gonna show him I won't."

The restroom door squeaks open again, and the sound of lipsticks and compacts clattering in makeup bags instantly stops, along with the gossip.

"Hey." Another girl wearing a blue-and-white skirt enters the mix. "Are y'all going to the party?"

"Why? Are *you*?" April asks in the bitchiest way possible.

"I'm not sure." The girl rifles through her purse "Your double pike looked great tonight, Madison."

Madison ignores the compliment. "I had that down freshman year."

"FYI, Grace," April says. "I dumped Christian, so feel free to follow him around like a puppy tonight, like you always do."

I don't know much about cheerleading, but these girls are on the same squad, which makes them a team. You don't gang up on a teammate.

"I don't follow him around," Grace says quietly. "We're just friends."

"Give it up," April snaps. "Everyone knows you're into him. It's embarrassing. Even before I broke up with him, you were always lurking around. I never said anything because I felt bad for you."

Okay . . . she's definitely a bitch.

"You should go for it," Madison says. "Maybe Christian will take pity on you."

The bitches burst out laughing.

Come on, Grace. Tell them to go screw themselves.

Grace stays quiet. All the pent-up emotions I held back during my conversation with Reed suddenly resurface. I slam my palm against the stall door, and it swings around and bangs against the next stall.

The three girls jump.

A quick assessment and I'm ninety-nine percent sure I have all the players pegged. The chesty brunette with freckles wearing too much eyeliner is the ex, April. The tall girl with a ponytail next to her—who looks like she lost a battle with a bottle of self-tanner—is Madison. And the petite girl fidgeting with the ends of her long, straight black hair must be Grace.

Based on the conversation, I was expecting Grace to be awkward or mousy-looking, but she's pretty—thick glossy hair, brown eyes, and rosy cheeks.

April glares at me from beneath her expertly coated lashes. "You're in the wrong bathroom. Visitors use the one on their side of the stadium." She crosses her arms and taps her foot, as if she expects me to scurry out.

I'm not a fan of power trips, and April is on a serious one. "Am I supposed to be intimidated? Because I'm just not feeling it. What else have you got?"

Madison puts her hand on her hip and stares. The whole scene is déjà vu from middle school.

April snorts. "You're obviously not from around here, so I'll let that go."

"Are you always this perceptive? What gave me away? My accent or the fact that you've never seen me before?" I ask. "I'm actually from a faraway place called Washington, DC. The president lives there, in a big white house called . . . *the White House*. Maybe you've heard of it?"

Madison and Grace stare at me wide-eyed, as if I'm the only person who has ever stood up to April.

April narrows her eyes. "I'd be careful if I were you."

"Or what? You'll throw lip gloss at me?" I almost laugh.

I'm done here.

Grace stifles a smile as I pass her on my way out, and I stop. This girl deserves a break. "By the way, your *friend*, and I use that term loosely"— I gesture at April—"didn't dump Christian. He dumped *her*. She was whining about it before you walked in."

"You bi—" April shouts at me as the door closes.

That was fun.

Sticking up for Grace cheered me up a little.

The stadium has emptied out for the most part, and the sight of the green field makes me feel like running. As a striker, it was my job to move the ball down the soccer field and score goals. The team relied on my speed.

I can't remember a time when I didn't play soccer. Dad spent hours dribbling alongside me—him with a standard soccer ball and me with a toddler-sized version. He stood in front of a flimsy net we'd made out of

PVC pipes, and played goalkeeper for hours so I could practice my corner shots. I lose myself in the memories.

"Hey! Watch—"

I look up in time to see a guy's broad chest before I walk right into him. My knee gives out, but he catches my arm.

"Nice save," he says, as if I'm the one who kept him from falling instead of the other way around.

I jerk away from him. The combination of hearing Reed's voice a few minutes ago and feeling a guy grab me from out of nowhere . . . it's too much.

"You okay?" Brown eyes that look even darker against his pale skin.

It's Owen, the mystery guy from the parking lot.

"I'm fine."

"You sure?"

Why won't my pulse slow down?

"Yeah. I have to go." I take off in the opposite direction, embarrassed.

I bumped into a guy and almost jumped out of my skin? This isn't me. I'm the person who never flinches during horror movies.

The leg brace makes me feel helpless. What if a stranger had grabbed me instead of Owen? Knowing I couldn't run or fight someone off terrifies me.

Or if someone tries to hurt me again.

Mom and Hawk are exactly where I left them. The Twins have returned from the locker room, freshly showered, and they swapped their football uniforms for jeans and T-shirts. The four of them are huddled together talking. They're probably discussing my fragile state.

They think I'm too traumatized to hang out at a stupid party. But I'm not the damaged person everyone thinks.

I *refuse* to be that girl.

I walk up behind the Twins and squeeze between them. "So when are we going to that party you were telling me about?"

CHAPTER 11
Bitches and Barn Parties

"I THOUGHT YOU said you weren't coming," one of my cousins says. Now that Christian and Cameron have changed out of their numbered football jerseys, I'm back to guessing which one of them is talking to me.

"I changed my mind."

The Twins each swing an arm over my shoulders and sandwich me in a bear hug.

"Just wait," one of them says.

"You'll love it," the other finishes.

Doubtful.

Mom's eyes well. "You're not leaving without giving me a hug, too. I'll probably be on the road by the time you get back to Hawk's."

"You aren't staying the night?" my uncle asks her.

"I already took today off, and I have an important meeting tomorrow."

"So where's my hug?" Mom opens her arms wide and I let her squeeze me as hard as she wants. "I'm going to miss you."

"Don't worry."

"It's part of the job description." She releases me.

The Twins trade uncomfortable looks. I want to get out of here as much as they do. The lump in my throat gets bigger every time Mom sniffles.

"I'll call you tomorrow." I give her another quick hug and walk toward the Twins, who perk up the minute they realize we're leaving.

She waves. "I love you, sweetheart."

"Me too."

"I'll take your things to the house," Hawk says. "Your mama will feel better after she gets a chance to give me instructions and boss me around."

The Twins fall into step on either side of me.

"Let's get outta here before they make us go eat dinner with them," one says.

"So what's the trick?" I ask as we walk to the parking lot.

"Run like hell before they catch us," my other cousin laughs.

"I mean the trick to telling you guys apart."

The twin in the green T-shirt nods in his brother's direction. "Obviously, I have cooler hair and I'm better looking."

His brother laughs. "Don't give up on your dreams, bro."

"Be serious. I don't want to guess who I'm talking to all the time."

"Nope. But I'll make it easy for you. Cam's shirt is blue. Mine is green," Christian says.

I wait for a serious answer, but that's all I get. "Come on. I'm smarter than your ex-girlfriend April. Give me a real answer."

Christian frowns, his thumbs hooked through the belt loops of his jeans. "How do you know about April?"

"I met her in the restroom. She was in full-on bitch mode."

Cam cuts between two trucks. "April gave you a hard time?"

"I'll set her straight at the party," Christian says. There isn't a hint of anger in his voice, but the comment strikes a nerve.

"She's not intimidating enough to give me a hard time. She was busy torturing another cheerleader." I turn to Christian. "And if anyone needs to be *straightened out*, I'll take care of it myself."

"I just meant I'd *talk* to her." Christian runs a hand through his damp hair, making it stick up in a few places. "I'd never put my hands on a girl."

Cam smirks, and Christian adds, "Not in a *bad* way . . . or without asking first. But if I have a girl's permission, then I'm all hands."

"I hope that sounded better in your head," I say.

Christian scratches his head and looks at Cam. "What did I miss?"

"TMI, bro," Cam says. "Keep that stuff to yourself."

"Right." Christian nods. "Sorry, Peyton. My bad. So did you tell April who you were?"

I laugh. "Who am I?"

"You're our cousin. Did you tell her?" he asks again.

"Sorry, I didn't realize you two were celebrities. Next time, I'll ask your ex to put a hold on the bitchcraft so I can identify myself properly."

I scan the parking lot and try to guess which pickup truck is Cameron's. "Where's your car?"

Cam gestures at the end of the row. "The gray F-150 with the lights on top is mine. Dale Earnhardt Jr. here burned out his clutch and he's too lazy to put in a new one."

"Why should I bust my ass fixing it when I have you to chauffeur me around?"

Cam unlocks the truck. "Keep running your mouth. It's a long walk to school."

Christian opens the passenger-side door and tries to help me climb in.

"I've got it." I try to pull myself up, but I'm not strong enough.

"It doesn't look that way from here," Christian says.

After a few attempts, I make it onto the running board and manage to haul myself up from there.

Christian hops in after me. "That seemed like a lot of work for no reason."

"I had a reason."

"Not a good one." Cam starts the truck and shifts it into gear. The engine roars and the seat vibrates. The thing sounds more like a monster truck than a normal pickup.

I cover my ears.

Cam pats the top of the dashboard and drives out of the parking lot. "She's not that loud."

We pass more farms, a Texaco gas station, and a diner with a blue neon sign on top that reads: THE BEST DINER IN THE WHOLE DARN STATE.

This isn't my typical Friday night. I should be at Tess' house, angling for a corner of the mirror while we put on our makeup together and debate which party to hit first. Between the private schools and the public schools like ours, we usually had at least two or three options.

Cameron turns off the main road and drives over the grass toward a cluster of cars parked in front of a long barn. A bonfire blazes off to the side. He pulls up behind a red pickup and pockets his keys.

I look around outside. "Where's the house?"

Christian points to a steep hill next to the barn. "At the top."

There's no way I'll make it up that slope. "I'm not sure my knee can handle a hike yet."

"The party isn't in the house. It's a barn party," Cam says, as if that will clear up any confusion.

Barn party isn't a term I heard a lot in DC.

Christian reaches for the door handle, and I catch his arm. "Hold on. I'm not going anywhere until we're clear about a few things."

"Okay. Lay it on us," Christian says.

Cam cuts in. "If you're nervous—"

"I'm *not* nervous." Okay, that's a lie. But I need this to sink in. "Number one: I don't need babysitters."

Cam tries again. "We never said—"

"I'm not finished. And number two: you both have to swear that you aren't going to tell *anyone* the truth about how I injured my knee—not your coach, not your girlfriends, not even your priest. I want to focus on rehabbing my knee, not answering questions about my ex."

"No worries there," Christian says. "We don't have girlfriends and there aren't any priests in Black Water. Only pastors."

"You're missing the point." I try a less subtle approach. "If you tell anyone what happened, I'll slip Ex-Lax into your lunch on game day."

Cameron's jaw drops. "That is wrong on so many levels."

Christian laughs. "She's not serious."

"Try me." I don't know if the Twins are trustworthy. I want to believe they are, but the situation with Reed proves that my instincts aren't as reliable as I thought.

"Your secret is safe with us," Cam says.

"We'll take it to the grave." Christian hops out and waits for me to lower myself down.

"If anyone asks, I fell down the stairs." Technically, it's true. "Don't offer up any details," I say as we cross the field. I need to keep the story simple. The more complicated it gets, the easier it will be for my cousins to make a mistake.

"Don't worry. We've got this," Christian says.

"If Christian doesn't screw up," Cam adds.

"I'm not the one who forgot to switch his tie at homecoming last year. That's how April caught us."

I get the feeling he's talking about switching more than ties. "Please tell me you didn't . . . Forget it. I don't want the details."

"You sure? It's a pretty good story." Christian grins.

"So is there anything I should know?" I walk between them, my head in line with their shoulders.

"Don't believe anything Titan tells you. He's a show-off and a pro at getting into girls' . . ." Christian hesitates, trying to edit his side of the conversation.

"Pants?" I finish for him.

"Yeah. Those."

The bonfire near a red barn is right out of a children's book. This one is a little shabby, and there's a keg sitting on top of a barrel beside actual haystacks. Fifteen or twenty people lounge around the fire, sitting on lawn chairs or blankets. The girls are clad in leather jackets or cute down coats. Some of them are wearing cowboy boots, but they look comfortable in them, like they're wearing sneakers.

My dark-wash jeans, layered tees, and Dad's leather jacket blend in well enough.

"It's about time." A good-looking guy the size of an NFL player walks toward us. His hulking frame makes the Twins seem average-size. He's wearing a Warriors letterman jacket over an untucked flannel shirt, jeans, and a baseball cap with an orange T on it. The scruff along his jawline adds to his white farm-boy vibe.

"I thought you bailed." The huge guy hooks his thumb around Cameron's, and they do a weird handshake.

"Our cousin just got into town." Cam nods in my direction. "This is Peyton."

The guy grins and sweeps his eyes over me. "Did your dad name you after Peyton Manning?"

It's a question people ask all the time. "No. My parents just liked the name." It was as close to the name of legendary soccer player Pelé as my mom would allow—a piece of information I'm not sharing with anyone in Football Country, USA.

The guy leans closer. "I'm Titan. This is my place, so let me know if you want anything, and I'll make it happen."

"Back off." Christian steps in front of me and jabs Titan in the shoulder. "She's our goddamned cousin."

"Just being friendly. Relax." Titan tugs on his baseball cap. "You didn't tell us she was hot."

Christian charges at him and Titan jumps back, hands raised. "Come on, man. I'm screwing around."

I grab Christian's shirt and yank him toward me. Then I smile at Titan. "It's nice to meet you."

"I need a beer," Christian grumbles.

As we walk to the barn, I take in the surroundings. Country music blares from a Bluetooth speaker perched on a bale of hay. Another dozen people hang out near the keg—girls flirting with other guys wearing quilted flannel coats or letterman jackets with jeans. Heads turn in our direction and people whisper.

I study the dented silver keg and try to ignore them. I'm not usually self-conscious, but the *RoboCop* brace changes things. It makes me feel different, even though the attention I'm attracting probably has more to do with the fact that I'm new in town than my knee brace.

"What's up, Darius?" Christian nods at a lanky guy wearing a University of Kentucky Wildcats Basketball cap.

Darius hands Christian and Cameron plastic cups and fills one for me. His tall brown frame towers over all of us. "You two played your asses off tonight."

Christian chugs the beer. "Don't we always?"

"That's what I like about you, Christian. You're a humble guy," Darius says as he hands me a cup.

"Thanks."

The Twins head for the bonfire. I slow down and let them walk ahead of me. They provide the perfect shield from all the strangers I don't want to meet.

Christian notices I'm lagging behind. "Come on, Peyton. We want to introduce you to everyone."

My cousins step aside and make room for me to stand between them. The people hanging out by the bonfire turn in my direction. Their expressions range from mildly curious to way too drunk to care.

"This is our cousin, Peyton. The one who's staying with us." Cam sweeps his arm from one side of the group to the other. "Peyton, this is everybody—Grace, Jackson, Tyrell . . ." He skips April and Madison.

Directly across from me, April stares with her mouth gaping open. "You've got to be kidding."

I flash her an exaggerated smile.

"What's that supposed to mean?" Christian asks her.

April looks like she's still processing the whole cousin thing, but she's trying to make eye contact with Christian.

"Maybe that's bitch code for 'nice to meet you,'" I say loudly.

Cam bursts out laughing and April's expression turns venomous. He ignores her and sits down next to Grace, like they're friends.

Christian picks up a beer from the six-pack next to April, cracks it open, and takes a swig without looking in her direction. "I heard about what happened. Don't give my cousin any more shit."

For a split second, April's alpha-chick facade slips. She catches herself and springs to her feet. "Is that what she told you?"

Great. Now she thinks I went crying to the Twins.

"If you want to ask me something, I'm standing right here." I stay calm. It will drive her crazy.

April puts her hands on her hips and glares at me, but it's Christian's attention she wants. "Your cousin was the one who was giving *me* shit," she says in an annoying high-pitched drawl.

Madison stands and positions herself next to April. The fur on the hood of her coat hits April in the face, and April swats it away.

"It's true," Madison says. "We were minding our own business, and she started in on us."

"For no reason?" Cam asks. "That's not Peyton's style."

The Twins have spent an hour or two with me. They have no idea what is or isn't my style, but Cam is right.

"This is *your* fault, Grace." April redirects her anger at the girl she was torturing in the bathroom.

"Mine?" Grace stares back at her, wide-eyed.

"This whole thing started because I was trying to keep *you* from making a fool of yourself."

Grace's face turns ashen. Her eyes dart to Christian and then to the flames. I know exactly where April is headed with this. She's going to out this nice girl in front of everyone, including Christian—the guy Grace has a crush on.

"Don't do it, or I promise you'll be sorry." My tone carries a warning, and April knows it's meant for her.

April narrows her eyes. "That sounds like a threat."

"Because it is."

"Don't do what?" Christian asks.

I look directly at April. "Nothing."

For a second, I'm not sure which way this standoff will go. Christian's ex might out Grace to spite me. If she's smart, she'll back down.

April flips her auburn waves with a dramatic sweeping motion that had to take practice. "I know what's really going on." She turns to Christian. "You were looking for an excuse to end things, so you sent your cousin to pick a fight with me."

Christian looks confused. "I had already ended things."

"I don't believe you," April says.

"No one *sent* me to do anything," I snap. "I'm not a puppet in the show you have going on here."

Madison puts her arm around April's shoulders. "This is your fault, Christian Carter."

Way to switch gears.

Christian snorts. "How do you figure?"

Madison points an acrylic nail at him. "You're always playing games with April. Could you be a bigger jerk?"

Christian throws up his hands, and beer sloshes out of the can. "What games? We broke up. End of story. Call me whatever you want. I don't give a crap."

Madison raises her chin. "That's because you are a total narcissist."

I'm impressed. Someone has been watching *Dr. Phil.*

"That means you're in love with yourself," she continues.

Not exactly the meaning of the word.

A black guy in a baseball cap sits up in his lawn chair, trying not to laugh. "I don't think you can be in love with yourself. You can like yourself a whole lot and all, but—"

"Shut it, Jackson." Madison puts a hand on her hip. "I watched a whole talk show about it. So don't tell me."

I was right about Dr. Phil.

Madison turns back to Christian. "You're emotionally abusing April, and it's not right."

"Abusing her? I wasn't even talking to her until you started up tonight," Christian says.

"I'm feeling emotionally abused too," Jackson mutters.

It's like I'm watching a bad *Saturday Night Live* skit, and I can't change the channel. "I'm taking a walk."

"Where are you going?" Cam looks worried.

I nod in the direction of the barn and lower my voice. "Over there. I'm not interested in joining the cast of this soap opera."

"I'll come with you." Cam grabs a beer from one of his buddies.

"Hang out with your friends. I'm fine."

Cam lets me go, but he stays in the same spot, craning his neck until it's too dark to see me.

I yank on the sides of the brace as I trek through the muddy grass—at least I hope it's mud. Finding a position that will make this stupid thing more comfortable is impossible. If my future on the soccer field weren't at stake, I would've trashed it already. I lean forward and give the brace a hard pull as I turn the corner. I look up in time to see a figure coming toward me in the darkness, but it's too late to stop. Our bodies collide and I lose my balance.

"Shit!" a guy calls out.

My knee buckles and I reach for the side of the barn, but my fingers barely graze the wood.

I fall backward and my mind flashes on the image of Reed standing at the top of the steps. My back hits something, and suddenly I'm being lifted. I blink hard, my eyes adjusting to the contrast between the darkness and the glow of the moonlight.

Owen looks down at me, his chest only inches from mine. His fingers press against the curve of my waist, and I realize his arm is behind me. My palms turn cold and clammy, and my stomach feels like a twisted towel waiting for someone to finish wringing it out.

"Sorry. I was reading a text." Owen steps back as if he's checking for injuries, and recognition flickers in his eyes. "Twice in one day. You must think I'm an ass."

"You just startled me," I manage, disentangling myself from him.

I take in the tousled dirty-blond hair that curls at his collar, his square jaw, and those warm brown eyes. It's hard to see them in the dark, but I remember from the football stadium.

He's gorgeous—the kind of gorgeous reserved for guys who don't know it.

"If we're going to spend this much time together, you should proba-bly know my name." He holds out his hand. "Owen Law."

I offer him mine, and his fingers curl around my wrist, grazing my pulse point.

"I'm Peyton."

Owen gives me a sheepish smile. "I know all about you."

CHAPTER 12
Sky Full of Stars

OWEN'S HAND LINGERS around mine a moment longer than I expect.

"You know what about me, exactly?" I ask.

And should I be worried?

"Well, I know the Twins are your cousins and you're staying with them. And I know your name. I guess that's not much, but it's something."

His phone rings, startling us both, and my hand slips out of his.

Owen answers and holds up a finger, indicating he wants me to wait. He offers the caller a gruff "hi."

Trekking through the grass took a toll on my knee, and I search for a place to sit. A tower of hay bales stacked against the barn is my only option.

"I don't want to talk about this again," Owen says under his breath, rubbing his hand over the back of his neck. "I need time to figure it out."

Sitting behind a barn in the dark, listening to a guy blow off his girl-friend, is too awkward for me. I start to get up.

Owen notices and abruptly ends the call. "I gotta go."

"Fighting with your girlfriend?" I ask in a way that comes off sounding more like a statement than a question.

He drops down on the hay bale next to mine, stretching his long legs in front of him, without giving me an answer. He notices that I'm still perched on the end of the bale. "I just sat down. If you take off now, I'll think it's because of me."

"Maybe it is." I keep my tone light and I scoot back just enough to make it clear that I'm undecided.

"Give me a minute and I'll walk back with you and protect you from the bears."

Bears?

My eyes dart to the tree line past the main barn. This is Tennessee—trees, forests, and the Blue Ridge Mountains. With my luck, I'll walk away and end up getting mauled.

I settle back against the hay.

Owen looks up at the sky and studies it with an intensity that makes me wonder if he's thinking about more than the stars. I've never seen a sky so dark or stars so bright. Without traffic lights or fast-food signs on every block, the moon is the only thing competing with the constellations.

"Ever feel like you're screwed no matter what you do?" Owen's question comes out of nowhere.

All the time. Part of me wants to say it out loud. "Once in a while."

"Any advice?" He gives me a half smile.

I don't know this guy, but he seems nice—and unhappy. I can relate.

He's waiting for me to respond. I shrug. "Sometimes life only gives you two options. Bad or worse. So you go with bad."

"Makes sense." He studies me like he's taking inventory, checking off boxes on a mental list. The competitor in me wonders how I'm scoring. What if I'm giving him advice about his girlfriend, possibly a delightful friend of April's?

The faint sound of laughter from the party floats through the air.

"Why did you come to Black Water?" Owen asks. "I'm guessing it wasn't for the social scene."

I tap on my brace. "I tore my PCL, the ligament that runs behind my knee. My doctor said I'll need a lot of physical therapy to get my knee back in shape, and I only have four months to do it."

"What happens in four months?"

"I'm a soccer player. I need to get back on the field in March, when the season starts."

"What if you need more time to recover?" It sounds like he actually cares about the answer.

"If I work hard enough, it will heal by then." *I hope.*

Losing my spot at UNC isn't an option. I practiced soccer drills with Dad every day after school and on weekends—and it paid off. I'm not letting Reed destroy my dreams.

"Don't they have physical therapists where you're from?" he asks.

"In Washington, DC? Sure."

"You left Washington, DC, to come here? Why?" Owen is smart and nosy. Not the best combination when I'm trying to keep certain parts of my life private. But he does have an amazing smile.

"Why not?" I counter.

"How about because Washington, DC, is a major city with museums and concerts and the subway, and Black Water is . . . Black Water."

106

"In DC, we call it the Metro, not the subway."

He smiles at me again. "In Black Water we don't call it anything, because we don't have one."

"That's the point. There are no distractions here."

"How did you hurt your knee?"

I didn't.

"I fell down a flight of stairs." It's the truth, but for some reason leaving out the details makes me feel like I'm trapped in a room that's too small and could get smaller any minute. "I'm a klutz when I'm not on the soccer field."

"That sucks. I'm sorry." Owen looks me in the eye and says it, like he really means it.

"It could be worse." But with my scholarship hanging in the balance, it doesn't feel that way.

"It still sucks."

Why am I letting Owen ask me so many questions? I've known him for fifteen minutes. The incident with Reed taught me how easy it is to misjudge someone. I thought he was the kind of athlete who would never resort to doping and cheating.

I've always relied on my gut instincts about people—the little voice in the back of my head. But I don't trust it anymore.

Owen cocks his head to the side and grins. "So do you still want to know if I have a girlfriend?"

Heat crawls up the back of my neck. "I never asked you that."

"When I got off the phone, you asked if I was fighting with my girlfriend."

"I was making conversation, not fishing." *Okay, I sort of was.* "I'm not hunting for a boyfriend if that's what you think."

"Your cousins made that pretty clear."

107

I'm going to strangle those two. "What did they say?" *So I know how much salt to dump in their breakfast tomorrow.*

Owen leans back against the bales. "I saw them coming out of the locker room after the game and I mentioned that we met, and they said you don't date."

The Twins are dead.

They made it sound like I'm joining a convent after graduation. The heat spreads from my neck to my cheeks. I should ditch Owen and go back to the party before this conversation gets more embarrassing.

But I want to stay.

The last three weeks have been full of lies and accusations, surgery and doctors' appointments, threats and depressing calls from an ex who won't stop calling me and a best friend who never wants to speak to me again. My conversation with Owen makes me feel normal. It's one of the few I've had in weeks that didn't revolve around my injury or Reed.

I want it to last a little longer.

I also don't want Owen thinking I'm convent-bound. "For the record, I do *date*. I'm just not interested in dating right *now*. There's a difference."

Owen holds up his hands in surrender. "I'm just telling you what I heard. Is that the reason you're back here instead of hanging out at the party?"

"No. I'm just antisocial."

His eyes flicker to my mouth. "I don't believe that."

I pull my hair back in a ponytail and secure it with the elastic around my wrist. Anything to keep from making eye contact with him. "You don't even know me."

Owen leans forward and rests his elbows on his knees. His arm grazes mine and he looks over at me. "Not yet."

"Peyton? Where are you?" one of the Twins shouts.

Owen hops off the bale. "Sounds like your cousins are looking for you."

A hulking figure rounds the corner. I'm not sure if it's Christian or Cameron until I see his green T-shirt.

Christian storms in our direction. When he sees Owen, he does a double take. "Owen? I didn't know you were here."

"I just stopped by to get Tucker," Owen says. "Some idiot freshman talked him into coming to the party. Garrett went after Tucker at the game so I just wanted to make sure nothing happened. I sent him home with his friend."

"Tucker is lucky he's got you to look out for him," Christian says. "You treat him like a kid brother."

"I'm trying to teach him how to look out for himself."

Christian nods and takes a quick look over his shoulder. "Does Titan know you're here?"

"No. And it's probably better if we keep it that way."

"Why? You two don't get along?" I ask.

"Something like that," Owen says.

Christian looks at Owen, then at me, and frowns as if it suddenly occurs to him that we were alone back here. "How did you end up back here with my cousin?"

"We just bumped into each other," Owen says. "I was protecting her from the bears."

Christian gives him a strange look. "What bears?"

Owen flashes me a sheepish smile. "Forget it. Too many beers."

He heads toward the front of the barn, and I feel a hint of disappointment. He's probably worried about getting his ass kicked by the Twins.

"You don't even drink," Christian calls after him.

Owen stops and looks back at me. "It was my mom."

"What?" I ask.

"On the phone earlier. That's who I was talking to," he says before he turns the corner.

A smile tugs at my mouth.

"What was that about?" Christian holds out his hand to help me up.

I swat it away. "Nothing."

"It didn't sound like nothing."

Using the bales for balance, I ease a little weight onto my right leg. The pain has ratcheted up over the last few hours, and I wince. Christian reaches for my elbow, but I slip out of reach. "I've got it."

"Has anyone ever told you that you're hardheaded?"

"I prefer *determined*. If I want to get my knee back in shape, I have to use it." I follow Christian around the side of the barn. Suddenly, I'm exhausted. I should've let him help me up.

Across the field, the bonfire spits orange flames into the darkness. A figure jogs toward us.

Is it Owen? Did he leave something behind?

"Did you find her?" Cam yells.

Christian gestures in my direction. "She's with me, isn't she?"

"I wasn't lost."

"Yeah, yeah," Christian says. "Everyone wants to hang out behind an empty barn with the cow shit and the snakes."

"Snakes?" I freeze.

"Not poisonous ones." Christian scratches his head. "At least I don't think any of them are poisonous. But I'm not really a snake guy."

"Oh my god. Stop talking about them." I stay glued to his side until we get closer to the light of the bonfire.

We catch up to Cam and he shakes his head at me. "Damn. You

scared the crap out of us, Peyton. You can't just wander off without saying anything."

What's left of my patience runs out. "Actually, I can. Stop treating me like I'm ten years old. We're all the same age."

"Technically, you're older," Christian says. "You turn eighteen three months before we do."

Cam makes a slashing motion across his throat. "Not helping."

"Are you two telling people that I don't date?" My hands move to my hips.

"Where did you hear that?" Cam asks innocently.

"Owen was here," Christian says. "He was hanging out with Peyton."

Cam looks confused. "Owen who?"

"Owen Law, you dope. Who did you think I was talking about?"

"He was *here*?"

Christian nods. "Yep."

"It's a party. Why are you guys acting so weird about it?" I ask.

"Owen doesn't go to parties," Cam explains. "I mean, he used to before . . ."

"Before what?" I ask.

Christian takes over. "Before his parents split up."

My cousins are acting weird. Maybe it's because they're friends with Titan, and he and Owen don't get along.

"So let's get back to the part about you guys telling people that I don't date."

Cameron looks around as if he thinks I'm talking to someone else. "I didn't say that. Christian did."

"Sellout." Christian punches his brother in the shoulder, and within seconds, they're circling each other and bouncing on the balls of their feet like boxers.

111

This is what I'm dealing with for the next four months?

I step between them. "I don't care who said it. Just don't say it to anyone else."

"In my brother's defense, that is what you told us," Cam points out.

"No. I said I wasn't *interested* in dating. There's a difference."

"We're trying to look out for you," Christian says.

The Twins have perfected their sad puppy faces, which makes it impossible to stay mad at them. "I appreciate it. But I know how to take care of myself."

Cam takes the car keys out of his pocket. "Ready to get out of here?"

"Yeah. I've had enough of April for one night," Christian says.

"I've had enough of her for a lifetime." I follow my cousins to the truck. Without houses or signs to use as landmarks, I have no idea where we parked.

Cam climbs in first and leans across the seat to offer me a hand.

"I've got it." I struggle to haul myself up.

Christian slides in next to me and shakes his head. "It wouldn't kill you to accept some help once in a while."

I'm not so sure.

CHAPTER 13

Tennessee Dreaming

THE TWENTY-MINUTE RIDE back from the party included lots of discussion about football, Christian's bad taste in girls, and whether or not Titan watered down the keg. After the long drive from DC to Black Water, the drama at the game and the party, and the effort it required to walk through a cow field, I'm wiped out.

Cameron nudges me. "Hey, Sleeping Beauty? We're here."

"I just closed my eyes for a minute," I mumble.

"Do you always snore when your eyes are closed?" Christian hops out of the truck.

"I do not snore." At least I don't think I do.

"Lighten up. It was a joke," Christian says. "Your sense of humor needs work."

I want to tell them that I wasn't always this serious—intense, stubborn, and independent, definitely. Serious is a recent development.

113

The porch light is on and another light glows inside.

"Pop always waits up," Cam says as Christian unlocks the front door.

The house is even prettier than I remember.

As a kid, I thought the sky-blue paint made the house appear as if it were floating in the clouds. With the white shutters and wraparound porch, it was easy to imagine fresh-baked pies cooling in the kitchen. Maybe there would've been if Christian and Cameron's mom hadn't died in a car accident when they were eight.

Cam holds open the door for me. "Pop. We're home. We've got Peyton with us."

"I didn't expect you to lose her." Hawk is standing in the kitchen doorway, wearing an orange-and-white University of Tennessee shirt that says GO VOLS and jeans that I'm ninety-nine percent sure are genuine Wranglers.

I point at Hawk's shirt. "What are Vols?"

"It's short for Volunteers," he says.

"Is University of Tennessee the big college around here?" I ask.

Christian jumps in. "The biggest. With the best Division One football team in the SEC. That's where me and Cameron are going next year. We were both recruited last fall, and we already signed our letters of intent."

"Congratulations. That's huge." I follow the Twins into the kitchen.

"Did you meet the boys' friends?" Hawk asks. "They're not as bad as they seem after you get to know them."

Christian opens the fridge. "The guys know they'd better behave themselves around Peyton."

Hawk nods his approval. "I hope so."

Not my uncle, too.

I shrug off Dad's jacket. "I don't need anyone to issue warnings for me."

"I'm sure that's true, but I still expect the boys to look out for you," my uncle says.

"Because I'm a girl?"

"Yeah." Christian takes a milk carton out of the fridge.

"Don't get her started." Cam snatches the milk from his brother's hand and drinks straight from the carton.

I wait to see if my uncle shares the Twins' chauvinistic view.

"Because you're their *cousin*," Hawk says.

Christian and Cameron exchange exasperated looks.

Hawk gestures to the fridge. "I was going to pick up some things at the grocery store, but your mom said you like to cook, so I figured I'd better take you with me. When it comes to cooking, peanut butter and jelly is my specialty."

Christian snaps to attention. "You cook?"

"More than just the frozen stuff?" Cam is grinning at me like I just told him that he won the lottery.

"Yeah. I can teach you guys if you want." Based on the Twins' reactions, I'm guessing they don't know how.

Christian laughs. "No thanks. Cooking is for chicks."

I glare at him. "I hope that's a joke."

"Why? Girls are better at cooking. It's a compliment."

"No. It's really not."

Hawk clears his throat. "Boys, why don't you show Peyton her room?"

"Good idea." Christian ushers me up the steps, while Cam returns the milk carton to the fridge.

"Wait up," Cam calls after us.

Hawk shakes his head and lets Cam slip in front of him.

The second-floor hallway hasn't changed. Mismatched frames hang on the walls, chronicling every important moment in their lives—a wedding photo of Hawk and Aunt Katie, icing smeared all over Hawk's face while Aunt Katie laughs; my aunt in the hospital, cradling two blue bundles in her arms; the Twins, as toddlers, covered in mud and holding kid-size footballs; and dozens of shots of my cousins on the football field at various ages.

One photo stands out from the rest. A little girl with dark brown pigtails, wearing a red soccer jersey with CUBA in white letters across the front. Her foot balances on top of the ball, and her hands are planted on her hips. Dad kneels beside me in a matching jersey, with his serious soccer expression—a sharp contrast to Mom's carefree smile as she pokes her head between us.

"That's you," Christian says, as if he's telling me something I don't know.

"Thanks for clearing up that mystery," I tease.

"Your dad was real proud of you," Hawk says. The Twins look away. Thinking about my dead parent probably reminds them of their mom. "He was as good as they come, even though I gave him a rough time when he started dating your mom."

"Why were you so hard on him?" Mom has told me bits and pieces of the story, but I want to hear Hawk's version.

"Your dad and I were in the same Recon unit in the Marine Corps, and he was a friend—those were two reasons right there. A man doesn't want his little sister falling for a Devil Dog who gets dropped into dangerous situations for a living. I wanted her to settle down with someone who would come home every night. But I brought your dad with me for Thanksgiving, and they fell hard for each other."

"Were you okay with that?" I asked.

Hawk laughed. "Hell no. I kicked your dad's butt when we left. He probably let me because he knew he had it coming. But it didn't stop him from calling and visiting your mom every chance he got. Then I had Sissy to deal with. After a while, I got used to it."

"And you stayed friends?"

"Only because your dad was such a good guy. He had a lot of honor. He respected your mom, and me. The day he asked your mom to marry him, he asked me first to make sure I was okay with it. He said that if he had a sister like your mom, he wouldn't have trusted a guy like him, either. Then he promised to take care of her."

"Great story, Pop. Can we show Peyton her room now?" Christian asks.

"The boys decorated it," Hawk says proudly.

"Thanks for telling me the story."

Hawk nods. "If you ever have questions or you want to know what happened—"

"I don't." Stories about my parents are one thing, but I don't want to hear the details about how my father died.

"Here it is," Cam says, stepping aside so I can open the bedroom door.

Suddenly, I'm worried. Visions of pink ruffles and fairy-tale princesses fill my head. I'm not sure if I can sleep in a pink room. I open the door, prepared to see a bed covered in rainbows, or something equally childish.

Don't be a brat.

When I see it, my first thought is that I must've walked into the wrong room. There isn't a shred of pink or a stuffed animal anywhere. The white furniture is accented with a sky-blue comforter and a cloud-shaped rug with a cute Japanese cartoon-style face. Above the desk on a pinboard, colored pushpins hold a Black Water High School Warriors decal, a picture of the Twins with their faces squished against a window, and an old photo of Mom and me.

"So do you like it or what?" Cam asks.

The surprising thing is that I do like everything in here. It doesn't resemble my room at home, but it has a cool vibe, unlike the princess nightmare I pictured.

"It's really nice." I take in the details. "You two picked out all this stuff?"

Christian rolls back on his heels and Cam studies the rug.

"Grace helped," Cam says finally. "But we drove her to Walmart."

"You don't like it." Christian sounds deflated.

"Actually, I do. A lot." I spread out the stack of notebooks and binders on the desk, nothing too cute or flashy, just the basics. Grace even threw in a decent mix of magazines—entertainment, sports, fashion, and a copy of *Southern Living*.

Hopefully, it has an article that covers how to deal with Southern high school divas.

Hawk and my cousins stand near the door, waiting for the final verdict.

"It's all great." I look around one more time.

"Why don't we let Peyton get some rest? She looks tired." Hawk steers the Twins to the door.

"I am pretty wrecked." I sit on the edge of the bed.

A muffled whimper and scratching sounds come from underneath it, and I fly off the mattress and stumble toward the dresser. "There's something under there."

What the hell is it? A huge rat? A raccoon?

Do they have wolverines in Tennessee?

"Relax." Christian bends down and picks up one side of the bed. "It's just Dutch. He gets stuck."

Reddish-brown paws poke out from beneath the bed skirt, and a moment later, the bloodhound's square head and floppy ears follow. Dutch crawls out on his belly. I'm not surprised he got stuck. The dog is a lot bigger than I remember.

I lean against the dresser and exhale. "I forgot about him."

Dutch turns his head toward me like he's moving in slow motion. The dog's droopy eyes and long ears make him look like a canine version of Eeyore from *Winnie-the-Pooh*.

Cam scratches the bloodhound's head as the dog lumbers into the hall. "You hurt his feelings."

Hawk puts a hand on each boy's shoulder and pushes them out of my room. "Let me know if you need anything." He pulls the door closed behind him.

For the first time since I arrived in Black Water, I'm alone. As much as I hate answering questions about what happened to my knee, and walking around in a brace, when I'm alone, the bad memories have room to stretch out.

Losing Tess is what hurts the most.

I'm not sure which is worse—the possibility that she and I will never be friends again, or the chance that I won't be the same when I get back on the soccer field.

It doesn't matter. Choosing one loss or the other isn't an option.

I'm stuck with both.

CHAPTER 14

High School and Hardcore Crushes

A STAMPEDE IN the hallway outside my bedroom jerks me awake. I slept most of the day on Saturday and used unpacking as an excuse to dodge my cousins' invite to hang out with "everyone" at the diner. Aside from the conversation with Owen, my Black Water debut at Titan's party was an epic fail.

The sounds of clattering pans, cupboards slamming, and shouting downstairs mean three things, none of which I'm happy about.

It's Monday.

The Twins are up.

And I'm starting at a new school.

I hate change, unless it involves turning the tide during a soccer game.

By the time I shower, get dressed, and apply mascara and lipstick-blush combo, the noise coming from downstairs starts up again. The stairs slow me down, but not enough to avoid the wrestling match taking place in the kitchen.

The Twins toss each other around with no effort.

"Boys. That's enough," Hawk warns from his seat at the table.

"Cam needs a workout. Didn't you see how slow his reaction time was on Friday night?" Christian grabs his brother around the waist and plows him into the wall.

I make a mental note that Christian is the one wearing the gray Warriors football T-shirt.

Hawk turns around in his chair. "If you put another hole in my kitchen, you'll both be dry-walling and painting this weekend."

"Yes, sir." Christian grins at Cam, who knocks off Christian's baseball cap the moment he looks the other way.

Christian picks up the hat and shakes it off before putting it back on. "Keep it up. You're taking your life into your own hands."

"I've heard that before."

The Twins eat their weight in eggs, bacon, and pancakes. Watching them scarf down plates of scrambled eggs kills my appetite.

"Aren't you hungry?" Cam asks when he notices I'm not eating.

"Not anymore." I push the bowl of oatmeal away and stick to coffee until the human garbage disposals finish breakfast.

Christian grabs a handful of bacon on our way out. "See ya later, Pop."

"I hope Black Water High treats you well on your first day, Peyton," Hawk calls after me.

I'm hoping the same thing.

High school sucks.

It's a universal truth.

Forcing hundreds of teenagers to spend ten months together is a fundamentally bad idea. Throw in a gym class, school dances, teachers on power trips, and a crapload of homework, and it increases the likelihood of disaster.

The same scenario is even crueler in a high school this small, with fewer kids to distract the predators from the weak and wounded zebras in the pack. The zebras at Black Water High are easy to spot from the parking lot, because other students actually follow them down the sidewalk, taunting them like a scene from an antibullying video.

Mom warned me that Black Water is small, but I think my middle school was bigger than this place. How many students could possibly go to school here?

Two hundred? Maybe three?

At a school this size, there's no way to blend in, which was my original plan—keep my head down, work my ass off in physical therapy, and go back to my uncle's house.

Things just got a whole lot harder.

I take a deep breath.

"You all right?" Christian asks as he opens the door.

I'm not confessing my insecurities to the Twins. "I shouldn't have skipped breakfast. I'm a little light-headed, that's all."

Christian frowns and pulls the door shut. "We'll hang here until you feel better."

A group of girls walks in front of the truck, talking and passing around a tube of lip gloss. The Twins check them out, discussing the candidates in the running to replace April.

I shove Christian. "You're both disgusting. Do you actually think those girls are interested in you?"

Christian flashes one of his admirers an I'm-the-bad-boy-of-your-dreams smile. "Pretty much. And if they aren't interested, I just need twenty minutes."

"Exactly twenty minutes? Not fifteen or twenty-two? What miraculous feat happens in that twenty minutes?" I realize the kind of response he'll probably give me. "Don't answer that."

Christian grins. "You sure? 'Cause I've got some good answers."

Cam reaches behind me and smacks his bother in the back of the head. "Don't talk about dirty crap in front of our cousin."

"I meant good answers like *funny* ones, you dope." Christian rubs the back of his head.

Grace walks by and peers at the truck through her curtain of black hair.

"Isn't that your friend?" I ask, hoping to shift their attention away from me.

Christian lays on the horn, and the girls jump. A tube of lip gloss flies in the air and lands on the ground.

A tall blond glares at him. "What's your problem, Christian?"

He leans out the window, acting innocent. "Sorry, ladies. My bad."

Grace smiles sheepishly and waves. If Christian doesn't know she likes him, he's clueless. "Are you coming in?" she asks him.

"Not yet," Christian says.

"Go ahead. I'm fine." I motion for him to get out.

"I'll stay," Cam says, suddenly grouchy.

I nudge Cameron. "I'm okay on my own, Cam. Seriously."

He leans back against the seat. "I'm good with waiting."

Christian hops out, grabs his backpack from the truck bed, and slings his arm over Grace's shoulder. "Change of plans."

Grace beams.

"That just made her day." It feels good to do something nice for someone else.

"Yeah. Christian is a real prize." Cam slips on a flannel with a quilted lining that looks more like a coat than a shirt, and messes with his hair. I can't put my finger on what it is yet, but there's something different about Christian's and Cameron's eyes.

"You should go with them," I say, but Cam doesn't move. He's not going anywhere unless I give him a reason. "I just need a few minutes to myself."

"I'll meet you in the office." He gets out and points at the main entrance. "It's straight through there. Miss Lonnie probably forgot you were coming."

Cam taps on the hood and takes off.

I slouch deeper into the seat and watch the students filter inside.

Senior year wasn't supposed to turn out this way. Tess and I spent most of last year mapping out every detail, and now she won't even speak to me.

My gaze drifts past the empty parking spaces to an SUV. A woman around Mom's age sits at the wheel, her face creased with worry. She's arguing with someone and gesturing frantically.

A guy is sitting in the passenger seat, and I recognize his profile and dirty-blond hair. Owen's broad shoulders hang slack as he stares at his lap. The woman must be his mother. At the barn party, when Owen said his mom was the person he'd been arguing with on the phone, I wasn't sure if he was serious.

Why is she so upset? And why does he look like he'd rather swallow nails than stay in the car for another second?

The conversation between them grows more heated, and Owen's mom bursts into tears. She buries her face in her hands, and he slumps against the passenger door. I shouldn't be watching them, but his expression looks so familiar.

It's the same one I see in the mirror all the time now.

Regret.

Owen says something and squeezes his mom's shoulder, but she doesn't stop crying. She stares straight ahead like a zombie.

He looks past her and catches me watching them.

My cheeks heat up. I turn to look away, but his eyes find mine.

A knock on the window scares the crap out of me, and I yelp. Cam waves, and I reach over and unlock the driver's-side door.

"Are you going to stay in the car all day?" he asks, clueless that he scared the hell out of me.

"I'm coming." I open the door and get out carefully.

My eyes flicker to the silver SUV. Owen's mom is backing out of the parking space and he's already across the street, walking up the sidewalk. He opens the door to the building, and at the last possible moment, he stops and looks back.

It's two seconds. Maybe less.

But when a boy looks at you like he's drowning and you're the only person who saw him fall in, it feels like forever.

CHAPTER 15

Warriors

THE FRONT OFFICE is small and cozy. Framed motivational quotes written in looped calligraphy and a collection of Beanie Babies crowd the counter.

Cam chats up Miss Lonnie, the gray-haired lady behind the counter, while she hunts for my schedule. The rosy circles of blush on her cheeks match her silk blouse perfectly.

I tune them out until Miss Lonnie says something that grabs my attention. "I hate to say it, but I'm worried." She toys with one of her huge pearl earrings. "A team without a quarterback isn't any different than having no team at all."

I don't remember anyone getting injured at Friday night's game, not that I saw much of it. With all the football talk afterward, wouldn't the Twins have mentioned it?

"Only thing worse would be a team without its linebackers," Cam says.

"Always looking for a pat on the back." She shakes her head at him. "Know your worth, Cameron. Don't rely on other people to remind you."

He looks away.

"Did the quarterback on your team get hurt?" I ask, rescuing my cousin from an awkward moment.

"Everyone on the team is fine as far as I know," Cam says. "Why?"

I drop my backpack on the floor. The extra weight—which isn't much since I don't have any books—has my knee aching. "She was talking about an injured quarterback. Was he from your team?"

Miss Lonnie smacks her hand on the counter and cackles. "No. He's the quarterback on my fantasy football team."

Fantasy football? Is she serious? The woman must be pushing seventy-five.

"It wouldn't be any fun if you win every year," Cam teases.

"It would be for me." She thumbs through the papers in front of her, plucks out a thick white card, and pushes it across the counter. "Here's your class schedule. Cameron knows where to find everything, since he's always roaming the halls when he's supposed to be in class."

The rotary phone on the counter rings. Miss Lonnie removes her gigantic clip-on earring before she answers it. She shoos us out with a wave. "Black Water High School, how can I help you?"

I scan my schedule as we leave the office. Precalculus first period, followed by AP English, chemistry, and lunch. European history and photography round out the afternoon. Who chose these classes? I don't know anything about photography, and precalc first period requires being alert at eight o'clock in the morning.

Cam reaches for my schedule. "Let me see."

I turn away before he snatches the paper. "I'm reading it."

He circles behind me and reads over my shoulder. "I want to see which classes you have with me or Christian."

I rattle off my schedule. "Happy now?"

"You don't have any classes with either of us. Just lunch," he complains.

"Are you worried that I can't find my way around this *gigantic* campus?" Knowing Cam, it's probably true.

I follow him around the corner to the vending machines, which are so old they don't take credit cards. Cam hunts in his pockets for change. One machine is stocked with packaged doughnuts and baked goods and the other one is full of candy and chips.

"No soda machine?" Weird.

"We've got two at the end of the hall. When the machines were delivered, the building supervisor, Mr. Kent, wasn't paying attention. He didn't notice where the delivery guys put them until after they left." Cam finds some change in his jacket and drops the coins into the slot. "Now he pretends this is where he wanted them all along."

I glance down the hall.

Owen is standing at a soda machine.

He's wearing earbuds and he seems oblivious to the noise around him. He pushes up the sleeves of his thermal, punches a number on the vending machine, and bends down to grab his soda out of the compartment. His forearm is covered with dark patches.

Are those bruises?

Those aren't the kind of bruises you get from bumping into things.

Owen stands and I turn away, but I'm not fast enough. His eyes are clouded with emotion, as if he's still sitting in the car with his mom. He sees me and the lines in his forehead relax. He shakes off whatever he was feeling and flashes me a smile that's the perfect combination of sweet and sexy.

It's the second time he's caught me staring at him this morning. I feel like such a loser.

"What are you looking at?" Cam asks.

"Nothing. Stop asking so many questions. I'm not a science fair project. Point me in the direction of my first class. Room A-four."

"Right this way." Cam lifts the backpack off my shoulder.

I reach for the strap. "I can carry it myself."

"If you want to put extra weight on your knee for no reason that's your call." He's stubborn, a quality we share.

"Fine."

When I turn around again, Owen is gone.

Cam walks me to class, and I find a seat in the back of the room.

I can't stop thinking about the bruises on Owen's arm until the bells rings and class starts. After that, I don't have much time to think about anything because precalculus sucks at Black Water just as much as it did at Adams.

It doesn't help that our teacher, Mr. Wickwheeler, is a beady-eyed jerk who probably became a teacher to torture kids. He gives everyone exactly two seconds to answer a question before he scribbles the solution across the whiteboard so fast that his comb-over flips the wrong way. He calls me Miss Rios, rolling the *R* in my last name in a dramatic attempt at a Spanish accent. When the prison bell finally rings, I'm tempted to lie to Mr. Wickwheeler and tell him that I'm Portuguese. Let him try practicing that accent.

Christian and Grace are waiting in the hall outside the classroom.

"You survived your first class with the Weasel," Grace says, holding out an open bag of SweeTarts. "Congrats."

"So I'm not the only one who notices the resemblance?" I pop a candy into my mouth.

Grace slows her pace to match mine. She's dressed like most of the other girls, in a cute flannel and jeans with hearts embroidered on the back pockets. But Grace brought her A game when she picked out her footwear—red cowboy boots.

"Everyone hates the Weasel. He's a jerk." She picks through the candy bag until she finds a pink one.

"He kept pronouncing my last name in a crappy Spanish accent."

Christian notices that we're lagging behind him and waits for us to catch up. "Who's a jerk?"

Grace shoves him. "Calm down, Wrecking Ball. We're talking about the Weasel. None of the guys here are stupid enough to bother Peyton."

"Wrecking Ball?" I ask.

"People call me that sometimes because of football," Christian explains. He turns to Grace. "But you never do, Gracie."

"Sorry," she whispers.

This conversation just got awkward.

A chorus of high-pitched laughter cuts through the hallway. April and Madison are at the end of the hall, entertaining a group of guys.

"Enemy forces at twelve o'clock," Christian mutters.

Grace steps away from Christian and lets him walk ahead of us.

"Don't let April intimidate you," I say. "She's a bitch."

"I'm aware. But she's a bitch who can make my life miserable."

"Only if you let her." Why am I giving Grace a hard time for wanting to fly under the radar when that's exactly what I'm trying to do? "I'm sorry. It's none of my business."

"Don't apologize. I think about telling April off at least ten times a day." Grace tucks her hair behind her ear. "But she's cheer captain, which means she picks the routines and decides who gets the prime stunts. I can't afford to get on her bad side or she'll stick me in the back row. Or find an excuse to kick me off the team altogether. A cheerleading scholarship is my only chance at getting into a decent college. My GPA isn't great."

"I get it."

"What's your locker number again?" Christian asks.

"I don't know. It's not on my schedule." That would be too easy.

"Are you sure?" Grace asks. "Usually it's on the back, at the bottom."

I scan the printout Miss Lonnie gave me. "Six sixty-six. That can't be right." I check again.

LOCKER #666.

"You got the Beast? Let me see," Christian says.

I hand him my schedule. "What kind of high school uses the symbol of the Antichrist as a locker number?" A month ago I would've thought it was funny. But now that I'm April's latest target, this is ammo.

Christian stops in front of my locker and checks the combination listed on the schedule. He opens the bright blue door and peeks inside. "No sign of the Antichrist or any weird satanic stuff. Just a couple of girls' phone numbers."

"Thanks." I take everything out of my bag except for a notebook and a pen.

"Incoming," Christian warns.

April zeroes in on me, her resting bitch face intact. "How's the first day going so far?" she asks. "Looks like they found you the perfect locker."

Madison laughs.

"Why do you have to start shit all the time, April?" Christian asks.

"I don't know, Christian. Why are you such an asshole?"

He lowers his voice. "You must've rubbed off on me."

April notices Grace standing beside me and acts shocked. "Seriously, Grace? I thought we were friends." This girl gives new meaning to manipulative, and Grace can't afford to piss her off. I don't want April to give her a hard time because of me.

"Grace's dad told her to show me around. He's a friend of my uncle's. So lay off her." I have no idea if it's true. Hopefully, April's and Grace's fathers aren't golf buddies.

"I'm going to class," I tell Christian.

I mouth *bye* to Grace, and I head down the hall.

Hopefully, I'm going in the right direction. But getting lost is worth it if it means I don't have to listen to April's annoying voice anymore.

Titan, the Twins' friend who threw the barn party, walks up beside me. He's a lot taller than I remember and he makes my cousins look average-size. His T-shirt strains across his broad chest, and he flashes me a well-practiced smile.

"How's your day going?"

"Fine, thanks."

"Did you have a good time at my party?" he asks.

Small talk. My favorite.

"Yeah. It was my first barn party." I read the room numbers on the classroom doors. Am I going the right way? I have no clue.

"Need some help finding your class?" Titan asks. "What's the room number?"

"B-nine. I thought I knew where—"

Before I realize what's happening, Titan literally sweeps me off my

132

feet—in a move that I'm sure he thinks is swoon-worthy. He slipped his arm under my legs like he had practiced this a hundred times.

It catches me off-guard and my pulse speeds up the moment he touches me.

"Put me down, Titan."

"What's the problem? I offer this kind of assistance to all the pretty girls with leg braces." He grins and makes a huge show of carrying me down the hall. "Coming through," he calls out so everyone will hear him.

How far away is my classroom?

The crowded hallway traffic parts like the Red Sea as people move out of his way. Screaming at him will just call more attention to us. It literally feels like every person in the hall is watching me, and I can't stand it.

I turn my face toward Titan's neck and hide.

It seems like it takes forever to get to my class. "Here you go," he says, bending down until my feet touch the floor again. "Door-to-door service."

I'm so annoyed, but people are still gawking. This will be lunchroom gossip for sure. But nothing anyone in Black Water says about me could be worse than what some of my friends were saying about me back home.

"That was so uncool," I say, just loud enough that he can hear me. "Don't pull that crap with me again."

"I bet you'll change your mind."

"Doubtful." I turn away and walk into my classroom.

Less than half the seats are occupied in the tiny room. I go straight to the back row and take out my notebook so I won't have to make eye contact with anyone. At least nobody in here saw Titan's performance in the hall.

I wish someone had asked before saddling me with AP English. I'd rather be in a regular section—easier homework and shorter novels.

The classroom door opens and I look up.

Owen walks in.

Maybe AP isn't so bad. Owen seems nice. Just because I'm not dating, it doesn't mean we can't be friends.

Owen trudges down the center aisle. I wait for him to notice me, but he doesn't even glance in my direction. I'm hard to miss—especially when he reaches the back row. I'm sitting two seats away from the aisle. It seems like he's trying *not* to look at me.

He sits down and takes out a notebook.

"Sorry I'm late." A slender black woman about Mom's age breezes into the room, carrying an armload of books. She's wearing a fitted black sweater with wide-leg black pants that would be considered classic and understated in DC. But there is nothing understated about her hair. It's amazing. She has long dreadlocks, dyed a rich shade of yellow-blond that almost looks gold. Thin braids are layered between her locks, and the sides are gathered on top of her head in a loose bun.

The teacher drops the books on her desk.

"Miss Ives? Are we starting a new novel?" asks a perky girl in the front row.

"Not today." Miss Ives puts on a pair of cat-eye glasses and I wait for the inevitable moment when she notices me.

Here it comes.

"Forgive me. This morning has completely gotten away from me. Class, we have a new student." She sweeps her arm in my direction, and the other students turn around in their seats.

My classmates stare, and I sit frozen in place like a deer in headlights.

Miss Ives purses her lips. "Miss Lonnie told me your name this morning. . . . Wait. Don't tell me."

Seconds pass and she doesn't seem any closer to figuring it out. A few students lose interest and go back to whatever they were doing. It's taking her too long. I have to say it or this will drag on forever.

"Peyton," I finally tell her.

"Peyton. That's it." Miss Ives snaps as if she remembered on her own.

Owen has his leg in the aisle and his knee bounces at record speed. His eyes dart from the notebook to the floor before they finally land on me.

Miss Ives launches into a boring recap of the way she introduced *The Stranger*, the novel the class finished last week.

I tune out.

This is the time when I'd normally text my best friend to report every embarrassing detail of the hallway incident with Titan. Instead, I try to pretend that Owen isn't sitting two seats away from me. I'm hyperaware of his every move. I can't look up without catching glimpses of him in my peripheral vision.

"We're doing something a little different today," Miss Ives says, and I refocus my attention.

"Initially, it might sound strange, but it's part of a larger activity." She seems more excited than the class. "And we'll be working in pairs. So I want everyone to find a partner."

Working in pairs on my first day?

What's next? A blood drive?

The class isn't big enough for much decision-making. A few people partner up right away, while the rest of us linger in our seats as if we think Miss Ives will forget about whatever she has planned if we don't move.

It's down to four of us—a guy with a fade, who is wearing a T-shirt with GO BIG OR GO HOME printed on the back; a girl smacking a wad of gum, whose sunburned skin looks leathery; Owen; and me.

I'm going for the gum smacker. Before I swing my leg toward the aisle to get up, she's already bouncing over to the guy in the clever T-shirt.

"Owen, it looks like you and . . ." Miss Ives taps her temple.

"Peyton," Owen says.

"Of course." She waves a hand in the air as if she was just getting to that part. "As I was saying, why don't you find a seat closer to Peyton so we can get started?"

Owen grabs his notebook and a pen and crosses to my side of the room. He catches the back of the chair in front of my desk and flips it around so it's facing me and he drops into the seat without a word. He doesn't seem like the same friendly guy I hung out with at the party.

Maybe he's upset about his mom.

"What now?" the gum-smacking girl asks midchew.

Miss Ives clasps her hands together. "Ladies, I'd like you to empty your purses on your desk. If you don't have a purse, take everything out of your backpacks except textbooks, binders, and class supplies. Gentlemen, go ahead and do the same thing. You may also empty your pockets."

"For real?" the guy in the GO BIG OR GO HOME T-shirt calls out.

"As real as it gets, Jordan," Miss Ives says. "Let's get everything on the desks."

Owen takes out his leather wallet and drops it on my desk. I match his wallet with my own and raise him a keychain and an energy bar. He steals a look at me, and I pretend not to notice.

An Asian girl with long, shiny supermodel hair sitting in the front row throws our teacher side-eye. "What if we have stuff in our purse that's inappropriate to take out?"

"Like what?" Miss Ives crosses her arms. "Are you referring to cigarettes or other contraband?"

The comment gets Miss Ives side-eye from everyone.

"I think she means *girl* stuff," Supermodel's partner, a cute guy in a plaid button-down, adds. "For when her *cousin* visits."

Supermodel whacks him with her purse. "Shut up. My *cousin* is none of your business."

"Settle down." Miss Ives adjusts her glasses, noticeably flustered. "If anyone else has items of that nature, please leave them in your bag."

Supermodel's partner tosses his wallet on the desk and points at it. "That means you might not want to open the inside pocket, Brit. Or maybe you do?"

Supermodel Brit stands up. "I want to switch partners."

"We're running out of class time," Miss Ives says. "We'll get started today and continue tomorrow. I want everyone to choose three items that are meaningful to you. Then share the items with your partner and explain their significance or what they represent."

Everyone groans.

"You might have to open the inside pocket after all," her partner teases.

Supermodel Brit ignores him. "What if we don't have anything that's important to us?"

"Look harder," Miss Ives says. "Check your pockets, inside makeup bags and pencil cases. For example, I carry a lucky penny in my bag."

Our teacher flits around from group to group while we search through our belongings.

"This sucks," Owen mumbles.

I ignore him and search for something impersonal to share. "I don't have anything."

"Nothing?" He seems annoyed that I didn't have any girly mementos in my backpack.

Our eyes meet, and I can't think of anything to say. Owen is gorgeous, and not in an obvious I-worked-my-ass-off-to-blow-your-mind way. His eyes take me in, drifting from my eyes to my mouth and it makes me nervous.

"Yeah, well, I don't have anything, either." Owen pushes the items I didn't even see off the edge of my desk and into his palm. Then he shoves his wallet into his back pocket.

At the party, he seemed nice.

Clearly, I was way off.

"You really know how to turn on the charm." I lay on the sarcasm and lower my chin, hiding behind my hair as I collect my stuff.

"What's that supposed to mean?" He sounds irritated.

"I guess that sweet boy-next-door personality was just for show?" I push my hair over my shoulder and my eyes drill into him. "Do you only break that out for girls in the dark?"

Owen stiffens. "Should I have gone with cocky-football-player-desperate-for-attention, like your boyfriend?"

He knows about Titan carrying me through the hallway. Did Owen hear about it from someone or did he see it for himself?

"Titan is *not* my boyfriend."

The bell rings.

"That's not the way it looked in the hallway." Owen stands and flips the chair around.

Now I'm pissed.

Miss Ives issues instructions about the personal items she wants us to bring tomorrow. I'm not paying attention. Owen swings his backpack over his shoulder and heads down the center aisle.

138

Maybe if I figure out how to get medical treatment for a fantasy football quarterback, Miss Lonnie will switch me to another English class. I turn my back to the door and put my things in my backpack.

Why do I care what Owen Law thinks?

I've only had one real conversation with him—two if talking to him for a minute at the game counts. And he's judging me?

I storm out of the classroom. Some football players are passing a ball in the hallway. The football sails through the air and skims the bottom of a banner hanging above the archway. BLACK WATER WARRIORS is printed in block letters across the top, with two lines of text underneath.

Players go for the win.
Warriors battle for it.

If I could reach the banner, I'd tear it down. I spent the last three weeks battling my heart out, and I still lost.

CHAPTER 16
Sucker Punch

"I'M LOOKING FOR Catherine Dane." I'm in the boxing gym at the YMCA after school, in search of the doctor who agreed to help me rehab my knee.

The woman keeps her eyes on the fighter in the ring wearing headgear. "You're looking at her, but nobody except my mother calls me Catherine. It's Cutter."

She looks like a mash-up between a delicate fairy and a dangerous assassin. Her platinum-blond hair is almost the same color as her skin and it's cut in a short pixie style that highlights her feminine features. Tess' hair is almost the same color, but it looks edgier on Cutter. Maybe it's the super-short cut or the rows of tiny hoops that run from her earlobes to the tops of her ears. She's short—maybe five foot two—but her body is lean and well-defined.

"Not what you were expecting?" Cutter cups her hands around her mouth and yells, "Lazarus, tell him to get those damn knees up."

Lazarus, the tall black man in the ring, with broad shoulders and salt-and-pepper hair, looks old enough to be my grandfather. But he has the strength of someone younger. He gives Cutter a thumbs-up, without losing his grip on the red pad the fighter is pounding.

The guy in the ring with Lazarus is a kickboxer. His knee kicks give him away. His knees hit the pad over and over, each impact pushing Lazarus back a little farther.

The sound of the guy's bare skin smacking the Vinyl triggers memories of Reed—images of him throwing an elbow jab or a shin kick in the gym, circling an opponent in the cage, the way he cracked his neck to the side before he moved in for the kill.

Cutter looks back at me. "So you're Hawk Carter's niece."

"Peyton."

"Hawk told me you're a soccer player and you took a serious hit to the knee."

"I fell down a flight of stairs and ruptured my PCL. There was also some damage to the cartilage."

"Did you bring your MRI?" she asks.

I slip the large white envelope out of my backpack and hand it to her. Cutter holds it up to the window behind her.

"The PCL ruptured here." She runs her finger along the film, like she's following a path. "Has your knee been giving out on you?"

"Not as much since I had surgery."

"Do you have a copy of the surgeon's notes?"

I hand her a manila folder. "Everything else I brought is in there."

Cutter flips through the pages, reading some closely and scanning others. "Your orthopedic surgeon thinks it will take four months to get your knee back in shape." She snaps the folder shut with one hand. "But with the right physical therapy regimen—*if* you work hard—I should be able to get you out of that long leg brace in four to six weeks and back on the field in about three months."

It sounds too good to be true. "Are you sure? Don't get me wrong. I'd love to get out of this thing tomorrow, but the orthopedic surgeon said—"

"Hands up!" Cutter shouts, watching the kickboxer. "Knee. Knee. Elbow. Knee." She turns her attention back to me. "I know exactly what Dr. Kao thinks. I just read her diagnosis and recommendations. She's a brilliant surgeon. Graduated second in her class from Harvard Medical School, completed her residency at Georgetown University Hospital, and she has published three articles about her arthroscopic surgery techniques. I'll give you one guess who graduated *first* in her class."

Cutter's crooked smile is a dead giveaway.

"You?"

She nods. "Damn right."

"I'm sorry if I offended you, Ms. Dane. I know you're helping me as a favor to my uncle, and I really appreciate it."

"Ms. Dane?" She laughs. "Drop the *Ms.* It's just Cutter. And I'm not offended. I'm used to people wondering why a Harvard Med grad with eight published papers in the field of sports medicine walked away from the operating room and the seven figures she was earning as an orthopedic surgeon." She cracks a real smile. "The truth is I like sports more than surgery and martial arts more than money."

Cutter notices something out of the corner of her eye and waves to get Lazarus' attention. "If he doesn't move faster than that, he's going to get his ass handed to him at the semifinals."

"I know exactly how fast he has to move," Lazarus says. "We're working on it."

Cutter returns to our conversation. "If you want to get back on the field, I'll help you. But you'll have to work for it. If I give you exercises, I expect you to do them. And if I tell you to rest, you rest." She walks toward a small office in the back of the gym and I follow her. "You're going to start in the pool. Walking. That's it. Did you bring a bathing suit?"

"Yes." I brought everything on the list Hawk left in my room, not that I expected to break out my bathing suit on day one.

Cutter points at a door across from her office. "The women's locker room is straight ahead. Walk for thirty minutes. Come see me when you're done."

"Okay."

The kickboxer throws a killer shin kick. His movements are fluid and controlled, unlike the brute force of Reed's fighting style. Developing that kind of control takes time. It requires practicing the same drills and techniques for years until they become second nature. Soccer demands the same level of discipline.

The guy lands an elbow strike, and Lazarus stumbles back. The fighter rushes to help him up, and my heart thumps in my chest.

I turn away and head to the locker room.

After thirty minutes of walking in the pool, I admit my knee feels better. The view certainly didn't hurt, either. Across from my lane, a window separates the boxing gym from the pool. A few guys showed up around lap twelve to shadowbox and work the speed bag, but none of them compared to the kickboxer in the ring.

Lean and cut to perfection, without the exaggerated definition of a bodybuilder, he has the type of body I love.

If I was dating and if he wasn't a fighter.

I pull myself out of the water and sit on the edge of the pool, wringing out my hair.

The kickboxer lands three body shots and a combination. Lazarus puts down the pad and makes a wide circle with his hand. The guy nods and circles the ring, hands resting on his hip bones and sweat running down his muscular back. He picks up a water bottle in the corner of the ring and takes a drink. He tugs on the black padded headgear, but Lazarus shakes his head and waves him back over.

I wrap a towel around my waist and let my eyes roam over his shoulders one last time. He's probably a jerk. I appreciate an amazing body as much as the next girl, but the way a guy makes me feel outweighs everything else.

Funny and smart are must-haves. If a guy hates soccer or cheesy horror movies, he won't last. Athletic and capable of doing his own laundry are pluses.

Reed had the pluses. He excelled at MMA—without doping—and he knew his way around the laundry room in his building. But he fell short in the must-haves department. Reed wasn't brilliant, but he was street-smart. And he wasn't exactly funny, but I didn't notice. I'd lost my father. My sense of humor back then was almost nonexistent.

In the locker room, I shower, change, and pull my wet hair into a ponytail. When I return to the boxing gym, Cutter is standing near the ring. She sees me and checks her watch. "Right on time. At least you know how to follow directions. That's more than I can say about most of the athletes I work with."

"Thanks. What's next?"

"I need to assess what kind of shape the PCL and surrounding ligaments are in—strength and range-of-motion tests. You probably did something similar with Dr. Kao. After I determine where to start, I'll design a physical therapy plan for you. I'll meet with you twice a week. I'll run through the exercises with you, track your progress, and make adjustments."

"Just twice a week?" I expected to see her more often.

She flips through a date book that's falling apart. "You caught me during football season. I'm a consultant for the University of Tennessee in Knoxville. They've got a wide receiver with an ACL tear and an offensive lineman who can't stay off the injured list, so my schedule is tight. But don't worry. You'll work out with my intern on the three afternoons I'm not here. Let me introduce you."

"Lazarus," Cutter shouts. The old man peeks out from behind the pad, and she motions to the kickboxer.

Lazarus understands her shorthand. He taps the fighter on the shoulder and points in our direction. The guy swipes a bottle of Gatorade off the mat, tips his head back, and takes a long drink as he walks toward us.

She can't mean . . .

"The fighter? He's your intern?"

Cutter gives me a strange look. "He interned with me for two summers. He knows his stuff. You'll be in good hands." She notices my apprehension and crosses her arms. "But if you don't trust me—"

"No. It's fine." I can't risk offending her.

"That's what I like to hear."

The guy stops behind the ropes in front of us, his head still tipped back as he finishes off the Gatorade. He looks at Cutter without even glancing in my direction.

She doesn't seem to notice. "This is Peyton. I'm setting up a PT program for her. You're going to work with her on the afternoons I'm at the university."

The guy crosses his arms and studies the mat, as if the dust at his feet is more interesting than this conversation. He obviously isn't thrilled. Working with me will probably cut into his training time. I put one hand on my hip and hit him with some attitude. I want him to know that I'm not happy about being stuck with him, either.

When he doesn't respond, Cutter loses her patience. "Are you waiting for an invitation? Take off your damn headgear and say hello."

The fighter pulls off the black headgear and drops it on the mat. Tufts of damp blond hair are plastered against his head, and trails of sweat run down his face.

"It's about time." Cutter turns to me and gestures at the ring.

"Peyton, this is Owen."

CHAPTER 17

Against the Ropes

OWEN STANDS ON the opposite side of the ropes, his eyes still glued to the mat. He's shirtless and barefoot, his body covered in a thin sheen of sweat. His black shorts hang low on his hips, and my gaze flickers to a set of perfect abs. He has the kind of body you see on twenty-five-year-old underwear models, not high school guys.

Heat spreads through my chest. Less than twenty minutes ago, I was in the pool drooling over his body.

Owen's body.

He finally raises his head and our eyes lock. A crease forms between his brows and he looks miserable, like he'd rather scrub this place down with a toothbrush than spend three afternoons a week working with me.

I turn away first, which gives me a ridiculous amount of satisfaction. This whole situation feels like a giant bitch-slap from the universe. My hand tightens on the plastic water bottle I'm holding and I shake my head.

"What?" Owen leans on the ropes, his shoulders tense.

"You're a *fighter*?" I spit out the word. Now I know where he got the bruises on his arms.

"Yeah." He stands straighter. "But unlike your boyfriend, Titan, who starts fights with anybody who looks at him the wrong way, I try to keep my fights in the cage."

"He's *not* my boyfriend!" Without thinking, I chuck the plastic water bottle at him.

Owen's eyes widen and he pivots out of the way, but the bottle pegs him in the side.

Lazarus winces and makes a hissing sound between his teeth. "Ouch."

"That must've hurt," Cutter says, smirking at Lazarus as he tries not to laugh. "I guess they already know each other."

The boxers in the back corner of the gym take a break to watch us, too.

"There's nothing wrong with her arm, that's for sure," Lazarus says.

Owen rubs the spot where the bottle hit him. "What's your problem?"

"You first."

He swipes a gray hoodie off the mat, shoves his arms in the sleeves, and yanks it over his head. Then he ducks between the ropes and jumps down from the ring. "What's that supposed to mean?"

My pulse pounds and the air feels heavy as if the room is getting hotter. Why did I make a fool of myself and throw that stupid bottle at him? Who cares if Owen gave me crap about Titan?

I want to get out of here. I walk toward the glass door that leads out of the gym. Owen rushes ahead of me and plants himself in front of the door, blocking my path. I could probably squeeze by him, but that would involve touching him—something I'm not doing after I just spent thirty minutes gawking at his body from the pool.

"Please move." I lower my voice. We're far enough from the ring that no one can overhear our conversation unless we raise our voices.

Owen looks down at me. "You can't leave. What about physical therapy?" He's watching me and I look anywhere but at him.

"Not your problem."

"It is if you walk out of here and Cutter gets pissed at me," he says.

"And that's not *my* problem." I avoid his eyes.

"What did you mean by 'you first'? I never said I had a problem with you."

I snort. "You made it pretty clear in English."

Owen clasps his hands behind his neck and stares up at the ceiling. "I just didn't think you were the kind of girl who would get mixed up with Titan."

"I'm not mixed up with anyone. You're making lots of assumptions. Titan is friends with my cousins and he offered to help me find my classroom. I didn't ask him to pick me up and make a big scene. But even if I did, that doesn't make him my boyfriend."

Owen looks a little embarrassed. "What if I apologize?" He sounds sincere, but he also already gave away that he doesn't want to piss off Cutter.

"It doesn't matter. I don't want to hang out with a fighter."

"First off, I'm not a *fighter*. I'm a kickboxer. Second, we won't be hanging out. Cutter will leave a long-ass list of exercises for you to do, and I'll help you do them."

I toy with Dad's dog tags and weigh my options. I can't afford to leave and risk offending Cutter. Not when she's the only person in Black Water capable of helping me get back on the field.

I walk back to the ring. I hear Owen's footsteps behind me. Cutter and Lazarus are exactly where we left them, except now they're huddled around Cutter's phone.

She taps on the screen. "That's after he won the bronze for the one hundred meter, in the Summer Olympics. Fifteen years later and he still looks great."

"If you say so," Lazarus says.

Cutter sees us and pockets her phone. "Did you two lovebirds work things out?"

"No," I say at the same time Owen says, "Yes."

"And we aren't *lovebirds*," I say.

Cutter dismisses my comment with a wave. "People fight for three reasons—survival, aggression, and attraction. When I lived in China, I watched pandas do the same thing."

Did she just compare me to a panda?

"The female pandas snapped and took swings at the males, and the males gave it right back. But they never hurt each other," Cutter explains. "That's how you know it wasn't aggression. Eventually, they would stop fighting and pair up. That's what happens when it's attraction."

"Then what?" I ask. "The pandas live happily ever after?"

Cutter smiles, as if she's pleased with herself for giving me what has to be the worst analogy I've ever heard.

"What about praying mantises?" I ask. "After they mate, the female bites off the male's head."

Dead silence.

Maybe I went too far?

Cutter laughs. "You catch on fast, Peyton."

"Actually, I do. That's why I won't need Owen's help." I feel Owen's eyes burning a hole through me. "After you show me the exercises, I won't have any trouble doing them on my own when you're at the university."

Lazarus rubs his head and eyes Owen. "She really doesn't like you. This whole thing is looking more praying mantis than panda."

Owen's cheeks flush.

"What the hell did you do to make this girl so angry, Owen?" Cutter asks.

He glares at me. "Nothing."

"We were partners in English class. We just don't get along," I say. "Oil and water. That kind of thing."

"Then you'd better work it out," Cutter says as she and Lazarus walk toward an office under the caged clock on the wall.

"Oil and water?" Owen sounds offended. "We've had a total of two real conversations."

"Four, including this one." I head for Cutter's office and Owen follows me.

The office door is open, but I still knock.

"Come in," she says.

The office walls are covered in posters of martial arts moves and photos of Cutter—at tournaments, hitting a tall piece of wood with wooden prongs sticking out of it, or bowing in front of an elderly Asian man. A bookshelf holds medical texts and journals, alongside titles like *The Art of War*, *The Heart of the Warrior*, and *The Adversary Within*. It's all a little too Zen for me, and the atmosphere suggests a level of calm that I'm not feeling.

"That was fast," Cutter says.

Owen clears his throat. "I think Peyton is right. The two of us working together is a bad idea."

The words sting, something I didn't expect.

Owen tugs on one of his hand wraps with his teeth. He unwinds the cloth in a long strip, tosses it on the floor, and starts on the other hand. "I'm not even your intern anymore."

Lazarus shakes his head, as if something bigger is happening here and it has nothing to do with me.

Cutter crosses her arms and studies Owen. "You might not be my intern, but unless you want to start paying me to train you, you'll help out when I ask." She points at the cloth strips. "And don't leave your wraps on my floor."

Owen picks them up and shoves them into the pocket of his hoodie.

Cutter spins the seat of her chair toward me. "And you have two choices. Option A: Do physical therapy with Owen, or Option B: Find someone else to help you. There is no Option C." She motions between us. "For either of you. Decide what you want to do and let me know," she says, shooing us out of her office.

Owen follows me and closes the door behind us. I lean against the wall outside Cutter's office and he walks over and stands beside me.

"I guess that means we have to work together." He doesn't sound any happier about the situation than I am, but it makes me feel like I'm the one forcing this on him.

Tension coils in my stomach. I want to let us both off the hook, but Cutter has me backed into a corner. "We'll meet up to satisfy Cutter," I say. "But you'll do your thing and I'll do mine. Minimal interaction."

Owen sighs. "Okay."

I turn to leave and I look back at him. "Don't look so depressed, Owen. I'm only here for a few months."

CHAPTER 18

Nobody Left to Run with Anymore

HAWK'S BLACK SUBURBAN idles in front of the YMCA. I can't wait to get out of here.

My uncle has his window rolled down, and a Southern rock song is playing. His arm is hanging out the window and he's nodding in time to the music as he taps the rhythm against the side of the SUV.

I circle around the front of the Suburban.

Hawk sees me and pushes my door open from the inside. He turns down the radio, just as the lead singer complains that there's "nobody left to run with anymore."

"Where are the Twins? Is everything okay?" They were supposed to pick me up.

"Coach extended practice until seven to go over the playbook. Cam texted me to see if I could swing by and get you."

"Sorry. I don't want to be any trouble."

"I don't mind at all. But I was thinking. You probably don't want your grease monkey uncle driving you around when the boys are tied up."

"Restoring classic cars hardly makes you a grease monkey."

"I've got an old Jeep in the garage that needs some bodywork, but it runs great. I'm planning to restore it and sell it when I have time. You could use it while you're here."

"That's really nice of you, but I can't take one of your cars."

What am I saying?

Driving equals freedom. I wouldn't be tied to the Twins every time I want to go somewhere.

"It was just a thought," Hawk says gently.

"Actually, the doctor never said I couldn't drive. At home I had nowhere to go, so I never thought about it. I'll check with her tomorrow. If she says it's okay, will you take a test drive with me?"

"It would be my pleasure. I survived teaching the boys to drive."

The Suburban passes the Best Darn Diner in the Whole Darn State. Black Water students sit in the booths next to the window.

"Doesn't Christian want to borrow it?" I ask.

Hawk laughs. "Your cousin already crashed one vehicle. I'm not letting him drive a car I'm planning to sell."

"What makes you think I'm a good driver?" I do have a clean driving record. I've never even had a ticket. Did Mom tell him?

"Just a hunch. And you'd be doing me a favor. It's better for the engine if someone drives it."

I'll have a car. Just thinking about it makes me smile. "Okay. Thanks."

Hawk nods his approval. "It's nice to see you smile. Don't let anyone take that away."

Somebody already did, but I'm finally ready to take it back.

"So how did physical therapy go?"

I twist wet strands of hair from my ponytail around my finger. "It went."

He glances at me from under the bill of his University of Tennessee Volunteers cap. "I'm not sure I like the sound of that."

"It was fine."

"Some people have a hard time with Cutter. She's . . . difficult."

"Actually, she was cool." Except for her terrible idea to have me work out with Owen. "How do you know her?"

"Cutter grew up in Nashville. I was working the door at a bar down there before I joined the Marine Corps. That's where I met her. She was already in med school, impressing the hell out of everyone—and pissing them off. Cutter was always getting herself in trouble. She came home to visit one weekend and I got her out of some. That's how we became friends."

"Why did she stop performing surgery? She said something about liking sports more than surgery and martial arts more than medicine."

"Cutter came out of operating room one day and handed in her resignation. Then she fell off the grid. Ten years later, she showed up in Nashville. She told me she'd been living in Asia. But she missed whiskey and Elvis, so she came back."

"Did she tell anyone why she left?"

We turn onto Hawk's street and he pulls into the driveway. "Some people want to live life on their own terms. They don't want anyone else deciding their fate. Cutter has always been that kind of person."

Hawk walks into the house and Dutch greets us, howling like he wants everyone in town to hear him. My uncle pats the bloodhound on the head with one hand and holds the door open for me with the other.

"You don't have to hold it open."

My uncle laughs and closes the door behind us.

"Your grandma would rise up out of her grave if I didn't." He drops his keys in a bowl on the table by the door. "It's a Southern thing. And if the boys don't hold it open for you, I'll send her after them, too."

It's easy to picture my grandma, a stubborn spitfire like my mom, haunting the Twins because their manners aren't up to her standards. I'd forgotten how funny my uncle is sometimes. He's cool, in the uncool way some adults manage to be cool.

"We have dinner around seven after the boys get home from practice," Hawk says on his way to the kitchen. He stops in the doorway and looks back at me with kind brown eyes that look like Mom's. "I know you weren't crazy about the idea of coming to Black Water. Seeing me every day can't be easy for you. But I'm glad you're here."

I wish being around Hawk didn't remind me of how Dad died—at least the parts I know. I don't blame Hawk. It wasn't his fault.

"That's not the reason I wanted to stay in DC." *Okay . . . it's one of them.* "I didn't want it to look like I was running away. I don't want him to think he broke me."

"I hear you. But leaving doesn't always mean you're running away. Sometimes you have to regroup before you go back and fight another battle."

"There won't be another battle. I already lost the war." And my best friend.

"Don't be so sure. You're a fighter like your mom. Don't let a pathetic excuse for a boy change that."

At the mention of Reed, a chill runs up the back of my neck. I excuse myself and go up to my Tennessee bedroom—that's what I've decided to call it. I unstrap my *RoboCop* brace and change into sweats and an oversize T-shirt.

I call Mom and fill her in on the first day. I tell her about my room and Black Water High. I give her the rundown on my classes, minus the Weasel, and I tell her about Grace. I don't mention April, Titan, Owen, or my demonic locker number. That stuff will just stress her out.

After I get off the phone, I'm out of distractions and my thoughts go straight to Owen.

What's my problem? Why am I thinking about him?

Because he's a hot smart-ass, who defended Tucker from bullies . . . who flirted with me behind a barn and promised to protect me from bears . . . who made my skin tingle when he touched me. But he's also a frustrating pain in the ass who thinks I'd be interested in dating a jerk like Titan.

Then there's the other thing about Owen. . . .

He's a fighter.

And I have to do PT with him.

I definitely didn't see the fighter part coming. Black Water is the land of football. Who kickboxes in a tiny-ass town in Tennessee?

Owen Law.

And he looks hot doing it.

I wish I could snap a picture of Owen and send it to Tess. She'd think he's good-looking too.

It's impossible to understand how much you need someone until that person isn't around. Losing Tess feels permanent, like there's no way to Krazy Glue our friendship back together.

A long howl followed by an even longer one comes from downstairs.

The front door slams, and it sounds like someone is dropping rocks on the floor downstairs. The howling stops and the bickering starts. The Twins are home.

On my way down to the kitchen, the scent of fried chicken wafts through the air and my stomach rumbles. Suddenly, I'm starving.

So what if Owen is at the YMCA when I'm there?

He's *one* guy.

One guy I have to work out with three times a week.

I'll ignore him during PT and avoid him the rest of the time. If he gives me any crap, I'll hand it right back to him. Or maybe throw more water bottles at him.

At the bottom of the steps, football helmets and pads are strewn across the floor in a trail leading to the kitchen. That explains the banging I heard. A week with Mom and she'd have the Twins putting away their gear and doing their own laundry.

I step around the pads and follow the smell of fried chicken.

The Twins mill around the kitchen, wearing grass-stained football pants with their sweaty Warriors football shirts. Cam opens the fridge and gulps milk straight from the carton—the only way I've seen him drink it so far. Christian tears open a party-size bag of barbecue chips, leans his head back, and shakes the chips directly into his mouth. There's no sign of the fried chicken I smelled, not even a KFC bucket.

Hawk points at the chips. "Put those back. We're about to eat. Go sit down."

Christian shakes the bag over his mouth before returning it to the pantry. He notices Cam walking toward the long farmhouse table, and he tries to rush past him. Cam catches on and grabs the back of his brother's shirt to stop him, but Christian is faster and he shoves Cam against the fridge.

Dutch raises his head from his spot underneath the kitchen table. Nothing fazes the bloodhound.

Cam regains his balance. "You're going to pull a punk move like that when I'm not paying attention?"

"Stay sharp, boy!" Christian yells back in an exaggerated Southern accent and a clipped tone.

"You'd better hope Coach doesn't catch you imitating him. He'll have you doing push-ups until your wrists break," Cam warns.

"That's enough," Hawk says, opening the oven. "Sit your tails down. And if one of you breaks my fridge, you'll spend the spring mowing lawns to replace it."

"That'll give Christian something to look forward to," Cam says, following me to the table. He pulls out a ladder-back chair for me at one end and drops into the chair beside it.

I gesture at the chair. "I'm not sitting at the head of the table. One of you should sit here."

Christian takes a seat across from his brother. "We're not allowed. House rules."

Hawk looks over his shoulder at us. "Don't make me sound like a drill sergeant. Go ahead and tell her why."

"We used to fight over that spot," Christian explains.

"Which always turned into a wrestling match," Cam says.

Christian shrugs. "One night we broke some dishes."

"Is that the way you tell it?" Hawk shakes his head and pulls a large foil pan out of the oven. "These two were rolling around and bumped right into their mother."

The Twins exchange embarrassed looks, and Hawk continues, "She dropped the Thanksgiving ham on the floor, platter and all. A Southern woman takes pride in four things—her kids, her appearance, her house, and her cooking. I thought she was going to put you both over her knee."

"How old were you?" I ask the Twins.

"Eight, maybe?" Christian guesses.

"Seven," Cam corrects him. "It was the year before . . ."

Their mom died.

Nobody wants to say it.

"Right." Christian's eyes cloud over for a moment, then he snaps out of it. "For the record, Cam started it."

Hawk carries two huge aluminum foil pans to the table and places them in the center. He makes another trip to grab biscuits, a ready-to-eat bag of salad, a glass bowl, and two bottles of salad dressing. The aluminum pans, extra-crunchy fried chicken, and breadcrumb-dusted mac and cheese look familiar, and I realize they're Stouffer's frozen dinners.

Stouffer's mac and cheese was a mainstay at Tess' house. I've eaten the fried chicken at plenty of potluck dinners, but never at home.

Before Dad died, he did all the cooking and nothing came out of a freezer pan. After we lost him, I took over the cooking. Resorting to frozen food would've been another reminder that he was gone—that everything in Mom's life and mine had changed. I wonder if it felt that way to Hawk and the Twins.

It's easy to forget that my cousins know how it feels to lose a parent, too.

Hawk rips open the salad bag and dumps it into the glass bowl. "Go ahead and eat."

No one reaches for the food. Are the Twins thinking about their mom?

"You like fried chicken?" Christian picks up the pan and holds it out to me.

"Yes." I take two legs and set them on my plate. "Thanks."

The moment the crispy brown coating touches my plate, the Twins descend on the pan like locusts. Water glasses wobble and silverware clinks as they reach across the table in a rush to fill their plates. Christian grabs four pieces of chicken and digs into the mac and cheese, serving himself three heaping spoonfuls. Cam shakes the bread basket above his plate as if he's planning to empty it.

Hawk rescues the biscuits before they disappear and offers the basket to me. "Help yourself."

Now I know why they didn't serve themselves right away. They were waiting for me.

Is it because I'm a girl or a guest? I want to ask, but it seems rude to lecture them about gender equality when Hawk just made me dinner.

For ten minutes, nobody says a word. Hawk and I eat at a normal pace, while the boys wolf down the family-size portions that are probably designed to feed ten people. They finally slow down after they kill what's left of the mac and cheese.

"We heard Titan was acting like an ass in the hall this morning before second period. Why didn't you say something?" Cam asks, watching me over the chicken leg he's eating.

"Because I handled it."

Christian stabs a biscuit with the butter knife. "We warned Titan not to pull any of his Romeo bullshit with you."

"Language," Hawk says.

"Sorry, Pop." Christian tears the biscuit in half and slathers it with butter, as if the conversation is over.

Hawk puts down his fork. "Does someone want to fill me in?"

I glare at Cam. "*Nothing* happened."

Christian snorts. "Yeah . . . Well, I nailed Titan at practice so that *nothing* won't happen again."

"Is *nailed* a football term? Because if it isn't, I'm about to get really upset."

"Not exactly." Cam glances at his brother.

"What did you do?" *And how embarrassed am I going to be at school tomorrow because of it?*

Christian scratches the back of his head. "I said he'd better back off or we'd have a problem."

That's not so bad.

"Is that all?" I ask.

"Yeah. Why are you getting so worked up?" Christian asks. "Titan was out of line."

"Out of line how?" Hawk leans forward and props his elbows on the table. Now we have his full attention.

"I made the mistake of asking Titan how to get to my classroom. Instead of giving me directions, he picked me up and carried me there," I explain. "It was ridiculous and embarrassing."

"He didn't ask," Christian adds, looking his dad in the eye. "He just grabbed Peyton and picked her up."

Hawk's expression darkens.

"He didn't grab me in a forceful way." I'm not making excuses for Titan. The guy is a total ass. I just don't want to misrepresent the situation.

"But you weren't expecting it, right?" Cam asks. "After what happened with . . . your knee, it seems like that might freak you out."

"Yeah. A little." I'm not sure what else to say. I didn't expect the Twins to think about the situation from my point of view. It's sweet.

"Titan always goes too far," my uncle says.

"Exactly. He had it coming." Christian takes another biscuit. "It was no big deal. Coach said it was a clean break."

I press my fingers against my temples. "You broke something?"

"Just his nose," Cam says calmly. "In football, we don't really count that as a broken bone."

"I think it's just cartilage anyhow," Christian adds.

"It's not just cartilage." I raise my voice and the Twins snap to attention. "Forget it."

Hawk looks Christian in the eyes. "Did Coach bench you?"

"Nope." Christian grins proudly. "He thinks Titan had it coming, too."

"You're lucky." Hawk's expression doesn't change. I can't tell if he's upset because Christian broke Titan's nose or because his son could've been benched.

"I know you two were just trying to help, but don't you see how stupid I look now? People will think I went crying to my cousins because a guy carried me down the hall." The leg brace already makes me look fragile and the Twins confirmed it by coming to my rescue in a situation that didn't require a rescue effort.

"Who cares what people think?" Christian asks, picking up a chicken bone.

"I care," I practically shout.

Christian drops the bone and Cam's eyes widen. Hawk raises his eyebrows and sits back in the chair as if he's waiting to see what I'll do next.

"Then I guess you don't want us to say anything to Owen?" Cam asks.

"About what?"

Cam clears his throat. "We heard you were arguing with him at the YMCA."

"Are you two spying on me?"

The Twins look confused, like they can't figure out why they didn't come up with the idea themselves.

"Boys?" Hawk asks.

"No," Christian says. "Rusty Thompson boxes at the Y. We ran into him at Circle K and he brought it up." Sometimes I forget how small this town *really* is, and how fast news travels.

"It sounded weird because Owen is so laid-back," Cam says. "Did something happen between you two?"

Short of a zombie apocalypse, nothing could get me to tell them what happened.

CHAPTER 19
A Girl Like You

THE SILENT TREATMENT is my superpower. It drives people crazy, and the Twins are no exception. On the way to school, they took a tag-team approach, alternating between cracking jokes and apologizing. By the time we pulled into the school parking lot, they were begging me to talk to them.

I remained stone-faced through it all. The silent treatment only works if I hold out long enough to make a point, and subtlety doesn't seem to have any effect on my cousins.

Starting the school day with precalculus and the Weasel sucks. Despite the dirty looks I throw his way, the Weasel continues to roll his Rs every time he calls me *Miss Rios* just like he did yesterday. One of us might not survive the next four months.

He'll hit the wall before I do.

After class, the Twins are loitering across from my locker, talking to

Grace. They try to make eye contact with me, but I ignore them and put away my books as quickly as possible.

Grace sees me and crosses to my side of the hall. Today she's dressed in a white V-neck tee, a fitted black leather jacket, and skinny jeans—a combination my friends back home wear all the time. Except none of them could rock red leather cowboy boots with it.

"Hey," she says. "The Twins told me about Christian's *chivalrous* behavior at football practice yesterday. Sometimes they act like idiots."

"I can't believe he broke his friend's nose. Who does that?"

"Christian just reacts. He doesn't think first. Cam is the levelheaded one. He usually talks Christian out of doing crazy things, but Cam wasn't happy with Titan, either. They're sorry for embarrassing you."

They do look pretty pathetic.

"I know they mean well. But they're like puppies. If I don't lay down the law now they'll be out of control, swinging at every guy who talks at me."

"You have to forgive them, or one of them will be texting me every five minutes. Consider this a purely selfish request."

"Okay. I just want them to suffer a little bit longer."

Grace laughs and keeps walking. "Deal."

I stop in front of my English classroom. I'm about to spend the next fifty minutes in the same room as Owen. The way I left things yesterday didn't mark the beginning of a beautiful friendship.

Owen is already sitting at a desk in the back corner when I walk in. He's stretched out in his chair, and my mind flashes to the sweatier and shirtless version of him. He looks up from the notebook he's scribbling in and tries to make eye contact.

I choose the desk in the opposite corner of the classroom and pretend to check my email until the bell rings. Miss Ives walks around to the front of her desk. Today her blond dreadlocks are arranged on top of her head in an intricate bun and the metallic oxblood lipstick she's wearing gives her light brown skin a golden glow. "I hope everyone brought in at least one object that holds special meaning for you."

Several students reach for their backpacks while the rest of us remain frozen in place.

Miss Ives scans the room. "If you forgot, find something in the next five minutes—or expect a zero for this assignment." The threat mobilizes us. My backpack has nothing in it except pens, two notebooks, a Dr Pepper Lip Smacker that Mom swears is the holy grail of lip products, my wallet, Ibuprofen in case my knee swells, and my cell phone. Unless I convince Miss Ives that my driver's license has sentimental value, I've got nothing.

My fingers reach for the dog tags around my neck out of habit. I'll just say they're my dad's. I don't have to cough up any details. Dead parents make people uncomfortable. Lifting the chain over my head, I gently lay them on the desk.

"Find your partner from yesterday and get started," Miss Ives calls over her shoulder as she scribbles furiously on the board.

English has officially dropped below precalc on the list of classes that suck.

Chair legs scrape across the floor and bags zip and unzip as the other students swap seats and find their partners. Not me. I'm hoping I'll be granted with the power of invisibility before Owen comes over here.

Scooping the dog tags off the desk, I clutch them in a death grip.

Owen flips a chair around and pulls it up to my desk. He sits on the edge of the chair and leans forward, arms resting on his knees and hands clasped.

"I heard about what happened between Christian and Titan yesterday at practice. I feel like a jerk for giving you a hard time about him."

At least we agree on one thing.

"An asshole like Titan couldn't score a girl like you."

The comment takes me by surprise and I look up. Huge mistake. Owen smiles at me and my anger dissolves.

"Is that a compliment?" I ask, hoping the question will distract him. If he keeps staring at me, I'll forget that I'm supposed to be angry.

He stops fidgeting with his hands and the corner of his mouth turns up. "Why? Are you one of those girls who can't take a compliment?"

I cover my mouth to hide a smile. "I have no issue taking one. I just wanted to make sure it wasn't another cheap shot."

Owen smiles, and my stomach flutters.

"You're not going to let me off easy, are you?" he asks.

"Not a chance."

Miss Ives walks down the center aisle toward us.

I kick Owen's foot under the desk, and he notices her a second before she descends on us.

"I don't see anything on the desk except pencils." She sounds disappointed.

Reluctantly, I open my hand. "I brought these."

Miss Ives sees the dog tags and her face brightens. "Excellent, Peyton. How about you, Owen?"

"I was getting mine." He digs through his backpack and pulls out a clean white hand wrap.

"Carry on." Miss Ives waves her hand and moves to the next group.

I point at the wrap. "Nice save."

Owen leans forward, so we're eye-to-eye. "You too. Except yours looks legit. That means you get to go first."

"You're not serious." I swallow hard.

He glances over his shoulder. "If we don't turn in something, we fail, right?"

I rub a stainless-steel tag between my fingers, and the raised letters that form my father's name press against my skin. I've touched them so many times that I recognize the shape of every letter and number stamped into the metal.

"These were my dad's."

Owen reaches across the desk and touches the edge of the tag I'm not holding. "Were?"

So much for avoiding the topic of dead parents.

"He was in the Marine Corps. He died in Iraq." The back of my throat burns. I don't trust myself to keep talking. It feels like someone punched a hole in my chest.

"When did it happen?" His finger is still touching the tag, and it grazes the curve of my thumb. Warmth spreads through me, and I feel safe enough to answer.

"A year and a half ago." I change the subject. "Is your dad around?"

His smile falls and his lips form a hard line. "My parents split up a couple years back. My dad and I don't really talk."

"Sorry." Now we're both uncomfortable.

I pick up the hand wrap on the desk. "Maybe you should tell me why this is important to you. Miss Ives is still making the rounds."

The tension in Owen's expression fades. "You don't think it will go over well if I say it was the only thing I could find in my bag?"

I tap on the cloth and pretend to give him a stern look.

Owen slips his thumb through the hole at one end. "I use these to wrap my hands before I train." He loops the cloth around his knuckles a few times. "I love kickboxing and my knuckles would get torn up without these."

I resist the urge to tell him that I know why he uses them. I wrapped Reed's hands for him all the time.

"You probably don't want to hear about anything related to kickboxing. Since you hate fighters." He glances at me, and my stomach somersaults.

My body needs to get the message that Owen is off-limits.

"I said I don't *like* fighters."

"That changes everything," he teases. "So what's the deal? There must be a reason. Do you puke at the sight of blood?"

"I'm a soccer player. I get scrapes and cuts all the time. Blood doesn't bother me."

"Do you think kickboxing and MMA are too violent?" Owen asks.

"Something like that."

"Kickboxing isn't about hurting people. It started as a form of self-defense in Thailand. For me, it's also a way to get out of my head." When I don't say anything right away, Owen gives me a sheepish smile. "That was a lame explanation."

"No. It made sense. I've just never heard anyone describe it that way. But I get it. Soccer is my escape—at least it was, before this." I tap on the brace and look away.

"Hey? Your injury doesn't change anything. You'll play again. You just need time to heal."

Owen isn't the first person to say I just need time, but the words mean more coming from him because he didn't have to say them.

I'll do whatever it takes to get back on the soccer field.

My knee will heal. Deep down, I believe that. But I'm not sure about the rest of me.

CHAPTER 20

Wishing, Wondering, and What Ifs

AFTER SCHOOL, CAM drives me to the Y without saying a single word the entire way there. I grab my bag the second the truck stops. "The reverse silent treatment, Cam? I'm impressed." I must be rubbing off on him. I reach for the door handle. "Thanks for the ride."

"Hold on." He takes an energy bar out of the center console and hands it to me. "You didn't eat lunch."

"I'm not a fan of cafeterias."

Cam taps the steering wheel. "Is that why you were hiding out in the library?"

"I wasn't hiding." I sink back against the seat.

The Twins noticed when I didn't show up at lunch, and they made

171

Grace check the girls' bathrooms in case I'd fallen like the old lady from a Life Alert commercial.

"They're the same way with me," Grace said. "Especially Cameron."

The Twins were standing in the hall next to the library when I came out with Grace, and they practically tripped over each other trying to make it look as if they hadn't been waiting.

Cam didn't speak to me for the rest of the afternoon—until a minute ago.

"Don't you need to get to practice?" I ask.

Driving me to the Y after school means one of the Twins has to miss the first fifteen minutes of football practice—an exception their coach isn't willing to make on a regular basis.

Cam checks the time on his phone. "Yeah. I've gotta go. Coach is already annoyed. We'll pick you up as soon as practice ends."

"Okay." I step on the running board below the door and lower myself to the ground.

"You forgot this." Cam leans over the passenger seat, holding out the energy bar. I take it and shove it into my bag.

Inside, I check in and go straight to find Cutter. Today, the boxing gym looks empty. I spot Lazarus sitting at a card table next to the ring, playing chess. He has his back to me and he's studying the board.

"Cutter is on the phone," Lazarus says without turning around. "She'll be out in a minute."

"Thanks." I inch closer and watch as Lazarus captures a rook. "Is it hard to play alone?"

He rubs the salt-and-pepper stubble along his jaw. "It depends. I like studying the board from both sides of the table. It reminds me of the old days when I used to box. Before the internet and fancy coffee with names nobody can pronounce."

Lazarus' dark brown skin is so smooth that it's hard to guess his age. "Boxing and chess." He winks at me. "Two of my three great loves. They both require strategic thinking. You have to plan your next move and figure out what your opponent is going to do at the same time. But it's a lot harder when someone comes at you with a right hook."

Boxing and chess? Boxing seems more like a test of speed, strength, and stamina than a game of chess in the ring.

"Were you good?" I ask.

Lazarus removes a stopwatch from his pocket and loops it around his neck. He winks at me. "One of the best."

"The best what?" Owen's voice catches me off guard.

I steal a look in his direction and the butterflies in my stomach do more than flutter. They nose-dive like fighter planes in a dogfight.

Owen is barefoot—and for some reason it's sexy. Black gym shorts hang low on his hips, and the fabric of the faded gray T-shirt he's wearing is thinner in some places, revealing the outline of the muscles underneath. It feels like the temperature in the gym just rose by thirty degrees.

Lazarus shakes his head at Owen. "I was telling Peyton that I'm the best padman and cutman on the East Coast. Start stretching. Then get your tail in the ring and I'll prove it."

Owen looks over at the man old enough to be his grandfather and grins. "Somebody is fired up today. And you're the best padman and cutman on both coasts."

Lazarus moves a knight on the chessboard and captures a queen. "You've never seen me fired up. But when I was young, I would've given you a run for your money."

The affection between them is reassuring. Lazarus seems like a man with character—someone who wouldn't waste time training a jerk.

"Ready to work out with Cutter?" Owen asks. He reaches for one of the higher ropes, takes hold of it, and leans back, using his body weight to stretch his hamstrings. Owen's T-shirt rides up, offering me a clear view of his carved abs.

High school guys aren't supposed to be this hot. Reed was solid as a rock, but he didn't have as much muscle definition.

Owen has a body that looks as if it's meant to be touched. I imagine dragging my fingers down his stomach.

Owen catches me staring.

Kill me now.

I never answered his question.

What did he ask me? Something about Cutter and PT?

"I was ready to start the day I got here," I blurt out, referring to PT.

Cutter steps through the doorway as I'm walking to her office. She's dressed in a plain T-shirt and a pair of black martial arts pants. The pant legs billow out when she moves.

"They're a present from my boyfriend," she explains when she notices me looking at them.

"The Olympian?" I ask. Last time I was here, Cutter was showing Lazarus a photo on her phone of an Olympic medal-winner. I shouldn't be nosy, but the Olympics are almost as cool as professional soccer.

Cutter stops and thinks about it for a moment.

"Sorry, it's none of my business."

"Peyton is talking about your new boyfriend." Lazarus snaps his fingers. "You know, what's-his-name."

"You mean Dale!" she says. "These aren't from him."

"He's *another* one of her boyfriends," Lazarus explains.

I have to ask. "How many boyfriends do you have?"

"Too many," Lazarus mumbles.

Cutter smooths her blond pixie cut. "They're not really my

174

boyfriends. They're men I'm dating." She turns to Lazarus. "And nobody judges a man if he dates more than one woman at a time. Why should I comply with ridiculous gender norms? Besides, the whole online-dating thing was your idea, Lazarus."

"Whoa." Lazarus holds up his hands. "Don't pin that on me. It was my wife Davina's idea," he explains. "She thought Cutter should go on an online-dating site and meet a nice man."

"That's exactly what I did." Cutter pats him on the shoulder. "I just met more than one nice man. What can I say? I feel like I'm on *The Bachelorette*. I'm living the dream."

Lazarus moves a pawn across the board. "Even I know that show is scripted."

I try not to laugh. I'd love to invite Cutter over to Hawk's for dinner so she can help me teach the Twins a lesson or two.

"He's just grouchy because he has to give Davina updates," Cutter says. "She's like a second mother to me. And just like my mom, she wants me to settle down. We don't have a lot of time today. UT's quarterback pulled a muscle in his shoulder, and I need to take a look at it."

I'm only scheduled to meet with Cutter twice a week. If she bails on our sessions, will it hurt my chances of recovering by March? I change into black leggings, a T-shirt with PROPERTY OF ADAMS SOCCER printed on the front, and cross-trainers.

Owen is already in the ring, hands wrapped and protective gear in place, talking to Cutter.

Lazarus leans against the ropes, listening.

As I get closer, I hear Cutter say, "You're not blocking on your left. Get that left arm up. Anyone you compete against will see that opening."

"I block when I need to. I've got it covered." Owen sounds irritated.

"Prove it." Cutter moves to the center of the ring and wags her fingers, urging him to come closer.

Owen circles her, his hands cupped loosely in front of his face.

She laughs. "Now you've got your guard up?"

He maintains his fight stance, keeping his guard up and the weight on the balls of his feet. He moves closer to Cutter, who hasn't taken a step or bothered to raise her guard. He throws an elbow, and she blocks it without exerting any effort.

"If you think I'm weak on the left, throw a punch," Owen says.

"The punch you don't throw is just as powerful as the one you do."

Owen rolls his shoulders and throws a combination—right elbow strike, a kick from the left, and a right hook.

Cutter ducks before Owen lands the hook. In a series of lightning-fast movements, she reaches over his left shoulder and around the back of his neck. She sweeps Owen's legs out from under him and pulls his head to the side. He lands on his back with her forearm jammed under his neck, forcing his head against the mat. After a moment, Cutter releases her hold and stands.

Owen coughs and sits up, jerking off his headgear.

"Seems to me like you should've blocked on the left," she says.

Owen steals a glance in my direction. "You made your point."

Cutter claps a hand on his shoulder as she walks past him. "Good. You can't afford a mistake like that in the semifinals." She ducks and slips between the ropes, exiting the ring.

Lazarus raises the red pad in front of Owen and slaps the front. "Let's switch things up. Work off some of that steam."

Owen nods and mumbles something, but I miss it.

"You're up, Peyton." Cutter waves me over to the corner, where she's laying out foam floor tiles.

For the next thirty minutes, she leads me through a series of stretches and exercises to test my range of motion. None of them hurt, but they aren't comfortable, either. She demonstrates the exercises she wants me to practice until our next session and draws stick figures on a piece of paper to represent each move.

"Owen will take you through some strength-training exercises after you walk in the pool. I'll go over your program with him before I leave." Cutter hands me the paper with the stick-figure drawings on it and heads out. "Thirty minutes in the pool, then meet Owen back here."

"Then I'll tell you more about her boyfriends," Lazarus calls to me from the ring.

"Be quiet, old man. Or I'll drop you off at the old folks' home," Cutter says on her way out. Both of them are grinning.

Lazarus adjusts his cap. "As long as I have Davina, steak sandwiches, and ESPN, I'll live in the belly of a whale." He picks up the pad again and turns to Owen. "Do your worst, kid."

Pools are meant for swimming, not walking. After ten laps, my eyes burn from the chlorine, and I didn't even go underwater. But I can't complain about the view. The window that separates the pool and the boxing gym offers the perfect vantage point for watching Owen.

He switched from hitting the pad to dodging six heavy ropes suspended from the ceiling while Lazarus sends them flying at him— which led to Owen taking off his shirt.

If I wasn't paying attention before, I am now.

Owen's broad shoulders and back shine, slick with sweat. That might seem gross to some girls, but I'm an athlete and I dated a fighter. Sweat comes with the territory. The ropes fly at Owen one after another, and Lazarus makes sure they keep coming. Owen bobs and weaves, avoiding the ropes every time.

Okay . . . he's fast. I'll give him that.

Owen stands near the ropes, head down and his hands on his hips, catching his breath. He looks up and I'm caught in his hold, swimming in brown eyes that confirm he's feeling the same way.

The glass window between us seems to disappear.

What if my knee was fine and I didn't have an ex who had pushed me down the stairs? What if I could still trust the little voice in my head?

What if . . .

Water splashes in my eyes, and I turn away. An old lady wearing a yellow swimming cap backstrokes past me in the next lane over, her arms slapping the water. When I turn back to the window, Owen isn't looking over here anymore.

Why am I so disappointed?

CHAPTER 21
Breaking My Fall

WHEN I RETURN from the locker room a few minutes later, I'm wearing black leggings and a fitted tank under my T-shirt, and showing considerably less skin.

There's a guy in the ring with Owen and it's not Lazarus. I recognize the fauxhawk. It's Tucker. He's wearing a T-shirt, sweats with a red stripe down the side, mismatched socks, and his high-top Vans.

"You have to stand up to those boys," Lazarus says from his seat at the chess table, "or they'll never leave you alone. That's the way it works. Take down the ringleader and the rest of them won't bother you anymore."

Tucker sighs. "That's not gonna happen. Garrett, the guy who has it in for me, outweighs me by a hundred pounds, easy. The only way I'm going to take him down is with a bulldozer."

"Size has nothing to do with it. Even if you can't take Garrett down, you can stop him from kicking your ass." Owen motions for Tucker to move to the center of the ring. "Come on. I'll show you."

"I'm not sure I understand," Tucker says.

Lazarus looks up from his chess game. "Stop talking, Tucker. You don't need to understand. Just pay attention."

I move closer to watch.

"So here's what I want you to do," Owen says. "Bend your wrist back like this, so the heel of your hand is facing up." Owen demonstrates the correct position, and Tucker mimics it with his hand. "Good. You're going to use the heel of your hand to strike."

"That means hit, right?" Tucker asks.

"Yeah. There are three parts of the body that are vulnerable on everyone: the eyes, hitting the nose up toward the bridge, and right here." He touches the hollow at the base of his throat. "If you strike any of those places with the heel of your hand, you should be able to stun the person long enough to take off—if the hit doesn't take them down completely."

Tucker looks at the heel of his hand. "What if I don't hit them hard enough, or in the right spot?"

"The nose is the easiest target. But you have to strike in an upward motion, like this." Owen demonstrates the move in slow motion, raising the heel of his hand up to Tucker's nose as if he's going to hit it. "There are a lot of nerves in the nose, so if you hit someone there, it hurts like hell and it will make their eyes water."

Tucker still looks unsure.

Owen motions toward him. "Try it."

Tucker performs the same movement, thrusting the heel of his hand upward until he reaches Owen's nose. "Like that?"

"Exactly like that."

He walks Tucker through the move over and over, explaining each step.

The first few times, Tucker's aim is off or he executes the strike incorrectly. With each failed attempt, he appears more dejected. "I'll never get it right."

"Try again," Owen says, sounding like Cutter issuing instructions.

"I've already done it ten times," Tucker complains.

"And we'll keep doing it until you get it. So are you going to try again or quit?"

"It's bad luck to give up in a boxing ring," Lazarus says.

"That probably only counts if you're a boxer," Tucker says.

"It counts no matter who you are," Lazarus says. "A ring is for fighting, not quitting. Sometimes you fight with your fists and other times you fight with your will."

"Come on." Owen gestures for Tucker to try again. "Stand up straight and concentrate. Visualize the move before you do it. See yourself executing each step."

"Okay." Tucker moves with more determination this time and shoves the heel of his hand at Owen's nose.

"That's it, kid," Lazarus calls out. "Like David and Goliath."

"I did it." Tucker stares at his hand. "Did you see that?"

Owen nods. "Yeah, and I can feel it, too."

"Oh yeah. Sorry!" Tucker stares at it as though he had just shot fire from his fingertips.

"We need to keep practicing, but you've got the hang of it." Owen gets up and notices me watching them.

"But what if the person is someone like you, and they really know how to fight?" Tucker asks.

"If you're not confident that you can do it fast enough, then you need a distraction."

"Okay."

Suddenly, I'm interested. Distracting an attacker is a solid strategy, in self-defense and sports.

Owen motions to Tucker. "Do you have a quarter?"

Lazarus stops playing chess and looks over as if he's curious, too.

Tucker pulls at the side of his sweats. "Not on me. I don't have any pockets."

"I've got one." Lazarus stands, takes a quarter out of his pocket, and holds it up next to the ropes.

"Thanks." Owen takes it and tosses it in the air a couple of times.

"What are you gonna do with it?" Tucker asks.

"Watch." Owen stands directly in front of Tucker, the way Garrett did in the parking lot at the football game. "So Garrett or some asshole is coming at you, right?"

Tucker nods. "Yeah?"

Owen tosses the coin, higher this time. It sails above Tucker's head, and Tucker looks up, tracking it. The moment Tucker looks away, Owen comes at him with a strike and pretends to hit him in the nose.

"I wasn't ready," Tucker says.

The coin hits the mat between them.

"That's the whole point. If you throw something in the air, nine times out of ten, the person will look up. That gives you enough time to make your move without them seeing it coming."

It's actually really clever.

Tucker picks up the quarter. "So this is my strategy?"

"Don't knock it. It works. You can do it with anything: car keys, a pen . . ."

"Guess I'll start carrying a quarter." Tucker grins at me and leans over the ropes. "You're Peyton, right?" Owen glares at him, and Tucker clears his throat awkwardly. "I'm Tucker. I'm a freshman at Black Water."

"It's nice to officially meet you." He obviously remembers me from the parking lot. "You look pretty good up there." I realize Owen might think I'm talking to him, and I blurt out, "Tucker."

"Thanks. Owen is teaching me some self-defense." He ducks between the ropes and jumps down from the ring. "But I've gotta go. My mom is picking me up in a few minutes. Thanks, Owen." Tucker grabs a skateboard that's leaning against the wall.

"You got a new board." It's nice to see Tucker riding again.

"Yeah." He pulls on a hoodie. "*Someone* left it on my front porch yesterday. I'll see you guys later."

"You did great," Owen calls after him.

After Tucker leaves, I say, "It's really cool that you're teaching him to defend himself."

Owen's eyes flicker to me. "I can teach you, too, if you want."

"I'm good. I already know how to take care of myself."

"Do you?" Owen shakes his head and holds up one of the padded red ropes. "Prove it."

"This makes it kind of hard." I tap on the top of my brace, annoyed that Owen would challenge me when he knows I can't accept.

"You don't have to go full force. I'll settle for a demonstration." He's still holding up the rope, and he makes a ridiculous sweeping gesture with his arm. "Your stage awaits."

Owen's smug expression seals the deal.

"Fine." When I walk over to the ring, Owen offers me a hand. I take it, and the moment his skin makes contact with mine, a rush of warmth starts at my fingertips and travels all the way to my toes. His hand slides around my back, and he supports my weight as I duck between the ropes. I lead with my good leg, and Owen's grip on my waist tightens as I ease my other leg through.

"Thanks." With both of my feet planted safely on the ground, Owen doesn't need to hold on to me anymore, but his hand lingers a moment longer.

I step back and toss my ponytail over my shoulder. "So now I do you?"

That did *not* come out right. Why do I keep saying the wrong things in front of him? It's like I'm cursed.

A slow smile spreads across Owen's lips. He leans against the ropes and crosses his arms, raising his shirt enough to show the sexy sliver of skin. If I didn't know better, I would swear he was doing it on purpose.

"You look cute when you're embarrassed."

"Cute?" I put one hand on my hip. "Puppies are cute."

He holds up his hands in surrender. "I take it back. You're not cute."

"What about my knee? You could hit it by accident."

"This is a demo, like when I was practicing with Tucker. I didn't hit him," he reminded me.

True. It was more like watching stunt people practicing for a fight scene.

"I'll come straight at you, no surprises." Owen stands in the center of the ring. "And you pretend I'm an attacker and show me how you'd get away."

"Okay. But be careful with my knee."

"Got it. Ready?"

I try not to think about how silly I'll look pretending to knee him in the groin. "Whatever."

Instead of running at me like people do in self-defense classes, Owen takes his time. He focuses on me, stone-faced, without taking his eyes off me for a second—like a predator tracking its prey.

The adorable and shameless flirt with the sexy abs is gone. It's strange, but I'm not scared of Owen. The look in his eye is nothing like the one I saw in Reed's eyes before he pushed me. Owen is pretending to be dangerous. Reed wasn't acting.

A few more steps and I'll be within his reach. I wish the circumstances were different—that I was different. And I could let him catch me.

Because I'd love to be caught.

The corner of my mouth tips up.

"This is serious, Peyton." Without warning, Owen comes at me.

I raise my good knee, mimicking the way I'd knee a real attacker. But I don't even get close.

Owen reaches over my shoulder and around the back of my neck, and puts his hand over my ear—almost like he's cupping it. The next thing I know, my body is turning away from him and my balance feels off. Before I have time to panic, Owen's arm slides up my back, like we're on a dance floor and he's dipping me.

He lowers me down to the mat gently, with his hand cradling my head. The sensation of his fingertips on my scalp sends a current tingling along my spine. Owen flips one of his legs over my body so that he's straddling me, without actually sitting on me. He stays on his knees, supporting his weight. One of his hands is still behind my head, and his other hand is planted on the mat next to my cheek. He leans over me, his face hovering above mine. His gaze drops to my mouth, and I suck in the tiniest breath possible. His lips part, and I imagine reaching out and touching his full bottom lip—running my finger down the indentation in the center.

Suddenly, he sits up on his knees, my body still pinned between his legs. His hands move to my wrists, holding them against the mat. He looks down at me with a cocky smile. "Still think you know how to defend yourself? A real attacker wouldn't break your fall."

For a moment, I forget about the reason I'm pinned against the mat. He must feel my pulse pounding against my wrists.

Why Owen? Why now—at the worst possible time?

"Did I hurt you?" Concern flickers in Owen's eyes.

"No. But I don't understand what happened. I started to turn and it felt weird."

"Like you were off balance?" he asks.

"Yeah."

"If you put your hand over someone's ear and pull them in the opposite direction from behind, it throws your inner ear out of whack. Your inner ear is what controls your equilibrium."

"Maybe I don't know as much about self-defense as I thought."

Owen releases my wrists and tucks the loose strands of hair that escaped from my ponytail behind my ear. "I'll teach you the basics if you want. It won't earn you a black belt, but you'll know how to protect yourself if someone tries to hurt you."

I look away when he says the last part. "You don't have to."

Owen helps me up, and I lean against the ropes, trying to make sense of everything I'm feeling. His arm skims my waist as he reaches for the rope behind me. He brings his other hand up to my cheek. It hovers there for a moment—frozen in place.

The same way I feel right now.

Finally, he tucks another strand of hair behind my ear and leans closer. "Let me teach you, Peyton. I don't want anyone to hurt you."

Too late.

I almost let the words slip out.

"You got quiet on me. Does that mean you're thinking about it?" Owen asks.

What were we talking about?

Self-defense.

Me and Owen rolling around on the floor together . . . his face inches from mine on a regular basis. Me wanting to kiss him.

"Peyton?" Owen watches me with an intensity that makes it hard to concentrate.

"Yeah. Sure." Why am I agreeing to this? "If we have time after PT and everything."

When he hears the last word, he smiles. He's still sweaty from training. Unlike most guys, he doesn't smell like a dirty pair of gym socks. It's crazy and I'd never admit it to anyone, but I think he smells like the ocean—clean and salty. And it's not helping with the attraction issue.

Owen holds one of the ropes I'm leaning against. If I move the slightest bit, the side of my arm would graze his hand. I inhale and get another hit of his intoxicating scent.

"I don't want a boyfriend," I blurt out.

It's a defense mechanism. Fight or flight. Except words fly out of my mouth and my feet stay planted on the floor.

Owen leans closer. "Who said I want to be your boyfriend?" His breath tickles my neck.

"You're right. I should've said that I'm not looking for a hookup." I step to the side and move out of reach.

"You don't seem like the kind of girl who randomly hooks up with guys." He's leaning against the ropes where I was standing a moment ago.

"What's that supposed to mean?"

Owen walks over to where I'm standing. "You're stubborn and you don't take any shit. And don't look at me that way. It's a compliment."

"Maybe, if you're a drill sergeant."

"You're the kind of girl a guy wants to keep around for a lot longer than one night."

I tilt my head to the side. "How many nights, exactly? Are we talking two or three, or a whole week? I want to keep my expectations realistic."

Owen looks down at me. "You're taking this all wrong. I wasn't saying I wouldn't *want* to be your boyfriend. I was just giving you a hard time. You made it clear you weren't available the first night we met. I believed you."

Part of me regrets it—the same part that told me how lucky I was the first night Reed kissed me. The part I can't trust anymore.

He takes a deep breath. "But we can still be friends, right?"

Unbelievable. I'm getting an updated version of the "let's be friends" speech from a guy I'm not even dating.

"Or do you have too many friends already?" he teases.

Getting closer to a guy I'm attracted to and I can't date is a bad idea—like playing with matches over a puddle of lighter fluid.

Owen holds his fists in front of him, like a boxer meeting his opponent in the center of the ring before a fight. "Friends?"

I don't believe that everything happens for a reason. Some things just happen, and you have to live with the fallout.

Miracles have explanations.

Love at first sight isn't an inexplicable phenomenon. It's science—biology and pheromones.

Owen is still holding out his hands. "Have you ever watched a boxing match?"

"Sure. Why?"

"Boxers touch gloves at the beginning of a fight as a show of respect."

"Are we going to fight?" I hold back a smile.

"Are you ever gonna go easy on me?"

"Probably not."

Owen grins. "I can live with that." He holds out his hands, still balled into fists between us. "Friends?"

I search his dark eyes for an indication that I'm not crazy to trust him. There's no way to be sure. I think about coincidences and excuses, giving up and fallout.

I ball it all up in my fists and touch mine against Owen's. "Friends."

CHAPTER 22
Things We Can't Forget

"ALL RIGHT, EVERYONE," Miss Ives says as she stands in front of the class the next day. "We're going to take a look at the next novel we'll be reading."

She walks around passing out books.

Owen is sitting across from me, and she hands him two copies of the book.

Please let it be a book I've already read.

Owen gives me a paperback, and the moment I see the cover my mood instantly changes.

The cover depicts a row of silhouettes, each carrying a large pack.

My gut wrenches as I read the title, hoping I'm wrong about the subject matter—and, at the same time, knowing I'm not.

The Things They Carried.

They. The soldiers on the cover.

With a trembling hand, I turn it over and skim the description on the back.

Groundbreaking.

War.

Memory.

Choppers.

Vietnam.

Bile rises in the back of my throat, and a firestorm of images from my nightmares rains down on me.

Dad sinking in the water—his heavy pack dragging him down. Water swallowing him as he thrashes. His hand raised, reaching for someone to pull him out, until he loses the battle and the water closes over him, as if he were never there at all.

Dad, hanging from a wire below a helicopter, focused and calm. The sound of automatic weapons firing, round after round. The helicopter jerking to the side as it is engulfed by billows of black smoke. The wire swinging, with Dad clinging to it. He's reaching again, but there's nobody left to help him.

I've had nightmares about those scenarios and all the other ways Dad could've died during a Recon mission. The nightmares started the day I found out my father was dead and I've been having them ever since.

But one nightmare haunts me more than the others, because it's the closest to what really happened that day, at least according to Mom. She knows the whole story—all the details I'm too terrified to hear. The part she told me is awful enough.

Dad and two of his Recon "brothers," on his fire team, moving silently through a crude stone tunnel, underneath a hotel in Fallujah. Darkness and the sound of their breathing, each time they inhale and exhale. In and out. In and out. The sound of the explosion inside the tunnel. He looks up when he hears an avalanche of rock sliding and cracking, just in time to catch a glimpse of the tunnel coiling before it collapses on them.

"Peyton?" Owen's voice shatters the images.

I focus on his face—worried brown eyes searching mine—his forehead furrowed and lips parted. I drop the book like it's radioactive.

Owen watches me for a moment without saying a word. In the background, Miss Ives drones on about the Pulitzer Prize and the canon of American literature.

"Peyton?" he tries again.

Say something.

But I can't find the right words. Or any words.

"Do you feel sick?" Owen puts his hand on my wrist, and the weight of it combined with the roughness of his fingertips calms me.

"I'm fine," I mumble. "I got light-headed."

His hand is still on my wrist, and I let the soft pressure of his fingers moving back and forth over my pulse point drag me out of what's left of the tunnel.

"You should go to the health room. I'll take you." Owen's hand slips from my wrist and moves to the back of his chair as he turns toward the front of the room. He's trying to get Miss Ives' attention.

"Please don't," I whisper.

He leans over the desk, keeping his voice low. "You look like you're about to pass out."

"I'm okay. I swear." I'm not and he knows it.

Miss Ives scrawls a name on the board. "The author, Tim O'Brien, was the only member of his unit to survive the Vietnam War."

Like Hawk.

"In his novel, he tells stories and anecdotes about the soldiers who died—the men he never forgot."

192

Like Dad, Rudy, Ghost, and Big John—the recon operators who died in the tunnel.

"O'Brien tells us about the things the soldiers carried with them—the physical mementos and reminders of home, like photographs and letters." Miss Ives continues talking, but I can't make sense of the words.

What did Dad carry with him?

Owen's eyes dart to the worn paperback. "It's because of the book, isn't it?" he whispers, leaning closer. "That's why you're so pale. Is it your dad?"

"I don't want to talk about it." I let my dark waves fall over my shoulder to hide my face.

"But he died in combat?"

"On a mission." I touch the spot on my shirt where Dad's dog tags rest close to my heart, under the fabric.

"You should tell Miss Ives. She'll assign you another book."

"I'm not telling her." I can't.

Owen rakes his hands through his hair. He hasn't taken his eyes off me. He's either worried or freaked out. "Are you sure?"

"Positive."

The details I just shared with Owen are more than I tell most people.

The rest of the period passes in a blur of discussion about the author, the significance of the novel, and other things I tune out. When the bell rings, Owen follows me out of the classroom and we walk down the hall together. He doesn't ask questions or make small talk to fill the silence. He just stays beside me, angling his body toward the hallway traffic so no one bumps into me.

"I'll catch up with you," Owen says as we pass the boys' bathroom.

I keep walking. "I'll be at my locker." *Burying this novel under whatever I can find.*

I'm not paying attention when I get there.

April and Madison are a few lockers away, laughing and whispering. They're probably talking about me. But then again, they seem to talk about everyone so who knows?

I turn the combination on the lock, watching them.

April gives me an icy stare, her long auburn hair pulled up in a tight ponytail with the front hair-sprayed halfway to heaven. It's getting colder outside, and they've swapped their jean skirts for skintight jeans. They look like they escaped from a Barbie Dreamhouse.

I pop the lock and open my locker.

The door flies open, and suddenly everything is falling out. I cover my head. Objects just keep falling and falling. I don't even have that much stuff in my locker. I try to back up and I stumble.

I hit the floor and my butt breaks my fall.

Suddenly, I realize what's tumbling out of my locker, and the familiar shapes and the sound they make when they bounce on the floor.

Soccer balls.

At least a dozen of them, rolling and bouncing across the scuffed floor of the hallway. Brand-new soccer balls. Someone spent a lot of money to embarrass me.

I sit up, determined to hold on to what little self-respect I have left. April and Madison, along with some of their friends, dissolve into hysterical laughter. They don't even try to hide it.

Bitches.

Getting up from the floor without putting too much weight on my knee is tricky. I'm still trying to get back on my feet when I feel a strong arm encircle my waist.

"Are you all right?" Owen whispers in my ear. He's behind me. He pulls me up, then circles around so he's standing in front of me.

"I'm fine."

But I'm not. I'm furious and humiliated.

It's such a juvenile prank, and instead of just laughing it off, I ended up falling on my ass. I want to pick up every single ball and chuck them at April's head.

I catch a glimpse of Christian charging down the hall, and he looks pissed off. He's heading straight for us.

"What the hell is going on?" he demands.

"April put a bunch of soccer balls in Peyton's locker," Owen says.

Christian picks up a soccer ball and walks over to April. "If you think screwing with Peyton is gonna get me to come back, you're wrong."

She knocks the ball out of his hand. "No one wants you back, and I'm not the one who did this."

Madison moves closer to April and crosses her arms. "She was with me in class the entire time. We have more important things to do than make a fool of your cousin."

Christian slaps his forehead. "Oh, well, if *you* say April was with you, that changes everything. Because you'd never lie for her."

I slip past Owen and push Christian out of the way so that I'm nose-to-nose with April. "Your little prank was funny. I would've done something like that in sixth or seventh grade."

April narrows her eyes. "Then you should tell the person who did it, because it wasn't me."

I square my shoulders. "I hope not, because I won't be in this brace forever. And I'm pretty sure I could still kick your ass with it on."

"Are you threatening me?" April sounds shocked. If what I have witnessed over the past week is any indication, I'm probably the first girl who has ever stood up to her.

"It's not a threat. It's a promise." I snatch the soccer ball out of Christian's hand and tap on the side of it. "These are a lot harder than they look. I've seen a couple of girls get their noses broken when they've taken a ball to the face."

April shrinks back. "If you throw that at me, you'll get expelled."

"Don't worry. I'd never come after you *on campus*." I smile at her, and it's a real smile. Then I chuck the ball at the locker behind her. It smacks against the metal, inches from April's ear, and she yelps.

People in the hallway laugh.

"Are you crazy?" she screams at me. "You could've hit me with that thing!"

"Exactly." I turn and walk away, knowing Christian is still standing between the two of us. I wouldn't put it past April to pick up a ball and chuck it at me when I'm not looking. Everything about her says *sore loser*.

The drama has attracted a small crowd, and a few people give me a thumbs-up while others laugh at April. It doesn't make the situation any less embarrassing, and the black-and-white balls rolling around the hallway are a cruel reminder of how long it's been since I've played.

I slam my locker shut as I pass it, kicking aside some soccer balls.

"I don't know why you're blaming me," I hear April say. "I'm glad I'm not with Christian anymore. I traded up." April looks over Christian's shoulder and waves to someone behind him.

A good-looking guy with dark hair rushes to April's side and puts his arm around her. "What's going on?" He's wearing a Warriors basketball hoodie, and he's at least a foot taller than everyone else nearby.

"Christian's bothering her again," Madison tells him.

The basketball player tightens his hold on April protectively and turns to Christian. "What's the deal? Are you bothering my girl?"

"Your girl?" Christian laughs.

"Yeah," the basketball player says. "You got a problem with that?"

"Seems like you're the one with the problem now," Christian says. "She's all yours."

Dylan takes a step toward Christian and pushes April behind him. "If you wanna be an asshole, we can go outside and take care of this."

"You really want to go there?" Christian steps forward. The two of them are only inches apart. "'Cause basketball season is coming up, and your team won't do very well if you can't play. I think we both know you can't take me."

Owen shoves his way between Christian and Cameron. "Nobody's going outside. Neither of you can afford to be benched."

"I don't have to worry about that," Dylan says. "Basketball season hasn't started."

Owen stares him down. "I said, nobody's going outside. Unless they're going with me."

Dylan backs off. "I don't have a problem with you, man. Why are you getting in the middle of this?"

"You don't need to worry about what I'm doing, or why I'm doing it," Owen warns.

"You're such a jerk, Owen." April tries to step out from behind Dylan. "For, like, two years, you haven't given a shit about anything, and now suddenly you're playing hall monitor? For the last time, I didn't put anything in her locker. And if I did, I'd take credit for it."

What does she mean about Owen not caring?

April turns on her heel and grabs Dylan's arm. "Come on, let's get out of here. This conversation is boring."

When she's out of earshot, I turn to Christian. "I appreciate you looking out for me, but I don't need your help with April. She might need a guy to fight her battles, but I'm perfectly capable of handling my own problems."

Owen rubs the back of his neck and stares at the floor. Christian frowns, looking confused. I turn my back on them and walk to class.

"Peyton, wait," Owen calls after me.

"I'm going to class."

As if on cue, the bell rings.

April is looking for attention. Unfortunately for me, Christian and Owen just gave it to her.

CHAPTER 23

Killer Smiles and Almost Kisses

CHEMISTRY PASSES IN a blur of periodic table elements and unbalanced equations. I can't stop thinking about the novel stuffed in my backpack. Reading it isn't an option. I'll have to find a summary online and hope Miss Ives doesn't come up with lots of in-class activities that leave me feeling like a gutted fish.

I catch myself picturing Owen's lopsided smile instead of copying the homework written on the board and I kill the thought.

He's off-limits.

One hundred percent not an option.

But if things were different and Owen wasn't a fighter . . . who knows?

The bell rings.

Books slam shut and chair legs scrape across the floor. I ease out of the chair quickly and try to keep up with everyone else, but I'm still the last person out of the classroom.

The moment I step into the hallway, I stop short.

Owen is standing next to the wall, thumbs tucked in the pockets of his jeans. He turns as if he senses me watching him.

"Ready?" Owen asks, pushing away from the wall.

Whatever he's referring to, I'm not ready for it. "For what?"

He falls in step beside me. "Lunch. I hear you haven't had the pleasure of eating in our one-star cafeteria yet."

How would he know that? Did the Twins tell him? Or did he ask?

"I'm not a fan of school cafeterias. We're allowed to eat off campus at my school."

"Isn't this your school now?"

"Only until March. Then I'm going home." I steal a glance at him. "I have to be ready to play by then, remember?"

"Right." Owen pushes his hands deeper into his pockets. "But you're here now, and you have to eat."

"And you're offering me a personal escort?" I brush my hair over my shoulder.

I'm totally flirting.

Could I be more obvious?

"It's a service I provide to all my English partners with killer smiles and knee braces. Don't let it go to your head." Owen cocks his head to the side, watching me.

I recognize the look. He's sizing me up. I'm used to seeing the expression on the faces of my opponents on the soccer field.

He thinks I have a killer smile. Not cute or sweet. Killer.

Suddenly it feels like I'm standing on the deck of a boat. Is my knee giving out? But it's not my bad knee.

Owen's smile, the thump of my heartbeat, the fluttering sensation in my stomach—my legs have transformed into ramen noodles because of this guy.

I reach for the wall beside me and Owen catches my arm. His rough fingers slide under my forearm and leave behind a tingling sensation. He cups my elbow, my arm resting on top of his, and I grab his biceps for balance.

"Sorry . . ." I stammer. "My knee gave out." It's the first time I've used my knee as an excuse without resenting it.

Owen's hand drops to my waist.

Not good.

Not the kind of good I'm looking for, anyway.

"Do you need help walking?" he asks.

Yes. I shake my head. "No."

The pressure of his hand on my waist makes me wonder how it would feel on my skin.

Owen scans my face. "Your cheeks are bright red, and you look like you're about two seconds from passing out. Are you in pain?"

"I just need some water." I'm still holding his arm and it makes me self-conscious.

Owen slides his arm behind me and moves next to me, as if he wants me to throw my arm over his shoulders for support. I've embarrassed myself enough already.

"I'm okay now," I say, trying to figure out what to do with my arm, which is hovering above his shoulders.

His arm lingers a moment longer, and his fingers trail over the material of my T-shirt before he releases me. "If you pass out, I'm not responsible."

I walk toward the cafeteria, the ghost of Owen's touch lingering. "I'll take the blame. I don't want to jeopardize the knight-in-shining-armor routine you've probably got going with the girls."

He studies the black marks on the floor. "No chance of that."

No chance I could put it in jeopardy, or no chance the girls think of him that way? The way he's inspecting the floor has me leaning toward option number two. I hate that something I said made his smile disappear.

"Anything I should know before we go in?" I ask when we reach the door.

He relaxes. "Don't eat the sloppy joes or the tuna melt. Or anything that looks like it's made with cream of chicken soup."

The clatter of plastic trays hitting tabletops and conversations overlapping on the other side of the door paralyze me. When was the last time I set foot in an unfamiliar school cafeteria? Freshman year?

Memories of the bitchy girls whispering about their so-called friends make me rethink the whole thing. I wasn't on the receiving end of any major drama back then, but that doesn't mean April and Madison and their army of clones won't target me here.

Eating is overrated.

I step to the side, away from the door. "I'm not all that hungry."

Owen lets the door swing closed. "Don't tell me you're one of those girls who only eats three pieces of lettuce and a carrot for lunch?" He takes a step toward me and lowers his head so we're eye-to-eye. "Because I know you wouldn't let anybody intimidate you."

"Maybe I'm not as brave as you think." I raise my chin. Owen has no way of knowing how much truth there is in what I'm saying. But it feels like he does, and it's unnerving.

He leans his shoulder against the wall, watching me. "Says the girl who threw a water bottle at me. And something tells me you were holding back."

I open my mouth, but I can't come up with a smart-ass comment.

The door behind Owen swings open, and he lunges toward me to avoid getting hit.

I back into the wall as Owen's broad chest flies at me. I bring my hands up in front of me and brace myself. His chest hits my palms and I hold my breath, waiting for his body to slam against mine. But it doesn't happen.

Warm air tickles my ear and I open my eyes.

Owen's face is inches from mine, his chest pressed against my hands, his ragged breathing echoing in my ear. His arms are extended on either side of my head, his palms splayed on the wall.

He caught himself.

"I'm sorry, man. I didn't know you were behind the door." It's a guy's voice, somewhere behind Owen. "You good?"

Owen lifts his head and pushes away from the wall to look at me. With every breath, his chest presses against my palms. "Are you?"

I'm not sure what he's asking, and with his body this close to mine, I don't care. "Am I what?"

"Good?"

I nod and Owen's arms relax. He lets out a long breath and leans his forehead against the wall above me. The rough stubble along his jaw brushes my cheek, and I shiver.

"You need anything?" the guy behind Owen asks.

Owen pulls back, his breath evening out.

I look up at him from beneath lowered lashes, and I'm immediately caught in the drag of his dark eyes. His gaze drops to my lips for a split second.

"We're good." Owen says the words softly, so I'm the only one who hears them.

CHAPTER 24

Powdered Cheese and Power Trips

THE TEMPERATURE IN the cafeteria drops from cool to subzero when Owen and I walk in together—at least, at the tables where April is holding court with her friends and some football players. She's wedged between Dylan and Madison, laughing ridiculously loud. The Twins are at an April-free table nearby, with their backs to us, so they haven't noticed me yet.

I wish I could say the same for Titan. He's sitting directly across the aisle from me, holding a burger. He's about to take a bite when he sees us and drops it onto his tray.

The burger-drop sets off Madison's drama-queen radar, and her eyes dart around the room until she spots Owen and me. She immediately turns to April and whispers in her ear.

I get in line behind the other students waiting to buy lunch. "This is like a bad scene from a movie."

Owen walks around and stands on the other side of me, blocking Titan's view. He picks up a red plastic tray for himself and takes another one for me.

"Thanks. But I'm just going to grab a snack." If the stench of boiled hot dogs and powdered cheese is any indication of what the Black Water High School cafeteria has to offer, I'll stick with junk food.

I sense Titan watching us and it annoys me. "What's Titan's problem? I talked to him for two minutes at his party."

Owen loads his tray with ham sandwiches wrapped in plastic. "This is a small town. New girls don't show up that often. He probably thought he had a shot with you."

I pick up a bag of mini Oreos. "Didn't the Twins give him the our-cousin-doesn't-date speech?"

Owen adds a stack of giant cookies and a slice of cake to his tray. "They probably did, but Titan does whatever he wants."

We pay the cashier, and suddenly it feels like everyone is staring at me—not with April's uber-bitch level of intensity, but it's still awkward. Tucker walks into the cafeteria carrying his new skateboard, shifting some of the attention away from me.

He drops the board, hops on, and coasts over to us. "How's your day going?"

I remember the way Owen's body felt pressed up against me before we came in. "Some parts have been better than others."

We pass April's table and Grace looks over from the last seat. I make eye contact and give her a quick smile, hoping April and Madison won't notice.

Cam sees me, picks up his tray, and heads in my direction. Christian stacks his sandwiches under his chin and follows him.

"Come on, Grace." Christian waves her over and waits for her to catch up.

Owen chooses the only empty table in sight. I wish it was further away from April. He sits across from me, with his back to them, and Tucker takes the seat beside him, creating a wall between April and me.

Cam sets his tray down next to mine and nods at Tucker. "What's up? I'm Cameron."

"Tucker. Nice to meet you."

Cam looks over at me. "I didn't know you and Owen had third period together."

"We don't," Owen says, digging into a slice of cake.

"You don't what?" Christian asks, catching the tail end of the conversation.

"Have third period together," Owen says between bites. "Your brother isn't happy that Peyton and I walked in together."

"What do you mean by *together*?" Christian loses his chin hold on the stack of sandwiches, and they tumble onto the table. A cellophane-wrapped square lands in Cam's mashed potatoes.

Grace pushes the sandwiches aside to make room for her tray. "Stop acting like such a baby, Christian. Do you think they started dating in the last three hours?"

Christian straddles the chair next to hers. "Stranger things have happened."

"Hi. I'm Grace." She waves at Tucker. "I think your locker is near mine."

Tucker grins. "Yeah. It is."

"This is Christian," Grace continues the introductions.

Owen looks over at me, and my stomach does a little flip. It didn't seem to get the message that we're just friends.

I'm attracted to him.

Any girl with a heartbeat would have trouble ignoring the pull of his sexy smile and beautiful brown eyes. I'm also attracted to half the guys on the Italian men's soccer team, and I won't be dating any of them, either.

It's a physical reaction, like an allergy.

I'll get over it.

I avoid meeting Owen's gaze, but it's not easy when he's across from me.

After what feels like forever, he balls up his napkin and tosses it on his tray. "You guys have nothing to worry about. Peyton made it clear that she's not interested in dating anybody. And even if she was I'm not her type."

Owen's comment stings, and I try to hide my disappointment. To be fair, I did tell him that I don't like fighters.

Laughter erupts at April's table and Grace shifts in her seat.

"Will April and Madison give you a hard time for sitting over here?" I ask.

"April has nothing to be mad about, and she has a new boyfriend to entertain her." Christian looks over at his ex. She stops laughing and snuggles up to Dylan.

"April isn't the only person who looks pissed," Cam says, tipping his chin in Titan's direction.

Titan is staring Owen down like he's trying to burn a hole through him.

"Could he act any creepier?" Grace scrunches up her nose. "What's his problem?"

"I am." Owen crosses his arms and makes eye contact with Titan.

The linebacker plants his feet on the floor and pushes his chair away from the table. The sound of metal scraping halts conversations around him as students at neighboring tables turn their attention to Titan.

Titan's expression makes me uncomfortable. "This makes no sense. I don't even know him."

"It's not about you," Cam says. "I mean, it is and it isn't."

Grace drops a half-eaten granola bar on her tray. "Thanks for clearing that up."

Christian watches Owen and Titan, like a ref prepared to break up a fight. "I thought you settled that shit last year."

Owen's jaw forms a hard line. "I guess Titan wants to un-settle it."

I'm not letting Titan use me as an excuse to dredge up whatever happened between Owen and him.

"There's too much testosterone at this table for me." I stand up and Owen jumps to his feet. More chair legs scrape against the floor, then Titan is on his feet—followed by the Twins.

"Could this get any more embarrassing?" Grace shields her face and looks in the opposite direction, avoiding April.

"So that's how it's gonna be?" Titan asks the Twins. "You're backing him up?"

Owen rolls his shoulders and subtly shifts his weight onto the balls of his feet, adopting a defensive stance. It's the opposite of what Reed would do in this situation—strike first, but go easy. Give the other guy a false sense of security and then attack.

The aisle that separates Owen and Titan seems dangerously narrow.

"Nobody is backing up anyone," Cam says, walking toward Titan. "We're trying to make sure you don't get benched on Friday night."

"That's not how it looks from here," Titan fires back.

Owen widens his stance. "Listen to Cameron. We both know I don't need anyone to back me up in a fight, especially not against you."

"Shit." Cam lunges for Titan, but he isn't fast enough and Titan slips past him.

In a blur of movements, Titan and Owen are within arm's reach of each other—Titan's hands clenched into fists and eyes full of rage, and Owen's expression calm and calculating.

Cam wedges himself between them, and Christian uses his chair as a step and jumps over the table to help.

"You should sit," Grace says. "If they start throwing each other around, it will feel like an earthquake."

I take her advice.

"Get outta my way, Cameron, or I'll lay you out," Titan warns.

Christian comes up beside Cam, and the Twins stand next to each other.

"Take it easy, Big Man, or all three of our asses will be watching the game from the sidelines." Christian's voice drops. "But if you threaten my brother again, you'll be watching it from a hospital bed."

"I've got this, Christian." Owen hasn't taken his eyes off Titan.

"You think so?" Titan points at Owen over Christian's shoulder. "That kung fu bullshit won't help you when I'm pounding your head into the ground."

"I'm right here." Owen opens his arms.

"Carters! Wallhauser!" A voice thunders through the cafeteria.

A short man about my uncle's age with blotchy skin and patchy muttonchops along his jaw marches toward us. Dressed in track pants, a white polo, and a Warriors zippered jacket, he has *football coach* written all over him.

He points at the Twins. "Step back unless you two want to play ball for a community college next year!"

The other football players at tables nearby sit up straighter. When the Twins and Titan don't move, the coach points at them and explodes. "Did I stutter? Move your tails or clean out your gym lockers."

The Twins snap to attention and back up.

"Sorry, Coach," Christian mumbles.

Dylan says something to his friends and laughs.

"You think this is funny, Mr. Rollins?" Coach demands, red-faced and angry. "Does Coach Graff know he's got a comedian on the basketball team? Should I get him in here so he can see how goddamn hilarious you are?"

Coach turns to April's table and points at one of the cheerleaders. "Natalie. Go to the gym and tell Coach Graff that I've got something he oughta see."

"Why did he have to pick her?" Tucker says under his breath.

Natalie reluctantly gets up from the table, her cheeks growing pinker by the second.

Dylan's face pales. "I don't think I'm funny, sir. Not even a little. I'm the opposite of funny." His eyes dart to Natalie, who is almost at the cafeteria door. "Please don't bring Coach Graff down here, sir."

Coach makes Dylan sweat it out for a second then calls out, "Natalie? Come on back and sit down."

Natalie looks relieved and rushes back to her seat.

"Take a walk, Rollins. Before I change my mind." Coach dismisses Dylan with a wave and eyes Titan and the Twins.

"Sorry, Coach," Cam mumbles.

Coach marches up to Cameron. "Sorry is for sissies and second-rate players. You play football for the Warriors. State champions four years running, with the highest recruitment rate to Division One colleges in Tennessee." He turns to Christian. "You want to show off for the girls? You can do push-ups on the field this afternoon for the first half of practice. Invite all the girls to watch."

"Yes, sir." Christian stares at the floor.

Tucker scrambles past me, carrying his skateboard, and runs up to the football coach. "I saw the whole thing, sir. Titan started it."

Coach examines Tucker and his fauxhawk. "Good lord, son. What happened to your head? Did some older boys get ahold of you?"

"No, sir." Tucker runs his hand over the short strip of hair on his scalp. "It's my haircut."

"You did that to yourself on purpose?" Coach shakes his head. "Where's your visitor's pass?"

"Um . . . I'm not a visitor. I go to school here, sir. I'm a freshman."

"Why haven't I seen you before?"

Does he think Tucker broke into the Black Water cafeteria to sample the epic mac and cheese?

"He doesn't take gym." Owen pushes his way past the Twins and stands next to Tucker.

The information throws Coach for a loop, and he studies Tucker like he's checking to see if the kid has two heads. "Why the hell not?"

"My family moved to Black Water two years ago," Tucker explains. "The requirements were different at my old middle school. So I never took—"

"I'm glad we cleared that up," Coach says, cutting Tucker off and turning to Owen. "I hope you weren't involved in this mess, Mr. Law. I'd hate to tell Cutter that you're using my high school athletes as sparring partners."

Owen rubs the back of his neck. "I wasn't—"

Coach puts his hand on Owen's shoulder and steers him toward our table. "I know it's tough without your dad around. My old man left when I was about your age."

Owen stiffens.

"You should think about wrestling again. You were damn good, and there's nothing like being a member of a team."

Owen was a wrestler?

"I'll think about it, sir." Owen maintains a respectful tone, but his rigid posture makes it clear that he doesn't appreciate the advice. He returns to the table, but instead of sitting down again, he grabs his tray. "I'll catch y'all later."

Tucker follows him.

Grace and my cousins didn't react when Coach mentioned the situation with Owen's dad. Does everyone know? Owen looked so uncomfortable.

It's hard to imagine what it would feel like if my dad had walked out on us. Whenever he left on a mission, all he wanted to do was get back to Mom and me. I knew there was a possibility he might not come home, but I never thought it would happen. Watching someone leave willingly is a different kind of loss.

The Twins drag themselves back to the table.

"Forty-five minutes of push-ups?" Christian complains. "I'm going to beat Titan's ass."

"It could be worse. Coach could've benched us," Cam says.

"He wouldn't have much of a defense without the three of us." Christian smashes one of his sandwiches inside the plastic wrap.

"I'm sorry," I say. "I feel like this is my fault. I don't know why Titan is acting like this. Owen and I are just friends."

Sort of.

"Titan will never buy that," Cam says.

"Why not?" I ask. "It's true."

Christian smashes another sandwich like a bored little kid. "Everyone knows guys can't be friends with girls. Not really."

Grace gives him an incredulous look. "We're friends."

"That's different," Christian says without missing a beat.

"How do you figure?" Cam asks.

Pain flickers in Grace's eyes for a second, then it's gone. "Christian doesn't think of me as a girl, that's why." She picks up her bag and gets up from the table. "I'm his sidekick, like one of the guys."

"Come on, Grace. That's not what I said." Christian reaches for her arm, but she yanks it away.

"You don't have to say the words for it to be true."

"Trouble in paradise?" April asks from her table.

"Do everyone around here a favor, April," Cam snaps, "and shut up."

April glances at her friends, embarrassed. "Screw you, Cameron."

Cam watches Grace walk out of the cafeteria.

"Grace!" Christian calls after her.

"I should find Grace." Christian crushes his trash and presses it into a ball.

"Why don't you leave her alone and stop jerking her around?" Cam asks.

"What are you talking about?" Christian sounds confused.

Cam leans across the table and looks his brother in the eye. "You *know* what I'm talking about. She doesn't deserve it."

"If I want your opinion, I'll ask for it," Christian says before he gets up and walks away.

"He's just going to make it worse," Cam says.

The sadness in his voice and the way he jumped all over his brother . . . something doesn't add up. Or maybe it does.

"Does Grace know how you feel about her?" I ask.

"We're just friends." Cam looks away, shredding a paper napkin in front of him.

I lean closer and lower my voice. "Come on, Cam."

He checks the area around us. When he seems satisfied that no one is eavesdropping, he props his elbows on the table. "You can't tell Christian anything." He lowers his head and rests it against his palm.

"I won't." I'm becoming an expert at keeping secrets. "But you should tell him before one of them figures it out."

Cam laughs. "No chance of that happening. Christian can't even figure out how he feels about Grace. In case you haven't noticed, most people act like Christian and I are the same person. Hell, some of our friends still can't tell us apart. Except Grace. And she only sees Christian. I'm background noise." He collects the trays everyone else left at the table. "Let's get outta here."

"What if you're wrong about Grace?" I ask as we leave the cafeteria. "Maybe if she knew how you felt—"

"Some things should be left alone."

"But if you don't take a chance, you'll never know."

Cam walks beside me, shoulders hunched. "At least I won't get my heart stomped."

It's a hard point to argue. I'm always surprised when I see people set themselves up to get hurt. They hold their hands over a fire, then they're shocked when they get burned.

"Looks like Owen cooled off," Cam says.

At the opposite end of the hallway, Owen leans against a bank of royal-blue lockers watching us.

"Should I be worried?" Cam asks.

"About what?"

"The fact that Owen Law is hanging out in the hall, waiting for my cousin."

"He's not waiting for me." I'm not admitting it to Cam, but Owen *does* look like he's waiting for someone. "He was probably at his locker when he saw us coming, so he waited. Isn't that what a good Southern boy would do?"

"Yep." Cam lowers his voice. "There's just one problem with your theory."

"What?"

"Owen's locker is on the other side of the building."

Without thinking, my eyes go straight to Owen. He's looking right at me and he stands straighter as we walk toward him.

Owen says something to Cam, but I'm not paying attention. I'm thinking about what Cam just said.

Owen's locker is on the other side of the building.

Suddenly, I'm the person holding out my hand. I see the fire, but I still want to hold my hand over the flames.

"I've gotta hit my locker before fifth period. Do you know how to get to your next class from here?" Cam asks.

I realize he's talking to me.

"I'll get her there if she doesn't," Owen says.

Cameron gives him a warning look.

"We're just walking," Owen says.

"Good to know." Cam takes off.

Owen smiles at me.

It's like there's a little girl inside me, holding a bunch of yellow balloons, and she releases them to take flight inside my chest.

CHAPTER 25

Caught Up

WHEN I FINISH PT that afternoon, I return from the locker room freshly showered to find Owen pacing in front of the ring with his cell phone to his ear.

"Come on, Mom. Pick up." Owen tugs at his hair like he's trying to yank it out. "It's bad enough that you're ignoring my texts, but now you're sending me straight to voice mail?" He stops pacing and leans against one of the ring's padded corner posts with his arm above his head and his forehead pressed against the padding.

"Don't do this, Mom. Please. Not tonight," Owen begs. He hangs up and hurls his phone at the floor. It hits the concrete and explodes. "Shit!" He grips the ropes and shakes them, shoulders slumped, and hangs his head.

I walk over, watching his shoulders rise and fall with each deep breath. In the dimly lit gym, his black track pants and hoodie make him look like a shadow.

"Owen?" I say his name softly and touch his shoulder. "What's wrong?"

He takes one hand off the ropes and lays it on top of mine, curling his fingers around the side of my hand. He slides his thumb under my wrist, sending a ripple of shock waves up my arm.

"My mom is playing her trump card. She doesn't want me fighting, and by the end of tonight, I won't have a shot at the regional championship."

"I need you to give me more than that. What did she do? I can't help you if you don't talk to me."

Owen's hand slides off mine and he turns to face me. The top of my head doesn't even reach his shoulder. "You would help me?"

"It depends on what we're talking about."

He tucks a loose strand of hair behind my ear, and his touch gives me goose bumps.

"There's nothing you can do, but knowing you'd help me means a lot." Owen scrubs his hands over his face. "My mom was supposed to be here twenty minutes ago so I could drop her at home and use the car. The semifinals are tonight outside of Nashville. If I'm a no-show, I'm disqualified and I can't fight in the finals."

"What about Cutter? Can you ride with her?"

He shakes his head. "She's meeting me there. UT has a big game on Friday night and they needed her at practice today. Even if I called her now, she wouldn't make it back in time to pick me up." He sounds defeated, and I understand. Getting disqualified without having a chance to compete isn't something I could stomach, either. "Maybe I could ask your cousins for a ride when they come to get you?"

"They're not picking me up today," I say calmly. "Practice doesn't end until seven, and Cam said it might run longer because we don't have school tomorrow. So I drove myself."

Owen's eyebrows shoot up. "Since when do you have a car?"

I take out the keys and dangle them from my finger. "My uncle let me borrow a Jeep he's working on."

"You've gotta give me a ride, Peyton. I'll do anything. I'll pay you or carry your books for the rest of the year. Whatever you want. I just need a ride."

"To a fight?" I take a step back.

Owen drops to his knees and steeples his hands. "Please."

I want to go to an MMA fight about as much as I want to walk into school naked. But how can I say no?

"I can't go to an MMA fight." The words slip out.

Owen stands, watching my every move. "What do you mean by *can't*?"

I pull the elastic off my wrist and work on gathering my hair into a ponytail. Anything to keep from making eye contact with Owen. "I meant *won't*."

"You don't have to go to the fight. You can drop me off," he says, switching gears. "If I can't catch a ride home with Cutter, I'll hitchhike back, and I'll do it with a smile. Just get me there."

"Fine. I'll take you. But I'm not going in."

"Seriously?" Owen throws his arms around my waist, picks me up, and spins around. "You have no idea how much I love you right now."

My heart slams against my ribs.

It's a figure of speech. People say it all the time.

I've said it. He doesn't mean anything by it, but I kind of wish he did.

Owen puts me down. He grabs his bag and lifts mine off my shoulder. "You're saving my ass, Peyton. I owe you."

"Come on." I lead him through the parking lot to the Jeep.

"Want me to drive?" he offers. "I know where I'm going. It'll be faster."

I hesitate.

"Worried I'll crash it?" Owen asks. "I'm a good driver and I have insurance."

I snort. "If you're such a great driver, why did you throw in the part about having insurance?"

Owen pats down his pockets. "Where's my—?"

"Your phone? You threw it on the floor."

"Right. Not my finest moment."

"It's okay. I threw my cleats out the car window once, after I lost a game."

He opens the car door for me and offers me his arm when I step onto the running board. I settle into the driver's seat and start the car while he runs around to jump in, but when I try to shift out of park, Owen covers my hand with his and stops me.

"Forget something?" He leans over and pulls the seat belt across my chest without touching anything he shouldn't. It's the sort of gesture you read about in novels, but nobody does it in real life.

Except Owen.

He straps the seat belt into place and secures his own. He doesn't say much during the forty minutes to the arena. He thanks me ten more times and fidgets with his hands—opening them, stretching his fingers wide, and then squeezing them closed.

"Are you nervous?" I ask. *Because I am, and I'm not the one fighting tonight.*

Owen looks over at me, and his dark eyes search mine. "Why?"

"Why what?" I've completely lost track of the conversation.

He flashes me a smile. "You asked me a question before you got distracted by whatever it was you were thinking about a second ago—which I know couldn't have been me, because you're *not* attracted to me and we're just friends."

I open my mouth, but I can't think of a single thing to say.

"But I'll catch you up anyway," he says. "You asked if I was nervous, and I asked why. Then you couldn't remember what you asked me." He winks at me.

"Are you always this cocky before a fight?"

"Have you always been this good at changing the subject?"

I lean my elbow on the armrest between us. "You changed it first. I guess you aren't comfortable admitting that you're nervous."

"Not as nervous as you are about watching it," Owen says.

"Nice try." I keep my eyes on the road so he can't read my expression. As much as I enjoy flirting with Owen, I'm not a fan of the fact that he can read me so well. "I don't like fights, or fighters. Didn't we cover this?"

"Have you ever been to an MMA fight?" He sounds so confident and sure of himself. The competitive side of me cringes.

"No." I hesitate before adding, "I've been to *more* than one." The moment the words leave my lips, I regret saying them. I'm only inviting more questions.

Owen's gaze darts between my face and the road. "When? Who did you go with?"

"My best friend's older brother is an MMA fighter. She dragged me along to watch his fights." Sort of true.

"And you weren't into it." He's not asking, which saves me from feeling like a total liar when I don't correct him.

The truth? I loved going to fights. The skills involved in MMA and the conditioning it requires impressed the hell out of me. Now the thought of watching a fight just reminds me of Reed.

Owen sighs. "So much for my brilliant plan."

"What plan?"

"The one where I talk you into coming to a fight and you see the error of your ways. Then you become an obsessive fan, beg me to bring you to all my competitions, and scream your lungs out when I win."

I laugh. "You're delusional."

"Okay. Forget the last part." He sounds hopeful.

"I'm guessing your mom doesn't come?"

Owen stiffens, then shakes it off. "Don't try to change the subject. I'm asking the questions. You used to like MMA, and now you hate it. What happened between then and now? Did you see someone get hurt in a fight?" He's working hard to connect the dots that I don't want connected. But he's on the wrong track, and every omission and misleading piece of information I give him sends him deeper into a rabbit hole.

"I'm not playing twenty questions. MMA isn't my thing. End of story."

"Come on. Give me something. Friends are supposed to tell each other stuff."

"Aren't you the guy who was giving me a hard time about the friends thing?" I ask.

"I'm not saying I *wouldn't* go out with you if the option was on the table, but it's not. I guess you'll just have to wonder what it would've been like since we're just friends."

"So what happened to make you hate MMA so much?" he asks.

I hate lying to Owen, but everyone has secrets. I'm entitled to mine.

Telling him won't accomplish anything. It won't make what happened with Reed any less painful or frustrating or unfair. It will just stir up those shitty feelings again.

It's not like every word I tell Owen is a lie.

This is *one* thing.

I told him how my dad died—something I usually keep to myself. He knows a lot more about me than I know about him.

"It's my turn to ask a question. You said friends tell each other things, and we're friends, right?" I'm using his logic.

"Unless you changed your mind." He smirks and I poke his shoulder.

"Stop. I'm serious."

"And you think I'm not?"

I roll my eyes. "Forget I asked."

Owen reaches over and tugs my sleeve. "Of course we're friends. Why?"

"Is everything okay with your mom? I wouldn't ask, but I saw her crying in the car the other morning, and then she didn't show up tonight."

"It's a long story, but the short version is that she thinks MMA is dangerous and she wants me to quit fighting. But she's never done anything as extreme as what she did tonight."

An LED sign up ahead reads: MMA REGIONAL CHAMPIONSHIP SEMIFINALS. I turn into a packed parking lot in front of an arena. It reminds me of the place where I saw my first concert.

Men and women carrying gym bags file through a side door while spectators line up at the main entrance. This is an amateur event, but the size of the arena and the number of competitors and trainers entering the building tells me it's still big time.

I park and Owen looks at me. "Thanks for the ride. I mean it. You saved my ass. I'll catch a ride back with Cutter, or I'll figure something out."

"What time does this end?" I don't want him hitchhiking.

"Around nine. Why? Did you change your mind about watching?" He looks hopeful.

"No. But I'll come back and pick you up. It's only two hours, and I've always wanted to check out Nashville."

"Are you serious?"

"Yes." I shove his arm in a flirtatious move that would make Lucia proud. "I'll meet you back here at nine."

Owen's eyes drift to the spot where I'm touching his arm. I move my hand, but he reaches up and presses his palm against mine, as if they're lined up on opposite sides of a window. He interlaces his fingers with mine and rests our hands on his leg.

"Can I ask you a question?" he asks.

Any question that begins that way is one I probably don't want to answer.

"Forget it. You won't tell me anyway."

For a girl who always picks *dare* in Truth or Dare, ignoring a challenge is impossible. "Reverse psychology? Am I that easy to read?"

"Just the opposite," Owen says.

"What do you want to know? The name of the first guy I kissed? The worst thing I've ever done? My deepest, darkest secret? Hit me."

"If you weren't taking a break from dating and I wasn't a kickboxer, would you have given me a shot?"

The inside of my mouth goes dry. What can I say? Admit that I'm attracted to him and that in an alternate universe I'd go out with him in a second? Doing anything other than making a joke or evading the question altogether is too risky.

"What kind of shot?" I'm giving him an out, even though I secretly hope he doesn't take it.

"The kind that ends with me kissing you good night."

I suck in a breath and end up coughing.

"I didn't mean to make you uncomfortable." Owen stifles a smile.

"It takes a lot more than a good line to make me uncomfortable." I throw him a sideways glance. "I bet you say that to all the girls who won't go out with you."

The corner of Owen's mouth tips up. "Actually, there aren't that many."

"Like you'd tell me if there were."

"That hurts, Peyton. Are you trying to break my heart?"

I shoot him an incredulous look, which isn't easy when he's fake pouting. "I'm not sure that's possible."

Owen brings our joined hands to his chest. "Every heart can be broken. Some just break more easily than others."

"Do you always flirt this much?"

"Only on fight nights."

I laugh. Owen makes me forget about the weight I'm carrying, and it feels good.

"What are you smiling about?" he asks.

"A girl can't smile?" I'm flirting again.

"If the girl is you she can do whatever she wants." Owen doesn't take his eyes off me, and it feels like he knows exactly what I'm thinking. "Are you sure you don't want to come inside?"

"You never give up, do you?"

Owen's expression turns serious. "Not if I want something bad enough."

CHAPTER 26
Fight Club

I'M STILL IN the parking lot when the steady stream of people entering the arena slows to a trickle. The fights will be starting soon. I planned to leave and go walk around in downtown Nashville, but I'm still staring at the side door that Owen used a few minutes ago.

What kind of fighter is he? Aggressive and always on the offensive—going after his opponent the second he hears the bell? Or is he slow and steady, like a marathon runner, pacing himself and wearing down his opponent in the process?

I slump down in the driver's seat, annoyed with myself.

Who cares how Owen fights?

He's a fighter. That's all I need to know. But I can't stop wondering.

That's it. I'm going in.

I'm overthinking this. I'll go in, watch a little of the fight, and leave. Owen will never know I was there.

I open the car door before I change my mind. The temperature has dropped, and it's cold. I should've brought Dad's jacket.

Owen's Black Water High hoodie is balled up on the passenger seat. I pull it over my head, and the salty scent of the ocean envelops me.

Why can't he smell like blue cheese or old sneakers?

I slam the door and cut across the parking lot to the main entrance. A woman perched on a stool near the door is playing *Word Wars*, a *Scrabble* rip-off, on her cell phone. She holds out her hand without taking her eyes off the screen. "Five dollars."

I dig a crumpled bill out of my pocket and hand it to her.

"Go on in." She points behind her with her thumb. "Just follow the hollering."

The moment I walk through the doors, I hear the familiar din— whistling and shouting, foot stomping and cheering.

I forgot how loud it was at these things.

Watching a fight is discount therapy—a way to let out your anger and frustration, while disguising it as enthusiasm for the competitors. I hesitate at the open doorway that leads to the fight floor. Mangled hinges frame the opening, as if someone had ripped the doors off, which sums up the vibe in the arena.

The moment I cross the threshold, it feels like I've stepped into a time machine, and it takes me back to one of Reed's fights.

Folding chairs are arranged around the perimeter of the octagon-shaped cage, but no one is sitting in them. A slim guy wearing red trunks soaked in sweat pummels his opponent with a series of punches to the ribs, following with a knee to the stomach. The guy doubles over, with the wind knocked out of him. This fight won't last much longer.

His right side is exposed.

Cover up.

Too late. The guy in the red trunks throws a kick, his shin landing hard on his target, and his opponent falls against the mat.

The crowd roars.

Why would anyone subject themselves to this level of physical punishment? I asked Reed that once after a fight.

He looked at me like I was crazy. "For the rush."

Soccer gives me a rush, too, but I don't have to get my butt kicked.

I glance at the doorway behind me. I should get out of here. This place reminds me of Reed, and he's the last person I want in my head. But if I leave, it's *because* of him, and that's worse.

I stay near the wall so I don't get bumped by someone rushing to the bathroom. I move closer to the cage, but not too close.

The fighters clear the cage, and two new competitors approach. I can't see them, and there's no spotlight as they emerge from the locker rooms. Nobody is airing these fights on cable. But they still matter. No one starts at the top.

Maybe Owen fought before I came in and I missed it. It's the universe's way of telling me that I should've stayed in the car. I'm about to go back out there when I spot Cutter's orange UT jacket.

"Bring in The Law," someone shouts.

Owen comes into view, flanked by Cutter and Lazarus, who are both talking to him.

Another thing you don't see at MMA fights are flashy satin robes. Owen is wearing nothing except a pair of black-and-yellow trunks.

They enter the cage and Owen raises a fist when the ref—doubling as the announcer—calls out his moniker: "Owen the Law."

Owen's opponent comes out next—"Rabid" Ricky Dio.

I see his hair before the rest of him—the top gelled and spiked so straight that it actually looks dangerous. Dio's hair is buzzed down to his scalp everywhere else and he looks rabid. His expression is a lethal mix of anger and anxiety.

Dio lunges at Owen and starts yelling. He's trying to psych Owen out. It's a page right out of Reed's playbook. Owen ignores him.

The ref calls the fighters to the center of the mat and talks to them. Then the trainers and cutmen exit the cage. Mouth guards go in and the bell rings, signaling the start of round one.

Dio goes after Owen like a man possessed. He's an offensive fighter, like Reed—pointing at Owen and talking smack. He hits Owen with a combination—a jab to the kidney, a flying knee to the stomach, followed by an elbow strike to the jaw.

The elbow lands hard and I flinch.

Owen shakes it off and stays calm. He blocks and weaves, letting Dio wear himself out.

Between rounds, Cutter and Lazarus rush back into the cage. Cutter bends down in front of Owen, who nods as she talks, while Lazarus ices and applies ointment to Owen's cuts to stop the bleeding.

By round three, Dio's spiked hair is holding up better than the fighter himself. The guy wasted a lot of energy going after Owen in the first two rounds and now he's paying for it.

Owen is patient and calculated. He waits for openings, and then he nails the guy with a power hit or combination.

I hold my breath every time Owen hems Dio up against the ropes.

"Come on. Go down already," I whisper.

Owen sweeps Dio's legs out from under him. When Dio hits the mat, Owen doesn't hesitate. In seconds, he's on the mat in front of Dio. Owen makes a fist and wraps his arm around the back of the other fighter's neck. Then Owen clamps his free hand around his fist, securing the guillotine chokehold.

It's over.

Dio must know it too, because he taps out—tapping the mat three times—the MMA version of giving up.

The ref calls the fight. "And the winner is Owen Law."

I shout and clap, along with the crowd.

Lazarus turns in my direction, and I hold my breath. He's looking right at me.

No . . . above me.

A caged clock hangs on the wall over my head. Lazarus checks the time, then turns back to Cutter.

My heart pounds and I duck behind a group of college guys wearing Tennessee State baseball caps who are arguing about the weight cap for welterweights.

"I'm telling you, it's a hundred sixty-five pounds," one of them says.

"Middleweight starts at one hundred seventy-five pounds," his friend counters.

The debate escalates. "Fifty bucks says you're wrong."

"You don't have fifty bucks, or I'd take that bet—and your money."

"Save your money," I say. The three college boys look back at me. "Welterweight ends at one hundred seventy pounds, and middleweight is above one-seventy."

They stare at me dismissively, as if I couldn't possibly be right.

Losers.

As I walk to the exit, I steal a glance at Owen, sweat-soaked and grinning from ear to ear, like he's genuinely happy. The rogue butterfly in my stomach flutters its wings.

Damn.

I've got to find a way to keep that from happening.

First, I have to get back in the Jeep, before Owen sees me.

I turn around and catch a glimpse of a guy in a red T-shirt coming toward me. I know that logo.

"Peyton?"

I recognize the guy's voice, but it takes me a minute to process— because his voice shouldn't be here.

"I thought that was you," Billy says. "What are you doing here?"

My throat goes dry when I look up and see Reed's friend and teammate staring at me.

"I came in to use the bathroom," I stammer. It's not even a decent lie.

Billy shakes his head, watching me. "You couldn't stay away, huh?"

"Stay away?"

He gestures at the cage. "From the fights. You miss it, don't you?"

Is Reed here with Billy?

My pulse races and I scan the room, panicked.

"Reed isn't here, if that's who you're looking for. I came on my own. My cousin is fighting. He lives in Nashville."

"Your cousin. Right," I mumble.

"Reed misses you. I know he'd want to hear from you. Hell, he'd take you back in a hot second."

"I don't miss him." My tone turns cold.

Billy gives me a knowing look. "Come on, Peyton. Why else would you be here? Or did you start fighting?"

"This would make it kind of hard." I point at my *RoboCop* brace, hoping Billy realizes how ridiculous he sounds.

He looks away. "I feel you. I said the same thing after Jen broke up with me. I used to hang at the football field at lunch, like I was waiting to pick her up from cheer practice."

"I have to go." I slip around Billy, desperate to get the hell away from him. I want to beg him not to tell Reed that he ran into me, but it's pointless. At least we aren't in Black Water.

I focus on the doorway that leads out of the arena.

"He wants you back, Peyton," Billy calls out.

My stomach knots, and an image of Reed, standing at the top of the stairs, flashes through my mind. I ignore Billy and keep walking—through the open doorway, down the hall, past the woman collecting tickets, and across the parking lot, until I make it to the Jeep.

I keep looking behind me to make sure no one is following me. When I climb into the car, I drop the keys in the cup holder beside me. I'm not willing to turn it on and risk attracting attention.

I sink lower in the seat, wishing I could disappear.

Running into Billy caught me off guard. All that garbage about Reed missing me and—my favorite part—that he would take *me* back if I just asked? What kind of sob story is Reed selling? After all the lies he told, I'm surprised he hasn't been struck by lightning.

What if Billy tells Reed his idiotic theory about me hanging out at an MMA semifinal because I miss him so much? Reed will never stop calling me.

Billy probably texted him the minute I walked away.

I spend the next hour sulking in the Jeep. The fights ended a while ago, and the flood of testosterone-pumped guys doing bad side kicks in the parking lot has cleared out. The fighters leave through the side door with their trainers, but there's no sign of Owen, Cutter, or Lazarus.

Maybe there's another exit, and I'm sitting here like an idiot while they're halfway to Black Water. The side door finally opens. Lazarus and Cutter come out and head straight for the parking lot. I watch the door, expecting Owen to follow them.

Where is he?

Cutter's truck drives by and turns onto the street.

There's still no sign of Owen.

Did he catch a ride with someone else?

I'm sure one of the MMA groupies in the arena offered to give him a ride. But Owen wouldn't ditch me. Would he?

I start the Jeep and back out of the parking space. The lot is deserted, except for a few cars that probably belong to employees. I flip a U-turn and circle around to the back of the building to check for another way out. There's an emergency exit door, with a dumpster blocking half of it. Only the Incredible Hulk could get out this way—not a reassuring thought after I was in there earlier.

As I circle back to the front of the arena, a nagging feeling tugs at me. Owen didn't leave the building with the other fighters—or Cutter and Lazarus. Either he lost track of time and he's taking the world's longest shower, or something happened.

I park near the side door. If I go through the main entrance, I might run into someone who works at the arena, and I'll get stuck explaining why I'm sneaking around.

I'm just looking for a guy I drove here—who isn't my boyfriend, and probably left already, while I sat in the parking lot, freezing my ass off.

That doesn't sound pathetic at all.

I stare at the dented red door. If it's locked, I'm leaving, and Owen will have to find his own way home. One hard pull and the door swings open.

Inside, the hallway is wallpapered with fight cards and posters for pro MMA fights, like the UFC matches Reed loved watching on TV. Fluorescent ceiling panels bathe everything in pale orange light. I pass the restrooms, where a woman is smoking a cigarette and mopping the floor in front of the ladies' room. Other people wearing staff T-shirts dart in and out of the hallway, pushing stacks of chairs or carrying huge trash bags over their shoulders. I don't see any trainers or fighters.

Come on, Owen. Where are you?

A man leaves the arena with a bag of garbage slung over his shoulder. He's wearing earbuds and singing along with the music.

I wave to get his attention. "Excuse me?"

"Need some help?" he asks, removing one of his earbuds.

"I'm looking for my friend. He fought here tonight. Are any of the fighters still around?"

"Not sure. They usually clear out fast. You can check the locker room." He points toward the end of the hallway. "Straight down."

"Thanks."

He notices my leg brace. "Are you a fighter?"

"Soccer player."

He raises an eyebrow. "Didn't know soccer was such a rough sport."

"Thanks again." I head down the hall, feeling less optimistic about finding Owen. It's probably a result of the Reed Effect—the way Reed turns everything to shit.

The locker room is dark and quiet. Locker rooms aren't quiet unless they're empty. Conversations, showers running, doors closing, and footsteps echo inside. But I still don't want to chance it and walk in on a half-naked stranger.

I take a step inside and whisper-shout Owen's name. When no one responds, I take another step. This time I call his name loud enough for a person without supersonic senses to hear. "Owen? Are you in here?"

"Give me a minute," a muffled voice calls out.

"Owen? Is that you?"

A moment later, I hear what sounds like "Hold on."

There's something weird about his voice. I'm not waiting.

I storm into the locker room, my steps echoing to announce my arrival.

Owen must hear them, too, because he calls out to me again. "Just give me a minute." He sounds strange.

"You've already had over an hour. That's how long I've been waiting in the parking lot for you."

"Peyton, don't come in here. Please . . ." He coughs and then sucks in a deep breath.

I stop at the corner where a bank of lockers begins. Owen is just on the other side. Why doesn't he want me in here? And why does he sound so strange? Did the fight take a bigger toll on him than I thought?

Owen coughs again, and I round the corner. "You'd better have clothes on, because I'm—"

The moment I see him, I lose my train of thought. He's sitting on the floor, leaning against the lockers behind him, still in his trunks. His hands are still wrapped, the white cloth stained red from the fight.

Why hasn't he showered or changed?

Owen sees me and takes a labored breath. "I told you not to—" he gasps, then sucks in a sharp breath. Even in the dim light, he looks pale.

My heart stalls.

"I'm okay," Owen mumbles, struggling to keep his eyes open. I rush over to him just as he loses the battle and they flutter shut.

CHAPTER 27

Just Friends

OWEN IS NOT okay.

I take off my brace and carefully lower myself to the floor beside him. I'm not worried about hurting my knee. Owen is in pain, and I don't want to do anything that might make it worse. I sit facing him with my legs tucked to the side, my thigh pressed against his.

"Is it your ribs? Are they broken?" That would explain his labored breathing. How could Cutter and Lazarus leave him alone in this condition?

"My bag." Owen tries to point, but it seems like too much effort, and his hand drops to the floor.

I scoot backward and reach the gym bag easily, which terrifies me. It's only a few feet away from Owen, and he couldn't get to it himself.

I unzip it for him. "What do you need?"

Owen's chest heaves with every breath as he gropes through the bag.

Whatever he's looking for, he's not finding it. I reach across his lap, grab the bag, and dump out the contents. Rolled hand wraps unfurl and land in our laps as energy bars and bottles of pain reliever clatter against the floor.

"Tell me what I'm looking for," I plead.

"My inhaler."

I push the items around, looking for the inhaler. I see it! I pick up the inhaler and put it in Owen's hand. He takes two puffs and closes his eyes.

"Should I call 911?"

His eyes fly open and he grabs my arm. "No!"

"Relax." I raise my hands so he can see them. "I'm not calling."

Unless he gets worse.

When Owen closes his eyes again, I grab a T-shirt from the bag and wipe the sweat off his face. My hand lingers on his jaw, my thumb only inches from his lips. I listen to his breathing until it evens out, our faces so close they're almost touching.

"I'm okay," he says, as if he senses me watching him.

Owen's breathing is returning to normal and he sounds like himself again. But without knowing exactly what's wrong with him—and why he needs an inhaler—I have no idea if I should be worried about anything else, like his pulse rate or blood pressure.

"No, you're not." Tears prick my eyes. I feel helpless. "I think we should go to the hospital and get you checked out."

The color still hasn't returned to Owen's cheeks, and his expressive eyes, which usually give away his feelings, look dull and glazed over.

His back stiffens and he shakes off the fog. "No hospitals. My medicine is kicking in. I'll be fine in a couple minutes."

"Why don't I believe you?"

His eyes drift past my face to the narrow space between his chest and mine. The way I'm leaning over him makes it look like I want to jump into his lap.

I pull back, suddenly self-conscious. "Tell me what happened. Did you take a bad hit? Tell me if this hurts." Without thinking, I gently run my fingers over Owen's rib cage. The moment my fingertips touch his bare skin, my nerve endings buzz.

"Nothing's broken," Owen says, staring at my hand. I yank it away, drawing even more attention to the fact that I was touching him.

The disadvantage of putting more space between us is that now I have a better view of Owen's chest—and the rest of his gorgeous body.

I pick up his inhaler. "Why do you need this?"

"I don't like talking about it."

I stare at him. "Then you'll have to get over it, because I just found you sitting on the floor of an empty locker room, gasping for air. You don't know how bad you looked. I thought . . ." My voice wavers. I can't say it.

Owen reaches up and trails a calloused thumb over my cheek. "I'm glad you didn't listen to me."

"About which thing?"

The corner of his mouth turns up. "Coming in here."

"Doing the opposite of what I'm told is my specialty." I hold up his inhaler. "So are you going to tell me why you need this?" I ask.

Owen rubs the back of his neck and frowns. He glances at his wrapped hand and brings his wrist to his mouth, tugging on the end of the wrap with his teeth.

"Stop." Taking his wrist, I quickly unwind the wrap—following it around his wrist three times and threading the cloth out from between his fingers and then back down to his wrist, before moving on to the next finger. After that, it's easy. Around the knuckles several times, then back down to his wrist and up to the thumb loop.

My thumb grazes the soft skin under his wrist, and Owen's pulse drums against the pad.

"Have you done this before?" Owen asks as I slip his thumb out of the loop and toss the other wrap aside. "You're better at that than I am."

"No," I say automatically, realizing my mistake. It takes practice to unwrap someone's hands. "You don't have to be a genius to figure it out," I add. "The . . . cloth stuff only unwinds in one direction."

Owen rubs his wrists. "Most people still need practice to do it that fast."

"I'm super coordinated, and don't try to change the subject to get out of answering my question." Which is exactly what I'm doing.

He takes a deep breath. "Is there any chance you'd be willing to put that question on hold?"

I cross my arms. "No."

Without a word, Owen stands and extends his hand to help me up. As soon as I'm back on my feet, he picks up my leg brace and gives it to me. I put it on, watching him from the corner of my eye. Owen's hands are on his hips and he's staring at the floor, the contents of his gym bag scattered around his feet.

But he won't look at me.

As much as I want to know what happened, he doesn't want to talk about it even more.

"You win. You don't have to tell me." I sigh. "I'll wait in the hall while you change, in case you need me . . . I mean, need help."

I turn to walk away and Owen touches my elbow. He lets his fingers slide down my arm until he's holding my hand. "Don't leave." He takes a deep breath and raises his eyes to meet mine. "I've got . . ."

Whatever he's about to tell me is difficult for him. Instead of pushing, I wait until he's ready to talk. I understand how it feels to need time. I rarely tell people that my dad is dead, but when I do, it takes me a minute to collect my thoughts.

Owen leans his shoulder against the locker and faces me. "I have asthma. It gets bad sometimes."

I've had teammates with asthma, but I've never seen any of them unable to catch their breath.

"A black eye is *bad*. You could barely breathe when I got here. What would've happened if I hadn't come looking for you?" The moment I ask the question, the truth hits me.

I care about what happens to Owen.

"Eventually, it would've let up enough for me to grab my inhaler. You walked in during the worst of it." He sounds so calm.

"What if your bag wasn't nearby?"

"It would've been okay, Peyton."

"You don't know that for sure." Before Dad left for a mission, he'd give me a bear hug and tell me that he would be okay. Even though high-risk ops were the norm for him, Dad believed he would always come home to us. Then one day he didn't.

"Don't dodge the question. What happens if you have an asthma attack and you don't have your inhaler?"

"Peyton—"

I'm not giving up that easily. "What would happen?"

"I wouldn't be able to breathe."

Something else occurs to me. "Does fighting increase your chances of having an attack?"

Owen sighs. "Yeah. But so does running across the street. Should I stop doing that, too?"

"If it keeps you alive."

"I don't want to live that way—avoiding anything that *might* hurt me." He looks directly at me.

"Normal people don't want to get hurt, Owen."

"Normal is overrated." He takes a step toward me. "I can't let my condition control my life. I don't want to play it safe all the time. I don't want to be afraid to go after the things I want and take risks . . . like this."

Owen wraps his arm around my waist and pulls me against him. When I don't protest, he slides his other hand up my back and into my hair. "Unless you tell me to stop, I'm going to kiss you."

He leans in, never taking his eyes off mine.

When his lips graze mine, it feels too good. The kind of good I want to feel a hundred more times. He brushes his lip against mine, and the contact sends shock waves through my body. He continues to tease me, tracing the seam of my lips with his tongue.

I part my lips. Owen accepts the invitation and kisses me for real.

My hands touch the bare skin on his chest and he moans—low and sexy. He tastes sweet, with a hint of copper from the cut on his lip. I loop my hands around his neck, and he tightens his hold around my waist, carefully turning us until I'm leaning against the lockers.

The combination of the cold metal against my back and the heat of Owen's skin against my chest creates a delicious burn inside me. Part of me knows I should stop kissing him, but the other part of me wins out.

Owen lets his hands trail up my sides, and he reaches over my shoulders and plants his palms on the lockers, boxing me in. His bottom lip is swollen from the fight and I brush my lips across it. His breathing speeds up and he deepens the kiss. I'm breathing just as hard, and our chests press together whenever one of us exhales.

When Owen finally pulls back and looks at me, his eyes are glassy and his cheeks flushed. "I knew that's how it would feel to kiss you."

"How?"

He leans over and whispers the answer in my ear. "Like it was worth the risk if you didn't feel the same way."

I do. That's the problem.

"We can't do this, Owen." I turn my head away and try to pull myself together. "We're just friends."

He touches my chin with his finger and turns my face back toward him. His mouth hovers in front of mine, so close that his breath teases my lips. It takes every ounce of self-control I have left not to kiss him again.

"If that's what you want . . ." he says.

It *is* and it *isn't*, but I can't say that without giving him an explanation.

When it's clear I'm not going to respond, Owen leans over to my ear and whispers, "We can be *just friends*. For now.

"As long as you aren't *just friends* with anyone else."

CHAPTER 28

Secrets

I'M STILL IN the hazy place between dreaming and waking, but I don't want the dream to end. It feels so real. Owen's hands tangled in my hair. His mouth finding mine over and over, nipping and tugging until my lips are swollen. I can't think about anything except what it would feel like to have his hands on me . . . because kissing Owen feels *too* good.

That's why it can't happen again.

The nagging voice in the back of my head is awake, reminding me that last night was a one-time thing. If I hadn't felt anything, then maybe I could sneak in a repeat performance. But a kiss like the one we shared—that kind of kiss isn't easy to forget.

My phone rings, and I grope around on the nightstand until I find it.

I check the caller ID, and it's not Reed.

"Hi, Mom."

"Hi, sweetheart."

I've talked to Mom a few times since she left, mainly to fill her in about PT and my classes.

"How is everything?" she asks.

"Okay, actually. I think I'm getting used to things here." *And I kissed an amazing guy I can't kiss again.*

"That's a good thing, right?" She sounds relieved. "Hawk said you have the day off from school."

"Yeah. The teachers have an in-service."

"How's school otherwise?"

"Not bad." *Except for Christian's bitchy ex that annoys the crap out of me, and the Twins' friend, who wants to pick a fight with the guy I kissed . . . the one I'm not mentioning.*

"That's all I get?" She's disappointed.

I'd love to tell her about Owen, but it will just worry her, and she'll ask questions about him that I'm not ready to answer.

Instead, I offer up more details about my classes. But I don't mention the novel we're reading in English. I also tell Mom about the way Lazarus plays chess against himself and how Dutch gets stuck under my bed. She loves hearing about the everyday things.

We're about to get off the phone when she gets quiet. "Is Reed still calling?"

"Yeah. But I never answer. Why? Is he calling the house, too?"

She doesn't say anything.

"Mom?"

"Reed calls more now than he did when you two were dating. He leaves ridiculous messages asking if I'll tell him where you are. He seems . . ."

"What?" If Reed is bothering my mom I'll sic Hawk on him.

"I don't know. Out of touch with reality is the best way to describe it."

"I know what you mean." The fact that Reed thinks I'd give him another chance proves it.

"Just don't talk to him, okay?" she asks.

"Trust me. That's not a problem."

"Good. I'll call you in a day or two, sweetheart," she says. "I love you."

"Love you too, Mom."

The moment I hang up my phone chimes with an incoming text.

are u up?

Cameron.

He probably wants to grill me about what I was doing last night. I ignore his text and, a minute later, another message comes through.

helping Pop haul crap to storage. text me when u get this.

I'm not ready to face the Twins and answer questions about last night.

Finding Owen in the locker room, in such bad shape, still has me reeling. By the time I got him in the car, he was so tired that he slept until I pulled up in front of his house to drop him off.

"Don't tell anyone what happened until we talk, okay?" he asked.

"I won't."

His secret wasn't mine to tell.

Owen was about to close the car door, when he bent down and poked his head back into the car. "My hoodie looks good on you."

A hoodie I just happened to sleep in last night.

What was I thinking? Kissing him was a huge mistake.

I kick back the covers and put on a pair of sweats. Now that I'm up, the familiar scratching sounds start under the bed. I lift the bed skirt and take a peek. Dutch is sprawled out on his belly.

"Maybe you should stop crawling under there if you can't get out." Dutch howls.

I'm not strong enough to lift the end of the bed without putting pressure on my knee, so I sit on the floor and use my shoulder to lift one corner of the bed high enough for Dutch to belly-crawl his way out. Once he's free, the bloodhound lopes across the rug and stretches out on the floor next to the closet.

I wash my face, brush my teeth, and try to decide what to do with the rest of the day. Normally, I'd just hang out and binge-watch women's soccer, but after last night I need a bigger distraction.

I consider calling Grace to tell her that Owen kissed me. I'd leave out the part about his asthma attack. Grace seems trustworthy, and I'm dying to tell someone. I scroll through my contacts to find her number, and my phone chimes again.

If Cam plans to text me all day long, it will drive me nuts. I open my messages, expecting to find another update on the crap hauling.

It's Owen. I'm on a loaner phone. You busy?

Seeing a message from him makes me smile.

not really. how are u feeling?

Three blinking dots in a speech bubble appear on the screen as he types.

Good as new. I was hoping we could talk.

I'm not sure how to respond. Is he asking to call me or see me? I test the water.

i'm free now if u want to call.

I hit send and immediately wish I could delete the message. It sounds like I'm asking him to call.

I'd rather talk in person. Can I pick you up?

Instead of overthinking it, I type back:

what time? i need to shower.

Ugh . . . Why did I mention the shower?

Is an hour enough time?

that works.

As soon as we stop texting, I jump in the shower.

I'm not one of those girls who take forever to get ready. I'm pretty low-maintenance in the makeup department—blush, lip gloss, and a little concealer if I stayed up too late the night before. My thick waves won't yield to a blowout, so my style choices are limited to ponytail or no ponytail. But today, I spend a ridiculous amount of time deciding between the two.

I finally settle on wearing my hair down. Owen has a way of looking at me that leaves me feeling exposed. My hair will give me somewhere to hide.

Choosing something to wear is more complicated. In an effort to make sure this doesn't seem like a date, jeans are the obvious choice. But then I have to decide whether to go with a long-sleeve T-shirt or step it up a notch and wear a sweater. After changing four times, I end up wearing the first outfit I tried on—jeans and my fitted, super-soft V-neck pullover, and a gray infinity scarf.

Dutch howls from downstairs, which means the doorbell rang and I didn't hear it. I peek out my bedroom window. Owen's SUV is parked at the curb.

Has it really been an hour already?

I do a quick check in the full-length mirror on the closet door. My perfectly arranged curls, "just bitten" lip stain, and black V-neck that hugs my curves make me look like I spent an hour getting ready. I flip my head forward and rake my hands through my hair to mess it up a little. Then I rub my berry-colored lips with a towel. The hair trick works, but my lips end up pinker.

The doorbell rings again and Dutch howls like crazy. On my way out, I throw on my oversize Adams High soccer hoodie. Nothing says *not really trying* like a ratty hoodie.

Why am I nervous? It's Owen. We're friends.

Friends who kissed last night.

I walk downstairs and open the door.

Owen's eyes skim over me, and all I can think about is the way his lips felt when he kissed me. His damp blond hair is finger-combed in the sexy-sweet look that he has perfected without realizing it. He breaks into a smile and shakes his head.

"What?" I look down at my outfit.

"You look even hotter with your hair all wild."

"Whatever." I close the door and slip past him. *Hot* isn't a word guys use to describe me. Cute? Maybe. But hot? No way.

Hot is for girls like April. I'm more of the girl next door type. After years of fighting it, I'm finally okay with it.

I cross the lawn and Owen rushes ahead of me to open the car door. When I get in, he raises an eyebrow. "No argument?"

"I've given up on this one."

Owen seems nervous, too. He turns on the radio, and then turns it off again. "There's somewhere I want to take you, if that's okay."

"Sure. Where?"

"I kind of want it to be a surprise." He glances over at me, and I melt a little. I start to say something, and he adds, "Before you say anything, I just want to remind you *friends* do surprises, too."

He knows me better than I thought.

"That's not what I was gonna say."

He grins at me. "Liar."

I try not to smile, and Owen laughs. He doesn't look anything like he did last night when I dropped him off. His cheeks have color again, and he's back to his adorable smart-ass self.

He takes the windy back roads instead of the street to get to the mystery destination.

"Where did you say we were going?" I ask innocently.

"Nice try. This is the scenic route to my house."

"Are we going to your house?" I'd love to see his room. You can learn a lot about a person from the things in their bedroom.

"No. The place I'm taking you is in the woods behind my house." He pulls off and stops in a clearing.

"The woods?"

"It's not like we're going camping. Pretty much everything around here is forest." He glances at my knee brace. "And it's not far or uphill." He wipes his hands on his jeans like his palms are sweaty. "I don't know why I'm making such a big deal about this. Now I feel kind of stupid. It's just this place. You'll see."

I get out before Owen has a chance to rush around and open the car door for me. He notices, but he lets it slide.

"You ready?" he asks.

"Yeah. I want to see this mystery place."

He reaches toward me, as if he's going to take my hand. Then he pulls his arm back and shoves his hand into his pocket instead. The kiss definitely complicated the just-friends plan.

The Tennessee forest is gorgeous. The trees are losing their fall leaves—shades of yellow, orange, and red that I've never seen before. "It's pretty out here."

Owen looks around at the woods he probably played in all the time as a kid. "Yeah, I guess it is. This is sort of my backyard. Just a little farther."

Suddenly, he seems nervous, like he's about to show me his bedroom.

The trees open up, revealing a path. This must be what he wanted to show me.

"Oh my god, Owen. Is that a tree house?"

"It's not really high up enough to be a tree house. My dad built it when I was a kid, and my mom is pretty overprotective. She was convinced I'd fall out. So it turned into a tree fort."

The tree house is nestled among three huge oaks. It's small with a flat roof, but branches and vines have grown around the outer walls, and now it looks as if it's part of the forest.

Owen's dad nailed four logs onto a tree trunk to serve as steps. Owen is right. It's not very high. The platform is just above his head.

Owen hops onto the first step and offers me his hand.

"I can't climb up there." If my knee gives out or I miss a step, I could end up in even worse shape than I am now.

"I'm not asking you to climb." He's still holding out his hand.

"Are you gonna lift me up with your Superman arm and set me up there?" I ask.

"You're such a smart-ass. Hop on my back. I'm gonna carry you up."

I take a step back. "No, you're not."

Owen jumps down and kneels in front of me. "Just hop on my back. It's four steps."

I don't move. After watching Owen pin Ricky Dios and put him in a chokehold, I think he's strong enough to carry two of me.

He looks up at me. "I'd never let anything happen to you." The way he says it makes it feel as though he's talking about more than just carrying me up the steps, and it gives me goose bumps in a good way. "Trust me, Peyton."

He doesn't know what he's asking. How impossible it feels to trust any guy after what happened with Reed.

But things are different with Owen.

We're friends, and my *friend* Owen won't drop me.

"Okay. But if you drop me, I will kill you."

Owen motions for me to hop onto his back. When I wrap my arms around his neck, it changes things. He hooks one arm under my leg. "Okay, ready?"

It takes him less than two minutes to pull us up the steps, but it feels like forever—and not because I'm afraid I'll fall.

We reach the platform and he sets me down, so my legs are dangling over the edge. It isn't high, but it must have felt like a tower when he was a kid.

Owen dusts himself off and ducks through the doorway. "You coming?"

I follow him inside.

The tree house is one huge room with two open windows, and right now it's full of leaves. I would've loved this when I was younger—having a place that was all my own.

"This is amazing." I turn in a circle and check out the space.

Owen's initials are carved next to the door, above NO GIRLS ALLOWED.

I tap on the words. "I'm not supposed to be in here."

Owen looks me in the eye. "You're an exception."

Coming up here was a mistake. I can't stop looking at his mouth, and all I can think about is the way it felt when he kissed me. If I didn't need his help to get back down, I'd take off right now.

Owen sits on the floor and pats the spot in front of him. "Come on, have a seat. This is as good as it gets."

From where I'm standing, it looks pretty good. I sit in front of him, and it's impossible to ignore his big brown eyes.

He's quiet for a moment. "I'm sorry if I scared you last night."

"I'm just glad you're okay. And I wish you'd told me."

Owen leans forward and rests his hands on my hips. With what seems like no effort, he gently pulls me forward so we're practically nose-to-nose.

"You're the first person I've ever wanted to tell. Only a few people know about my condition—my parents, my doctors, and now you."

He must be exaggerating. "What about your friends?"

Owen shakes his head. "Nope."

"Why didn't you tell them?"

He looks away. "I didn't have any symptoms as a kid. Then two years ago, I had an . . . attack. Everything changed overnight. The doctors wanted me to stop kickboxing and wrestling, and I was spending more time at their offices than at practice. So I quit the wrestling team. I started avoiding my friends. I didn't want to tell them what was going on. That's why Titan has a problem with me. We used to be friends."

"Really?" I can't picture Owen and Titan hanging out.

"Titan wrestled, too. When I quit, he took it personally. He said I bailed on the team. He was right."

"You should've told him why you quit. You don't have anything to be embarrassed about," I say gently. "Lots of people have asthma."

"The type I have isn't common, and I have to manage it. I wasn't used to having any limitations, and suddenly I had tons of them. The last thing I wanted to do was tell my friends and get stuck answering a bunch of stupid questions."

"Maybe they wouldn't have been stupid?"

"I guess I was scared," he admits. "I didn't feel like myself anymore."

"I get it." I feel that way all the time now. "But Cutter and Lazarus must know?" I can tell from his expression that he hasn't told them. "Cutter is your trainer. She shouldn't be in the dark."

"Cutter might not look at me the same way if she knew. I know you don't understand, but it could change things."

He's right. I don't understand. He's taking unnecessary risks with his life because Cutter and Lazarus *might* see him differently?

"Do you honestly believe that?"

Owen studies the weathered boards on the floor. "It changed things with my dad. It changed *him*."

I scoot closer to Owen and touch his hand. "What do you mean?"

"My dad was a kickboxer. He started training me as soon as I could walk. Mom says I was a natural, so my dad kept training me—every single day except for Thanksgiving and Christmas."

"That seems a little extreme." I don't want to judge, but Owen doesn't sound thrilled about it.

"Extreme is a good way to describe him. My dad's dream was to compete in the Olympics or fight in Thailand, at Lumpinee, a famous boxing stadium. Only the best of the best compete there. But he didn't make the cut. So his dream became my dream."

"That's a lot of pressure for a kid."

Owen nods. "But it was the only thing I knew. And pissing my dad off was dangerous."

He means literally.

I can see it in his eyes.

"Did he hurt you?" I thread my fingers through Owen's and he closes his hands around mine. He gently pulls our hands toward his chest and I move even closer.

"Yeah. But not as bad as he hurt my mom."

The world around me stills.

"He hurt her?" The words sound like a whisper when I say them.

Owen clutches our intertwined hands against his chest. "He pushed my mom around all the time when I was growing up. Sometimes he hit her. I tried to stop him, but he was stronger than me, and he was a better fighter. So I started studying jiu-jitsu at twelve. It's the only martial art that's popular here because it's great training for wrestling. I couldn't beat my dad at kickboxing, so I changed the game. I had to do something to protect my mom."

Owen looks away. This can't be easy for him to talk about. "A year later, I had the attack. When the doctors diagnosed me, my dad went ballistic. He didn't want a 'defective son.' That's what he said to my mom right before he threw her across the living room."

"Oh god."

"That was the first time I really tried to fight him. I lost and he bailed." He takes a deep breath. "I didn't have anyone to train me. It's not like there are a ton of martial arts instructors hanging around Black Water. But I was interning for Cutter, and I knew about her background in martial arts and Lazarus' experience training boxers.

"At first, Cutter didn't want to do it. She was already pissed off because I told her that I didn't want to follow through with the internship. I think Lazarus talked her into helping me. She agreed to train me and I started competing in MMA. I realized that my body could still do what I needed it to do."

"But you told me that fighting increases the odds of you having an attack."

"Sure, if I'm not careful. And last night I wasn't. I should've used my inhaler before the fight. I don't know what I was thinking. But none of that means I can't fight."

"Why are you telling me all this? I mean, why me?"

"Well, I sort of had to tell you about my asthma." He gives me a sheepish smile.

"That's true." I let out the breath I'm holding.

Owen scoots forward so his knees are on either side of mine. "But I'm glad I told you the other stuff, too."

"Me too." I swallow hard. "But last night . . . that can't happen again."

"An asthma attack? I agree," he says, acting serious.

"You know what I'm talking about."

"You mean when we kissed." His eyes lock on mine, and I can feel him kissing me again.

"I don't want to date anyone," I blurt out.

"I know you felt something when I kissed you. And I haven't been able to think about anything else since. Just tell me why you won't give this a chance. That's all I'm asking."

I want to give him a reason, but I can't tell him the truth.

He ducks his head so he can look at me. "What are you thinking?"

That I let things go too far, and now I'm in over my head. That I can't stop thinking about you, either, and it scares the hell out of me. And I really wish you would kiss me again.

But I can't say any of those things. I look down and let my hair fall over my face.

"Talk to me, Peyton."

"I can't." The words come out as a whisper.

The silence stretches too long and Owen inches closer. "How about if I go first?"

I peek out from behind my hair. "Okay."

He catches on to my hair trick and brushes the long waves off my shoulders. His fingers graze my neck, sending a shot of heat through my body. "I think someone hurt you, and now you're scared of getting hurt again."

257

Talking about this, even when I'm not doing the talking, is harder than I expected.

"My last relationship ended badly." I try not to think about the night of the party. "It was complicated. We had a lot of the same friends, and people took sides. His side."

"I'm sorry." Owen touches my leg and runs his hand back and forth between my knee and my ankle.

"I don't really want to talk about it," I say softly. "I just want to focus on getting my knee back in shape. And I'm not here for that long. There's no point in dating anyone."

By *anyone*, we both know I mean him.

"Why? Because you're going back home? You'd be going to college in the fall anyway."

"I just can't."

"But you did feel something. Right?"

I can't lie. My heart is beating so hard he can probably hear it. And I don't want to lie to him about anything else.

"What do you want me to say?" I look away and watch the leaves rustling on the tree branches outside.

He presses his fingers against my back. "I want you to admit that you felt something when I kissed you. I need to know I didn't imagine it."

"I felt something, but it doesn't matter. Whatever this thing is between us, it can't happen. So I'm trying not to think about it, and you're making it really hard."

Owen's hand grazes my cheek, and he tucks his finger under my chin and gently turns my face toward him. "I don't think I can turn off the way I feel about you. I wasn't looking to get involved with anyone, either. I'm taking off as soon as I graduate to backpack around Europe and Asia." He hesitates. "But I can't help it. Every time I look at you, all I can think about is holding you and kissing you. Making you smile."

It takes me a second to recover. "We're attracted to each other. Sometimes that happens with friends."

I'm trying to reason away my feelings, and I'm doing a terrible job.

Owen traces my jawline, and his fingers trail down the side of my neck. His hand pauses there, his thumb against my shoulder and his fingers curved around so they're touching the back of my neck. It's the way you touch someone before you pull them in for a kiss and I want him to kiss me even though I shouldn't.

"If you really don't want anything to happen between us, I'll back off. But it's going to be hard, and it's not what I want." He rests his forehead against mine. "And it's been a long time since I've wanted anything. But if you don't want a boyfriend, I don't have to be your boyfriend. I'll take whatever I can get."

I pull back just a little. "I don't want to get hurt again."

Owen takes my face in his hands, and his lips brush against mine. "I promise I won't hurt you."

Part of me believes him.

CHAPTER 29
Lie to Me

OWEN DROPPED ME off an hour ago and I'm lying on my bed, staring at the ceiling. I can't stop thinking about the way his hands felt on my skin—how it felt to kiss him and hear him whisper my name. My genius plan to keep my distance and not let him get too close was a total fail.

My phone vibrates.

I hope it's Owen.

I check the caller ID, but it's not him. I don't recognize the number, but it has a DC area code. It has to be Reed. I should ignore it and let the call go to voice mail. But there's something about him calling now that sets me off, as if he knew I was feeling amazing and he had to ruin it.

"What do you want?" I ask without confirming that it's Reed.

"Peyton? It's so good to hear your voice. I didn't think you'd pick up." Reed sounds sweet and heartbroken, which is impossible since he doesn't have a heart.

"What do you want?" I ask again.

"I want you to come home. Lucia said your mom sent you to a fancy rehab center for athletes and you aren't coming back for five or six months, or something crazy."

I actually smile. Only Lucia could figure out a way to torture Reed. When I get home I'm going to buy her the reddest lipstick I can find.

"You don't need to worry about when I'm coming back. Nothing has changed. I didn't want to see you before I left, and I still don't."

"I miss you."

"Get used to it."

"Tess misses you, too." He's trying to manipulate me.

But what if he's not?

"Don't call me again, Reed." I hang up before he has time to say another word. He calls back two seconds later, but this time I don't pick up. I add the number he called from to a long list of blocked numbers.

Does Tess really miss me? Because I miss her, especially when something amazing happens. She's still the first person I want to tell.

Maybe she's ready to listen.

I take a chance and hit speed dial on my cell. The phone rings three times. Either she's not around or she still doesn't want to talk to me.

I'm about to hang up when someone answers.

"What do you want?" Tess snaps from the other end of the line. It doesn't sound like she has had a change of heart.

"I want to talk."

"Does that mean you're ready to explain why you lied to me?" The anger in her voice takes me by surprise. It's the tone Tess uses when she talks about her father, a man she hates.

"Tess—"

"I've thought about this over and over, and maybe you weren't trying to hurt me, and I was just collateral damage." A hint of sadness creeps into her voice, and for a second she sounds like my best friend again. "It's the only explanation I can come up with that makes any sense."

Not the only one.

"Sometimes relationships change people and make them do stupid things," she says. "Is that what happened?"

All I have to do is say yes and I'll have my best friend back.

But I can't.

"I've never lied to you before, Tess, and I'm not going to start now. I was telling you the truth. Reed pushed me. He admits it when he calls me. I'm not confused."

"Right." Tess sounds even angrier than before. "Call me when you're ready to be honest. Or don't call me again."

CHAPTER 30
Roadkill

"WHEN THE WORLD around us doesn't make sense, we find ways to make sense of it ourselves." Miss Ives is talking about the novel, but it feels like she's talking about my life.

"The author, Tim O'Brien, tells us a lot about the items from home the soldiers carry—photographs, comic books, good luck charms, a pebble—because these objects are more than just reminders of home. But O'Brien also writes about the intangible things the men carried, like hope, sorrow, and fear."

I swallow hard, but my throat feels like it's stuffed with cotton. Owen scoots his chair a little closer to mine.

Miss Ives leans against the front of her desk and watches the class, searching our faces for a reaction. "I want each of you to keep this in mind as you're reading. Ask yourselves what each of the soldiers is carrying—because at the end of this unit, I'm going to ask you to write an essay about the things *you* carry. Not the objects you brought in when we started the novel, but the intangible things you can't hold in your hand."

Her statement is met by a chorus of groans from the class.

Whatever. I'll make up something poignant and meaningful—BS that will pass for introspection. English teachers love that kind of stuff. I won't write anything personal. So why does it feel like I'm choking on a baseball every time I swallow?

Owen nudges my knee with his. It's his way of asking if I'm okay without asking. I smile to reassure him.

I'm relieved when the bell finally rings, and I rush out the door. Thanks to Miss Ives and Tim O'Brien, I dread English class. But even a depressing war novel can't kill my mood today.

"Why are you smiling?" Owen asks once we're in the hallway.

"I'm not."

"I know a smile when I see one," he says. "And that was a smile."

We walk down the hall side by side, close enough for his hand to graze mine, which it does more than once.

"Would it be wrong if I told you that I really want to hold your hand?" Owen asks, reading my thoughts.

"Friends don't walk around school holding hands." I move closer and let my hand brush his.

"*Just friends* do," he whispers.

We pass the hallway Owen takes to get to his locker. "Maybe my *just friend* wants to stop by his locker so he doesn't have to bum paper off everyone."

"Mine is too far away. I'm saving trees. No one uses all the paper in their notebooks anyway. I think my time is better spent escorting you to your locker."

We get to my locker, and he leans against the one next to mine, watching me. I spin the lock but I keep missing the numbers.

"Having trouble?" he asks. "Maybe you're distracted."

I'm so transparent.

"No. I've got it." I'm still looking at Owen when I open the door. I catch a glimpse of something falling. It's coming right at me.

Is it more soccer balls?

A girl screams, and the object hits me for a split second before Owen bats it away. It happens so fast that I don't even see it. Owen pulls me next to him, and I look at what fell out.

A mound of gray fur lies on the floor—a tiny leg and a long paw jutting out from underneath it.

My stomach heaves, and I cover my mouth.

Owen puts his arm around me. "It's okay."

Cameron jogs toward us. He spots the ball of fur in front of my locker and my proximity to it. "Where the fuck did that come from?"

"Peyton's locker." Owen says the words slowly, through gritted teeth.

"What is it?" I peek at the pile of fur. It's some kind of animal.

A crowd gathers. This is a repeat of the soccer balls, but a hundred times worse.

Cam yanks a T-shirt out of his backpack and uses it to pick up the dead animal. "It's a rabbit."

That's when I notice the rabbit's body is flat. It's not just a dead rabbit.

It's roadkill.

I want to scream, but there are too many people around and I'm willing to bet one of them is the person who did this.

Cam holds the carcass away from his body and turns his back to me so I don't have to look at it.

"What have you got there, bro?" Christian calls out. He's grinning, like he thinks Cam is messing around or pulling a prank. I can't see Cameron's face, but his expression must be serious because Christian's smile instantly vanishes.

"Someone put this in Peyton's locker," Cam says.

"Are you shitting me?" Christian slams my locker door closed hard enough to dent it. "Who did it?"

April is standing next to her locker with Dylan, and her smug expression makes me want to strangle her.

"I'm pretty sure I know." I slip past them and storm down the hallway. Owen and the Twins follow me.

"You're sick, you know that?" I shout at her.

April's expression changes from amusement to confusion. Not that I buy her act. She starts to say something, then she sees what Cam is holding.

"You think I did that?" She points at the roadkill dangling from Cam's hand.

"You or your piece-of-shit boyfriend," Christian says.

Dylan drops his backpack and gets in Christian's face. "What did you call me?"

"You heard me."

"I'm not a sick asshole like you," Dylan fires back. "I'd never put anything like that in a girl's locker."

I stare April down. "Then she did it on her own."

"You think I go around collecting roadkill?" She eyes the rabbit, scrunches up her nose, and looks at me. "That I'd pick up that disgusting thing?"

"You hunt. Dead animals don't bother you," Cam says.

"I haven't hunted with my dad in years. And it's not like we ran over things and then went back and picked them up." April's eyes dart to the carcass.

"You went from soccer balls to a dead animal? That takes commitment." I shake my head as if I feel sorry for her. "You had to drive around and look for it. Then you had to pick it up and put it in your car, drive to school and carry it in here. Personally, I would've puked. Did you put it in a bag, at least?"

People in the hall start whispering and April looks around, frantic. "It wasn't me! I put the soccer balls in your locker. I admit it. Are you happy now? But I don't know anything about a note, and I did not touch that *thing*." She points at the flattened rabbit.

As much as I can't stand April, I don't think she did it. But I'm not sure if Dylan was involved.

Dylan points at Christian. "I bet you put it in there yourself so you could come over here and start shit or get April in trouble."

Christian's eyes cloud over. "What did you just say?"

"*You heard me.*"

Christian lunges at Dylan and slams his back against the lockers. Dylan throws a hook and catches Christian in the jaw, stunning him just enough for Dylan to slip out of Christian's grip.

"Fight!" someone shouts.

Dylan plows into Christian, but he has trouble moving the linebacker more than a few feet.

"Heads up, Cameron. Here comes the cavalry," Owen says, watching four tall guys sprint down the hallway toward them.

Cam drops the dead rabbit and cracks his neck. "You take the two on the left."

"No. I'll take the two on the right. Beck Johnson wrestles," Owen says. "If he gets you on the ground, you're screwed."

Cam cusses under his breath. "I'm gonna get benched."

Christian and Dylan hit the floor, and within seconds they're grappling in the middle of the hall. Dylan is taking a beating.

"Get off him, Christian!" April shrieks.

"Peyton, get out of there," Owen yells.

April scurries out of the way, and I head in the same direction. She seems like she knows the drill.

The tall guys, who look like basketball players on Dylan's team, don't say a word before they start swinging.

Cam leans forward and charges. He catches the two around their waists and tackles them. The other two go straight for Owen, but they hesitate. "We don't want any trouble, Owen," one of them says.

"Then walk away, Beck," Owen says. "It will be hard to defend your title as state wrestling champ if you can't wrestle."

The other guy isn't as smart as the wrestler. He moves to the side and tries to sucker punch Owen.

Owen blocks the punch with almost no effort, grabs the basketball player by the back of his neck, and slams the guy to the floor.

"Teachers!" someone yells, and students scatter.

Owen grabs Christian by the back of his shirt and hauls him off Dylan. "Your coach is coming."

Christian points at Dylan. "We're not done."

Dylan scrambles to his feet. His nose is bleeding all over his Warriors basketball T-shirt, and his face is red and blotchy.

Owen walks up to Dylan and stops in front of him. Even though the basketball player is a head taller than Owen, he shrinks back.

The football coach and another man wearing a Warriors warm-up jacket call out names. "Rollins! Carters! Law!"

Owen takes a step closer to Dylan. "If I find out that you had anything to do with this, or you knew anything about it, I'm gonna break my rule about only fighting guys with my level of training. And I'm going to come after you."

Dylan swallows hard.

"And if anything *else* happens and I find out that you have anything to do with *it*, I'm gonna come after you again. And we'll see how well you play basketball with two broken arms. You and your boy Beck can share a hospital room."

Owen steps back just as chaos erupts.

The football coach is yelling at the top of his lungs. He shoves Dylan's friends toward one side of the hall and Cam toward the other. Cam looks fine, but the other two guys who went after him didn't fare as well.

"Christian Carter!" Coach shouts.

The coach wearing the warm-up jacket lays into the basketball players.

Owen turns toward me.

"Not so fast, Mr. Law." Miss Ives marches down the center of the hall with her hands on her hips. "I think you should stay right here while we sort this out."

CHAPTER 31
Handsprings and Happiness

THE HALLWAY FIGHT earned Owen, the Twins, and Dylan and friends three weeks of morning detention—a disciplinary action the principal cooked up as a way to keep the Twins on the football field. The possibility of detention must not worry April, because she had the guts to mess with my locker again. This time she left a note taped inside with a message written in huge letters: GO HOME. NO ONE WANTS YOU HERE.

Whatever.

April can write all the notes she wants as long as she doesn't put anything gross in my locker. I didn't mention the note to Owen or the Twins. The last thing they need is more detention.

Coming to the football game tonight wasn't my idea. Cam guilted me into it with, "Don't you want to come support me and Christian and Grace?"

Well played.

Grace is my only girlfriend in Black Water, and her spot on the cheer squad means everything to her. So unless I want to hang out at one of her practices, which would involve unnecessary exposure to April and Madison, the only time I can watch her perform is at a football game.

Christian and Cameron bugged me to come, too, so I'm killing two birds with one stone.

The home team side of the stadium is packed. I spot Miss Ives sitting near the front, wearing a Warriors jacket and a blue scarf.

The cheer squad is already on the field, hyping up the crowd. April is front and center, gesturing and issuing orders.

Tucker stands up and waves at us from the middle of the bleachers. There are two empty spots next to him.

"Looks like Tucker saved us seats," Owen says, moving aside so I can walk in front of him.

"That's weird, considering I didn't decide to come until a little while ago." I feel Owen's fingertips touch the small of my back as he walks behind me, and my spine tingles.

"I guess he was hoping." The flirty way he says it makes it clear that Tucker wasn't the only one.

I peek over my shoulder at Owen. "You don't even like football."

He glances at the stands. "I thought that was our little secret."

"We're starting to have a lot of those." I make my way up to where Tucker is sitting at the end of the row.

"I knew you'd end up coming." He grins and scoots over.

"I'm being supportive."

On the field, the band plays a new song and the cheerleaders move into position, fanning out to form the shape of a star. April is the front tip of the star. She claps three times, and the rest of the girls snap to attention. The routine consists of lots of marching, jumping, and pony-tail tossing. But I have to admit, the stunts look difficult and each girl's movements are perfectly synchronized.

"They're good," I say.

Tucker leans forward and watches. "Just wait. They haven't even gotten to the stunts yet."

"He's got a crush on Natalie Wynn." Owen reaches behind me and messes up Tucker's hair.

Tucker looks around as if he's worried someone might have over-heard. "I don't. We're just friends."

"Who's Natalie?" I ask.

Owen points at the field. "The brunette. Third from the left, in the front row."

"Isn't she the girl from the cafeteria?" The one Coach picked to go find Dylan's basketball coach. The poor girl was so embarrassed.

"That's her," Owen says.

Natalie is pretty. She looks younger than the other girls on the squad. I nudge Tucker with my shoulder. "She's cute."

He blushes and shakes his head. "I *don't* have a crush on her."

"Whatever you say," Owen teases.

When the band hits the chorus, all the cheerleaders rush to the center of the field and begin assembling a pyramid. The taller girls on the squad form the base. Another group forms the second tier. The cheer-leaders waiting to take their places boost up the other girls. Grace is the last cheerleader to join the pyramid. The two girls on the tier below Grace link hands to form a platform for her. Grace stands, her arms stretched out in a V.

"She's so high up." I bite my bottom lip and hold my breath.

"Relax," Owen says. "She does this all the time."

I curl my fingers around the edge of the bleacher. Owen takes his hand out of his pocket and casually places it next to mine. I love the way it feels when he touches my cheek or his fingers brush mine.

Secretly, I'd love to hold hands with him whenever I want.

The girls supporting Grace toss her in the air. I hold my breath and tighten my grip on the bleacher and Owen slides his fingers between mine.

Grace does a flip and lands perfectly.

The girls under Grace toss her into the air again, higher this time.

I squeeze Owen's fingers between mine, and he rubs his thumb back and forth across the side of my hand.

Grace does another flip and then a half twist. The girls form a net with their arms and catch her.

I exhale, but my heart rate doesn't return to normal. I'm not sure it's possible with Owen holding my hand.

The cheerleaders break down the pyramid in reverse order, beginning with Grace. As each tier disassembles, the girls from that tier finish with stunts. When the girls at the bottom do handsprings across the field, the crowd applauds.

Owen slides his hand off mine so we can clap, too.

"I don't know why April is the team captain," I say. "The whole routine builds up to the pyramid and Grace's big finish. Without her, they'd just be a bunch of girls doing cool flips and back handsprings."

"True," Owen agrees.

"That's why the flier is so important," Tucker explains.

If Grace has a key position on the squad, why is she worried about April leaving her out of their routines?

"What if Grace was sick or something? Could one of the other girls fill in?" I ask.

Tucker steps on the end of the skateboard at his feet and catches the top with his hand. "Not unless there's another flier on the squad. Bigger schools usually have at least two. Black Water had two fliers last year, but the other girl graduated."

"So without Grace, the squad would be screwed?"

Tucker nods. "Pretty much. And they've won the state finals two years in a row. The group stunt is a big part of that."

Grace must know the importance of her position. Why does she put up with April's crap?

"Do you have sisters?" I ask Tucker.

He gives me a weird look as he passes his board back and forth from one hand to the other. "No. Why?"

I try not to smile. "You know a lot about this stuff for a guy who isn't on the cheer squad and doesn't have any sisters—or a crush on a cheerleader."

Tucker stifles a smile. "Okay, maybe a little one."

"Another takedown by Cameron Carter!" the announcer shouts through the loudspeaker.

On the field, Cam springs to his feet, freeing the player pinned beneath him. Christian and Titan rush over and take turns shoving Cameron, grabbing the front of his helmet, and shouting at him—universal signs of approval in the language of football. I'm not interested in the sport, but watching my cousins play is impressive.

"I wonder what it's like to be that big." Tucker steps on the end of his skateboard again. When the front flips up he reverses the sequence, doing it over and over, the way some people pace or twirl their hair.

"Lots of girls don't like big, overdeveloped guys," I tell him. "They usually spend more time in the gym than they do with their girlfriends."

"Is that so?" Owen asks. He's almost the same size as the Twins.

"That's what I've heard."

Tucker grins and steps on the board again. "You're coming to the party after the game, right?"

Owen waits for my answer.

"Whose barn are we going to this time?" I ask.

"This is way cooler," Tucker explains. "It's at an abandoned grain mill outside of town. It was shut down two years ago when the new grain processing plant opened in Black Water. A mill isn't really good for anything else, so the place has been empty since then. It's the kind of place urban explorers are always trying to find. Half wrecked and full of rusty machinery."

"And people throw parties there?" In DC, the police would be all over a spot like that, and the party would last five minutes. "Won't someone hear the noise and call the cops?"

"Nobody ever goes back there," Owen says. "One side of the building is condemned."

"Why didn't you say so? That makes it so much more appealing."

Owen leans over and brings his mouth so close to my ear that his breath tickles my neck. "I can think of a way to make it even more appealing. Come with us."

He must know what he's doing to me.

The fact that Owen wants me to go makes me happy and scares me at the same time. I shove him away playfully. "I'll think about it."

Tucker looks at Owen. "That's girl code for yes."

CHAPTER 32
Urban Explorers

BATTERY-OPERATED LANTERNS ARE scattered throughout the main section of the huge factory. Metal skeletons of abandoned machinery create a dangerous maze, and the place smells like a cross between wet newspaper and a petting zoo.

"It stinks in here." I scrunch up my nose.

The Twins sniff the air like bloodhounds.

"Smells okay to me," Christian says.

Cam shrugs. "Me too."

"It's rot, from the residue in the machines," Grace explains.

"Oh, *that* smell. That's normal." Christian surveys the room. "Let's find the keg."

Grace follows him, with Cam glued to her side.

Owen and I hang back with Tucker, who is watching the door intently.

"Are you waiting for someone?" I ask.

Tucker looks behind him, as if he thinks I'm talking to someone else. "Me? No."

Owen tries not to laugh and ushers us in the direction where Grace and the Twins went.

"So what do you think?" Tucker asks. "It's cool, right?"

"Yeah. But I see why it's condemned." We pass what looks like a rusted printing press. "I should've gotten a tetanus shot."

"The condemned section is on the other side." Tucker drops his skateboard and lets it roll ahead of him before he hops on. "It's not that bad. Just be careful where you walk."

The mill has a creepy steampunk vibe. I've never been inside any kind of factory before. I don't put a lot of thought into how things are made, unless it's soccer gear.

The truth? I thought mills were obsolete in general. In DC and Maryland, factories are clustered together in industrial parks. People don't build them in the middle of the woods.

"Why would someone leave all this machinery behind?" I ask. "Isn't it worth something?"

"Most of this equipment is outdated, like this place," Owen says. "It was probably cheaper to leave it here. A country singer from Nashville was going to buy the place and turn it into a bed and breakfast. Then the northeast section of the building collapsed during a big storm and the singer backed out."

I hear laughter and see more lanterns glowing in the next section of the building.

"Tucker." Owen waves him over and Tucker hops off the board. "Stick with us or the Twins. And stay away from the condemned side. Okay?" He's treating Tucker like his kid brother.

"Got it."

Owen touches my waist as we walk through a dimmer section of the mill.

Grace and the Twins are just ahead of us, and they stop when they hear Tucker's skateboard.

"Come on," Christian calls from where he's standing near a huge machine. "Everyone is back here playing Bullshit."

"No one can come up with a new drinking game?" Grace asks.

Christian shrugs. "You know what they say: Don't fix what isn't broken."

Cam watches Grace and his brother without saying a word. It's not like him, but he's been preoccupied since we left the game, tracking Grace's and Christian's every move.

On the other side of the rusty machine, people are sitting on crates around a makeshift table, playing cards. Titan is pouring beers from the keg behind him. April is perched on Dylan's knee, nuzzling his neck and whispering in his ear, and Madison is hanging out by the keg, flirting with another basketball player.

The game has already started.

Tucker rolls in on his skateboard and Titan looks up from his cards. He flashes me a crooked smile that would pass for sexy if I didn't already know that he was full of himself. He turns his attention back to the game and calls out, "Bullshit."

"Your funeral." Dylan picks up some cards from the discard pile and flips them over so they're face up. "Like I said, two eights."

"You know what that means!" someone shouts.

"No excuses and no do-overs," a girl teases.

"When have I ever asked for a do-over?" Titan hops off the crate.

"Where is he going?" I ask Grace.

"He has to go down to the condemned section of the basement and bring something back up with him to prove he didn't chicken out."

"But that part of the building collapsed." My stomach churns. I don't like it in here. It feels too cramped.

"I know. It's stupid," she says. "But people never get sick of playing it."

"Keep my seat warm," Titan says, grabbing a can of beer. He jogs to the far corner of the room and ducks through an open doorway.

He went down there.

I try not to think about it, but I can't stop watching the door and imagining this place falling down around us.

After nine minutes, Titan still hasn't returned. I seem to be the only person worried about him getting crushed if the building collapses. I can't stand the guy, but I'm not sure how much more of this I can take.

A figure bursts through the basement door.

Thank god.

Titan holds up a long pipe over his head. "I've returned! Don't try to rush me all at once, ladies."

"How do we know that's really from the basement?" Dylan asks. "You could've found it on the stairs."

Titan's lips form a hard line. "Are you saying I'm lying?"

Dylan doesn't respond right away. He's either stupid or looking for a beatdown. "It's part of the game. You've gotta have proof."

Titan makes a sweeping motion from one end of the room to the other with his hand. "You see any other pipes lying around here, genius?"

He's right.

"It's dark," another guy says. "Who knows?"

One of the cheerleaders struts over to Titan. "Don't get worked up, y'all. I'll settle this." She examines the pipe like a museum curator and says, "It looks legit," without providing any explanation.

Dylan seems satisfied. I hope he realizes that cheerleader just saved his ass.

April is standing behind Dylan with her arms crossed, and she looks annoyed. But she's not paying attention to the game—and, for once, she isn't staring at me. Her attention is focused on Christian and Grace, who are whispering and laughing a few feet away from me.

Christian leans against the wall, looking down at Grace, who is at least a foot shorter than him. Truthfully, they just look like they're talking. They're not hanging all over each other. But I doubt Cameron or April see it that way.

Cam is sitting on a crate at the makeshift table where everyone is playing Bullshit, and he has an unobstructed view of Christian and Grace. He slams a beer, crumples the plastic cup in his hand, and tosses it onto the floor.

"Your cousin looks pissed," Owen says.

"I know."

Cam motions for one of his teammates to hand him another beer, and he slams that one, too.

"I'm gonna grab a beer," Owen says. "Can I get you one?"

"No thanks." I'm watching people play a drinking game that involves scavenging crap in a condemned building—there's no way I'm drinking tonight.

"I'll be back." He smiles at me, then heads for the keg.

I'm so focused on Cam that I don't notice when Owen sits down on a crate around the table until he calls out to my cousin. "Cameron, are you gonna play with us or what?"

Cam tears his eyes away from his brother and refocuses on the game.

"What the hell is Owen doing?" It was rhetorical, but Tucker answers me anyway.

"He's trying to keep your cousin from killing someone." Tucker flips the front of his board back and forth.

But what if he loses and he has to go into the basement? Did he think about that?

It's probably filthy and dusty—the worst possible conditions for someone with asthma. Not to mention the fact that it could collapse at any second.

Christian puts his hand on the wall and shifts position so he's standing in front of Grace and her back is against the wall. He has her boxed in with his arms, and it almost looks as if he's leaning in to kiss her. But I'm standing off to the side, and from my vantage point, I realize he's just whispering in her ear.

Unfortunately, Cameron and April don't have the same angle. Cam stares at them, wide-eyed. Then his face falls, and he pounds another beer. If April wasn't standing at the table, I'd just go over there and tell Cam that it's not how it looks.

The conversation stirs around the card game.

"Bullshit," Titan calls out. "Let's see those cards, Owen."

I hold my breath. Owen flips over his cards from the top of the discard pile. "Three sixes."

Thank god.

Titan looks annoyed. Now that Owen is playing he's taking the game more seriously.

"Titan already went down to the basement once," says a perky cheerleader.

Owen points at the beer in front of Titan. "Then start drinking."

"Drink!" everyone shouts while Titan chugs it.

Two girls wander over from behind the tanks. I've never seen them before, which doesn't mean much. But they look older, closer to college age than high school. They're checking out the guys. I'm relieved when they look past Owen and focus on Cameron instead.

"Do you know those girls?" I ask Tucker.

"Nope. They're probably from West Valley, or they graduated from there. It's a lot bigger than our school."

The girls whisper and do a double take when they see Christian. With all the giggling they're doing, you'd think they had never seen a set of twins before.

Christian still has one arm up against the wall, but he moved to the side, giving me—and the girls—a clear view of his profile. The two girls stroll in Christian's direction. He stops talking midsentence and looks over at them. The tall redhead wags her fingers at him in a sexy wave. He tips his chin at her in acknowledgment and smiles.

Grace's shoulders sag as she watches the exchange. She turns her back on Christian and walks away. But he catches her arm.

The redhead and her friend snicker at Grace's reaction, which is not okay with me. I walk toward them, and just before I pass by, I veer to the left as if I'm going to plow right into them. It startles them both, and the redhead yelps.

"Oh, sorry. I didn't see you," I say in a sickeningly sweet tone.

The girls back off, but they linger.

"Come on, Grace. Don't be mad," I hear Christian say. He reaches for Grace's arm, but she snatches it away.

"If you're going to flirt with other girls, the least you could do is wait until I'm not standing right in front of you. But that would require you to notice me in the first place."

Christian frowns and scratches the back of his head. "What are you talking about? I always notice you."

She laughs. "You pay attention to me when you're in between girl-friends, Christian. Or when there's no one else around for you to flirt with. I'm tired of being your backup."

"You're not." Christian looks completely baffled. "I don't under-stand where this is coming from."

"That's the problem. If you paid any attention, you'd know. I'm tired of playing stand-in until you get back together with April or you find a new girlfriend." Grace storms away and walks right past me.

April smirks. "Trouble in paradise?"

Grace stops walking and turns around to face her nemesis. "Do you ever get tired of being such a bitch?"

Nobody in the room moves.

I'm not even sure anyone breathes.

Everyone is in a state of shock—including April. It takes her a moment to recover. Then she turns into a pit viper. "I don't know, Grace. Do you ever get tired of chasing a guy who has zero interest in you? I mean, if Christian was going to ask you out don't you think he would've done it by now?"

Christian bristles. "Oh, hell no."

He starts toward Grace, but I step in front of him and block his path. "Don't."

"Good luck at the state championships without a flier," Grace tells April as she walks away.

"Grace, wait," Christian calls after her.

I step in front of him and block his path so he can't follow her. "Leave her alone. She needs some space."

Christian scrubs his hands over his face. "I don't understand what the hell just happened. Why is she mad at me?"

"Are you serious right now?"

"Yeah. Why?" He's clueless.

"Maybe you should have listened to what she said."

I don't notice Cameron until he's only a few feet away.

"What did you do to Grace?" Cam shoves Christian so hard that he staggers.

Christian regains his balance and gets in his brother's face. "What's your problem? Are you trying to get your ass kicked?"

Cam laughs. "I don't know. Do you have someone to help you?"

The Twins shove each other back and forth.

Owen drops his cards and jumps over a crate to get to them before they kill each other. Titan and the other guys on the football team rush over just as Cameron throws a punch. Owen catches his arm, and the Twins go ballistic.

"You think you can take me?" Christian shouts.

"Any day of the week, and twice on Sunday," Cam says.

Owen and the football players try to run interference, but they have their work cut out for them.

I'm worried about Grace.

I leave the mill through the same door we came in, but I can't see anything. I forgot how dark it is outside. I take one of the lanterns near the door and look around. There's nothing else out here except grain silos. She probably went back to the car.

"Grace? Are you out here?" I hold up the lantern and turn around slowly, hoping to see her.

The wind rustles the leaves on the ground, and a branch snaps behind me. I whirl around, the lantern swinging back and forth in my hand. "Grace?"

The tiny hairs on the back of my neck stand on end.

Someone is out here.

You're imagining things. Stop being paranoid.

I take a deep breath and turn back to the parking lot, holding the lantern out in front of me.

Another branch snaps.

A figure moves between the trees, not far from where I'm standing.

I tighten my grip on the lantern, and the light shakes in front of me.

"Grace?" I try again. Suddenly, I feel stupid. It's probably April and Madison trying to scare me. "Whoever is out there, stop screwing around. You're pissing me off."

I scan the darkness, but nothing moves.

Maybe April sent Dylan out here? I don't think he's smart enough to find his way around in the dark.

There's another blur of movement in the shadows, and I jump. Am I close to the parking lot? I'm not sure.

But I know someone is watching me.

CHAPTER 33
Quicksand

THE SOUND OF leaves crunching starts again in a rhythmic pattern, like footsteps.

"Peyton, are you out here?" Owen calls from the darkness.

I'm so relieved to hear his voice that I can barely speak. "Yes."

Owen touches my shoulder, and I flinch. He ducks his head so he can look at my face. "You don't seem okay. What are you doing out here, anyway?"

I take a deep breath and fight off the panic. "I came out here to look for Grace. I thought she might have gone back to the car. But it's so dark that I got turned around, and I couldn't figure out where we parked."

I'm not sure if I want to tell Owen the rest. "Before you came out, I thought I heard someone following me. That's why I freaked a little."

Owen slides his arm around my shoulders protectively. "Did you see who it was?" There's an edge in his voice.

"No. It was probably just April trying to scare me."

Owen rubs the top of my shoulder. "April was inside. She was still there when I came out to look for you."

"Maybe it was Madison. Or Dylan. He'd do anything April says."

"They were both inside, too." Owen's expression hardens. "It could've been someone from East Valley. The football teams are rivals. Not as bad as Spring Hill, but it could've been one of the players trying to start shit."

My stomach feels queasy. I don't like the idea of anyone following me, for any reason.

The sound of another branch snapping startles me. More leaves crunch—louder this time.

Owen whips around and steps in front of me. But when the figure comes into view, I immediately recognize his gait.

"Hey. Have you guys seen Grace?" Christian asks.

I step out from behind Owen. "No. I was looking for her. I think she might have gone back to the car."

Christian trudges past us. "I'm gonna go find her. I guess I messed up again."

Owen takes my hand as if it's something he does all the time. "Come on. Let's go back inside."

"No thanks. I'm not interested in watching you and Cameron take stupid risks."

Owen seems confused. "You mean the game? It's no big deal. We play all the time."

I slip my hand out of his and wrap my arms around myself. "Did it ever occur to you that you could get killed? If that part of the building caves in . . ."

I can't say it.

"That's not gonna happen. The building has been like this for years."

"Now you're a structural engineer?" I ask, frustrated. "That part of the building is condemned for a reason. If it's unstable, the roof could cave in. Someone could get trapped down there, or worse."

An image flashes through my mind—a dirt ceiling crumbling over my dad's head—and I shudder.

Owen notices and starts to take off his jacket. "Are you cold? You can have my coat."

"No, I'm fine."

"I didn't realize the game bothered you so much. I won't play. I'd rather hang out with you anyway. Come on. I want to show you something cool."

"What?"

"You're not good at surprises."

I pout. "Fine."

Owen leads me around the side of the building to a crumbling concrete staircase that leads down to a padlocked metal door.

"I'm not going in the basement. Did you miss the whole conversation we just had?"

He walks down two steps, our joined hands stretched out between us. "All the damage was on the north side of the building."

"Are you sure?"

"One hundred and ten percent. A bunch of newspaper articles came out about it. They had inspectors here and everything." He shoves his hand into his pocket and pulls out his phone. "Want me to look it up?"

"No. I trust you," I say without thinking about it. "I mean . . . I believe you. But what's worth seeing down here?" I'm imagining a dark basement full of more rusty machinery. "There are probably rats."

"I'll protect you from the vermin." Owen grins. "I protected you from the bears, didn't I?"

"Fine." I follow him down the steps. "But if I see a rat, I'm gone."

"Deal." He reaches the second-to-last step and jumps down.

I notice the padlock again. I sigh dramatically. "Oh well, I guess we can't go in."

"I just need a minute."

Owen hunts around near the door and holds up something.

"Is that a rock?"

"That's what the millionaire who invented these wants you to think." He slides a panel off the bottom of the rock.

It's a Hide-A-Key. We had one for our garage when I was a kid.

Owen holds up the key. "Behold."

He unlocks the padlock and takes it off the door. "You know I did that to impress you, right?" His tone is playful, but there's also something serious about the way he says it.

"I'm impressed you found the plastic rock."

He grins and pushes his shoulder against the heavy metal door. It opens slowly and makes an awful scraping sound. "I can't wait for you to see this. Nobody knows about it but me."

Owen keeps talking, but I'm not listening anymore.

On the other side of the door, a tunnel stretches out in front of us.

Metal walls rise up from the cracked concrete floor. The ceiling is standard elevator height, and the tunnel is wide enough for three people to walk side by side.

Owen steps inside and turns back to look at me. The moment he sees my face, he realizes something is wrong.

"I can't go in there." I'm shaking my head back and forth, over and over, and I can't stop.

He rushes back to me and cups my cheek with his hand. "What's wrong? You look like you're going to pass out." He touches my forehead as if he's checking for a fever.

"I can't go in there," I repeat. It's only the second time I've said it out loud, but the words keep repeating over and over in my head.

Owen looks back at the tunnel. "Are you claustrophobic? It's okay. It's not that far. And I'm gonna be with you the whole time."

I can't find the words to explain what's wrong.

He takes my hand. "Maybe if you close your eyes, I can walk you through."

I don't know if that actually works for people with claustrophobia, since I'm not one of them. I don't know if they can feel how close the walls and the ceiling are, even with their eyes closed. I feel it all. And I'm not even in the tunnel yet.

"If you don't want to try, it's okay." Owen touches the side of my face.

I don't want to feel this way every time I walk up to a football stadium with the wrong type of entrance or an underwater exhibit at an aquarium. I don't want to see rocks and earth raining down on my father, crushing him, wondering how long he stayed alive.

Did he suffocate? Or try to dig his way out?

How long did he survive under there?

I'm sick of feeling like a hostage in my own body. "I want to try."

"Are you sure?"

I nod.

Owen takes my hands and he backs into the tunnel one step at a time. The toes of my boots touch the strip of metal that runs across the threshold, and I can't go any farther. My feet feel like they're trapped in quicksand and it's swallowing me inch by inch.

Earth and rocks raining down on me.

"You can do this. I know you can." Owen tugs my fingers gently, but my feet still won't move.

The quicksand rises another inch, and my heart thrashes in my chest.

Owen offers me an encouraging smile.

I wish there was a way to let him inside my head so he would understand why this is so hard for me without me having to tell the story. I never talked about it with Reed. Tess and my mom are the only ones.

But I want to tell Owen.

"I—" My voice wavers. "I'm not claustrophobic. My dad died in a tunnel. His team was under a hotel in Iraq. There was an explosion, and the tunnel—" My voice cracks. "It caved in."

Owen immediately pulls me against his chest and hugs me. "I'm so sorry."

Tears burn my eyes, and I bury my face in his jacket. I choke back my tears, but I can't swallow them all. "I don't know the details, but none of them made it out."

He kisses the top of my head. "It must be hard not knowing."

"I don't want to know. My mom and my uncle have been trying to tell me since the day it happened. But I can't handle it. I already have nightmares."

Owen hugs me tighter. "Maybe what you're imagining is worse than what really happened?"

"Or my version isn't nearly as horrible." I hesitate. "I hate talking about it. My best friend, Tess, is the only person I've ever told."

"What made you tell me?"

I pull away. "I'm not sure."

"You're not sure, or you're scared to admit the reason?" Owen puts his finger under my chin and gently turns my face toward him. He dips his head and kisses me softly. "Why is it so hard to admit you have feelings for me?"

"Because . . ." I try to turn away, but there's nowhere to go. I rake my fingers through my hair and flip it to the side in an unsuccessful attempt to hide my face.

"Are you going to finish that sentence?" He isn't letting this go.

I'm raw from talking about Dad and I can't find a way out of this conversation.

"Because if I admit that I have feelings for you then I'll have to *do* something about them!" I blurt out. "There. I said it. Are you happy now?"

He's smiling. "On a scale of one to ten, I'm at about an eight."

"Stop."

"I can't." Owen's expression turns serious. "If I stop, I'll never find out why you won't give us a chance. What are you so afraid of, Peyton?"

"You don't understand. I can't afford to make any more mistakes. I've already made too many."

"So this thing between us is a mistake?" His eyes search mine. "Because the way I feel when I'm with you feels like the opposite of every mistake I've ever made."

I don't want to admit the truth, not even to myself. But I find the courage to say it.

"Me too."

CHAPTER 34
Battle Scars

OWEN THREADS HIS fingers through mine, and we circle around to the front of the mill. After trying, and failing, to conquer my tunnel phobia and telling Owen about the way my father died, my emotions are fried. I'm ready to get into bed, crawl under the covers, and call it a night.

But not until I find Grace.

As we clear the tangled overgrowth snaking up the corner of the building, I see a pale circle of lantern light in the darkness.

I squeeze Owen's hand. "There's someone near the entrance."

What if it's the person who was following me?

"One of the football players probably came outside to puke."

"Owen?" Tucker calls out.

"Or it's Tucker," Owen says.

"Is that you, man?" Tucker asks he walks toward us.

"Yeah. What are you doing out here alone?" Owen asks.

"I'm not alone." Tucker's lantern light bounces in the darkness. As he gets closer, I make out the silhouette of someone walking beside him—a girl.

The girl steps into the light. It's the pretty cheerleader Tucker has a crush on. What's her name? Nicole? Noelle?

Tucker stands next to her, grinning like the happiest guy on earth. "This is Owen and his"—he catches himself—"*our* friend Peyton."

It sounded as if he was about to introduce me as Owen's girlfriend. I'm sort of disappointed that he didn't.

"I'm Natalie," the girl says brightly. She's wearing Tucker's quilted zip-up jacket, and it's big on her. She looks at me. "You're Grace's friend, right?"

"Yeah. It's nice to meet you."

"I thought you were going to hang out with Christian or Cameron until we came back," Owen says.

"We were, but they're sorta busy," Tucker says. "That's why we were looking for you two."

"Busy doing what?" I'm not sure I want to know.

"Your cousins went looking for Grace. She was sitting in Cameron's truck and when she saw the Twins, she locked the doors. Your cousins were trying to get her to roll down the window and talk to them, but she wouldn't."

"That's when they started fighting," Natalie adds.

"Who? Grace and the Twins?" I ask.

"Just the Twins," Tucker explains. "They were still going at it when I took off to find you."

We follow Tucker to the parking lot.

I hear the Twins before I see them. Christian and Cameron are rolling around in the dirt and punching each other like overgrown kids.

"You're both acting like total jerks," Grace yells from Cam's truck.

"Stay here," Owen grumbles.

Tucker raises his hands and steps back. "No argument from me."

"Be careful," I say.

"Drinking messes with your coordination, and your cousins drank way too much." Owen trudges over to the Twins. He grabs Cam by the back of his jacket and hauls him off Christian.

Cam staggers and looks around, disoriented. He sees Owen, but the way Cam is squinting, I'm not sure he recognizes him. "What the f—"

"Don't be stupid," Owen tells Cam as he drags Christian to his feet. "I don't want to mess up that pretty face of yours, Cameron."

"Owen?" Cam brushes the dirt off his clothes. His forearm is scraped and bloody, but otherwise he looks fine. "Where did you come from?"

"The land of Not Completely Drunk and Stupid," Grace shouts from the pickup.

"Grace . . ." Cam wanders toward the truck, but Owen stops him.

"I'd let her cool off for a while."

I climb into the truck with Grace, who looks angry enough to kill the Twins. "Are you okay?"

"No." Grace crosses her arms.

The Twins start arguing, and Owen shoves them in opposite directions to keep them separated.

I lean across the seat and yell out the driver's-side window. "You're both acting ridiculous."

"I'm sorry, Grace," Christian says.

Grace looks over at me. "Why don't I believe him?"

Grace and I ended up driving Cam's pickup back to Hawk's. The Twins were staying at Titan's, and Cameron didn't want to leave his truck at the mill overnight. Grace didn't seem like she was in the mood to do Cam a favor, but I think she wanted to come hang out and talk.

Hawk stocked the kitchen with some of my favorite foods—powdered doughnuts, Lucky Charms cereal, and chocolate milk. We took the cereal and doughnuts up to my room, and now I'm watching Grace pick the marshmallows out of the box.

Dutch is watching, too. Every once in a while she tosses him some of the crunchy cereal, which she has stripped of marshmallows.

"I meant to tell you earlier, but you were amazing during the cheer routines tonight. I don't know how you let those girls throw you into the air like that."

"I'm used to it." She tosses Dutch some cereal, and he springs to his feet. I've never seen that dog move so fast. "I've been in cheer since I was young. Fliers have to be small and I was always the smallest kid in my class, so it was sort of a given." She pops a handful of marshmallows into her mouth. "After what I said to April tonight, I won't have to worry about cheerleading."

"April won't let you quit if it means risking the squad's chances at the state finals. And even if she didn't care about losing, your coach will."

"You think so?" Grace sounds hopeful. I remember her saying she needs a cheerleading scholarship.

"Just wait until your coach hears that the squad doesn't have a flier. I bet she calls you in to her office and asks you to come back before the end of the day on Monday."

Grace smiles. "It's nice to have a real friend looking out for me."

I break a doughnut in half and pop a piece into my mouth. "Maybe you want to tell your real friend what's going on between you and Christian?"

"Nothing, I guess. One minute it seems like he might actually like me, and then the next minute he's flirting with other girls right in front of me. This isn't new. It's been going on for years. And I know what you're thinking. If he liked me, he would've said something by now."

"I didn't say that."

"But it's true. I just didn't want to see it. After tonight, I can't pretend anymore." She crosses her legs and twists the frayed threads on the bottom of her jeans. "And I feel awful about dragging Cameron into this mess."

Is that what she thinks happened? "Nobody dragged Cam into it. He went after Christian on his own."

Grace hugs her knees. "Cam feels like he has to protect me."

"I don't think that's it." I can't say more without betraying Cam's confidence.

Grace falls back on the bed. "Talking about me is depressing. I want to hear about you and Owen. Please tell me there has been kissing."

I cover my face with my hands and groan. "There has and it's only making things harder."

"What things? It sounds like everything between you two is going perfect."

I don't believe in perfect anymore—not perfect days or perfect relationships. But I have to admit that when I'm with Owen it feels pretty close.

I fall back on the bed next to Grace and I stare at the ceiling. "Have you ever made a mistake that you can't forget about no matter how hard you try? And you just don't want to make it again?"

"What kind of mistake are we talking about? I've made lots of them."

"The kind that involves dating a guy for seven months and finding out that he wasn't the person you thought he was." It feels good to finally say it out loud.

"I've never had a boyfriend for longer than a month, so that's a *no*. But it sounds awful." Grace is quiet for a moment. "What happened?"

"I'm not sure if I'll ever know for sure. My ex, Reed, changed while we were together. I didn't even notice at first. My dad died a little less than a year before Reed and I started dating, and I was still a mess. Reed helped me through it. He didn't get upset when I was distant or preoccupied, which was most of the time."

"He sounds really sweet."

"That's why it was so hard when he changed." I rest my chin on my knees and try not to think about how much I've lost in the last year and a half. "Reed is an MMA fighter, like Owen."

"No way."

"Trust me. I know." It still seems crazy when I think about it. "Reed is really serious about MMA. It's his whole life. He's a year older than me, and after he graduated last year, he started competing and training other fighters full-time. He was obsessed with making it into the UFC."

"What's the UFC?" Grace asks.

"It stands for Ultimate Fighting Championship. They organize most of the big pro fights on TV."

"Your ex must be really good."

"He is, but he was so obsessed with getting on the UFC's radar and going pro that he started cheating."

Grace twists her shiny black hair around her finger, hanging on every word. "Isn't there a ref watching the fight the entire time?"

"Not that kind of cheating. Reed was taking performance-enhancing drugs." Every time I think about it, my stomach ties itself into knots. "Reed was using steroids, which is prohibited in MMA, like it is in most sports. I didn't catch on right away, but based on the changes in Reed's behavior, I think he was using for at least two months before I finally figured it out."

"I'm sorry. That must have been so hard." Grace breaks the last doughnut in half and hands me a piece. "How did you find out? Did he tell you?"

"I found the drugs in his gym bag."

"Seriously?"

This is my opening.

If I chicken out now, I might never tell her and I want Grace to know. But it's harder than I expected.

"Finding his stash wasn't the worst part."

Grace doesn't ask any more questions. She waits until I'm ready to tell her the rest.

"We were at a party, and I went out to Reed's car to look for something. That's when I found the drugs. So I confronted him. He admitted the steroids were his, but he refused to stop doping, so I broke up with him."

Bits and pieces of my conversation with Reed flash through my mind. . . .

I was going to stop after the fight.

A couple of months . . . that's all I need.

After the tournaments I've got coming up. I'll stop. I swear.

You have to choose right now—me or the drugs.

This is the hard part. "Reed refused to accept the fact that I was breaking up with him. He got angry and flew into a rage." I take a shaky breath, picturing the scene. "People talk about 'roid rage, but I didn't really understand what it meant until that night. Reed turned into a different person. It was like he was a stranger."

"What did you do?" Grace's voice is a whisper.

There's no way to prepare her for what I'm about to say next. I can't find the right words. It's too painful and ugly. "Remember when I said I hurt my knee falling down a flight of stairs? I left something out. Reed pushed me."

Grace's eyes go wide and tear up. She points at my brace. "That's how—?"

"Yeah." Seeing Grace on the verge of tears triggers the same reaction in me. I press the inside corners of my eyes and take a deep breath to hold them back.

"Did you press charges against him?" she asks.

"No."

"Why not?" she blurts out. "Oh my gosh. I'm *so* sorry. I'm not judging you. I just hate that guy for hurting you."

"Don't feel bad. It was a hard decision, and the situation was complicated because Reed's sister is—I mean, she was—my best friend. Tess loves him so much. I just couldn't do that to her." *And look how it turned out.* "But I wanted Reed to pay for what he did to me. So I reported him to his trainer instead. I knew if Reed wanted to keep competing, he'd have to submit to a drug test for PEDs. It's league protocol. I thought he'd test positive and his trainer and his mom would get him help." I close my eyes to keep from crying. "But that's not how it turned out."

Grace scoots closer to me. "What do you mean?"

A tear runs down my cheek and I wipe it away. "Reed figured out how to beat the test and the results came back clean. He had already convinced people that I was *confused* about what happened the night of the party. He said he never pushed me—that he was just trying to grab my arm when I started falling. The test results made it look like he was telling the truth and a lot of people believed him—including Tess."

"People believed him?" Grace demands.

"Enough to call my house and threaten me." This part of the story doesn't seem as dramatic in my head. But it's hard to describe how much it hurt to have everyone doubt me.

How much it still hurts.

"That's why my mom sent me here to stay with my uncle. The threats really freaked her out, and Reed kept calling and showing up at our house. . . . It was too much for her."

"Does Owen know about any of this?"

"No! I don't want him to feel sorry for me or treat me like I'm fragile, on the verge of breaking."

"I'd never say anything to him," Grace says calmly. "You can trust me."

I nod and take a deep breath.

"Now I understand why you're not sure if you want to get serious with Owen. After all that, I'm surprised you didn't swear off dating altogether."

"I did." But I wasn't expecting to meet someone like Owen.

"But you like Owen," Grace says as if she understands. "Are you worried about letting things get serious with him because he's a fighter, like your ex?"

"It's not that." I tell her exactly how I feel without worrying about how it will sound. "I'm scared to get close to him because I don't trust my judgment and I can't afford to make another mistake." My eyes flicker to the brace strapped around my leg. "Look at what the last one cost me."

What I don't say is the other thing I'm thinking.

There's no "letting myself get close" to Owen. I'm already close to him. If that's a mistake, it's too late, because I've already made it.

CHAPTER 35

Unraveling

TODAY I ASK Owen to take me through my exercises *before* I hit the pool. I need to burn off some energy—at least that's what I'm calling it.

Watching Owen through the gym window while I'm in the pool is becoming more unbearable every day. The tension from being so close to him and seeing the way he moves in the ring has me wound so tight that I can't think about anything else when I look at him.

I've never met a guy who affected me this way—a guy I wanted this much.

I've wanted guys to kiss me before, but I want Owen to *touch* me— every inch of me. And I want to touch him.

I didn't feel this way with Reed. We slept together, and it was good. But not mind-blowing, tension-inducing good. I never lost track of a conversation because I was daydreaming about Reed's hands all over me.

I know it would be different with Owen.

I'm standing at the end of the pool, staring at the water and imagining *how* different, when an old lady in a flowered swim cap clears her throat. "Are you using the lane?"

I snap out of it. "Yeah. Sorry."

I adjust the strap of my black one-piece and quickly braid my hair. My eyes dart to the glass wall, out of habit. Usually, Owen is working out or sparring in the ring.

Not today.

He's standing in front of the window, watching me.

And it's so incredibly hot.

A rush of heat burns down to my core. I should smile and act casual, or jump in the pool—anything except stare at him like I want to take off his clothes.

"Miss? Are you getting in?" the lady asks impatiently. "It's bingo night at church, and it's my turn to spin the wheel."

Bingo night breaks the spell, and I ease into the pool, painfully aware that Owen is probably still watching.

"I'm sorry," I tell her again. "I won't be long."

Cutter graduated me from walking to swimming laps, which cuts down on the amount of time I can spend drooling over Owen.

A swim class finishes, freeing up the other lanes. Now it's just Bingo Lady and me. I count my strokes, anything to distract me from the window. But I'm getting tired faster than usual.

Bingo Lady finishes before me and rushes off to spin the wheel.

I steal a look at the window.

The gym is empty.

Owen and I are often the last ones to leave, but I don't see him. He wouldn't take off without telling me. I check the clock on the wall. No wonder I'm tired and the gym is empty. I swam twice as long as I normally do.

I pull myself out of the pool. Water drips down my legs, and I lean to the side and wring out my braid, leaving puddles behind me as I head for the showers.

The entrance to the women's locker room is next to the glass door that leads to the gym.

Owen pushes it open and walks toward me without a word.

My heart throbs at the sight of him—his broad shoulders and muscular chest, his intoxicating brown eyes, and full lips that beg to be kissed. He picks up my striped towel as he passes the chair where I left it, stops in front of me. He holds the towel between us, our toes almost touching. "Hi."

"Hi." I should feel self-conscious standing here, dripping wet, in nothing except a bathing suit. But I don't.

Owen opens the towel, slips it around my waist, and uses the ends to pull me toward him.

My chest touches his, and the thin layer of wet fabric between us emphasizes how little clothing we're both wearing.

My fingers graze his waist as my hands slide down and rest above his hip bones. "I'm dripping on you."

"You can do whatever you want with me, Peyton. Just don't break my heart." His tone is sexy and playful, but there's a hint of seriousness, too.

The gym door opens behind him.

"Hey, Owen? I need a favor." It's Charlie, the guy who works at the front desk. "It's bingo night over at the church and nobody brought the doughnuts. Y'all are the last ones here. Any chance you can lock up for me when you leave? The older folks get real upset if there aren't any doughnuts."

"No problem," Owen says without taking his eyes off me.

Charlie waits for Owen to turn around. But Owen doesn't move.

"All right, then. I'll leave the keys in the boxing ring," Charlie says. "How about that? Just toss 'em in the mail slot after you lock the front door. I've got another set at home."

Charlie rushes back out the glass door and through the gym.

Owen and I are alone—as in the only people in this building.

His eyes glaze over. "You are so beautiful."

Owen touches my lips with his, but he doesn't kiss me. He just brushes his lips over mine, back and forth, until I can't catch my breath. He pulls the towel tighter, and I feel how much he wants me.

I slide my arms around his neck and tilt my head to kiss him.

He pulls back so our lips barely touch, teasing me.

"Kiss me, Owen. Please." I run my finger down the back of his neck and continue the path along his spine.

When I reach his shorts Owen's mouth crashes into mine. Firecrackers explode inside my chest as his tongue slides into my mouth. The kiss is hungry and impatient, and I don't want it to end. He tries to move down to my neck, but I recapture his lips with mine.

My skin is burning up from the heat building inside me, but I'm still soaked and I shiver.

Owen brings the towel up around my shoulders and nuzzles my neck. "You're cold."

"I'm fine."

"Let's go inside. You need to change out of this thing." He hooks his finger under the strap of my bathing suit.

I don't want to change, or do anything that involves being any farther away from him than I am right this second. "Only if you come with me."

Owen draws back and looks at me. He's trying to figure out if I meant it the way it sounded. "Only if I get to carry you." He leans close to my ear. "You don't know how crazy it made me when I saw you in Titan's arms, in the hallway."

"That wasn't my choice."

"I know." He cups my face in his hands. "But when I touch you, I want to know that it's your choice."

"Owen? Will you take me to the locker room?"

"I'll do whatever you want, Peyton. Haven't you figured that out by now?" He bends down, scoops me up in his arms, and carries me into the women's locker room.

It's dark except for the safety lights plugged in along the baseboards. In the corner, two chairs and a sofa are arranged like a sitting area in a department store.

It's colder in the locker room, and my teeth chatter.

Owen notices. "You *are* cold."

"I'm okay."

He carries me to the counter, where clean towels are stacked next to a basket of body lotion, brushes, and Aqua Net hair spray. "Grab some towels."

"Why?"

He kisses the top of my head. "Don't be stubborn."

I pick up a few towels with a huff, and Owen carries me to the sitting area.

"It's warmer over here," he says, gently lowering me down onto the sofa. He kneels on the floor in front of me and wraps the towels around my body.

"I feel like a burrito."

"You look like a burrito. A pretty burrito." He looks around. "Where's your locker? I'll get your clothes."

I tug on his shorts so he'll come closer. "I'm warm now. I don't need clothes." *That came out wrong.* "Other clothes."

"You can't stay in a wet bathing suit."

"Maybe . . ."

He wraps his arms around my waist. "What?"

"You could warm me up?" It sounds like a bad pickup line.

Owen searches my face.

I lean forward and kiss him, and his uncertainty disappears. He reaches inside the towels and wraps his arms around my waist. My pulse pounds faster than before, as if my body was just waiting for him to pick up where he left off.

He slides my bathing suit strap off my shoulder and kisses his way up my neck. Then his hands drift lower. He traces a path along my collarbone. When his fingers brush over the wet fabric covering my chest, another rush of heat makes me shudder.

"Come here." I lie back slowly, keeping my arms looped around his neck so he follows. The towels are tangled around me, and Owen tugs at the one wrapped around my waist and lowers his body between my legs carefully, so he doesn't lean against my knee.

He runs his hand along my body slowly—down the side of my breast to my waist, then farther south to trace the edge of my bathing suit. My body reacts in ways I've never experienced before.

His hand lingers at the boundary. "Is this okay?"

"More than okay."

He slips his hand under the material, and I gasp.

Oh god.

His touch is gentle—slow and deliberate.

I can't think.

Owen holds himself up with one arm, and from this angle his face is directly above mine.

I tug on the other strap of my bathing suit. "Take it off."

"That's not what this is about. I wasn't trying—"

"I *want* you to take it off."

"Are you sure?" He touches my cheek. "I don't want to hurt you."

I realize what he means . . .

He thinks I'm a virgin.

Why am I surprised? It's the classic double standard. Guys can sleep with as many girls as they want, but girls are supposed to save themselves. But I'm not double standard compliant.

I push up onto my elbows. "I'm not a virgin. Sorry to disappoint you."

"I was talking about your knee."

Oh, right.

"Sorry."

"It's okay. I love the way you say whatever you think. Come here." He slides his arm behind my back, supporting my weight, as I loop my arms around his neck again.

I nip at his neck and work my way up to his ear, tracing the curve with my tongue. "I love this," I whisper, letting my tongue slide into his ear.

"Shit, Peyton." He groans. "What are you doing to me?"

Owen pulls down my bathing suit strap, leaving a trail of kisses in its place. He seems surprised when I slip my arms out of the straps. He looks down at the wet fabric clinging to my chest and watches the material inch lower when I inhale. He shifts between my legs, and every muscle in my body tenses.

He groans again. "You feel so good, Peyton. I want—" He hesitates. "We should stop."

I look up at him. "What were you going to say before that?"

He shakes his head. "Nothing."

"You said you wanted something." I slide my hand between us and rest my palm against his stomach below his belly button, my fingers teasing. My hand drifts lower, and he sucks in a sharp breath.

"Tell me what you want, Owen."

"I want to know what you feel like." He brushes his thumb between my legs. "Here."

My breath catches and I bite my lip. "Owen . . ."

He brings his mouth to my ear. "I want to know what it feels like to be inside you."

The words hum through my body and I ache for him. "That's what I want, too."

Owen pulls back to look at me. "Are you sure? Because—"

"I'm sure."

"Shit." He buries his face in my neck. "We can't. I don't have anything."

He means protection. "Not even in your wallet?"

"My wallet is at home. I forgot it this morning."

"Wait." I start to sit up, and my head hits Owen's chin. "Sorry."

"I'm okay." He rubs his chin.

"I think I have something in my purse. In the locker." I point down the hall.

Owen springs off the sofa. "What number?"

"Two ten."

He bolts around the corner and I hear a crash.

"I'm okay," he calls out.

I barely have time to catch my breath before he returns with my purse and my knee brace. I motion for him to hand me my bag. I lean over the front of the sofa and dump everything out on the floor. Owen sits next to the mess and watches me scatter the contents of my purse until I find the black pouch.

I hope it's still in here.

"I found it!" I hold up the black foil packet.

Owen grins at me.

"What's so funny?"

His eyes dart to my chest. "Nothing. I just like the view."

I look down. I forgot to pull up the straps of my bathing suit before I leaned over, and I'm giving him an eyeful. "I hope you like the rest of the view just as much."

Owen is still sitting on the floor, and he wraps his arms around my waist. "Is that a joke? I think *the view* is gorgeous. You are gorgeous. Every inch of you."

Not every inch.

Without thinking, I put my hand on my knee to cover the scars.

Owen slides his fingers between mine and moves my hand away. Then he plants a soft kiss on each of the four scars around my kneecap. "*Every* inch of you."

He eases me back down on the sofa and puts a pillow under my knee.

"It's fine. Come here." I tug on the waistband of his shorts.

"Hold on." Owen reaches down and picks up something.

"I am *not* wearing my knee brace the first time we're together." This is so embarrassing.

"For me? Please?" He kisses my neck. "I won't be looking at your knee. Trust me."

"You seriously want me to wear it?" He nods and I roll my eyes. "Fine."

Owen slips it on carefully and fastens the straps. He props up my leg and wraps my other leg around his waist. "I'll make you forget you have it on."

His eyes travel down my body, and I'm aching for him all over again.

He leans forward, still holding my leg around his waist, and kisses me slowly. He traces the top of my bathing suit, grazing my breasts with his palm. "Can I help you take this off?"

"Mm-hmm." Suddenly, I realize how *much* of me Owen is about to see. It's dark in here, but not that dark.

He starts by peeling down the top of my bathing suit. When it reaches my waist, he pauses to look at me. I close my eyes as he works the suit down farther. Down my hips and thighs. Over my legs. The damp bathing suit hits the floor, and I feel his smooth skin as he slips off his shorts. He leans down and kisses my stomach, working his way up to more sensitive areas.

"Peyton. Look at me."

I open my eyes and Owen's face is directly above mine.

"Are you sure about this?"

"Positive." I hold up the foil packet. "Wait. Do condoms expire?"

This one has been in my bag since I was fifteen. Mom gave it to me after she read an article full of statistics about teens and sex.

"Everything expires," he says. "But they're good for a long time."

"Define a long time."

"A few years maybe? They don't have a ten-year shelf life like Twinkies, if that's what you're asking." He takes the packet from me and points to a spot near the bottom. "You have to check the expiration date."

Probably something I should've known about my "just-in-case" condom.

I squint and read the numbers. "It's good for another six months. And the Twinkie thing is an urban legend."

Owen rips the packet and I stop talking, my body humming with anticipation. His mouth hovers over mine, and I tug on his bottom lip. He makes a sexy rumbling sound in his throat and lowers himself between my legs. When he's close enough for me to feel how much he wants me he stops. I wait to feel the pressure of his body against mine.

When he doesn't move, I tug on his waist, urging him the rest of the way down. Tension pulses in my belly—and everywhere else.

I want him so bad.

He traces a line from the curve of my breast to my hip bone.

"Owen, please . . ." I squirm underneath him and he almost gives in.

"You don't know many times I imagined this. How it would feel to be this close to you." His voice is deeper now and thick with desire. "How it would feel to touch you."

He slides his hand between my legs, and my whole body shudders. "I thought about it, too. All the time. I wanted you to touch me."

"Is that what you want now?" His fingers continue to tease me and I can't think.

I shake my head. "No . . . I want more."

Owen can't hold back any longer.

Our bodies collide, and I feel every part of him.

It feels *too* good, like he memorized a map of my body and he knows every inch of it by heart. The push and pull between us creates the perfect rhythm. The intensity builds and sensations I've never experienced ripple through me over and over.

I moan. "Owen . . ."

"I love it when you say my name."

Another wave of bliss rolls over me, and I'm unraveling.

It's happening to Owen, too. "Peyton."

It's the last thing I hear before we come undone.

"Peyton?" Owen whispers. "Are you awake?"

Of course I'm awake.

I can't fall asleep naked on the sofa in the locker room at the YMCA. But if he thinks I'm sleeping why is he trying to wake me up?

What if he's about to give me the *just friends* speech that I've given him so many times?

Oh god. What if he regrets . . .

I stop myself.

Owen isn't that kind of guy.

My little voice is right about that much.

He brushes the damp hair away from my face and kisses the top of my head. He thinks I'm sleeping.

"If I had you . . . maybe I would do it," he murmurs.

What's *it* and why would I have anything to do with his choice? I focus on the other part—

If I had you.

CHAPTER 36
A Tiny Crack

AFTER THE EPIC night at the Y, a little over a week ago, Owen and I settle into a routine. English class together with lots of flirting and lunch in the library if I can dodge the Twins. Those are my favorite times. We talk about everything and nothing. Sometimes we sit in the stacks and hold hands. Other times we do homework together like a regular couple.

Since we slept together, Owen hasn't pushed about dating or giving him a shot. We both know that's what we're doing. Part of me wishes he would bring it up, because my answer would be different now. At the same time, things feel right—the kind of right that isn't forced. The kind you ease into.

The only downside to sleeping with Owen is that I want to do it again. But that requires being alone—a lot more alone than you can get in the library. So when he texts me and asks if we can go to the movies and *somewhere else*, I can't think straight for the rest of the day.

The Twins seem extra suspicious when they get home from practice. Cam knocks on my door three times to borrow three different supplies he needs for his homework, which makes no sense because he does most of it in class. He's actually really smart—something I'm sure he doesn't want his football buddies to know.

Christian, on the other hand, is less stealth. While I'm getting ready, I hear him pacing in the hallway.

I finally get sick of waiting for him to knock, and I open the door. "Did you want to come in?"

"No, why?" He looks around like he thinks I'm talking to somebody else. "I'm just walking."

"You've been walking out here for fifteen minutes. Are you sure you don't need something?"

"I'm just worried." Christian leans against the wall.

Christian, worried? About what?

Cam comes out of his room. "What's going on?"

"I was just telling Peyton that I'm a little worried," Christian says.

Cam nods as if he knows what we're talking about. I'm glad someone does. "We're both a little worried."

"About?"

"This thing with Owen," Cam says. "I know you said you two are just friends, but—"

"We don't want to see you get hurt," Christian says.

"Owen is . . ." Cam clears his throat and Christian jumps in. "Owen is a complicated guy. He has a lot of stuff going on."

"Like what?" He goes to school and the gym, and competes. That's it, as far as they know. But I'm not about to enlighten them.

316

"He's not going to college," Christian says. "Did he tell you that? He's taking off right after graduation. He's going backpacking around Europe or something."

"And?"

"Do you really want to get involved with a guy who is just going to take off?" Cam asks.

"I'm only here until March," I remind them. "If Owen and I decided to get involved, the fact that he's going backpacking around Europe in the fall wouldn't factor into the equation."

"Wouldn't you feel bad if he was gone and you'd never see him again?" Christian asks.

Cam glares at his brother.

This conversation is too weird for me. "I don't know what you two are up to, but I'm getting dressed."

"Where are you going?" Christian asks.

I give him a stern look. "Not that it's any of your business, but Owen and I are going to the movies. Is that okay with you?"

"The movies sounds like a date." Christian looks to Cam for confirmation. "Right? That sounds like a date."

Cam nods. "Yeah, it does."

"If you're so interested in dating, maybe you should find a girlfriend, Christian," I say.

He crosses his arms and frowns. "I don't want a girlfriend. I had a girlfriend. She was a pain. Worse than a pain. Why do I have to get a girlfriend just because you're going to the movies?"

"You don't have to find a girlfriend because I'm going to the movies, just like I can go to the movies *without* having a boyfriend."

"If you don't want a girlfriend maybe you should stop leading Grace on," Cam mumbles.

Christian looks at his brother like he's crazy. "Where the hell did that come from? Me and Grace are friends. She knows that."

"And you don't like her more than a friend?" I shouldn't get involved in this, but I'm happy the conversation has shifted away from me.

"I don't know." Christian rubs the back of his head. "Why are we talking about this?"

"I agree with Cam. You're sending Grace mixed signals. You're always flirting with her, but then you claim the two of you are just friends. It's confusing."

"Confusing for who?" Christian asks.

"For everyone," I say.

"Maybe what you and Owen are doing is confusing," Christian fires back.

Nice one.

"I need to finish getting dressed." I wave my fingers at them and close the door.

I scroll through Owen's texts from the past few days. Sweet, flirty, attentive—the kind of messages a boyfriend would send. And my responses have *girlfriend* written all over them.

It's time to get real and tell him that I'm ready to take a chance and see where this goes.

Tonight.

I wear my hair down and decide on jeans and a soft gray sweater layered over a stretchy tank.

Owen texts when he's on his way and I start getting nervous. How am I going to tell him that I changed my mind about our just-friends status?

I think we should give things a try? That sounds awful.

I really like you? A lot? More than a lot? That's worse.

I'm still wrestling with my options when the doorbell rings. I rush downstairs and open it.

Owen smiles at me. He's dressed in jeans and a flannel with the sleeves rolled up—the kind of shirt that's super soft and perfect for cuddling.

"Hey. You look great," he whispers.

"You look pretty good, too."

"Did you pick a movie?" he asks as he comes inside.

"I was thinking we could skip the movie."

He leans close to my ear. "Did you want to spend some time in the women's locker room?"

I shove him and laugh. "I want to talk."

"Hmm. Now I'm curious." He hooks his thumbs in the pockets of his jeans and looks down at me. "I want to talk to you about something, too. Then we can hit the women's locker room."

"Hey, Owen," Christian says. He's standing at the top of the stairs, watching us. It's annoying and creepy at the same time.

Owen tips his chin at him. "What's up?"

That's when Cameron turns the corner at the landing. The Twins exchange conspiratorial looks. Now they're both watching us.

Christian clears his throat. "This thing going on between you two . . . It's a bad idea."

For a second, I think he's joking.

"We're just going to the movies," Owen says.

Cam walks halfway down the stairs and stands below Christian. "It's nothing personal, Owen."

Who do they think they are?

I turn on the Twins. "What the hell is wrong with you two? We're going to the movies, not eloping."

"You've been spending a lot of time together. Things can happen," Cam says. "You can end up having feelings for someone that you weren't expecting."

"Are we talking about me, Cam?" I ask pointedly. "Or you?"

Cameron looks away. "I'm just saying that sometimes feelings sneak up on you."

"And if they did, would it really be that bad?"

Christian watches Owen, who hasn't looked up once.

Why is Owen so quiet? I bet he's trying to stay calm so he won't lose it and pummel my cousins. I've never seen him so uncomfortable. He looks lost—the same way he did the day I saw him sitting in the car with his mom before school.

"You don't want to get attached to him, Peyton," Christian warns. "Trust me."

"Trust *you* to give me dating advice? That must be a joke. You don't even have the guts to tell Grace that you're not interested in her. Are you just going to string her along until she leaves for college? Or are you planning to keep her around as a backup for holidays and summer break?"

Christian scowls. "You can give me shit me if it makes you feel better, but it won't change anything. Getting involved with him is a mistake."

"Why, Christian? Is he a serial killer? A bank robber? What's so terrible that I can't handle?"

"I think we should go," Owen says softly.

I keep my eyes fixed on the Twins. "No. I want an answer. Is this about Owen being a fighter? Because I don't care."

"It's not about that," Cam says. "We just don't want to see you get hurt."

"You already said that, and I'm not a child. I can make my own decisions."

Owen gives the Twins a pleading look. "I would never hurt her."

"Maybe not on purpose," Christian says.

"Then what's the problem?" I yell.

Cameron curses under his breath. "You can't get attached to him because—"

"Because what?"

"He's gonna die," Christian blurts out.

For a second, I can't make sense of the words. "What do you mean, *die*?"

Christian slumps against the wall. "Sorry, Owen. But she's our cousin."

I look at Owen, but he won't make eye contact with me. "Owen?" When he doesn't say anything, I turn back to my cousins. "Is this about his asthma?"

The Twins look at each other, and Cam says, "Owen doesn't have asthma."

"You're wrong. I saw him have an attack."

Owen finally looks at me. "I was going to tell you, Peyton. I swear."

"Tell me what?" A strange feeling comes over me. This is how glass shatters. It starts with a tiny crack, and the pressure causes it to splinter.

"Owen, do you have asthma?"

He stares at the floor. "No."

It feels like someone punched me in the gut, and I reach for the door to steady myself. "You lied to me?"

"I was going to tell you."

"Tell me what? I don't even know what we're talking about."

"I have a condition," Owen says.

"Like a disease?" *What if it's cancer?*

"No. It's a genetic condition. I was born with it. I didn't know until two years ago." Owen looks at me like he knows what he's about to say will crush me—and destroy us both.

"Something is wrong with my heart . . .

"I could die tomorrow."

CHAPTER 37
Heartache

AFTER OWEN LEAVES, the world collapses around me.

He lied to me.

He lied to me and he might die.

Someone knocks on my door. "Peyton? It's Christian."

"Go away."

"I wanted to see if you were okay. Do you need anything?"

"Not from you."

I walk into the bathroom and turn on the shower full blast. Maybe that will get rid of him. I don't want to know why Christian and Cameron kept Owen's condition a secret, or how much they know about it. The Twins should have told me.

The real question is why didn't I figure it out myself?

How did I miss the signs?

Again.

The night I found Owen in the locker room after the semifinals, I should've realized he wasn't telling me the whole story. Why didn't I ask more questions?

What's wrong with me? Is something inside me broken?

I've always relied on my instincts—on and off the field—and they've never led me astray. Until Reed.

Did he screw up more than just my knee?

And if he did, how do I fix it?

Suddenly, I'm panicked. I want somebody to tell me it's not true. I almost call Lucia, but what would I say? *I fell for another guy who was lying to me and I had no clue.*

I can't do it.

I curl up on the bed and listen to the voice mail from Dad that I saved on my phone. Hearing his voice makes me cry all over again, but it also reminds me that I'll be okay.

After I listen to Dad's message for the third time, I put my phone on the nightstand. Every few minutes it vibrates.

Owen alternates between calling and texting me. I let the calls go straight to voice mail and I don't respond to his texts. But I still read them.

> **I screwed up. I'm sorry.**

> **Please call me.**

> **I want to explain.**

> **I should've told you.**

I'm an idiot. But I can't lose you.

You mean so much to me.

I send Owen one text before I crawl under the covers and go to bed.

not enough for u to tell me the truth.

I hit send and turn off my phone.

At school the next day, I avoid Owen.

At the end of first period, I pretend to feel sick and I spend second period in the health room, which gets me out of English class. The Twins run interference, even though I'm barely speaking to them. After school, I skip PT.

Now I'm in my Tennessee bedroom, where I've been holed up for hours.

My cell phone rings, and I check the number before I answer. The list of people I'm not speaking to keeps growing.

It's Grace.

"What's up?"

"Promise you won't hate me?" she asks. When a friend leads with that question, it's never good.

"Why would I hate you?"

"Well . . ." She stalls. "I sort of told Owen that I'd give him a ride to the fight tonight. He cornered me after cheer practice and asked if you were okay. Then he hit me with all these questions: 'Does Peyton hate me? Will she give me a chance to explain? Do you think she'll ever forgive me?' It was awful. I wanted to change the subject, so I asked if he was nervous about his big fight."

The regional championship.

"Owen said he didn't have a ride because his trainer was coming straight from UT. Maybe he'd take the bus or hitchhike. He looked so miserable. So I offered to give him a ride. He was going either way. I didn't want him to go alone. I'm sorry."

"It's fine." But it's not. If there's something wrong with Owen's heart, he probably shouldn't be fighting at all.

"I have to pick up Owen and Tucker in thirty minutes. I just wanted to tell you before I left."

"Come get me. I'm not letting you and Tucker go by yourselves. You've never been to an MMA fight."

"Are you sure that's a good idea? You're not even speaking to Owen."

"And I'm not going to start now. Just pick me up."

"Okay." Grace hesitates. "I'll be there in a few minutes."

By the time I change and get downstairs, the Twins are already standing by the front door, wearing their letterman jackets.

"Are you two waiting for someone?" I ask.

"Grace is picking us all up," Christian announces. "We're coming, too."

"What do you mean? How do you even know about this in the first place?"

"I know everything that happens with Grace," Christian says.

Cam glares at him. "What he means is that Grace told me. I talked to her right after you did."

"We're not letting you two go to some wrestling match alone," Christian says.

"It's not a wrestling match. It's an MMA championship fight."

Christian waves me off. "Close enough."

"What makes you think I want to be stuck in the car with you two?" I'm still hurt, and this is the most I've said to my cousins since they outed Owen.

"You probably don't." Christian keeps his eyes trained on the floor. "We're just gonna have to keep telling you we're sorry."

"And we'll try to find a way to make it up to you," Cam adds.

"What if I still don't want you to come?" I ask.

"We're coming either way." Christian's mind is made up.

"Fine." I sound like I'm in sixth grade again.

Grace honks, and the Twins follow me outside.

I pause by the front door when I realize Owen and Tucker are already in the car. Owen gets out and holds the passenger door open.

Christian heads straight for the front seat.

"Shotgun," Cam says.

I catch up with them and settle the argument. "I'm sitting in the front."

Christian and Cam pile into the back seat with Tucker, which doesn't leave much room for Owen. But he squeezes back there, too. I feel him watching me, but I try to ignore it.

"Scoot over." Cam elbows his brother.

"There's nowhere to go," Christian complains. "I'm bigger than you."

"Don't start that crap again," Cam says. "You're not bigger than me. You just take up more room. Maybe it's your ego."

"My ego? What are you talking about?" Christian snaps. The tension between the Twins is getting worse.

"How come the four of us are crammed back here when I have a truck?" Christian grumbles.

"I think you mean I have a truck," Cam says.

Christian waves him off. "Whatever. Same difference."

"If I remember correctly, you two weren't supposed to be coming," Grace points out. "So if you want a ride, don't complain."

"Peyton, will you talk to me?" Owen pleads.

"I don't have anything to say."

"But I do. I'm sorry for lying. I didn't know how to tell you."

Christian clears his throat. "It feels like I'm watching a sappy scene in a chick flick, but I can't pretend to go to the bathroom so I can hang in the lobby until it's over."

"Nobody gives a shit what you think, Christian," Cam barks. "Everything isn't about you. They're trying to talk."

"We're not talking." I don't want to be in the car with Owen any more than I want to watch him fight. But I'm also terrified that the fight could trigger another attack.

What would've happened if I hadn't been there the night I found him in the locker room struggling to breathe? Or if I had waited in the car fifteen minutes longer before I decided to go inside and look for him?

I can ignore Owen, but I can't turn off my feelings for him.

I stare out the window while Grace drives, and the Twins bicker and complain about the radio station—and each other. Tucker talks to Grace and Owen and I stay quiet.

We finally make it to the arena. This building is a lot bigger than the one where the semifinals were held. When Grace parks, I'm the first one out of the car.

As I walk toward the main entrance, I feel Owen watching me. I'm so aware of him, even now. Part of me wants to forgive him, but it would only make things harder.

Now that I know about Owen's heart, nothing can happen between us. I can't let myself fall for a guy who's putting his life at risk all the time. Losing my dad was hard enough. I can't imagine losing a friend, or . . . I don't even know what to call Owen.

Owen catches up with me. "Peyton. Can I talk to you for one second?"

I shake my head, keeping my back to him. "You need to concentrate on the fight tonight. You don't need to worry about me."

"I'll always worry about you." He's next to me now.

Cutter and Lazarus are waiting for him by a side entrance.

Thank god.

It's probably my only way out of this conversation.

"I'll talk to you afterward," Owen says, as if we were having a real conversation.

I keep my eyes on the door and keep walking.

Cam jogs up next to me. "You okay? Don't lie."

"No." I sigh. "But it doesn't matter."

Cam opens the door for me. "Listen. I know Christian and I weren't happy about the idea of you dating Owen, but it's not because he's a bad guy. You said you didn't want to date a fighter, and—"

"He's gonna die?" I cut in. "I'm quoting you."

Cam pulls out his wallet as we walk up to the ticket window. "We just didn't want to see you get hurt. But we shouldn't have told you the way we did."

"I think what you meant to say is that you shouldn't have kept it secret from me."

"Yeah. That too." He crams some money under the window. "Five tickets, please."

"Twenty-five bucks." The woman counts the crinkled bills, then slides the tickets under the partition.

Christian, Grace, and Tucker catch up with us, but it's too crowded for all of us to walk next to one another, so they fall in line behind Cam and me.

"I'm sorry we didn't tell you. But we gave Pop our word that we wouldn't tell anyone," Cam says.

"Are you saying Hawk *told* you to lie to me?" I can't handle another betrayal.

"Not just to you. To everybody."

"I don't understand."

Cam glances back at Grace and Tucker and lowers his voice. "Owen's dad was a piece of shit. He made your ex seem like a Boy Scout. After Owen was diagnosed, I guess things got really bad between his parents. Pop and Owen's mom were friends in high school, so she came over to ask him for advice.

"Christian and I were eavesdropping and we overheard Owen's mom talking about his heart condition. Later on, when we fessed up to Pop, he lost it. He made us give him our word that we wouldn't tell anyone."

"So Owen didn't tell you himself?" I ask.

"No way. Owen was mad when he found out we knew. And we never told anyone—not even Grace."

Maybe Owen was telling the truth when he said that I was the first person he'd ever wanted to tell.

"And I'm sorry you're miserable," Cam adds. "It seemed like Owen made you happy. So I guess I'm wondering if the fighter thing is such a big deal."

I choke out a laugh. "It doesn't matter if it's a big deal anymore. We're done. You understand that, right? There's no going back. He didn't just keep his heart condition a secret from me. He lied to me about it. He told me he had asthma."

Cam maneuvers halfway in front of me to shield me from the crowd. "I don't know why he lied, but it must be hard to have a condition that serious."

"I don't want to talk about this." I swallow hard. It feels like there's always a knot in my throat. Everything about this situation sucks. After the nightmare with Reed, I thought something positive was finally happening in my life.

We enter the main arena. The cage is set up in the center of the room. Green rubber-coated chain-link encircles the octagon-shaped mat, rising up around it like walls, and then curving to form a dome. It reminds me of the enclosure for the birds of prey at the zoo.

This venue is larger and less run-down than the arena where the semifinals were held. It has newer seats, a fresh coat of paint on the walls, and concession stands that sell more than hot dogs and beer. But this place is packed and people are sweating, so it reeks as bad as the other arena. The majority of the spectators are men, drinking beer from plastic cups.

We find our seats. Tucker and Grace are excited because we're sitting in the front row.

Grace points at the cage. "Those are Owen's coaches inside the fence-thingy, right? You mentioned one of them was a woman."

"The fenced-in area is called a cage or an octagon," I say.

"Cutter—the woman—is Owen's head trainer, but Lazarus works with him, too. Tonight he's here as Owen's cutman."

"What's a cutman?" she asks.

"Like in boxing," Tucker says.

"I don't watch boxing."

"A cutman fixes you up between rounds," Tucker explains. "Keeps the swelling down if you get hit in the eye, and stops the bleeding if your face gets busted open so you can go another round. That kind of stuff."

I'm relieved Tucker is doing the talking instead of me.

"If Owen's trainers are in the cage does that mean the fight is about to start?" Grace asks.

"Yeah. In ten minutes if they start on time," Tucker says.

"Why is Owen out here?" Cam nods at an archway on the opposite side of the cage that probably leads to the locker rooms. "Isn't he supposed to wait for them to call him or something?"

"Technically no. That only happens in big-ticket fights. But he shouldn't be wandering around ten minutes before a fight."

Owen looks right at me, and he heads in my direction.

What is he thinking?

"I think he's coming over here," Grace says.

I get up to walk outside, and Owen picks up his pace.

"Peyton, wait." He touches my arm, and I pull away.

"What are you doing out here?" I ask. "You're supposed to be in the locker room getting ready for your fight. Not out here talking to me."

Owen paces in front of me. "I can't fight without talking to you first. There are things I need to tell you."

"Whatever they are, they can wait. You have to get your head in the game." Excelling in a sport requires mental and physical prep.

"You won't take my calls and you dodged me all day at school. How am I supposed to explain if you won't listen?"

I lower my voice. "Owen, this is a championship fight. You can't do this. You've got to focus on the fight, or you could get hurt."

"Don't use my condition against me."

"I'm not using it against you. I'm stating a fact. You shouldn't be in the cage. But if you're going to ignore your doctors' advice, the least you could do is take it seriously." I turn away. At this point, I'm a distraction. "Go back to the locker room. The fight is starting in a few minutes."

"I don't care about the fight," he says.

"Of course you do. Or you wouldn't have lied to everyone."

Owen looks at me the same way he did the morning I saw him in the car with his mom—like he's drowning and he wants me to save him. But I can't, because I'm drowning too.

"That's not why I lied," he says. "You don't know how hard it is. I'm a time bomb without a countdown clock. I have no idea what's going to happen—or when. I just . . . I need you to understand."

"Isn't that sweet," a familiar voice says, and my blood runs cold.

How did he find me?

Reed circles around from behind me, his attention focused on Owen. "But take my word for it, Peyton isn't the most understanding girl out there."

TJ and Billy stand behind Reed like they're his bodyguards.

"Who the hell are you?" Owen demands.

Reed laughs. He looks worse than the last time I saw him. His skin is broken out along his jawline, and he's sweating like he just finished fighting. I wonder how much dope he has in his system.

"Peyton didn't tell you about me?" Reed tries to hide his irritation. "I'm her ex-boyfriend. Which makes *you* the rebound guy."

Owen's shoulders tense.

I want to intervene and say something, but my feet are stuck in quick-sand again. The last time I was alone with Reed, he was standing at the top of the steps after he pushed me. I've imagined seeing him again, and it didn't feel like this.

I know Reed won't touch me in front of all these people, but some-how my fight-or-flight response didn't get the memo.

"This is your ex?" Owen asks.

I try to respond, but all I can do is nod. I can't find my voice.

"Everything okay?" Cam asks as he comes up beside me.

I've never been so glad to see him.

Christian, Grace, and Tucker are trailing behind him. When Grace sees me, she rushes over. "What's wrong? You're totally pale."

"That's him," I whisper.

Her eyes flash to Reed and she stiffens next to me. "Oh my god. What's he doing here?"

Realization hits me.

Reed didn't come here looking for me.

"I'm fighting tonight, sweetheart," Reed says. "It's classic. Ex-boyfriend versus rebound guy."

"Hold up," Christian says. "This is the guy?"

Billy crosses his arms and squares his shoulders, and TJ leers at Grace.

"What guy?" Tucker whispers to Grace.

Reed tries to make eye contact with me. "So you've been telling every-one about me, Peyton? I guess you miss me more than I thought." He has always been cocky, but not like this. I wonder if Tess' big brother is still in there somewhere. I doubt it.

"Yeah. We heard all about you," Cam says, his tone icy.

Owen moves closer to me. "What's going on? Peyton, look at me."

I shake my head.

"She's fine," Grace says, trying to cover for me.

"She's not fine." Owen reaches for me as if he's going to pull me into the safety of his arms.

I want to say I'm fine, even though I'm not. But I can't speak. If I start talking, I'll have to interact with Reed, and this nightmare will be real.

Cam touches my arm. "Let's go. You don't need to talk to him."

"Does someone want to tell me what the hell is going on?" Owen asks.

Reed ignores Owen and looks at me. "It's not too late to come back."

TJ eyes Grace from where he's standing beside Reed. "And you can bring your friend with you. She's just my speed."

"What the fuck did you just say?" Cam's voice comes out as a growl, and before TJ has time to make a smart-ass comeback, Cameron tackles him, fists flying.

Reed smirks and steps out of the way.

"Cameron!" Grace shouts. "Stop!"

The ref sees TJ and Cam grappling on the floor and signals a huge man wearing a yellow EVENT SECURITY T-shirt.

Grace looks at Christian. "Do something!"

"I wouldn't," Billy warns.

Christian's hands curl into fists at his sides. "Or what?"

One fight is bad enough. If Christian and Billy get into it, someone is definitely going to get hurt. But the man working event security shows up before one of them takes a swing.

TJ and Cam are jockeying for the upper hand, but on the ground TJ has the advantage.

The security guard grabs TJ by the shoulder and jerks him back as if he weighs nothing. Cam gets back on his feet and goes after TJ again.

But the huge guy catches Cameron in a headlock. "You need to cut that shit out unless you wanna get hurt."

"Let him go," Christian says.

The giant of a man gives Christian a dismissive look. "I'll let his ass go outside, 'cause they're both out of here." He keeps Cam in a headlock as he walks up the aisle, and he shoves TJ forward with his other hand.

"I'm going to make sure Cam is okay," Grace says. She rushes up the aisle, and I'm left with Reed and Owen, who look like they want to tear each other apart; Christian and Billy, who are squaring off; and Tucker, who looks like he's just trying to stay out of their way.

The ref walks over to the edge of the cage and calls out to Owen and Reed. "You two aren't supposed to be out here. Get in your corners, unless you both want to be disqualified."

I spot Reed's trainer in the corner opposite Cutter, and he signals Reed.

"It was fun catching up," Reed says, looking right at me. "We should do this again after the fight. We can celebrate my championship win."

Billy laughs.

Owen's posture has turned to stone. He might not know exactly what's going on, but he knows something is wrong.

Reed notices Owen staring him down. "Why is he looking at me like I'm the bad guy, Peyton? Let me guess. You told them your little fairy tale about me pushing you down the stairs? Did someone actually believe you?"

CHAPTER 38
The Machine

OWEN DOESN'T MOVE. His gaze darts between Reed and me.

He's putting the pieces together.

Without warning, he lunges at Reed. "Did you hurt her?"

Christian grabs Owen and drags him away from Reed.

Owen reaches over Christian's shoulder and points at Reed. "If you touched her I'll tear you apart!"

My whole body is shaking, and I try not to cry. I don't want to do anything to fuel Owen's rage. Anger blinds a fighter. It has them fighting their demons instead of their opponent.

"Get your fighters in their corners!" the ref yells at Cutter and Reed's trainer.

Cutter exits the cage, and she's on the arena floor before Reed's trainer. She pushes past Reed, bumping his shoulder so hard that he actually moves. He looks impressed.

She marches up to Owen. "I don't know what's going on over here, but you'd better get your ass in that cage right now, or I'll forfeit."

"You can't do that." Owen watches Reed over her shoulder.

"Watch me."

Lazarus surveys the scene from behind the rubber-coated chain-link.

Owen's eyes flicker to me and Cutter turns in my direction. "Peyton? Are you all right?"

Tucker slings his arm around my shoulders, like we're at an eighth grade mixer. He gives Cutter the thumbs up. "She's good."

Reed's trainer finally makes an appearance. "Michaels! Inside!"

Reed smiles at me. "We can talk later. This won't take long."

"I'm gonna take you apart in there," Owen shouts at him.

Reed starts to walk away, then stops and points at Owen. "Second round. That's when I'll knock you out."

"Hey." Cutter snaps her fingers in front of Owen's face to get his attention. "You better get your head straight before this fight starts."

Owen clenches his jaw and watches Reed walk away.

"Look at me when I'm talking to you," Cutter barks. "You need to focus on the fight in that cage, not the one out here. Do we understand each other? We'll figure out the rest after you kick his ass."

"Yeah. Okay." Owen nods, but he's still tracking Reed and his body language hasn't changed. He doesn't seem focused.

"Get moving." Cutter waits until Owen starts walking and she follows him.

Owen enters the cage and walks to his corner, where Lazarus is waiting. Cutter and Lazarus are both talking to him, but Owen keeps looking over at Reed's corner, where my ex appears uncharacteristically calm.

"This isn't good," I tell Tucker and Christian.

"What do you mean?" Christian asks.

"Reed is acting weird. He's too calm. Usually, he's on the offensive from the second he enters the cage. This is the regional championship, and Reed is hanging out in his corner like he's bored."

"Owen will kick his ass," Tucker says. "Right?"

After watching Owen in the ring, I wouldn't have doubted him for a second. But the guy in the cage tonight isn't the same Owen I've watched so many times in the gym. There's nothing calm and calculated about his expression or his posture. Tonight Owen looks like he's running on a dangerous mix of rage and adrenaline.

An announcer enters the cage with a mic and hypes up the crowd.

I try not to look to the right, where Reed's team is getting him ready, but the way Reed is behaving worries me. Billy walks around the outside of the octagon and sits in one of the empty seats in the front row, behind Reed's corner.

I catch a glimpse of the girl next to him, the pale blond hair she never wears down hangs loose around her face. She has her feet on the seat and her arms wrapped around her legs.

Tess looks up and she sees me.

She doesn't give me a dirty look or turn away. She opens one of her hands as if she's going to wave at me. Instead she holds it open like she's pressing it against a window. I hold up my hand, too.

Billy turns to tell Tess something and she lets her hand fall back to her leg.

"Who are you waving at?" Christian asks.

"Nobody."

The microphone crackles and the announcer's voice booms through the arena. "From the nation's capital, Washington, DC, weighing in at one hundred seventy-nine pounds, Reed 'The Machine' Michaels."

Reed holds up his hands and the crowd cheers.

Lazarus rushes over to the announcer and tells him something. The announcer nods and returns to the mic. "And from Knoxville, Tennessee, weighing in at one hundred seventy-two pounds, Owen 'The Law.'"

"Why did he say Owen is from Knoxville?" Tucker asks.

Cutter and Lazarus are watching me.

"Maybe he just got it wrong," Christian says.

No. Lazarus gave the announcer the wrong information on purpose.

The trainers and cutmen follow the announcer out of the cage.

The bell rings, signaling the start of round one.

Owen comes barreling out of his corner, throwing punches, knees, and elbows.

Reed blocks most of the strikes, and he doesn't launch the lethal offensive I'm used to witnessing. He's playing games—letting Owen come after him, blocking punches instead of throwing them, and showboating instead of trying to pound his opponent into the floor.

Reed hasn't shut his mouth since the round started. He knows how to psych someone out during a fight. Intimidation is his specialty. What is he saying?

Round two is a replay of the first round—Owen throwing sloppy combinations, Reed taunting him, and Cutter screaming her lungs out from behind the chain-link. Reed turns up the intensity a minute before the bell—probably trying to make good on his promise to knock Owen out in the second round. Reed throws a jab followed by a right low kick that clips Owen's leg hard. The knockout doesn't happen, but Owen is wearing himself out fast.

Round three and four are a blur of round kicks, slashing elbows, and boxing punches, like hooks and crosses.

I rub Dad's dog tags and wince every time Owen gets hit.

Christian notices. "Don't be nervous. I think Owen is playing your ex so Reed will underestimate him."

"That's not what he's doing. I've seen Owen fight before, and he's better than this." Reed lands two flying knees into Owen's side and I turn away. "He's distracted because of me."

"Can you blame the guy? After what Reed did . . ." Christian can't even stand to say it.

Tucker knows he's missing something. But he also seems to sense that I don't want to talk about it, and he doesn't ask any questions.

Christian shadowboxes as if he's in the ring fighting along with Owen. And even Christian winces when Owen takes a slashing elbow to the forehead that draws blood.

Reed follows the elbow with another jab-low kick combo and lands both.

"Your ex really has a thing for low kicks." Christian wrings his hands in front of him.

"No. This is new. He's trying to take one of Owen's legs out. That would give him a huge advantage."

The bell rings and Lazarus rushes into the cage to try to stop Owen's forehead from bleeding. Cutter goes easy on him. Her mannerisms are more encouraging than critical.

When Owen comes out of his corner for round five, he doesn't look good. His head is still bleeding and his eye is starting to swell shut.

For the first few minutes, Owen concentrates on blocking Reed's attacks. Owen doesn't look steady on his feet. With each punch, Owen appears more and more dazed—and Reed knows it.

Reed backs up, intentionally moving closer and closer to the cage.

I realize what he's doing before Owen seems to, which makes no sense. It's a move Owen should see coming. But he doesn't, and it feels like I'm watching a car accident in slow motion.

I'm out of my seat. "Owen, get out of the way!"

Reed jumps and pushes off from the cage with his left leg and throws a right hook. His fist hits Owen in the temple and Owen goes down.

The crowd goes wild.

"Did you see that Superman punch off the cage?" someone yells behind us.

"Come on, Owen. Get up," I whisper like a mantra.

Owen struggles to get back onto his feet, and he barely makes it up. He sways and the ref starts counting. He leans against the chain-link wall of the cage, still dazed. Then the ref does the unthinkable and calls the fight.

After the fight, Christian waits by the cage with me. I'm hoping Owen will come out so I can try to explain. I never would've wanted him to find out the truth this way. I can't even think about the fight. Owen lost the championship because of me.

"You okay?" Christian asks.

"No." For once, I admit how crappy I feel.

"I can't believe he lost. That's rough. I mean, at least when we lose, I can usually blame it on somebody else."

"It's my fault." I watch the hallway that leads to the locker room.

"Your ex messed with his head. And his friend sure as hell messed with Cameron's." Christian scratches his head. "What the hell was all that about? I mean, don't get me wrong—I want to wipe the floor with those guys, too. But the last few weeks, Cam's been going off the rails."

I watch him, waiting for the pieces to fall into place. But after a moment, it's clear they haven't. Maybe it would be easier for everyone if I told him about Cam's feelings for Grace. Would Christian go ballistic? Or would he understand?

After tonight, I'm not willing to meddle in my cousin's life to find out. But there's nothing wrong with dropping a few hints. "Cam seemed really upset when Reed's friend insulted Grace."

"That's what I mean. I'm usually the one who flies off the handle first. Cam looked like he wanted to rip that guy's throat out. He's definitely pissed off at me about something. He's probably just taking it out on everyone else. The other day in practice, he tackled me so hard I thought I'd knocked one of my teeth out."

"Did you do anything to him? I mean, can you think of a reason he might be so upset?"

Christian frowns and rubs his forehead. "I dunno. Pissing people off is kind of my specialty. He's all over me about everything. My manners, the way I talk to Grace, my moves on the field. Look." Christian nods at the hallway across from us. "Somebody's coming."

It's not Reed. The guy isn't tall enough to be Owen. It's probably Billy.

I rub Dad's dog tags between my fingers.

Please, please don't let Reed come out next.

I'm not ready to face him. I hate him for what he did to Owen, but I also didn't expect my reaction, the way my pulse sped up when I saw Reed, like I wanted to bolt. It felt like I was back at the bottom of the stairs again. Just seeing Reed triggered panic, as if emotions have their own version of muscle memory.

Lazarus comes out of the locker rooms, wringing his hat between his hands.

The moment I see Owen, my heart sinks.

Cutter has her hand on the back of his neck, and he's staring at the floor. I can't see his face, but I know it must look bad. He's wearing sweats, with his hood pulled up.

"They're coming over here."

"Well, we're standing near the exit," Christian says.

I wait for Owen to look up, but he doesn't. Cutter sees me and says something to him. She must hate me. I lied to her, too. And I cost Owen the fight.

Lazarus walks by first and squeezes my arm as he passes.

Cutter gives me a sad smile. "You should go in case he comes out this way."

She means Reed.

"I just wanted to make sure Owen was okay." My voice sounds strange and far away, like it doesn't belong to me.

Owen stops next to Christian and finally looks up at me. I shudder when I see his face. He has stitches above his eye, secured with butterfly tape. His whole face is swollen, and the shadows of bruises are forming along his jaw and cheekbones.

"I'm so sorry."

The look on Owen's face tears me up inside.

"I'm sorry, too," he says. "Guess I wasn't the only one hiding something."

"Come on, kid." Cutter puts her hand on Owen's shoulder and steers him toward the exit. "You need to get home and put some more ice on your face."

"I'm gonna go with Owen," Tucker says.

We watch them leave. Christian slings his arm around my neck. "Let's get outta here. I don't want to see your ex or his loser friends."

I nod and follow him to the car. I'm numb inside.

Cameron is in the front seat talking to Grace, and he gets out when he sees me. "You okay?"

The moment he asks, I burst into tears. "No."

Cam hugs me.

I get in the car and Grace hugs me, too. "We saw Owen across the parking lot. He looked awful—"

"He lost."

Grace hugs me tighter. "It's not your fault."

"Then whose fault is it?"

"It's Reed's. That guy is . . ." She shakes her head. "Sorry. I shouldn't say anything. You were with him for a long time."

"You can say it," I tell her.

"He's a total asshole."

"I second that," Cam says, and Christian adds, "Third."

Grace drives, and it's quiet until my phone rings. My heart leaps.

Please be Owen.

"Who is it?" Grace sounds hopeful.

I check the display. "Unknown caller. That means it's probably Reed."

"Give me the phone." Christian practically jumps between the seats trying to grab it.

I yank the phone out of his reach. The last thing I need is for this situation to get any worse. I answer the phone and immediately hang up.

Within seconds, it rings again and I do the same thing: answer and hang up.

I turn off the ringer, but I still hear the phone vibrate every time Reed calls. By the fifth time, I'm tired of answering and hanging up, so I just let it go to voice mail.

"That guy has some serious problems," Christian says. "You think I could take him in a fight?"

I'm not sure if he's asking Cam or me, but I'm the only one with the answer. "No."

"Why'd you say it like that? You didn't even think about it," Christian complains.

"I don't have to. He's a trained MMA fighter. You're a football player. It's not the same."

Christian scowls. "I fight plenty."

"Not in a cage."

"It might be a nice change of pace if nobody got into a fight," Grace tells him. "You could settle your problems without beating anyone to a pulp."

After Reed keeps calling for twenty minutes, I want to throw my phone out the window. "I have eight voice mails already."

Christian holds out his hand. "Seriously, give me the phone. I'll talk to him. He'll never call you again."

What could Reed possibly have to say that requires eight messages? He's probably gloating.

"What the hell does he want?" Cam asks.

"He's a stalker," Grace says. "Who knows? The guy isn't exactly stable." She glances at me. "No offense."

"I'm not with him anymore. Feel free to insult him whenever you want. I'm going to see why the hell he keeps calling."

I listen to the first message.

"Peyton. You obviously know it's me, because you keep hanging up. I feel bad about beating the shit out of your new boyfriend. Actually, I don't. But I feel bad about making you feel bad. I mean, I just won the championship, and I can't enjoy it because you're not here. If you'd give me a chance to explain, we could work this out. Call me back, or pick up when I call. This whole thing is a big misunderstanding. We can work this out. I love you."

A misunderstanding?

I hang up and lean back against the seat.

"What did he say?" Grace asks. "Is he threatening you?"

"No. He wants to talk so we can get back together." I'm tired of Reed and his manipulative crap.

Grace looks over at me. "You're kidding, right?"

I shake my head and shrug. "No. He had a whole pitch."

"Let me have the phone," Cam says.

"It's an unknown number. You can't call back."

"I want to listen to the messages." Cam motions for me to give him the phone.

I hand it over. "Delete them when you're done."

Christian slides toward the middle of the seat, and Cam angles the phone so they can both listen.

Grace pouts. "I want to hear, too."

"We could put it on speaker," Cam suggests.

"No!" Grace and I shout at the same time.

The Twins huddle in the back seat, cussing and whispering to each other.

"Peyton? How many of these did you listen to?" Cam asks after a few minutes.

"Just the first one. Why?"

"We're on number three. Wait." Cam looks at his brother. "Is he crying?"

Christian nods. "Oh, yeah. He's definitely crying. Or he's faking it. It's hard to tell. I mean, I don't cry, so I'm not an expert. What do you think, Cam?"

"Why are you asking me? I don't cry, either. But it sounds like that's what he's doing."

I lean my head against the window. It's too much.

By the fourth voice mail, Christian and Cameron are perched on the edge of the seat with the phone angled so Grace can hear at least some of the message. If Owen hadn't just lost the championship . . . if he didn't have a heart condition and if I weren't staring at my *RoboCop* brace . . . this might be funny.

"Okay, number six is the best. The best meaning the worst," Christian tells me. "He's playing a song."

"I don't want to know."

"You don't," Grace assures me. "Oh my gosh, you guys. Get that away from my ear. I can't take it."

"I bet he's gonna start singing it himself in number seven," Cam says.

Christian scratches his head. "He might switch it up and play a new one."

"Bet you fifty bucks he sings it himself, whatever it is."

Christian nods. "You're on."

I have no idea what was on message seven—if Reed did or didn't sing, or pledge his undying love—because that's when I break down.

CHAPTER 39
A Different Kind
of Heartbreak

OWEN DOESN'T SHOW up at school the next day. Not that I expected him to after the beating he took last night.

It's Friday and everyone is pumped for the football game tonight. The players are wearing their jerseys and the cheerleaders are dressed in their uniforms. Half the student body is sporting bright blue greasepaint on their faces.

I sit in my classes like a zombie.

My teachers must notice because they leave me alone. The Weasel lets the whole class period go by without calling on me.

After lunch, I get a text from Owen.

Can we talk? Meet me in the library after school.

I watch the clock for the rest of the day.

When the last bell finally rings, I take the back stairwell up to the library. I stand in the hall outside the door for ten minutes before I'm brave enough to face Owen.

He lied to me, but now he knows that I lied to him, too.

But my lie cost him his dream.

What are you supposed to do when the one thing that gave you hope is gone?

The librarian is busy checking in books, and she smiles when I pass her desk.

Owen is waiting in the stacks where we've eaten lunch together so many times. He's sitting on the blue carpet with his back against the wall. His face is cut and bruised and it hurts to look at him.

"Hi." He sees me and the expression on his face breaks my heart into a hundred pieces.

"Hi." My voice is hoarse from yelling at the fight last night. Or maybe it's from crying.

I sit on the floor in front of him—close enough so that nobody will overhear us talking, but far enough away to stop myself from throwing my arms around him.

Owen's knuckles are wrapped in gauze and he pulls the frayed ends. "I'm sorry for what I said after the fight."

"That you weren't the only person hiding something?" My eyes flicker to his face. "Don't be sorry. It's the truth."

"I saw the look on your face when I said it. I hurt you." He frowns and a deep crease cuts between his brows. "You've already been hurt too much."

I inch closer to him, leaving space between us. "I shouldn't have lied to you, but I didn't want anyone to know. After it happened, I felt so helpless. I didn't want to feel that way when I came here."

"That's part of the reason why I didn't tell anyone about my heart. If that makes any sense." He hesitates. "Will you tell me what happened? I need to know."

I close my eyes and nod.

When I open them again, Owen moves over to sit closer to me.

"There isn't much to tell. Reed started doping behind my back and I didn't realize it for months. We were at a party and I found his stash in his car. I confronted him outside. There was no one around. Thinking back on it now that probably wasn't the smartest idea."

Owen takes my hand. "A girl shouldn't have to worry about getting into an argument with a guy if they're alone. You didn't do anything wrong."

"Thanks." It's nice to be reminded. I lean my head against his arm.

"What happened after you confronted him?"

"At first, he said the drugs weren't his. Then he realized that I wasn't buying it and admitted it. He wasn't going to stop, so I broke up with him. That's when he got angry. It was like watching Bruce Banner turn into the Incredible Hulk. Or maybe the Hulk had been there all along and I just didn't see it. He started yelling at me and pushing me."

Owen puts his arm around me and pulls me close.

"There were steps behind me and he knew it." My voice cracks. "He pushed me again and I fell back."

Owen moves in front of me and I wrap my arms around his neck.

"I was so scared." It's the first time I've said those words and the moment I say them tears roll down my face.

"Nobody will ever hurt you that way again." Owen hugs me tighter. "I'm so sorry. I wish I had been there. I'd never let anyone hurt you."

When I finally stop crying, Owen dries my face with the bottom of his T-shirt. "Are you okay?"

"Yeah."

Owen's expression . . . there's something wrong.

"What is it?" I touch his face and he tries to turn away. His eyes are glassy, like he's about to cry. "Owen? Look at me. Are you okay?"

He shakes his head. "He hurt you and I let him get away with it."

"That's not true."

Owen wipes his face on his sleeve. "He was talking so much shit about you in the cage. About how you were so in love with him and you couldn't handle it when he broke up with you."

"When *he* broke up with *me*? He said that?"

Owen takes a deep breath. "I knew he was lying, but I kept thinking about how scared you looked when you saw him, and that crack he made about you telling people that he pushed you. I should've beaten the shit out of him."

He coughs and suddenly all I can think about is the way he looked in the locker room when he couldn't breathe. I cling to him until his breathing evens out again.

I lay my palm on the middle of his chest. "What's wrong with your heart, Owen?"

He puts his hand on top of mine. "I have a genetic defect that causes arrhythmias—abnormal heart rhythms. It's called Brugada syndrome."

"I've never heard of it." Not that I'm up to speed on cardiology.

"It's rare. Before the doctors diagnosed me I had no clue what it was, either. They almost didn't figure it out at all."

"What do you mean?"

"I passed out during wrestling practice. My coach thought I was dehydrated or something. But it happened on school grounds so they sent me to the hospital. The doctors checked me out and ran a bunch of tests. They even did an EKG and it was normal. The cardiologist asked my mom all these questions about our family history. One of them was if anyone in our family had died young, under strange circumstances. We didn't know it then, but that's a red flag for Brugada syndrome.

"My mom told him about my older cousin, who died a few years earlier, at eighteen. He was a swimmer, headed for the Olympics. But he drowned in his pool. They did an autopsy and there was no sign of a head injury, so he didn't hit his head and there were no signs of an aneurysm or a stroke. After my cardiologist heard about my cousin, he did another EKG. I guess they have to look at a specific spot where the lungs and the ventricle meet to know if a person has Brugada syndrome. And I have it."

I'm terrified to ask the next question. "So you could have a heart attack?"

He squeezes my hand. "Worse. I won't go into cardiac arrest at all. My heart will literally stop beating. Unless someone like a doctor or a paramedic happens to be around with a defibrillator and they get my heart restarted—I'll die."

It physically hurts to hear him say it.

Then there's the part he isn't saying.

I've watched enough medical dramas on TV to know that a defibrillator isn't a sure thing. In those scenes, a doctor is usually performing chest compressions on a heart attack victim when the nurses show up with a crash cart. When the machine is charged, the doctor shocks the patient with the paddles. Then she waits.

Sometimes the patient pulls through and their heartbeat zigzags across the monitor. Other times, the patient continues to flatline.

"Are there warning signs? So you can get to a hospital in time?"

"Not always." Owen takes my hand off his chest and traces shapes on my palm—a circle, a star, and finally a heart. "And the symptoms are common stuff like shortness of breath and fatigue, so it's easy to miss them."

A tear escapes and runs down my cheek.

Owen reaches out and brushes it away with his thumb. "This is the reason I didn't tell you—or anyone else. My heart could stop five minutes from now or five years from now. There's no way to predict it."

I hear what he's saying, but it doesn't make sense. Owen is young and healthy. And his heart is just going to stop one day, with no warning?

"But the doctors can fix it, right?" I hear my dad's voice in the back of my head, and I repeat the words he'd said so many times: "Everything can be fixed."

Owen stares at the floor. "Except me."

"What about surgery?"

"There's only one. A surgeon attaches this thing they call a shock box to my heart. It's sort of like a pacemaker, but it works differently. If my heart stops, the box shocks it so it will start beating again."

Thank god there's a solution. "When can you get one?"

"I don't want one."

Is he serious? "Why not?"

"I'd never be able to compete again, or play contact sports, run long distances—"

"So what? You get to live."

"I'm not sure I want to live that way. That's why I'm not having the surgery."

Reality hits me and I finally hear him.

Owen, the guy I'm crazy about—who is only six months older than me—is going to die. And not when he's eighty or ninety or a hundred.

And I'll never see him again.

Like Dad.

I take his face in my hands.

When we slept together, I shared myself with him in ways I never had with anyone else. But I didn't share my heart with him that night.

He already had it.

He had it the moment we became friends—and our friendship is more important to me than anything.

"You can't die, because your mom needs you. Tucker and Cutter and Lazarus need you." I tilt his face toward mine. "I need you."

"I need you, too. But I didn't think about how selfish it was to let you get attached to me."

I cock my head to the side and smile. "Who says I'm attached to you? Maybe I'm just using you for your body."

He pulls me in for a hug. "I'm okay with that."

Owen holds me tighter, as if I'm the life preserver that's keeping him from drowning. He doesn't realize I can't save him—because I'm full of holes and I'm drowning, too.

The bell rings and we head out to the parking lot.

Christian and Cam see us and they rush to catch up, but they hang back and give us some privacy. They've been following me around all day like bodyguards.

"You're gonna be late for practice," I call out to them.

"You let us worry about practice," Christian says.

Owen hitches his thumbs in his pockets. "Are they following you because of me? They don't think I'd ever—because I wouldn't. Never."

Clearly I'm not the only one who thinks my cousins look like body-guards. The last thing I want is for Owen to think it's because of him.

"It has nothing to do with you. They don't think that, and I don't think that. They're worried I'm going to have some kind of breakdown. They were following me around the kitchen this morning, too."

Owen nods. "Good. I mean, not about following you, but I'm glad they know I'd never hurt you. You know that, too, right?"

"I do."

"I wish I'd known you when it happened, so I could've done something. Because I sure as hell didn't do anything in the cage."

"That's not true. Reed messed with your head. You're a better fighter than he is."

"It doesn't matter now. He won. I lost. It's over."

"It's my fault."

"Don't say that." Owen touches my arm. "Please. Come on. None of this is your fault. I understand why you didn't tell me."

I stop next to Cam's truck.

"I can drive you to the Y," Owen offers. "I have my car."

"It's okay. I'm not sure I feel like going today. Not because of you. It's just been a rough couple of days." *Without you.*

All of a sudden, I get a strange feeling someone's watching me. The tiny hairs on the back of my neck stand on end. I felt the same way the night outside the mill.

Christian and Cameron pick up their paces and catch up with us.

"What the hell is that piece of shit doing here?" Cam asks.

My gut tells me he's talking about Reed before I see him. He's standing on the sidewalk in front of the parking lot—technically not on school grounds. TJ and Billy are with him, pushing and shoving each other like idiots. Reed isn't the only one who has put on a lot of muscle quickly.

356

"I don't know what he's doing here, but I'm going to find out," Owen says.

I grab the sleeve of Owen's jacket. "Let's just leave."

Grace squeezes between Christian and Cameron, but there's no way the two of us can keep my cousins and Owen under control.

"Peyton's right," Grace says. "Let's go. She doesn't have anything to say to him, and neither do we."

"I've got plenty to say to his friend," Cam says, zeroing in on TJ. "And I'm gonna tell him while I'm pounding him into the ground."

"Please don't do this," I beg. "Reed is just trying to get a rise out of you guys. I have no idea what he's up to, but I promise you it isn't good."

The three guys keep walking. Reed narrows his eyes when he sees me with Owen. It's subtle, but I know that look. He's angry, even if he doesn't want anyone to know it.

I slip past Owen and rush ahead of him. "I have nothing to say to you, Reed. I want you to leave and stop following me around."

Reed makes a fist and holds it over his heart. "That hurts, Peyton. But I'm not here to see you."

"Then what the fuck do you want?" Owen cuts in front of me and squares off in front of Reed.

Christian and Cam fan out and flank Owen, Cam in front of TJ and Christian in front of Billy.

"What should we do?" Grace whispers.

I throw up my hands. "I don't know. But this is going to get out of control real fast."

"I'm glad to see you up and around," Reed says to Owen. "When you hit the mat, I wasn't sure you were gonna get back up."

To Owen's credit, he doesn't react. Today he's in control. "I would've gotten up if the ref hadn't called it."

"What do you think, Billy?" Reed asks.

"He was laid out. I'm not sure he would've gotten up," Billy says.

"I wouldn't put money on it, either," TJ adds.

"You two are such assholes," I say to Reed's friends. "Thank god I don't have to hang out with either of you anymore."

Reed's eyes dart back and forth between TJ and Billy. He's waiting to see if one of them is stupid enough to say something disrespectful to me, but they know better.

Reed seems satisfied and picks up where he left off. "That's actually what I came to talk to you about, Owen. When I beat a guy in the cage, I want to make sure he knows he's been beaten. And all this bullshit about the ref calling it early screwed that up for me."

"I was getting up."

Reed's smug expression turns menacing. "Prove it."

Just when I think there's no hope, I see Titan jogging across the parking lot toward us. Either he'll stop the Twins from starting World War III or he'll tip the scales in their favor. I won't feel the least bit guilty if Reed and his friends are outnumbered.

"Everyone needs to chill," Titan says, catching his breath. "Coach has eyes on you."

Titan looks over at the gym. The football coach is stationed out front, arms crossed, staring directly at us.

Christian and Cam look over and see him, too. "Shit."

"He said if any of us gets into another fight, we're benched for three games."

Christian raises his eyebrows. "Three games? There's no way he'd do that."

"Coach said he'll lose three games before he'll let his players disrespect him," Titan says.

Cameron turns back to TJ. "My coach just saved your life."

TJ laughs. "You don't even know how funny that is, man. I could take you without breaking a sweat."

Cameron moves to take a step forward, and Titan grabs his jacket and jerks him back. "Get your head out of your ass right now, Cameron. Coach is serious. He's still pissed off about the cafeteria."

"We've gotta go anyway," Reed says. "I'll call you later, Peyton." He tosses out the comment casually, like we're still dating and I don't hate his guts. "And, Owen? If you want to finish what we started in the cage, I'll be at that abandoned mill outside Black Water tonight at nine." Reed looks at me and smiles. "You know the one I'm talking about, right? Where you partied last Friday night."

My blood runs cold. "You were there?"

"I have to keep an eye on my girl. Even if she's telling lies," Reed says.

"There's a name for that," Grace says. "It's called stalking."

I ball my hands into fists at my sides. "How did you find me?"

"I was working on tracking you down when Billy said he saw you at a fight in Tennessee."

"So what did you do? Check all the high schools in Tennessee until you found me?"

"I didn't have to. Billy said you were wearing a hoodie with 'Black Water Warriors' on the back."

Owen's hoodie.

How could I be so stupid?

"I wouldn't leave my girl here all alone in a town where she doesn't know anybody—except those two." He looks over at the Twins.

Owen balls his hands into fists at his sides.

"I'm not *yours*, Reed. I never was."

Owen looks Reed in the eyes. "Peyton doesn't belong to anyone."

Reed pretends he isn't listening. "Did you say something?"

"I'll be there tonight," Owen fires back. "Did you hear that or do I need to repeat it?"

I whip around and face Owen. "No, you won't," I say under my breath.

Anger is coming off Owen in waves. "He has probably been following you the whole time you've been here."

A little over a month.

Reed stretches and cracks his neck. "Well, not the whole time. A guy's gotta sleep. But I was checking in. You've got a nice school, by the way. I like the banner in the hallway. 'Players go for the win. Warriors battle for it.' It's catchy."

My blood pressure takes a nosedive, and suddenly I'm light-headed. I grab Owen's arm to steady myself. Reed has been inside the school.

"You put the note and the dead rabbit in my locker, didn't you?" I should've known.

Reed whips around and grabs TJ by the throat. "A dead rabbit? That's what you put in her locker?"

TJ grabs Reed's wrist. "You said to scare her."

Reed shoves him away. "We'll talk about that bullshit later."

"You're a sick bastard." Owen is starting to lose it.

The Twins step in front of him. "Not here, man."

"Peyton is right." Reed heads for the street, with TJ and Billy trailing behind him like stray dogs. "I'll see you tonight, Owen. Nine o'clock."

Owen's chest heaves, rising and falling too fast, as he watches Reed go.

"We'd better get our asses to practice," Titan tells the Twins. Their coach is still standing out front, watching them.

The guys take off.

"I want to talk to Owen for a minute," I tell Grace.

"I'll wait for you by my car," she says.

"Calm down, Owen. Please." He looks almost as angry as he did last night.

"I'm calm. I'll deal with him tonight."

"You can't meet him tonight. He's talking about an underground fight."

"Whatever. It's a rematch."

I stand in front of him and touch his face to get him to look at me. "Have you ever been to an underground fight?"

He shrugs. That's a no.

"There are no rules, no refs, no cutman, and no paramedics if something happens. It's last man standing, literally."

"Then I'll be the last man standing."

"Did you hear what I just said?" I ask. "There are no refs. No bell. No doctors. No equipment if something happens to you. If your heart—"

"I don't care about that."

"You don't care if you *die*? Is that what you're saying?" I can't stand it. "I'll be fine."

"You don't know that. Reed fights dirty. And he has clearly gone off the deep end. He's on steroids, Owen."

"I have to go." Owen's eyes lock on mine. "He hurt you." He runs his thumb down the side of my cheek. "I can't live with that. Whether you want to be with me or not, I can't just suck up the fact that he pushed you down a flight of steps and pretended like it didn't happen. He could've killed you."

This isn't just about me, even if Owen doesn't realize it.

"I understand why this is so hard for you. You couldn't protect your mom and we didn't know each other when Reed pushed me, so you couldn't protect me, either. But risking your life won't change what happened to your mom. And she wouldn't want you to take this kind of a chance."

"I can't just let him get away with hurting you."

My frustration turns to anger. "Don't act like you're doing this for me."

"I'm not doing it *for* you. I'm doing it because of you. Because of what he did to you."

"No, you aren't. You're doing this for yourself."

That gets his attention.

Owen looks at me, his eyes full of pain. "I don't care about myself."

"That's the problem. I do. And if you care about what I want and what would hurt me, you won't go tonight. Because if something happens to you, that would hurt me more than anything Reed has ever done."

"You can't say that."

"I'm saying it. I'm telling you that I don't want you to go. And if I matter to you as much as you say I do, you won't."

Owen drags his hands through his hair, like he wants to yank it out. "What if you can't play again because of him? What if you lose your spot at UNC?"

"Don't do that. You don't have to worry about my knee or what happens with UNC. That hasn't changed since yesterday. What you should care about are my feelings. And I'm telling you that it will hurt me more than anything if something happens to you—especially if Reed is involved. He wouldn't ask you to meet him if he didn't have an ulterior motive. He's been following me around. His friend put a dead animal in my locker. Doesn't that show you there's something seriously wrong with him?"

"I have to do this."

"If you go there tonight, I won't be waiting afterward—not as your friend or anything else." A tear escapes and runs down the side of my face.

"Don't say that. We're more than just friends, and no matter what, we'll always be friends."

"Not if you do this. I can't watch you self-destruct." I've been down this road before. Owen is nothing like Reed, but the conversation feels familiar.

"It's gonna be fine, I promise." Owen reaches for me, but I pull away.

"It's me or the fight, Owen. You have to choose."

The look in his eye gives me the answer before he says it. "Don't do this, Peyton. I can't let him get away with what he did to you. He physically *hurt* you—so bad that you needed surgery."

"You didn't hear a word I said." I back away, and my heart feels like it's being ripped to pieces.

"You don't know how much you mean to me, Peyton. I swear—"

"If you're going tonight, I do." I turn away and walk straight to Grace's car without looking back. On the other side of my tears, the cars tilt and blur.

Grace is sitting on the trunk of her car and she hops off when she sees me. She gives me a huge hug. "What happened?"

"He didn't pick me."

CHAPTER 40
Broken and Battered

NOW THAT OWEN is gone and I'm with Grace, I burst into full-blown tears. She keeps asking me to tell her exactly what happened, but I can't stop crying long enough to get out more than a few words.

The Twins are at football practice and Hawk is consulting with a client in Nashville, so we go back to my uncle's house.

Once we're in my room, I finally calm down enough to talk to her.

Grace hands me the box of tissues on the desk.

"Thanks for coming over. You're a really good friend."

Grace shrugs a little. "I know. But it's easy to be a good friend when you only have one."

I switch from ugly crying to ugly nose blowing, until I use up all the tissues. "I'm not your only friend."

"Christian and Cameron don't count. Guys and girls can't be friends, remember?"

I force a tiny smile, and it makes my face hurt.

"Want to tell me what happened?" she asks.

"Owen is meeting Reed tonight. I told him what underground fights are like, but he wouldn't listen. I literally begged him not to go."

"What did he say?"

"That he couldn't let Reed get away with hurting me. I told Owen that if he actually cared about me, he wouldn't go. But nothing I said made a difference." I'm not giving her the whole story.

"I know how he feels. Both times I've seen Reed, I wanted to punch him in the face. It's hard to know that someone hurt my friend, and Owen thinks of you as a lot more than that."

As much as I don't want to betray Owen, I have to tell someone about his heart and the real risk he's taking. Because I have no clue what to do next.

"Owen shared something with me in confidence, and normally I would never repeat it. But if he's planning to meet Reed tonight, that changes everything. If I tell you, it will stay between us right?"

"Of course. I swear."

I take a deep breath. "Owen has a heart condition."

"Like high blood pressure?"

"No. It's a genetic defect called Brugada syndrome. The type Owen has is super rare. It affects his heartbeat." My voice cracks. "His heart could just stop beating."

Grace gasps. "How do they restart it? CPR? Or does someone have to jab him in the chest with a giant needle full of adrenaline, like in the movies?"

A tear runs down my cheek.

"Those aren't options for Owen. The only way to restart his heart is with a defibrillator. And there's no guarantee it will work. But if his heart *does* stop, unless he's near a hospital or somebody just happens to have a defibrillator in the trunk of their car, he'll die." The last word catches in my throat.

"I had no idea. He's such an amazing athlete. Are people with heart defects supposed to compete in MMA?"

"Owen shouldn't be involved in any contact sports, but he doesn't care. He's convinced that he's going to die, so it doesn't matter. It's like he's given up." I wipe my face and blow my nose. My phone rings. "I don't want to talk to him."

Grace checks the number. "It's not Owen. It's Tess."

"That's Reed trying to be stealth." I can't believe he's calling me after everything he did.

I take my phone from Grace. "Stop calling me, stop texting me, and leave me the hell alone," I say before he has a chance to get a word in.

Someone sniffles on the other end of the line. "Peyton? It's Tess." Her voice sounds so small and far away.

"Tess? Is that you? Are you okay?"

She chokes back a sob. "No."

"Where are you?"

"At a motel." She takes a shaky breath. "I know you were telling the truth about Reed."

"You do? Did he admit it?"

"He didn't have to." She coughs, half crying.

"Where are you? I'll come pick you up."

"We're staying at the Howard Johnson in Bay Creek. Is that too far?"

I check the GPS on my phone. "Bay Creek is about twenty minutes from here."

"I don't want you to come here, in case he comes back. There's a Circle K up the street. Want to pick me up there?" she asks.

"Wherever you want."

"Okay, I'll meet you there."

I slip on Dad's jacket. "I'm leaving in a minute."

Tess is quiet for a moment. "I should've believed you. I'm sorry."

"It's okay."

She hangs up, and I stare at the phone, stunned.

"What happened?" Grace asks.

"I don't know. Tess asked if I could come pick her up. She knows I was telling the truth about Reed. Maybe she caught him using. I don't think he'd admit it."

"After meeting him, I agree."

An awful feeling builds inside me. There was something about Tess' voice that sounded off.

"There she is," I tell Grace as she pulls into the Circle K parking lot. Tess is huddled against the wall, her blond hair peeking out from beneath an oversize hoodie. It's not her look. It's sloppy and so not Tess.

Grace parks, and I get out. "I'll wait here," she says.

The moment I step under the streetlight I know something is wrong.

"Thanks for coming to get me," Tess says. She's staring at the ground, her hands in the front pocket of the giant hoodie.

"What happened?" I ask her. "How did you figure out I was telling the truth?"

Tess slowly raises her head and pulls down the hood. One side of her face is black and blue from the top of her cheekbone to the bottom of her jaw. I've had enough bruises to know those aren't fresh. But the cut on her swollen lip is.

"Reed did that?" I almost can't believe it. It was one thing to hurt me, but I never thought he would hurt Tess.

"Yeah. He's done it a few times. Just not like this. He's really bad now, Peyton. He's taking all kinds of stuff."

"What set him off?"

"I found some of his pills. It's his new thing. I said something. I must have picked the wrong day of his cycle—who knows? This is what he's like now. But that's not why I called."

That's *not* why she called? Has she seen her face?

"Come on, get in the car." I don't want to run the risk of Reed seeing her.

Tess gets in the back seat. "Hi," she says to Grace. "Thanks for picking me up."

Grace's eyes go wide when she sees Tess' face, and Tess pulls up her hood again. "Are you okay?" Grace asks her.

"No. But I'm not worried about me. Reed is going to hurt your boyfriend."

"He's not my boyfriend. But—"

"Reed is going to hurt him. I heard him talking to TJ and Billy about it."

"Are those losers doping, too?"

"TJ is for sure. I don't know about Billy. I hate them both. Reed is so pissed off about that guy Owen. He's so paranoid now. He's convinced that Owen is the reason you won't get back together with him. You can't let Owen go tonight."

"Yeah, well, that ship has sailed."

"No, Peyton, I'm serious. Reed is going to fight dirty. And if Owen doesn't lose, and lose bad, Reed, TJ, and Billy are going to jump him when he leaves the fight."

My heart plummets. Owen might be able to beat Reed, but he can't take all three of them. Not after a fight, with a heart condition he ignores.

"Call Owen and tell him not to show up. The last few underground fights Reed has been in . . ." She takes a deep breath. "One of the guys ended up in the hospital. I heard another guy is all scarred up. Reed dipped his wraps."

"What?"

"Reed told me stories about guys dipping their hand wraps in crushed glass."

"Stop." My stomach threatens to turn inside out. "Oh god. We have to tell Owen."

I call his cell, and it goes straight to voice mail. Then I text him. Nothing.

"What are we gonna do? We can't just show up at the fight," Grace says. "We can't stop Reed and his jacked-up friends ourselves." She's right.

There's only one way to save Owen.

It will destroy his future as a fighter, but it will save his life.

"I have to call the cops and report the fight."

"Tell them there's gambling," Grace says. "This is a small town. If you mention gambling, they'll check it out."

I look back at Tess. "If I call, you know what's going to happen."

"I know."

"What's gonna happen?" Grace asks. "Fill me in."

"If Owen and Reed get arrested at an underground fight, they'll both

369

be kicked out of the league. They won't be able to fight anymore. I mean, not on a competitive circuit." I look at Tess when I say, "And that means no prize money."

Tess nods. "Someone has to stop him."

Owen's future as a competitive fighter will be over. Even though part of me feels like I'm saving him because he shouldn't be fighting anyway, that's his decision. But knowing Reed is trying to hurt him and could possibly kill him? I can't ignore that.

"I'll call the police. Keep calling Owen's cell, Grace."

We're fifteen or twenty minutes from the mill. The fight is supposed to start in five minutes. It could be over before we even get there. I can't waste any more time. I dial the number.

"Nine-one-one. What's your emergency?"

CHAPTER 41

Street Fighter

"YOU CAN'T GO in through the front," Tucker says. "There are cops everywhere, and they're not letting anybody inside. So far, every guy who has walked out of there has ended up in cuffs."

"What about Owen? Have you seen him?"

Tucker shakes his head. "No. And I've been looking. Your cousins are around here somewhere, too, but nobody's seen him."

"Thanks."

I take off with Grace and Tess beside me. I don't have time for anything except finding Owen.

Police cars are parked on the grass in front of the mill, and the flashing lights on top of the cop cars make it easier to see out here. A small group of middle-aged adults who clearly weren't involved in the underground fights watch the cops cuff people as they come out of the main entrance.

Tucker scrambles to catch up with us. "Where are you going?"

"I have to find Owen. Who are those people?" I point at the group of middle-aged adults. Now that I'm closer, they look more like senior citizens.

"I don't know. Probably the closest neighbors, or people who follow the police cars. People actually do that here. Nothing ever happens, so when people see a cop car, they want to know what happened."

"Then I guess I'll be one of those people." As we get closer, I scan every face, looking for Owen.

A burly cop walks out with Billy, whose hands are cuffed behind his back. He passes him off to another officer, who has more than a dozen other guys in cuffs sitting on the ground in a row.

Grace cranes her neck to get a better look. "The cops are definitely not messing around."

"I told you, they're arresting everyone," Tucker says.

An officer spots us and walks over. "What are you kids doing here?"

"We saw all the police cars coming this way, and we wanted to see what was going on," Grace says innocently.

"Well, now you've had a look. It's time to go home." He points behind us. "So go on back to your car." The officer gives Tucker a disapproving look. "And I know your mama wouldn't want to know you're over here, Tucker. Just be glad you weren't inside. Now, get on out of here."

The whole time the cop was talking, I've been looking for Owen. He's not sitting on the ground with the group in handcuffs. But neither is Reed.

We walk away to satisfy the officer. He watches us for a moment, then loses interest and goes back to the business of arresting people.

We only have to walk a few yards before we're hidden by the darkness.

"So what's the plan?" Tucker asks.

"I know another way inside," I tell them as Grace texts madly.

"Christian and Cam are already here," she says. "They're on the roof."

"What? Why?"

"They climbed into the ducts when they heard the cops come in."

"Did they see Owen?"

Grace shakes her head. "No, I already asked. Christian says they're waiting until there aren't as many cops inside, and then they'll start looking again."

What if Owen doesn't have that much time?

I check my phone to see if he texted me, but of course it's dead. I probably drained the battery with the dozens of texts I sent him that went unanswered.

"I can't wait that long," I tell Grace. "I'm going in."

She tucks her phone into her pocket and pulls her long black hair into a ponytail. "Let's go."

I lead the way as we approach the mill from the side. We stay close to the trees, so the cops won't see us.

"I can't see anything. It's too dark." I keep one hand in front of me so I don't walk into a tree branch. "And my phone is dead."

"I have a flashlight. You can borrow it," Tucker says.

He hands me something that doesn't feel like a flashlight. "Tucker, this is a pen."

"Press the end. Not now. It's really bright. But I've got my phone."

Luckily, the flashing lights from the police cars illuminate the front of the building, which helps me judge if I'm walking in the right direction.

As we pass the front of the mill, we work our way closer to the building.

"Someone's texting me," Grace says. "But I can't read it without turning up the brightness on my phone."

"Let me see it," Tucker says. I can't see what he's doing, but he's messing around with Grace's phone. He turns up the brightness a tiny bit. "I still can't read it," he whispers. "He tucks it under his shirt to hide the light. The light gets brighter as he turns it up a little more.

"Who's over there?" a man calls out. A streak of light from a flashlight waves back and forth in our direction.

Grace grabs Tucker and pulls him away from me. The light catches the two of them.

"What are you two doing over there? Stay where you are," the officer says.

Grace makes a shooing motion with her hand. "Go!"

I step deeper into the shadows closer to the trees. I feel terrible leaving them behind, but I'm more worried about Owen. I work my way to the concrete steps Owen brought me to once before. The moment I see them, my pulse goes into overdrive.

Am I really going to do this?

My legs shake as I walk down the steps. I remove the padlock the way Owen showed me, but I can't bring myself to open the door. There's a real tunnel on the other side—not one at the entrance to a football stadium. It's dark, underground, and completely sealed off, meaning there's no way out until I get to the other end—which I can't see.

My hands are shaking so hard I can barely open the door.

I can do this.

My dad didn't have anyone to swoop in and rescue him, but I might be able to save Owen. I can't let fear stop me. But this isn't a normal fear. I'm dealing with a panic attack–inducing phobia. I'm trapped in the quicksand again, and it's rising fast. Instead of imagining the tunnel I'm about to enter, I picture Owen in the locker room the day I found him after the semifinals, pale and gasping for air. He could be on the other side somewhere right now, in even worse shape.

I can do this.

I look up at the sky, and for the first time since my father died, I talk to him. To the sky and the darkness and the heavens and the constellations—all the places I can imagine his spirit roaming free.

"Help me, Dad," I whisper. "Please." I touch the dog tags around my neck. Mom's right. He is still with us. I can hear his voice as clearly as if he were standing in front of me.

Aim, kick, release.

I can't remember how old I was the first time he said it, but I remember the hundreds and hundreds of times he said it after that first day. *Aim, kick, release.* For every shot, those were the steps, and we practiced them over and over, passing the ball back and forth in the backyard.

"You can't focus on winning the game or scoring goals," he'd said. "You have to focus on that one kick in front of you. Whether it's a pass or you're taking a shot, that one kick has to be the most important one you make, and you do it every time. That's how you win."

I. Can. Do. This.

I clutch the dog tags in my sweaty palm. I swallow, but my mouth is so dry it feels like swallowing sand.

Aim. Kick. Release.

Focus on the next kick. That's all. I just have to focus on taking one step, and then another. And I have to keep taking them until I make it to the end.

I cross the threshold, and the walls tilt. The concrete floor seems to shift, like I'm walking on a rope ladder. I close my eyes and extend my arms for balance.

Aim. Kick. Release.

The first step feels impossible. My leg's too heavy, and I can't raise it.

What if Owen's heart stops and no one's there?

I lift my foot and take the first step. My body sways until I touch the ground again. I hear Dad's voice in my head repeating the same thing over and over like a mantra: *Aim. Kick. Release. Aim. Kick. Release.*

As I move my foot, I deconstruct my movements. I bring my knee up, put my foot down, and then switch legs and do the same thing. Knee up, foot down, then switch sides.

Up. Down. Switch.

I keep my arms extended. I can't reach the walls, which is probably a good thing. It makes the space seem larger.

It's more like a room than a tunnel.

I'm playing mind games with myself. My knees start to shake, and I close my eyes. It's too hard to look. I know how far I've gone, and that if I look back, I won't be able to see the entrance anymore.

Up. Down. Switch. Up. Down. Switch.

The mantra becomes automatic, and I start counting my footsteps.

Seven. Ten. Fourteen.

My knees shake and knock against each other, and the urge to puke my guts out hits. I take deep breaths through my nose, trying to settle my stomach.

Twenty-eight. Thirty-five. Forty-one.

The only light comes from Tucker's flashlight pen, but my eyes are closed anyway. Until the pounding starts. Not just pounding . . . foot-steps. Coming fast.

Maybe it's Owen.

The footsteps echo louder, reminding me that I'm still in a tunnel.

Where are they coming from?

My heart beats wildly as the sounds grow louder. A beam of light bounces off the tunnel walls, getting closer and closer. I can make out a silhouette, but not much more. Broad shoulders and a muscular body race toward me.

The floor still feels like it's shifting beneath my feet, and another wave of nausea hits. I gag and cover my mouth.

The person running toward me isn't Owen.

It's Reed.

CHAPTER 42

Losing Faith

REED AND I see each other at the same time and he stops.

"Peyton? What are you doing down here?" His voice sounds strange, like I'm underwater. "Worried about your new boyfriend?" He drops his gym bag at his feet.

"Is—is he okay?" I stammer.

Reed holds the flashlight between us, and the light casts an eerie glow on his face. "I don't know. The little bitch didn't show."

"Owen isn't here?"

"I figured he was with you. But I'm glad you're here. I wanted a chance to talk to you alone."

I'd rather eat nails.

Reed seems oblivious to the fact that I can't stand him.

"If you want to talk, let's do it outside." I start to turn around, but Reed blocks my path.

"No, we should talk now, while we're alone. I think that's part of the problem. We had a misunderstanding and other people kept getting involved. That's when everything got out of hand." His demeanor has completely changed, and he's playing the apologetic ex.

"Other people 'getting involved' wasn't what caused the problem. What you're doing to yourself is the problem."

He scratches the back of his head. "What do you mean?"

The tunnel walls look as if they're getting narrower, squeezing closer to Reed—and me. I take a shuddering breath.

Don't let him see how scared you are.

"Please don't play this game with me. I broke up with you because you were doping. Then you decided to push me down a flight of stairs. I don't really think there's much left to talk about. Unless you want to discuss the fact that you've been stalking me and leaving dead animals in my locker. Because that kind of stuff definitely shows a girl how much you love her."

Reed's jaw twitches, and I scoot my feet back rather than taking a step. If he senses fear or weakness, he'll attack.

"I told you I was sorry about your knee. I didn't mean it. Nothing like that will ever happen again. And you can't blame me for wanting to check up on you. You just disappeared."

"Reed, I think we should get out of here. The cops are searching the building and arresting everyone. They already have a bunch of guys hand-cuffed out front, including Billy. It's only a matter of time before they come down here."

"First, they have to find the entrance to tunnel in that thrashed-out basement."

"You found it."

I can't see the end of the tunnel from here, which means it isn't as close as I thought. Suddenly, I'm dizzy.

"And then I covered it up."

"With what? It's a tunnel, not a porthole." The panic is getting worse.

"I don't want to waste any more time talking about cops and tunnels," Reed says, moving closer. "I want to talk about *us*. I messed up. I admit it, and I'm sorry. But we belong together. You know that. I just *won* the regional championship. Aren't you happy for me? Everything is going to be great now. Just give me one more chance. I won't screw it up."

The tunnel walls look like they're expanding and contracting around us. I know I'm imagining it, but it feels so real. I can't leave because I'm stuck listening to Reed's bullshit. The panic recedes and another feeling replaces it.

Rage.

"We don't belong together, Reed, and we're never going to end up together. I saw what you did to Tess."

He flinches.

"Yeah. I saw her face. You haven't changed; you're getting worse. If you could do that to your own sister—"

"Shut up," he growls.

"Reed, please. You need help. Can't you see what this is doing to you?" I don't actually care if he gets help anymore. Too much has happened. Seeing Tess' face was the final straw. But right now I'll say anything to get away from him.

"I still love you, and I'm not giving up. I went easy on that guy Owen, but if you won't give me another chance and you start screwing around with someone else, I'll make him pay." Reed narrows his eyes. "And I'll enjoy every minute of it."

The voice in the back of my head whispers to me, *Do whatever you can to get away from him.*

My instincts failed me the night Reed pushed me. I didn't see it coming. But now I know what I'm looking for—the empty look in his eye. My little voice is right this time, and I need to listen.

The tunnel is cold, but Reed is sweating. I wonder how long ago he took a dose and what that means for me.

Get away from him. Now.

There's no way I can outrun him. Not when my knee still isn't a hundred percent.

I flash on an image of Owen and Tucker in the ring, when Owen was teaching him self-defense. The palm strike doesn't require a lot of strength to execute, and an attacker's size doesn't matter unless you can't reach the person's nose.

Still . . .

I haven't really practiced.

What if I try it on Reed and it doesn't work? It might set him off.

My heart pounds against my rib cage, like it's trying to break out. I'm not sure if it's because of Reed or the tunnel.

"What we have isn't the kind of thing you walk away from, Peyton. And once we work things out, our relationship will be different. You'll see. I'll stop doping, if that's what you want."

He's lying, and he's not even doing it well.

Reed paces back and forth in front of me.

"You'd really quit?" I pretend his answer matters to me. Maybe it's the wrong move, but I don't have time to think it through. It's a Hail Mary—a last-ditch effort to save myself—and right now it's my only shot.

Reed stops pacing and stares at me for a moment. "Yeah. I swear. Then we can pick up where we left off."

Like nothing happened.

That's what he means.

"You can quit just like that?" I ask. "Isn't your body used to that stuff now?"

"People quit all the time. Other guys on my team have done it. You just stop." He smiles and moves closer. "You don't know how happy that would make me. One chance. That's all I'm asking for. I won't screw things up this time."

You'll just punch me in the face the first time I piss you off.

Reed reaches out to tuck my hair behind my ear, and I try not to cringe. His touch makes my skin crawl. "I knew you'd come around. What we have is special."

I'm playing a dangerous game. And the huge smile on his face tells me that if I lose, I'll lose big.

"I've really missed you, Peyton. Things haven't been the same. Even winning doesn't feel the same without you. I think that's why I've been so stressed out."

Stressed out? Is that what he's calling it?

The sound of muffled voices drifts into the tunnel from somewhere inside the building.

Reed doesn't seem to notice. He's busy planning our future. "We could get an apartment together in the fall. We'd save a lot of money, and I could still help my mom."

He seems to have forgotten that I'm going to college. But I'm not about to remind him—not when the improvement in his mood is buying me time.

Suddenly, the air in the tunnel feels heavier and it's hard to swallow.

What if I don't make it out of here?

My chest squeezes tighter and tighter.

I hear Dad's voice in the back of my head. *It's now or never, kiddo.*

I doubt this is the scenario Dad envisioned when he said it, but that doesn't make it any less true. I'm running out of time.

It's getting harder to breathe. Any minute, I'm going to have a panic attack and start hyperventilating. Or Reed is going to want some kind of confirmation that I'm giving him another chance—like a kiss.

My throat spasms.

Shit.

Thinking fast, I fake-cough into my elbow to hide my real reaction. "You okay?"

I'm not confident enough to attempt a heel strike on Reed. I'd rather rely on human nature. I slide my phone out of my back pocket without Reed noticing. When he turns around, I toss it up in the air. Reed looks up, just like Owen said people do if you throw something above their heads.

I bring my knee up as hard as I can, and it lands squarely between Reed's legs. He doubles over.

I take off running. It's the first time I've tried to run since the surgery, and it feels awkward. I'm off-balance and not moving at top speed, but I'm running.

"Peytonnnn!" Reed shouts.

So much for incapacitating him. I just keep putting one foot in front of the other.

I see the door.

It's not much farther.

The voices behind me get louder, but I can't turn around. Losing one second might be the difference between making it out of here or Reed catching up to me.

The door is so close, and a pale light glows on the other side. Maybe the cops found the side entrance.

I'm going to make it.

I cross the threshold at the same time my knee gives out, and my body crashes against the stone. People shout my name.

In a blur of movement, a figure rushes past me.

It's Owen.

Why didn't he stop?

When I look back at the tunnel, I understand.

Reed is only a few feet away.

Owen throws an elbow and catches Reed in the jaw. I hear the sick crack of Reed's skull as it hits the tunnel wall. But it doesn't take him down.

Reed pivots and tries to sweep Owen's legs out from under him, but Owen catches him in a headlock. Two cops come barreling down the tunnel, from inside the building.

The voices I heard must have been theirs.

Reed must've done a shitty job of hiding the tunnel entrance.

One cop grabs Owen and throws him against the wall, and the other officer grabs Reed.

I point at Owen. "He didn't do anything wrong. He was trying to help me."

The cops don't respond. Either they can't hear me over Reed's non-stop string of profanity, or they're not interested in my opinion.

Owen cooperates while the cop pats him down and cuffs him.

"Someone told me there was a party here tonight," Reed yells at the officer who is stuck dealing with him. "I don't know anything about fighting and gambling. Do I sound like I'm from around here?"

A third officer emerges from the tunnel carrying Reed's gym bag. "I found this in there."

"That's his bag." I point at Reed. "And it has drugs inside."

"That's not mine," Reed says. "It was on the floor of the tunnel when I got there."

"He's lying."

The older cop nods at the bag. "Let me take a look inside."

The officer unzips it and fishes around. He takes out the same black box I found the night Reed pushed me. He opens it and tilts the box so the older cop can see the contents.

"That's not my bag!" Reed shouts.

"I can prove it's his. There's a gym membership card in one of the inside pockets. It has his picture on it."

"You bitch!" Reed turns and tries to charge in my direction.

The cop holding his arm jerks Reed back. "Let's go check out the back of the squad car." He flips over Reed's gym ID and adds, "Mr. Michaels."

I didn't single-handedly take Reed down with a palm strike, but I got away from him.

And I went into the tunnel—and not just for five minutes.

I was in there for a long time, and I held it together well enough to deal with Reed. No one talked me through it, except Dad. I faced my demons and I kicked one of them in the balls.

All around, tonight feels like a win.

A cop leads Owen around to the front of the mill behind Reed and his badge-wielding escort.

Owen looks back at me. "I kept my promise."

Owen promised he wouldn't hurt me and he didn't.

In front of the mill I see Tess, Tucker, and Grace in the glow of the red-and-blue flashing lights. Tucker waves at me and tries to talk his way past the cop in charge of keeping the small group of nosy people away from the building. Tess is with him.

Grace is busy yelling at Cam, while a cop yanks him off TJ. Why is Cameron wearing his football pads and uniform?

"Peyton, you're okay!" Christian calls out from the lineup of hand-cuffed guys sitting on the ground. He's wearing his football uniform, too.

The cop supervising the lineup notices me. "Are you all right, Miss? You don't look so good."

"I'm okay."

I look for Tess, and I see her walking toward me. "I told the police about the drugs. I had to do it. It's the only way Reed will get help. He won't stop on his own."

She nods, her lip trembling. "I know. And I want my brother back."

I'm not sure if the brother she's talking about still exists. For Tess' sake, I hope so.

I search for Owen in the lineup.

"He's over there next to Cameron," Grace says, trudging over to us. "Maybe Owen can talk some sense into him."

Owen is sitting cross-legged in the dirt with the Twins. Out of the three of them, Cam's the one who looks like he was involved in an underground fight. At least Owen isn't in the back of a squad car, like Reed.

"Why are the Twins wearing their football uniforms?" I ask. "Did they come straight from the game?"

Grace shakes her head and smiles. "The game didn't end until thirty minutes ago. They walked out during halftime."

"They just left in the middle of the game?" I ask.

"Yep. Cameron almost left before the game even started. He freaked when I didn't show up with the rest of the squad." Grace gives me a shy smile. "I texted him—and Christian—to tell them you were in trouble, but they were already on the field. Coach makes the players leave their phones in the locker room, so they didn't read my text until halftime. Then they took off."

Without thinking, I reach for my phone to call Hawk. I need to tell him what happened and ask him to meet me at the police station with bail money, for the three bravest guys I know.

Then I remember my phone is gone. It's on the floor of the tunnel.

Shattered.

I'll never hear Dad's message again.

But it's okay.

I remember everything about my father—his unruly dark hair and his lopsided smile; how he ate guava paste straight from the package and he squeezed just hard enough when he caught me in a bear hug; the way he could bounce a soccer ball on his knee for fifteen minutes without dropping it and he cussed at the TV in Spanish if Cuba was losing a soccer game.

I remember the way his voice sounded when he cheered me on from the sidelines and how it sounded different when he told me he loved me.

I don't need the phone anymore.

The memory of Dad's voice is all I need.

And I'll carry it with me.

CHAPTER 43
The Things I Carry

WHEN I COME downstairs in the morning, Hawk is sitting at the breakfast table drinking a cup of coffee, with Dutch stretched out at his feet. My uncle looks like he's been awake all night.

I pour myself a cup and sit across from him. "Did you get any sleep?"

Hawk shakes his head. "Not yet. It took a while to bail out the boys, and then they wanted to give me a minute-by-minute recap. But old men like me don't need much sleep."

Dutch howls as if he agrees.

"Don't let Mom hear you say that. You're only two years older than her," I remind him. "Are the boys okay? Getting arrested couldn't have been much fun."

"I don't know about that. Christian was excited to cross it off his bucket list. And your friend Grace waited at the police station until Cameron was released, and he seemed real happy about it."

The cops had probably still been taking my statement. It felt like I was answering their questions for hours.

"I think Grace was waiting for Christian. She's had a crush on him for a long time."

Hawk considers it for a moment. "She might be over Christian."

"Why would you say that?" I ask.

"Well she was kissing Cameron in the parking lot."

"Are you sure?"

He nods. "Positive."

Hawk leans back in his chair and rubs the scruff on his chin. "The boys filled me in after I bailed them out. They said your ex-boyfriend was arrested for drug possession."

"Yep." I take a sip of coffee. "He'll get kicked out of the MMA league."

"I hope that makes it easier to put this behind you and exorcise that demon."

"I think so, but I need your help to face another one." I take a deep breath. "Will you tell me what happened to Dad the night he died?"

"I've been waiting for you to ask me that question for a year and a half. In my head, I've rehearsed what I'd tell you a hundred times. But now that you're sitting in front of me, I can't remember a word of it. How much do you want to know?"

"Everything."

"All right." Hawk stays quiet for a moment. This can't be easy for him to talk about. "We were doing a BDA—a Battle Damage Assessment—in the basement of a hotel in Fallujah that had been fire-bombed. The insurgents were using the basement to house guns and supplies. An air strike had already leveled the area. It was a routine mission for us. That's what we thought anyway.

"We went in as a five-man fire team. Your dad as team leader and sniper, Rudy as point man, Mad Dog on the radio, and Big John as our gunner."

"Why weren't you in the tunnel with them?" It's the only reason my uncle is here to tell the story.

Hawk's eyes cloud over and he clears his throat. "I was guardian angel that day. That's what we call the team member assigned to overwatch."

"What does that mean exactly?" I was used to listening to Dad talk shop with Hawk and other recon operators. On a good day, I understood about half of what they were saying. Force recon was such a tight-knit brotherhood that the men had developed their own shorthand for everything.

"My job was to find high ground and use optics to keep eyes on the area—watching for unfriendlies and anything out of the ordinary. I also manned the comms between our team and base. Mad Dog was on the radio giving me the rundown of what they were seeing, and then I relayed information to base. Mad Dog was on the radio with me when it happened."

A knot forms in my throat. "What happened?"

"One minute everything was going according to plan. Then, out of nowhere, there was an explosion. The basement must've been rigged. The insurgents had buried Howitzer munitions under pressure plates in the floor. We'd seen that kind of thing before. When those bitches blew, they could take out a Humvee."

"So Dad probably died right away?"

"In close quarters, with an explosion that big, I'd bet my life on it. Once the area was secured, I went in with the rescue squadron to recover—" Hawk looks at me.

"The bodies," I finish for him. "It's okay. You can say it."

My uncle nods. "We had to dig them out of the rubble. Your dad had two things on him that weren't Marine Corps–issued—a blue string tied around his wrist and a picture of you. The day we left for Iraq, your mom cut a piece of string in half, and she tied one half to your dad's wrist and the other half to hers. She said the string would keep them connected. The string was something new, but that picture of you wasn't. It was falling apart, because your dad carried it in his pocket on every mission. I'd like to think that in the end, he found peace knowing that he had a little bit of you with him."

I think back to Tim O'Brien's book and Miss Ives' assignment. The soldiers in the novel carried tangible and intangible things—photos and pebbles, hope and fear. That's when I realize what the picture of me really meant.

I'm the thing my dad carried.

I kept him grounded and got him through the rough times. The way he helped me in the tunnel.

A moment later, I hear footsteps on the stairs. Then the Twins wander into the kitchen.

Christian holds out his wrists for Hawk to see. "Check out the bruises from the handcuffs. I bet they'll last until Monday."

Hawk takes a sip of his coffee. "Most people wouldn't be this happy about getting arrested."

"I was helping Peyton. That's all that matters, right?"

Cam makes a fist, and Christian taps his fist against his brother's.

"Well, you might not be as happy about it once Coach gets ahold of you for walking off the field," Hawk says.

"Are you saying we shouldn't have left?" Christian asks.

"Of course you should've left. I'm just saying I don't think Coach will see it that way."

Cam opens the fridge and takes out a milk carton. "Christian is getting pretty good at push-ups."

Christian balls up a kitchen towel and pelts Cam with it. "Shut it. No one asked you."

Cameron raises the carton as if he's about to do his usual. But then he stops, opens the cabinet, and takes out a glass.

Progress.

Christian walks over and squeezes my shoulder. "You okay?"

"I'm good."

"Have you talked to your mom again?" Hawk asks. "She should only be a few hours away."

"I called her from the police station."

Hawk's expression turns serious. "That boy is lucky I didn't get my hands on him."

"Don't worry, Pop. We took care of it." Christian pushes past Cam and rifles through the fridge. He takes out a carton of eggs and stares at them like they're an alien food source.

I wait for Christian to ask me to make scrambled eggs. He looks over at me.

Here it comes.

"Go ahead, ask," I tell him. After the Twins walked off the football field to come after me last night, I'll cook them anything they want.

"I was just wondering if you'd . . . teach me how to make scrambled eggs," he says sheepishly.

For a second, I'm not sure if I heard him correctly. But then I see the shocked expression on my uncle's face.

"You want me to teach *you* how to make them?"

"Us," Cam says. "I want to learn, too."

"What happened to *cooking is for chicks?*" I'm not trying to give Christian a hard time. I'm actually curious.

"I changed my mind." Christian takes out the bowl he's seen me use. "I mean, you're not staying here forever. Not that I want you to leave, but I figured I'd better learn 'cause Pop's scrambled eggs suck."

Hawk points at him. "Now you'd better learn how to cook those eggs, because I'm not making you breakfast anymore after that."

I walk over to the counter and take the carton. "You're going to need a fork, too."

Christian tries to crack an egg into the bowl, and he ends up crushing it into his hand instead.

"Nice." Cam laughs. "Try to get some in the bowl, bro."

"You have to tap the egg against the edge of the bowl." I demonstrate with another egg. "Like this."

"Now you tell me." Christian rinses his hands under the faucet. "That seems like the kinda thing you should've said at the beginning."

Cam picks up an egg. "I'll do the cracking." He does a slightly better job and he manages to get most of the egg—along with all of the shell—into the bowl.

"See? It's not as easy as it looks. You suck, too," Christian says.

Cam wipes his hands on his sweats. "Cooking is trickier than it looks."

I take another egg out of the carton and hand it to Cam. "Try again. If you can stop a two-hundred-pound guy from tackling you, then you can make scrambled eggs."

I stand between the Twins, watching them compete to see who can get the least amount of eggshell in the bowl.

I'm going to miss them when I go back home.

They're not who I thought they were when I arrived in Black Water. But I'm probably not the person they were expecting, either.

The doorbell rings, and Dutch howls. Hawk checks his watch. "Your mom couldn't have made it here this fast."

Cam wipes his hands on a dish towel. "Actually, it's Grace. I invited her to come over. You know, after she waited for me—" He glances at Christian. "I mean *us*, last night."

"We both know she wasn't waiting for me." Christian takes a fork and stirs the eggs in a circular motion instead of beating them.

Cameron jams his hands in the pockets of his sweatpants. "Are you cool with that?"

"It's a little late to ask now. You already kissed her," Christian says. "But it's cool."

"I heard about the kissing," I call after Cam as he rushes to answer the door.

"One kiss," he yells back.

Christian is still stirring the eggs like cake batter.

"You have to beat them." I take the fork and show him, but Christian snatches it back and angles the bowl away from me.

"I've got this. You can start teaching again when we put the eggs in the pan." He points the fork at me and accidentally flings raw egg across the kitchen. "Whoa. Like I said, this cooking thing is harder than it looks."

Dutch howls again when Cam opens the front door.

I nudge Christian with my shoulder. "That was pretty cool of you."

"I don't know what you're talking about. I knew Cameron and Grace were meant for each other the whole time."

He's lying, but I don't call him on it. "You'd better be careful, Christian Carter. People might find out you're a sweetheart."

"Shh. Keep it down. Grace is here. That kind of talk would ruin my reputation." He takes out a frying pan and a stick of butter. I try not to laugh when he drops the whole stick in the pan.

"How many eggs are you planning to make, exactly?" I ask.

"What? Too much?" Christian reaches for the hunk of butter in the center of the pan.

"Don't touch—"

He touches the butter—and the pan—and yanks his arm away. "Damn. That's hot!"

"Come here." I turn on the faucet and blast the cold water. "Put your hand under. Maybe we should start with something easier than scrambled eggs."

I catch a glimpse of Grace and Cam in the hallway. He whispers something in her ear, and she smiles at him. I've never seen him look so relaxed. And happy. I wish Owen was here, too. But he's talking things out with his mom.

"Hi, y'all," Grace says as she walks into the kitchen. Cameron is next to her, with one of his fingers looped around one of hers. She looks nervous.

"Want some coffee?" I ask.

She yawns. "I could drink a whole pot."

Christian looks over, and Grace lets go of Cameron's finger. She wraps her arms around herself and walks toward the counter tentatively.

My uncle gets up from the table. "I'll be right back. I'm gonna call and check on Sissy."

Grace waits for Hawk to leave and turns to Christian. "I just . . ." She hesitates. "I just wanted to make sure that you're okay with me and Cam." She looks over at Cameron, who's smiling at her.

I wait for Christian to laugh it off or make a joke. Instead, he gives her his sad puppy face. "I'm not saying it's easy to see you with someone. But if you and Cameron are happy together, that's what counts. So I'm good with it."

Christian winks at me.

"Thanks." Grace beams with pride and walks back over to Cam.

Christian says, "Let's get back to the eggs. Exactly how much butter are we talking about?"

Just when I think I have things all figured out, life throws me for a loop.

CHAPTER 44
Happily Even After

THREE MONTHS LATER . . .

I WAKE UP in the hospital for the third day in a row. Every muscle in my body aches from sleeping in a chair, but I've never been so happy to feel like crap. And I know Owen must feel worse.

I lace my fingers between his and rest my cheek on his leg. The first two days in the hospital, he was so out of it from pain meds that I wasn't sure if he knew I was here.

His fingers tighten around mine for a second, and he stirs in his sleep.

I end up falling asleep, too. I have the best dream. Owen running his fingers through my hair, smiling at me. The dream feels so real that I don't want to wake up.

"Peyton?" He's calling my name, and I love the sound of his voice.

I rub my eyes and feel Owen's hand sliding through my hair.

I lean over him. "How do you feel?"

"Good enough to do this." He catches me around the waist and pulls me closer. He coughs, and I pick up the giant plastic cup on the table. It's full of crushed ice and water.

"Here." I bend the straw so he can take a sip. "Are you all right?"

"My throat is just scratchy. Come here."

I lean over him. I can't believe how happy I am that he's awake.

"Closer. I can't see you," he says.

I lean in a little more. "How do you feel? Seriously?"

"Like I got run over by a truck."

I laugh as a tear runs down my cheek. "I'm so glad you're okay."

"Remember what you promised me before I went into surgery?"

"Which thing?"

"The one about how I can have anything I want afterward?"

To prove how confident I was that he'd make it through the surgery, I promised Owen that I'd give him anything he wanted. "So what do you want? Since you get to pick anything."

"I don't know what the rules are about going *in the pool* now that I've got an Arc Reactor implanted in my chest."

"Iron Man jokes? Seriously?"

"It sounds cooler than shock box."

Owen gave up so much when he decided to have the surgery—just to give himself a chance at having a life. Something most of us take for granted.

The surgeon implanted an ICD—an implantable cardiac defibrillator—in Owen's chest that will shock his heart if it stops. Like most people, Owen calls it a shock box and he knew that getting one meant he'd never be able to fight again—or play any contact sport. His whole life would change. "At least I'll have a life," he said.

The day of the surgery, Owen was more worried about his mom and me than about himself. I know he was scared, but he still went through with it.

Owen touches my sleeve. "What are you wearing?"

I have on my uniform. "Oh, I have a game. But I'm gonna skip it. I have someone who can cover for me."

"No." Owen shakes his head. "It's bad luck if you skip it."

"Now you're superstitious?"

"You have to go. I'm pretty sure an army of nurses will show up any minute to start poking at me and taking my temperature."

"I don't know about that, but your mom will be here any minute. She won't leave unless she knows I'm here."

"She's a good mom."

The door opens a crack, and Owen's mom pokes her head in. "You look great today, sweetheart." She smiles. It's the first time I've ever seen her smile.

"You have to go," he tells me. "I'll hang out with my mom."

I don't want to leave.

This feels like the beginning of something, and I don't want to miss any part of it.

"Okay, but I'll be back as soon as the game's over." I kiss his forehead.

"I think you missed."

"What?"

"I think you missed my lips," he says.

I have no idea what the rules are about kissing after heart surgery, but I don't want to test the boundaries. Plus his mom's standing right across from me. I kiss him gently, our lips touching just enough.

"Come here. I want to tell you something," he whispers. I bring my ear closer to his lips. "I decided what I want."

"Your mom is here," I remind him.

"It's not about going to the pool."

"Okay. What do you want? You get to pick anything."

"Look at me." The way Owen says it reminds me of other times he said it.

"Are you finally going to tell me?"

He gives me a half smile. "I want to be more than just friends."

My heart melts.

I kiss him again. "Done."

As I walk out, Owen's mom calls after me. "Good luck."

I'm practically flying by the time I get to the soccer field.

Owen is awake and he's mine. And he's going to be around for a long time. That's what my little voice is telling me, and I trust it again.

I strap on my athletic brace and tie my cleats. I jog onto the field, slow—not striker speed.

A dozen fourth-grade girls swarm me.

"Who's starting?" one of them asks.

"I don't know. Let's look at the list. Whose turn is it?"

They crowd around my clipboard and read over my shoulder.

My knee still isn't a hundred percent. It's not even eighty. There's no way I can play this season, but UNC let me defer until next year.

By then, I think my knee will be completely healed.

And if it's not? I'll figure something out.

I used to believe that everyone gets one perfect day sometime in their lives—if they were lucky. But I had it all wrong. We don't get one perfect day. We get a lifetime of *imperfect* days, and it's up to us to decide what we want to do with them.

Some days are hard, and they leave us feeling like we just got our asses kicked. That's the way I felt after Reed pushed me and wrecked my knee—broken and battered, with a life that would never be as whole as the one I had before.

But broken and battered can become broken and beautiful.

I'm working on that part now, and I'm okay with it.

I'm not looking for a happily *ever* after.

I want a happily *even* after.

The kind of happiness you have to earn. The kind you find after a broken heart or an injured knee. After a mistake that feels impossible to fix.

It's the *even after* part that matters.

I already have the *happy* part.

Author's Note

THIS WAS A difficult book for me to write. It dredged up a lot of painful memories. At one point in my life, I found myself in a situation like Peyton experiences in *Broken Beautiful Hearts*. I was dating an athlete who had started doping and I had no idea. Like Peyton, I broke up with him as soon as I found out. And like Peyton, I paid a price when the guy flew into a rage.

My inner circle of friends believed me when I told them what happened. But the mutual friends my ex and I shared did not. He was protective of me and he always stepped in if a girl was in trouble. He was *that* guy. He also adored me and everyone knew it. People couldn't believe he would *hurt* me. I must have just misinterpreted the situation . . . right?

Wrong.

I knew *exactly* what happened and I stuck to my story. But some people still didn't believe me.

Looking back now, there are things I didn't do that I should have done:

- I did not report the incident to the police.
- When my ex-boyfriend started stalking me, I didn't file a restraining order because, like Peyton, I thought it was "just a piece of paper." But a restraining order is more than that. Even if it can't stop the person from hurting/stalking you, a restraining order establishes a pattern of behavior that might help you later.
- I also didn't reach out for help.

If you are ever in a situation like this, please reach out for help. You deserve to be heard—and believed.

Resources

BREAK THE CYCLE

Break the Cycle inspires and supports young people ages 12–24 to build healthy relationships and create a culture without abuse.

https://www.breakthecycle.org/learn-about-dating-abuse

LOVEISRESPECT

Loveisrespect's purpose is to engage, educate, and empower young people to prevent and end abusive relationships.

http://www.loveisrespect.org/
Text loveis to 22522*
Call 1-866-331-9474

THE NATIONAL DOMESTIC VIOLENCE HOTLINE

Operating around-the-clock, seven days a week, confidential, and free of cost, the National Domestic Violence Hotline provides lifesaving tools and immediate support to enable victims to find safety and live lives free of abuse.

http://www.thehotline.org/
1-800-799-SAFE (7233)

RAINN

RAINN (Rape, Abuse & Incest National Network) is the nation's largest anti-sexual violence organization. RAINN created and operates the National Sexual Assault Hotline.

https://www.rainn.org/
1-800-656-HOPE (4673)

Acknowledgments

This book would not exist without the support and hard work
of these Beautiful people.

Jodi Reamer, my amazing literary agent—for listening to my crazy ideas and encouraging me to see where they lead, and shepherding my books into the world.

Erin Stein, my publisher and editor at Imprint—for pushing me to take chances in my novels instead of letting me play it safe. Your unwavering belief in my characters and my ability to bring their stories to life on the page keeps me going.

Natalie Sousa and Ellen Duda—for designing a book cover that exceeded my expectations and included a heart that doesn't look cheesy.

Christine Ma, my copy editor—for catching my mistakes and for loving Owen from the first read.

The whole "Beautiful" Team at Imprint: Nicole Otto, Natalie Sousa, Ellen Duda, Jessica Chung, Rhoda Belleza, and John Morgan. And the "Beautiful" team at Macmillan: Jon Yaged, Angus Killick, Allison Verost, Molly Brouillette Ellis, Kelsey Marrujo, Kathryn Little, Ashley Woodfolk, Lucy Del Priore, Mariel Dawson, Julia Gardiner, Gaby Salpeter, Teresa Ferraiolo, Jennifer Gonzalez and her sales team, Melinda Ackell, and Raymond Ernesto Colón.

Writers House, my literary agency—for representing me and *Broken Beautiful Hearts*. Special thanks to Cecilia de la Campa and Alec Shane.

Kassie Evashevski, my rock star film agent—for your intelligence, creativity, and passion. But most of all, for championing this book and everything I write.

Holly Black, Carrie Ryan, and Danielle Paige, my friends and extraordinary YA authors—for reading this book so many times, giving me notes to make it better, and for all the supportive texts and calls.

Dhonielle Clayton, my friend and an über-talented YA author—for taking the time to sensitivity read this book—and for giving the book such a wonderful quote.

Sarah Weiss-Simpson, my assistant—for organizing my life so I have time to write and for being a great friend.

Chloe Palka, my social media manager—for your expertise and creativity and for typing my messy handwritten chapters. You are the coolest.

Erin Gross and Yvette Vasquez, my BFFs—for always having the answers, cheering me on, and yelling at me when cheering doesn't work. You are two of my best friends.

Cora Carmack, Dhonielle Clayton, Abbi Glines, Elle Kennedy, Katie McGarry, Danielle Paige, Jennifer Niven, and K.A. Tucker, a group of authors whose novels I admire—for giving *Broken Beautiful Hearts* such amazing quotes. There aren't enough cupcakes in the world to show my appreciation.

Sargent Rudolfo "Rudy" Reyes, 1st Reconnaissance Battalion, Team Leader OEF/OIF, United States Marine Corps; cofounder of FORCE Blue; my friend; and a tireless warrior with a new mission—saving and improving the lives of veterans—for sharing your knowledge and experiences with me so I could bring Hawk and Peyton's dad to life on the page. And for helping me come up with a realistic (and scary) scenario for Peyton's dad's death.

Dr. Stephanie Jacobs, MD, cardiologist—for coming up with a heart condition that met my long list of criteria and then explaining it to me.

Vania Stoyanova, my friend and photographer—for making me look cool in my author photos, especially the one in this book.

Lorissa Shepstone of Being Wicked, my graphic designer—for designing my amazing new author website, along with postcards, bookmarks, business cards, and swag.

Benjamin Alderson, Caden Armstrong, Katie Bartow, Yvette Cervera, Bri Daniel, Andye Eppes, Jen Fisher, Vilma Gonzalez, Kristen Goodwin, Erin Gross, Sara Gundell, Ruthie Heard, Mara Jacobi, Taylor Knight, Hikari Loftus, Caden Sage, Evie Seo, Tracey Spiteri, Amber Sweeney, Natasha Tomic, Ursula Uriarte, Lauren Ward, Jenny Zemanek, and Heidi Zweifel—for being my think tank and offering your insight, creativity, and support. It means so much to me.

Eric Harbert and Nick Montano, my secret weapons—for being the guys who watch my back.

Alan Weinberger, my rheumatologist—for making sure I don't fall apart.

Librarians, teachers, booksellers, bloggers, bookstagrammers, booktubers, and everyone who helped spread the word about *Broken Beautiful Hearts*—your passion for reading and love of books is an inspiration. Thank you for everything you do and for reading my books.

My readers—for supporting me, sticking with me when I write new books and series, encouraging me on social media when I'm down, encouraging your friends to read my books, sending me letters and fan art, and sharing your stories with me. You bring my books to life.

Mom, Dad, Celeste, John, Derek, Hannah, Alex, Hans, Sara, and Erin, my parents, stepparents, siblings, and sisters-in-law—for your love and encouragement. Thank you for always being there.

Alex, Nick, and Stella—for your love and support. I couldn't do any of this without you.